*To my love,
a.k.a! Joe..
with best regards.'
Tom Risser
march 2016.*

NAKED TREASON

The Insurgent's Debutante
Baghdad Mistress

Tom Risser

SIGNALMAN PUBLISHING

Naked Treason
The Insurgent's Debutante Baghdad Mistress
by Tom Risser

Signalman Publishing
www.signalmanpublishing.com
email: info@signalmanpublishing.com
Kissimmee, Florida

Cover design by Duncan Long
www.duncanlong.com

ISBN: 978-1-940145-59-4 (sc)
        978-1-940145-60-0 (ebook)

Library of Congress Control Number: 2015959496

SP-1-16a

To The Corps. Semper Fi!

ACKNOWLEDGMENTS

A number of associates offered vital guidance in the preparation of this novel. I am indebted to Ms. Edie Mackie, Dr. Firas Naji, Dr. Slava Gaufberg, Dr. Paul Lesser, Mr. Patrick Wardell, CDR Richard Young, USN (ret.), and COL Michael Lesavage, USMC (ret.) for their helpful suggestions. Exceptionally helpful were the insightful observations of the accomplished novelists Susan Patterson and Katherine Hall Page. I am grateful to Ms. Jennifer Mackie for splendid editorial assistance. I was inspired to write by the intrepid men and women of the USMC 6th Civil Affairs Group. But most of all, I am grateful for the expertise, devotion, sacrifice, and courage of all who have served in the proud uniform of that national treasure which is the United States Marine Corps.

PREFACE

During and after the two World Wars, the American public came to identify and idealize some of America's greatest warriors. Sergeant York from WWI, and Jimmy Doolittle and Audie Murphy from WWII were, and in older families still are, household words. That situation has drastically changed, due to a number of factors. The U.S. military evolved into a professional organization, with no draft of duty to national service for all young men. Furthermore, most Americans have no personal relationship with anyone currently serving in the U.S. military, either active or reserve forces. Fewer members of congress are U.S. military veterans than at any other time in our national history. After the mass demonstrations against the Vietnam War, the military was denounced by the general population, and has not fully recovered in liberal circles. And in this globalized world, replete with massive international visitors to the U.S., the possibility of attacks by our enemies on our military heroes and their families right here in the U.S is credible, diminishing the incentive for individual warriors to accept widespread recognition. As a consequence, the public's perception of the modern American warrior is molded principally by our entertainment media. Sylvester Stallone's social misfit character John Rambo – without family, love, work, civic contribution – is prominent in many Americans' minds as the epitome of the modern American soldier. The truth, of course, couldn't be further from this perception.

The typical modern American military member is a man or woman with solid family ties, most with romantic partners if not spouses, and commonly are parents. These accomplished citizens commonly have created a history of contributing to their communities, both before and during their military service. With the contemporary U.S. military's emphasis on education and training, most modern soldiers (here also alluding to our soldiers, sailors, airmen, Marines, and Coast Guardsmen) are highly trained professionals – trained not just in their technical specialties, but also in leadership skills, preparing them to be able to assume command in battle if their chain-of-command is interrupted. And like their predecessors in the U.S. military, they are dedicated patriots, committed to their oath of office to, "Protect, preserve, and defend the constitution of the United States of America." Since the terror attacks of 2001, our soldiers have deployed in massive numbers to the combat zones of the Middle East, facing fearsome conditions and ferocious enemies, and have maintained a stellar standard of courage under duress. Many, of course, have paid the price of death or serious injury.

Although this novel features a totally fictitious plot and characters, it accurately reflects the ethos of the U.S. Marine Corps on deployment to Iraq in the 2005 - 2006 time frame. Written during the author's service there with the USMC 6th Civil Affairs Group in Ramadi and Fallujah, it reflects the rich culture of lifestyle, support services, language, organization, weaponry, and tactics while in those dangerous places. The singular exception of an element in the novel which, in fact, never occurred in that time frame, is romance and lovemaking in the combat zone, which was strictly forbidden, and, in fact, rarely if ever occurred. The author created that aspect of the story in artistic license to generate a spicy story line, but the Marines were scrupulous in avoiding such activity while deployed to Iraq.

But what is totally real in the novel is the display of splendid leadership, exceptional physical prowess, exemplary military bearing, intense camaraderie, remarkable ethnic diversity, incisive wit, superior training, raw courage, and brilliant devotion to duty of our military members deployed to the war zones. Men and women like Major Matt Baxter and Captain Chris Curtis are ubiquitous in our modern military. Their integrity, gallantry, and intelligence is the norm for those who allow us to sleep peaceably in our beds at night because they stand ready to protect us.

Another distinctive feature of this novel is the explanation of the nature of traumatic injuries, and medical approaches to treating those injuries. Contrary to Hollywood depictions, gunshot wounds commonly do *not* cause the victim to instantly drop motionless to the deck. Unless the traumatic injury impacts the brain or heart, the victim's functions are usually preserved, albeit perhaps transiently. Characters in the book exhibit a potpourri of traumatic wounds.

The author hopes that readers find the story entertaining, but at the same time, acquire new insight into the character and quality of those valiant men and women who wear the cloth of our nation, and go into harm's way to allow us to live so prosperously, peacefully, and joyously in these spectacular United States of America.

CHAPTER ONE

LOSS OF A HERO

Tuesday March 8, 2005

Four minutes and seven miles into its flight, the drab green helicopter clawed its way noisily through the cool desert night air, climbing to its planned altitude of 600 feet above ground level. Having launched at 0220 h, Legacy 23 had lifted off Marine Corps Camp Blue Diamond's helo landing zone with a full load of one pallet of freight and eleven passengers, plus its two .50 caliber machine gunners and the two Marine pilots up front in the cockpit. Lieutenant General Stanley Sienkiewicz could have blocked the other passengers from boarding, but he was always the team player, popular with all of his twenty thousand subordinates. As the senior Marine in Iraq, his command extended over six major bases, and some thirty small field sites (FOBS = Forward Operating Bases). At fifty-four years old, he was trim, muscular, fit, handsome, smart, and tough as nails. Thirty-three years in the Corps after four years at the Naval Academy had honed his leadership skills till he was at his peak in decisive, inspirational, innovative command.

It was March 8 2005, just under two years since Saddam's military had collapsed under the thunderous attack of U.S. forces. The weather at this time of year was like fall in New England—clear, relatively dry, no bugs, and gentle temperatures. The occasional rain storm transiently converted the ubiquitous Iraqi dust to a sea of mud, but most of the troops preferred dealing with tenacious mud in cool air to clouds of powdery dust in the stultifying summer heat.

General Sienkewicz had visited Blue Diamond, a rather small but important base, to meet with his commanders there, and pin medals on a number of his beloved Marines. Six purple hearts: he loved pinning those on in the field, because it meant the Marine's injuries were minor, and they didn't require MedEvac. Four meritorious promotions: ahead of schedule, but based on superior performance in the war zone. Two Privates-First-

Class became Lance Corporals that day, and two Lance Corporals became
NCOs – non-commissioned officers – as corporals. Two Marine Corps
Achievement Medals, a Marine Corps Commendation Medal to Cpl Hobie
Sanders for personally silencing an enemy machine gun that had pinned
down his rifle team, and a Bronze Star for Sergeant Patrick Wardrell, who
had braved withering enemy fire to approach the trench that six insurgents
were shooting from and dispatch them with his M-16 and two grenades.
What a pleasure it was to reward competence, and especially courage in
combat! And always a joy to remind him that America could still recruit
strong, disciplined, fearless young men and women to become the world's
best professional warriors.

Now winging his way back to his headquarters at Camp Fallujah, the
General's thoughts were with his battle plans for abolishing the flow of
arms and fighters from the Syrian border, via the Euphrates River valley.
He could barely see in the darkened cabin his fellow passengers, eight
Marines including three woman Marines, a Filipino cook from Blue
Diamond, and a USAID American civilian worker. Strapped into his
canvas seat facing the opposite wall of the cabin, his earplugs took the
edge off the high-pitched whine of the hydraulic pumps inside, and the
screeching jet engines outside. The whop-whop of the fore-and-aft rotors
vibrated the cabin synchronous with the sound. With his Kevlar helmet,
goggles over his eyes, neck cowl pulled up over his neck, chin, and mouth;
flak vest with ceramic armor and hundred rounds of ammunition for the
M-16 slung over his shoulder and the 9 mm pistol strapped on his hip, he
was weighted down heavily. But he was comfortable despite the cool air
rushing in the machine gun portals, and out the aft end of the cabin, where
the ramp was retracted upward but the cowling to close in the ramp from
the top was left open.

Seeing the young Marines, General Sienkewicz was reminded of his
own four children entering young adulthood. His oldest, Stan Junior, age
twenty, was a senior at the University of California San Diego, a member of
ROTC (Reserve Officer Training Corps), and planning a stint if not a career
in The Corps. At 18, Hannah, a freshman at the University of Colorado,
planned a career in the health sciences. Always good with her hands,
and a real people-person, she was thinking of becoming an ultrasound
technologist. At sixteen, Luke was a three-letter athlete, and planned
on becoming a rock star. And the miracle child, the one God delivered
without request, his beloved nine-year-old Molly, was sweeter'n cream.
He smiled in the darkness just picturing her cherubic smile. The image of
her Mama, Joyce, who was the devoted, loving, smart, and handsome wife

every man prayed for, then appeared, and prompted a broad smile in the darkness. Four months without the joy of her touch, General Sienkewicz longed for her presence. And the kids. How sweet it would be in three months when they all congregated to welcome him home, and allocated a week to family time to make up for his long separation abroad.

Lost in his reverie, and because of his ear plugs and the cacophonous aircraft noise, General Sienkewicz didn't hear the sound of light and heavy machine gun fire erupt from six hundred feet below him, but he suddenly saw dust from the pallet in front of him kicking up as bullets tore through the cargo and on through the roof of the helo. Then he felt the sharp sting of a round penetrating his left lower arm, and in the dim light saw three Marines begin writhing in their seat belts, shot through the floor and seat, into their buttocks, and up into their abdominal and chest cavities. Two young men and one young woman mortally wounded within seconds. Several hydraulic lines suddenly began to spew hot fluid into the cabin, and sparks erupted from suddenly dangling wire ends.

From their positions in the forward cabin, both machine gunners saw the sudden eruption of flashes and tracers below them and opened fire with their own ferocious weapons, aiming their stream of tracers at the source of tracers and muzzle flashes below them. But there were so many. Through their NVG's they could see the insurgents firing heavy machine guns from three pickup trucks, and some thirty other insurgents firing their AK-47's upward at them. One of the pickups suddenly erupted in flames as the .50 cal penetrated its gas tank, but the other two continued their deadly accurate fire. Up in the flight station, the command pilot took a 12.7 mm [.50 cal] round through his right thigh, and on through his lower jaw, through his brain, and the heavy slug continued right through his helmet and the roof of the helo, splattering the pilot's brain tissue on the ceiling. He slumped forward in his seat belts, lifeless. The copilot saw red warning lights flashing from both engines as well as the hydraulic systems, and knew he needed to land immediately before he lost control of the 6-ton aircraft, held up by the two flimsy-looking rotors of four blades each. As he eased the collective down to reduce lift and descend, an AK round sliced through the side of the helo and into his lower abdomen. In pain and bleeding, but still alert and in control, he continued the descent as bullets ripped apart his instrument panel and windscreen.

Back in the fuselage, the port gunner was now down, having taken two rounds in his left leg, and one in his neck. His armor plates had deflected three others from his chest, but he fell when his left leg gave way, and was striving to squeeze his left neck to staunch the arterial blood spurting from his lacerated carotid artery while the starboard gunner continued pouring fire down on the enemy.

The USAID worker was hit in both thighs and bleeding profusely. The first three Marines hit were now motionless, leaning forward in their seatbelts, dead from catastrophic internal hemorrhage. Two other Marines had taken rounds in the legs, but were shouting to prepare for a hard landing. Miraculously, three Marines were untouched, but the helo was still taking rounds, and its thin skin did nothing to slow the lethal slugs. One mildy wounded female Marine was creeping forward to operate the port .50 cal, but she suddenly dropped and lay on the floor writhing, having taken a round in the groin and up into her abdomen. As she fell, the starboard gunner fell backward; his helmet had deflected two rounds, giving him an enormous bell sounds and jolt, but he maintained his poise and continued firing. But then a third round struck him just under his helmet at his left temple, exploding his brains out the right top of his head, and he collapsed in a heap. Another of the uninjured Marines ran forward and began returning fire with the port .50 cal. The General sat back in his seat, knowing that the tubular aluminum support for the fabric seat was designed to give way in a hard landing, sparing his spine.

The helo hit hard because its hydraulics were nearly gone by the time it touched down, and the copilot's coordination was off as he grew weak and sweaty with shock. The blades flexed violently and chopped off chunks of the roof, hurling blade parts and aluminum skin and spars for two hundred yards. The remainder of the fuselage roof collapsed downward two feet, bent by the massive weight of the jet engines and transmissions, as the sides and floor cracked open. The copilot switched off the engines, but the fuel lines and tanks had ruptured. Yellow-red tongues of fire began licking up both sides of the mortally wounded helo. The two uninjured Marines unbuckled and ran aft. M-16s bouncing in their slings, they clambered through the narrow opening above the still-retracted aft ramp. The machine gunner emptied his cartridge case toward the enemy, then leaped from the aircraft. Except for the General, the other passengers were too injured to evacuate the doomed aircraft, and the fire began to advance toward the interior of the ruptured fuselage.

The General unstrapped and hobbled to the forward port door, where all three .50 cal gunners lay still, faintly illuminated by the flames outside, eyes open and fixated dead ahead. The General could see the three Marines outside, now joined up and running away from the muzzle flashes approaching from the south. As bullets zinged nearby and clinked into the airframe, the General half-climbed, half-fell the three feet to the ground and began also to run north, away from the aircraft and his pursuers. Catching up with the Marines, the four ran through the darkness, each of them repeatedly stumbling on the irregular desert terrain in the dark.

The sound of other running footsteps came up behind them, and the Filipino cook whispered loudly, "Don't shoot, don't shoot, I am Miguel Fuentes from the Blue Diamond Chow Hall."

Suddenly the desert was brilliantly illuminated. The boom followed in a second as the helo exploded. Those who survived the landing but could not escape were killed by the blast, and the fire set about cremating their remains. Ammunition began cooking off inside the fiercely burning fuselage, providing staccato pops and cracks.

If the pursuers hadn't seen the fleeing Americans before, they were readily apparent in the three seconds of brilliance from the explosion. Stopping to aim their weapons, a fusillade of slugs whistled through the air. Most Iraqis are poor marksmen, but twenty-four of them together raises the odds of a hit to a near sure thing. Six of them had been felled by the helo's .50 cals. Regardless all the rounds missed with the first volley, but others were following.

The two surviving pickups roared as they turned toward the burning helo from a mile south of its crash site. The first one hit a six-foot deep ravine, such that it nosed in and stopped abruptly, hurling the front seat occupants through the windshield. The two in the back became missiles as they hurtled through the air, both breaking their necks as they thudded into the dark sand. All four men were now motionless, as the ruptured radiator of the pickup hissed up a cloud of steam and the aft wheels slowly rotated five feet above the ground. The two men ejected through the windshield had the top of their skulls ripped off by the windshield housing, dead in a microsecond.

But the second pickup was lucky, and had no ravines in its path. Its lights snaked out onto the sand as it wildly pitched and bucked its way toward the fleeing Americans, now only a half mile away. The twenty-four insurgents on foot were running toward the Americans as well, stopping occasionally to fire off a few rounds. Because they were untrained thugs rather than disciplined professional soldiers, three insurgents shot compatriots in front of them in the back, when insurgents in the rear stopped to shoot at their quarry. But the pursuit persisted, eight miles from Camp Blue Diamond, unknown to the thousands of highly trained, awesomely armed US servicemen just a few miles away, because the helo's radio's had been shot up at the onset of the attack.

The woman Marine on the left was the first to go down, taking a round just below her armor plate on her left flank, penetrating her kidney and fracturing ribs both in back and front. The others realized that they could not hold off the much larger force coming at them, so they ran on. Suddenly, another six-foot ravine appeared before them and they tumbled into it. Marines are excellent shots at up to five hundred yards, but it was dark and unlike their enemy they had no night vision goggles, their usual equipment lost in the chaos of the downed helo. The pickup was now racing forward two hundred yards off to their right, unable to determine their location. Suddenly they heard the popping sounds of an M-16, and heard screams as the downed Marine a hundred yards back opened fire on the enemy at nearly point blank range. The M-16 was answered with a fusillade of automatic weapons fire, and it fell silent. But four more insurgents were down; now it was seventeen plus the four in the truck, against the four Americans. The General asked Miguel if he could shoot a 9 mm pistol. When Miguel nodded, the General handed him his Beretta and three additional magazines, instructing him to stuff them in his pocket and to hold his fire 'til commanded to shoot.

Trembling with fear and anticipation, the two Marines, Miguel, and the General waited until the enemy closed to less than fifty yards, and they could make out their silhouettes. Then their M-16s began popping, and six insurgents dropped, mortally wounded in their torsos. Three of the remaining group began racing forward, and the Marines dropped them with another round of firing. The eight remaining insurgents dropped to the ground, and began crawling forward. There was minimal moonlight, and the insurgents had now lost their NVGs. Peering into the night, Miguel saw movement and aimed the pistol. The General followed his lead, and saw the outlines of a head. Even with his penetrated left arm, the General released two quick rounds. The insurgent lay quivering, one round in the head and one through his shoulder into his chest.

Seeing his brother shot, the insurgent beside him stood up to charge. All four of the fugitives opened up on him, and his chest was shredded by six rounds as he fell to the earth. But muzzle flashes were a giveaway, and the six remaining insurgents opened fire. A round blasted through Miguel's forehead; the back of his head exploded, coating the wall of the trench with hair, skull fragments, and brain tissue. One of the Marines jerked backward, his left shoulder shattering as an AK round tore through it. Now the Americans could hear the pickup turning around five hundred yards behind them to return to the battle.

The General directed the Marines to move laterally in the ravine, away from the site of their muzzle flashes. After silently creeping twenty yards over, leaving Miguel's crumpled body where it lay, they saw three insurgents appear at the edge of the ravine. A fusillade of M-16 fire, and all three were silenced with rounds to the head, neck, and chest.

Now their chances were more reasonable: two wounded and one intact Marine, against three intact insurgents. But the pickup with the heavy machine gun was now approaching, skewing the odds wildly toward the enemy. With NVGs, the pickup saw the Americans and opened up with its 12.7 mm. But the truck was bouncing, sending the shot wide and killing one of the insurgents with three shattering blasts through his head and chest, ripping a six-inch diameter chunk out of the back of his chest, and causing his head to literally explode. The Americans crept further up the ravine, feeling rock fragments from .50 cal rounds above them pelting their helmets and uniforms. Meanwhile, under cover of the distraction of the pickup, one of the insurgents had circled around in front of them and was laying in wait. As they crept along with the pickup approaching, the insurgent in front leveled his AK and released two rounds into the first form he saw. The General jerked backward as both rounds penetrated his upper abdomen, ripping his aorta and fracturing his spine and spinal cord. Conscious but knowing he was mortally injured, he fired a burst toward his assassin as he crumpled to the deck. The volley went high, kicking up the dirt in the trench just above the insurgent's head.

The injured Marine immediately fired a burst at the muzzle flash, and the insurgent took a round to the temple, and crumpled, lying still. By now the insurgent in the back had crept forward, and dropped the Marine with the shoulder wound with two rounds to the low back below his armor plate. Whirring and firing, Lance Corporal Robert Green, the lone African-American Marine on the helo, caught the insurgent with a burst to his chest. As he did, the pickup replicated the error of its partner and tumbled headfirst into the ravine twenty yards from where Lance Corporal Green stood. Because the pickup had been advancing slowly, its crew were stunned but not killed. Lance Corporal Green was on them in a second. As the driver and front passenger shook their heads free of their daze, he caught them each with a burst to the head. The two gunners who had hurled forward on to the earth were trying to stand up when he leveled them both with a volley at each barely visible torso.

The desert abruptly went silent. The lights of the pickup pointed into the ravine, its tail lights beaming into the sky. LCpl Green heard receding running footsteps, and realized that there was an insurgent survivor, either with the ground force or with the truck. Overwhelmed with fatigue, grief, fear, and anger, he knew that pursuit in the dark was far too dangerous, and the insurgent seemed to have had his fill of battle that night.

Extracting extra magazines from the pack of his deceased buddy, LCpl Green crept back to the crumpled form of General Sienkewicz and was disheartened to find him still and lifeless. Searching his uniform for any classified documents which might aid the enemy, he removed a number of papers and stuffed them into the cargo pockets of his desert cammie trousers. Softly uttering a short prayer for the General and his comrades, LCpl Green stood up and examined his compass. Determining that the base was southwest of him, he knew that it couldn't be more than six to ten miles. Saying another brief prayer for his other fallen mates, and asking God for strength to find his way home, he began trudging toward the lights on the horizon, which he knew to be the insurgent-laden city of Ramadi—and where Camp Blue Diamond is situated.

Meanwhile the air traffic controllers at Camp Fallujah, forty miles east of Blue Diamond, realized they had a problem when they couldn't raise the General's H-46 on the radio. Within five minutes, two heavily armed Cobra helicopter gunships were lifting off, heading toward Camp Blue Diamond. The pilots saw the burning hulk of the General's aircraft from fifteen miles out in the clear desert air, and directed that a heavily armed convoy and an advance air team set out from Blue Diamond for the site immediately. So the Quick Reaction Force was augmented with extra vehicles. The fifteen-vehicle convoy was en route to the crash scene within another ten minutes, bristling with machine guns, grenade launchers, and tremendously powerful air support. Two Huey H-1 helicopters lifted off from Camp Fallujah with three Navy corpsmen (medics) aboard each.

The Hueys homed in on the Cobras' guidance, and landed amid massive clouds of desert dust some fifty yards from the crash site. Quickly determining that there were no visible survivors, they were preparing to lift off again when they heard distant shouting. It was the voice of Lance Corporal Green exclaiming, "U.S. Marine here, U.S. Marine here." Running toward his voice, CAPT John McCarty challenged him for his name, rank, unit, and how he got there. When he replied in his distinctively American urban patois, Hospitalmen Third Class Rich Osman and Lee Harman ran to him and escorted him back to the Hueys. After they were airborne, the Navy corpsmen tended to the multiple bleeding wounds on the left side of his face and neck, inflicted by the stone fragments kicked up by the pickup's .50 cal rounds when he had been in the trench. He was peppered by at least forty separate wounds, but they were all superficial, and his eyes had been protected by his ballistic goggles, such that he would fully recover.

The convoy trip to the crash scene took forty-five minutes. One Humvee rolled over in the irregular desert terrain, but the Marines were belted in and were uninjured. Hooking a tow cable to its undercarriage, another Humvee pulled it right side up, and all continued forward. At the crash site, they held vigil while the fire burned itself out.

Informed by LCpl Green of the ground battle, the Marines located their dead and recovered them. They also recovered the enemy dead, along with their weapons and documents. Two white phosphorous incendiary grenades, which burn at 4,000 degrees Fahrenheit, were tossed into each pickup to ensure that there would be no salvageable parts for the insurgency. Then the convoy mournfully turned back to Camp Blue Diamond. General Stanley Sienkewicz had pinned on his last medal, congratulated his last Marine. He died in battle, seeking to establish a world of justice and peace for his descendants. Fourteen other honorable Americans and one courageous Filipino were lost forever. But the battle was just beginning.

CHAPTER TWO

AMERICAN MILITARY WOMANPOWER AT ITS BEST

Wednesday, March 9, 2005

Captain Christine Curtis, USMC, arose at her usual 0530 hours, refreshed. At age twenty-eight, she had developed the discipline to maximize her productivity every day, but she also had the insight to make each day a joy to celebrate. A Marine since graduating from tony Elizabethtown College in southern Pennsylvania at age twenty-one, she had reported directly to Marine Corps Officers' Candidate School at Marine Corps Base Quantico, Virginia, for 10 weeks of vigorous physical, mental, and leadership training. An accomplished athlete, she found the physical portion challenging but far from overwhelming, unlike several of her female classmates who were lost from the Corps because they couldn't tow the mark. Then she was on to another portion of the same base for the Corps' celebrated TBS, as The Basic School is fondly known. TBS is the grinding, self-challenging, six-month gauntlet that every officer of the United States Marine Corps must negotiate. Now knowledgeable in military history, tactics, land navigation, GPS use, pistol, rifle, grenade, an array of machine guns, combat martial arts, water and land survival techniques, and military leadership skills, she was also physically tuned to perfection.

Christine liked arising this early to do her daily physical training, or PT, a mantra to Marines. A talented athlete since childhood, she had been the star pitcher of her high school softball team back in Watertown, New York, and had led her soccer team to the state finals as the fearless goalie who deflected even the most violent shots. At Elizabethtown, a regional soccer powerhouse, she once again became the nemesis of opposing forwards and halfbacks, guarding her goal with ferocious tenacity. And she placed admirably in conference finals in women's doubles tennis.

Slipping her graceful, silky-smooth legs into her green PT shorts and matching green T-shirt, she pulled on her running shoes and bounded out of her "can," the trailer she shared with one other female Marine officer. Here at Marine Corps Base Camp Blue Diamond, on the Euphrates River in the heart of the Sunni Triangle and the Iraq insurgency, she loved the crisp desert air during her usual two laps around the scenic base for her light routine of three miles. Stretching her firm and powerful muscles, she alternately touched her toes with the opposing hand and did repetitive squats. Dropping to the sidewalk, she did twenty-five picture-perfect push-ups, then leaped to the ubiquitous USMC chin bar and did ten graceful pull-ups. Women aren't required to do any; the USMC minimum for men is three. Then she was off on her run.

Built by Saddam Hussein to both accommodate and banish his sociopathic son Uday, Camp Blue Diamond featured some twenty-five lovely buildings, all handsomely covered with a façade that looked all the world like expensive quarried sandstone but was in fact two-inch thick beige-tinted, molded concrete, mortared onto a base of concrete block. Unfortunately, Uday's spectacular palace had been blasted with aerial bombs by the US Air Force during the 2003 Iraq invasion, but parts of it were still in service as troop berthing. Nearly all the other buildings were unblemished, and pressed into service as office space or berthing.

Sturdily built, Saddam's buildings were all "hardened," in other words relatively safe from aerial bombardment with rockets and mortars. The Marines' "cans" offered no such protection, so they were all surrounded by sandbags piled chest-high. Still, any explosive coming through the roof would be instantly lethal to those inside.

Except for the Euphrates shore side, the base was entirely surrounded by a twelve-foot high concrete wall. Guard towers bristling with machine guns and grenade launchers and manned by grim young Marines, protected the entire perimeter. Occasional desultory infantry attacks by suicidal insurgents were readily repulsed by a fusillade of withering fire from the towers. The roads leading to the massive gates were encumbered with alternating Jersey barriers that required sharp criss-cross turns by entering vehicles, preventing suicide bombers from getting up a run to challenge the gates. The Marines had learned these techniques the hard way in Beirut, Lebanon in 1981, when a suicide truck bomber had leveled their five-story barracks building at Beirut International Airport, resulting in the instantaneous loss of some two hundred and forty Marines.

Bounding down River Road, the main line of Blue Diamond, Christine greeted each group of Marines passing her with the usual, "Rah," the abbreviation for the always-appropriate Marine salutation of "Ooh-rah", also a creative exclamation for virtually any event which a Marine encounters. Alternatively, Marines occasionally simple growl at each other, with a scowling face, of course. Elite professional warriors share a rich and eclectic culture which promotes their esprit.

With a pleasing light sweat, her muscles engorged and limber, Christine darted into her can to retrieve her shower gear and headed for the shower trailer, some 50 yards distant. Running water is rarely available in forward bases, so the availability of shower trailers was a privilege denied most American warriors in Iraq. Signs in all such facilities admonish, "Navy showers only." All those in the US maritime services know this means to turn on the water and soak yourself for one minute, lather your entire body with the water off, then use two more minutes of water stream to rinse yourself. Although it sounds austere, forward deployed military members know that even a three-minute Navy shower is sheer luxury and are grateful for the privilege. Even the women, with the special bathing needs of long hair.

Slipping out of the shower and toweling herself down, Christine reveled in the beauty of her body: lustrous light brunette mane, graceful but muscular arms, perfect uplifted breasts, a tight abdomen, and legs shapely all the way to her flawlessly rounded derriere. Sliding into her underwear, then the desert cammie uniform, careful to keep from dragging any portions of it on the muddy floor, Christine was radiant. She expertly twisted her shining hair into a bun on the back of her head, per USMC standards, allowing her 8-point military headgear or "cover" to make just the right rakish fit. She tugged on her boots and tucked the trouser-bottoms up under the elastic blousing straps, a system designed to prevent insects from creeping up the boot onto bare skin of the leg. Finally, Christine buckled on her holster belt, bearing her USMC-issue 9 mm Beretta automatic pistol. Although the uniform fits loosely to allow full body motion in combat, her graceful curves and perfect physique were apparent nonetheless. Even in their bulky desert-beige boots, military women are a marvelous addition to the otherwise drab desert vista for their male counterparts.

CHAPTER THREE

SUSPICION

Wednesday, March 9, 2005

Striding briskly to her office in one of Uday Hussein's elegant buildings, now divided into military office cubicles by plywood partitions, Christine was greeted at the door by Corporal Carmine Carbone, a twenty-three year-old iron-tough combat veteran who worked for her in the Judge Advocate General, or JAG office. Cpl Carbone was the senior enlisted man in the office, supported by Lance Corporals John MacClure and Duncan Longe, both smart and capable young Marines. Christine had requested service in the Naval Investigative Service (NIS), which is the Navy and Marine Corps' FBI, and is located on every such base in the world. Having selected this military career path, Christine believed that her contribution to The Corps was to maintain its honor and integrity by rooting out those who couldn't hold its banner high. But instead she was assigned to this legal office in a communications battalion.

"Did you hear?" Corporal Carbone asked. Exceedingly reliable, Corporal Carbone was always up on the latest developments. He was a superior leader and role model for the two lance corporals and the private first class (PFC) who worked for him.

"What happened?" Christine replied.

"A bad one—really bad. General Sienkewicz: KIA. The whole helo —fifteen Marines, a couple civilians, both pilots—all dead. Only one guy survived."

"When did it happen?"

"Didn't you hear the commotion? About 0200 the Quick Reaction Force fired up and headed out the east gate. Came back about six."

"Gosh, no, I didn't hear anything. I've trained myself to tune out all the shooting at night, or I'd never get any sleep. I did see the convoy this morning, but didn't pay it much mind–looked like any other. Do they know what happened?"

"The SIPR says they were *shot* down, about ten miles east of here. But they never got off a radio call, so our response was delayed." [SIPR is encrypted, classified military internet].

*Christine's mind was racing. The loss of a **General** was a very serious matter in the military. Of all the helo flights in Iraq, very few carried General officers. Was it a coincidence that **this** helo was shot down, or was there something more sinister going on here?*

She sat down at her desk, lost in thought. *General Sienkewicz was such a superb officer, a respected mentor, a fantastic role model, and a dear fellow. Oh my Lord,* she thought, *four kids. And he was so close to them all. Those poor kids. And Mrs. Sienkewicz, such a gracious lady. Always taking care of the other wives, being there for them in their inevitable life crises. I feel so bad for them.*

Christine's intellectual side was already searching for associations, correlations, evidence of a trend. If the shoot-down was simply random enemy action, the event was out of her lane. But if there was reason to think it was something else, something involving an intelligence leak, then it was *entirely* in her bailiwick.

"Corporal Carbone, is Major Azaz in yet?"

"He was in earlier, Ma'am, but he went out to do PT."

Christine signed on to her classified computer, and called up the 2nd Marine Expeditionary Force (II MEF) webpage. Selecting "SigEvents," she brought up all of the contact with enemy forces over the past twenty-four hours. A few mortar rounds fired at Camp Ar Ramadi across the river last night. A Marine wounded with small arms fire (SAF) in Fallulah. *That damned sniper is still taking a toll,* Christine thought to herself. *He's hit 5 Marines over the past 2 weeks. One was saved by his helmet, and one by his body armor, but 3 were hit—one dead, now 2 badly injured.* "Gotta get that bastard", she whispered. "He's way too good".

Then there it was, near the end of the day's events. "USMC H-46 crashed seven miles east of Ramadi. Both pilots, both gunners, 10 Marines, 2 civilians KIA. General Officer KIA. One survivor WIA. Aircraft destroyed. Reportedly shot down by ground fire."

My Lord, she thought, *fourteen of our guys lost, both pilots, civilians, the General. What a disaster.*

Major Farouk Azaz was her officer in charge (OIC). Born of Egyptian parents in Michigan, he was fluent in Arabic language and culture. But he was also red-white-and-blue-blooded American, who would risk his life to help the Detroit Tigers win the pennant. Raised Muslim but married to an Irish Catholic girl, they compromised and periodically attended together services at the Unitarian Church in Jacksonville, NC, home of Camp Lejeune. But they both honored their roots as well, such that she periodically attended Mass, and he mosque.

"Good morning, Captain Curtis," Major Aza greeted Christine with a concerned expression. "Bad night, huh?"

"The worst," she responded. "General Sienkewicz was such a prince."

"As good as they get," he agreed. "I really admired his style. If I ever made flag rank, I'd want to carry myself like him." Pausing, Major Azaz positioned his boot on a chair and leaned over on his knee. "Any thoughts about what happened to them?"

"I'm pondering that now. It's relatively rare for our choppers to take fire. I don't know if that's because they only fly in the dark, because of their gunners, because they vary their flight route, or because they're lucky, but Mohammed doesn't usually like to fight in the dark."

"Well, it's up to the air guys to review it. We've got a lot on our own plate here. Where do you stand on the court martial?"

"I'm coming along with it, Major, but it's not ready yet." Hesitantly, Christine paused, then continued, "Major, I'd like to walk down to the COC and chat with the air guys about this crash. This could possibly involve us." ["COC" = Combat Operations Center, the planning center for all USMC operational activities].

"That's a pretty heavy statement, Captain. Do you have anything to suggest there's something fishy here?"

"It's just a feeling, sir. I'll have the court martial out in plenty of time, and I'd really like to pursue this a little. General Sienkewicz was one of my heroes."

"All right, Captain, if you're confident you're on speed with the court martial, go for it."

"Thank you, Sir, I really appreciate it," Christine said, relieved she could make some effort to right the terrible wrong that occurred to her Marine brothers and sisters the previous night. Standing up and straightening her blouse, she strode to Corporal Carbone's desk, palming the butt of the 9 mm Beretta automatic pistol strapped to her right thigh. "Corporal Carbone, I'm going to the air ops office at COC. Be back in an hour or so."

"Yes ma'am. I'll call down there if anything comes up."

And with that she was out the door. Striding briskly down River Road, she barely noticed the graceful date palms lining the road, the crystal-clear blue sky, the dry gentle breeze typical of Iraq's wide-open spaces, or the gently flowing Euphrates on her left.

Birds flitted among the rich bunches of dates suspended at the bases of the palm fronds. All went un-noticed by Christine as she pondered further the night's loss. *Lots of flights every night, and they're all in harm's way,* she reflected. *Gotta be sure we're doing all we can from the ground side to keep them safe.*

Past the chow hall with its three-foot thick roof of earth and timber to protect dining Marines from indirect fire. Past the Morale, Welfare, and Recreation Shop (MWR), with its pool tables, ping-pong tables, board games, video games, books and magazines, all available twenty-four hours to accommodate the shift-working Marines. Past the base laundry and under the massive middle "gate," an arch like the Arc de Triomphe in Paris, graceful despite its ten-story high stature, with machine gun emplacements covering its top deck, all covered over with cammie netting to obscure the Marines from enemy snipers. Past the motor pool, where teams of male and female Marine mechanics were servicing huge seven-ton trucks and the heavy up-armored Humvees. Turning left into the access road of what was Uday's second major palace on the camp, Christine skirted the steel I-beam gate mounted on a single wheel and glanced at the red-white-and black Iraqi flag painting the breeze beside Old Glory. Past the sentry's shack, where the Lance Corporal's "Ooh-rah" was answered with her gentle "Rah." Up the marble steps, through the grand, heavy wooden front door and into the sweeping three story marble lobby. Left through the ramshackle door mounted on the hastily-erected plywood wall, she turned right into the twenty-foot high room and passed row after row of eight-foot high plywood walls separating banks of desks, finally stopping in the last compartment, the air office.

Chapter Four

Check The Stats

Wednesday, March 9, 2005

Major Matt Baxter sat behind his desk, staring intently at his computer screen. He had a five-o'clock shadow due to being urgently summoned to the office at 0400 when word came back of the crash of Legacy 23. A graduate of "The Cradle of Naval Aviation," Naval Air Station Pensacola, Florida, the coveted golden wings of a United States Naval Aviator glittered above the embroidered "U.S. Marines" on his left breast pocket. Fifteen hundred hours of flying the same model helicopter that crashed, the H-46 Sea Knight, had instilled in him an enormous fund of knowledge about that aircraft. The H-46 has a distinctive appearance, and is accordingly nicknamed "The Bullfrog" because of its wide aft end, housing the main wheels.

It is said that there is no substitute for experience, and Matt had plenty of it. It is also said that you never truly know a subject until you teach it, and he had done that, too, as an Instructor Pilot at Middle River Marine Corps Air Station, adjacent to Camp Lejeune, for two of his 17 years in the Corps. An honor graduate of Baylor University, Major Baxter had an incisive mind, an aviator's derring-do, and a Marine Corps officer's forcefulness. At five foot eleven and a hundred and seventy-five pounds, his thirty-eight-year-old frame was a bundle of muscle in a perfect "V" configuration. He looked like the toughest guy on the base. And Marine Corps bases are full of tough guys and gals.

The cammie uniform doesn't allow the wearing of ribbons, but Major Baxter rated six rows of them. During the 1991 Persian Gulf War, he had been deployed with the battle force, fresh out of training in the H-1 Cobra Gunship. He had proven to be one of the rare helo pilots designated an Ace for shooting down no fewer than three Iraqi attack helos. Although

27

his ship was damaged by A-A fire as well as the near-miss detonation of an Iraqi air-to-air missile, and taking shrapnel in his left arm and leg, he had stayed in the fight with his gunner. They proceeded to turn back an Iraqi convoy bearing down on a battle-depleted U.S. unit. In that convoy, they destroyed three troop-carrying trucks, as well as a battle tank and an armored troop carrier. The latter two each had an explosive and terminal meeting with a Maverick missile. For his heroism and superb airmanship, the Major was awarded the coveted Navy Cross with "V" for valor, the second-highest award an American fighting man can receive, after the Congressional Medal of Honor.

The other rows of ribbons on his chest included the Marine Corps Air Medal with bronze star in lieu of second award, the Bronze Star Medal with Combat V, the Meritorious Service Medal, an Army Commendation Medal (for turning back that Iraqi convoy threatening a U.S. Army unit), the Navy and Marine Corps Commendation medal with two bronze stars, the Navy Achievement Medal with one bronze star, the Combat Action Medal, and the Purple Heart. His lesser awards included the Sea Service Medal, the Battle E Medal, the West Asia Campaign Medal, the Kuwaiti Liberation Medal, the Overseas Service Medal, and the Joint Service Medal. In his dress uniform, his chest was truly a mosaic of professional military achievement, and all eyes were glued to it in admiration whenever he walked into a room. A very senior major, he was in zone for promotion to Lieutenant Colonel.

"Good morning, Major Baxter," Christine offered with a subdued smile. She had seen him a number of times PT'ing on base, and had occasionally been at a chow hall table where he was part of the group. His physique was not lost on her discriminating eye. She knew his reputation to be one of toughness, fairness, and intense loyalty to The Corps and his Marines. Two of his people had been injured by an Improvised Explosive Device (IED) two months earlier, and he had gone overboard in keeping track of them and their families as they underwent medical care at each level.

Looking up, he offered, "It's not so good a morning in the air office, Captain. But hello. What brings you our way?"

"The accident," she responded. "Major Azaz suggested I check in with your shop to see if there are any issues we might be able to help you with," she responded, stretching the truth.

"It's still really early in the investigation, Captain. I don't have anything yet. Any ideas?"

"Do you have a listing of all enemy fire on our helicopters, with or without loss of the aircraft? I think that's the right place to start."

"Yes, it's published every day on the II MEF (Marine Expeditionary Force, a subunit of the 2nd Marine Division) website and put out on SIPR, but I keep a separate listing for all incidents involving Marine aircraft in Iraq. I don't do Army and Air Force incidents—they keep track of those themselves." [SIPR = Secret Internet Provider Receiver, the military's classified and encrypted internet].

"Whatever you have will let me get started, Major," Chris responded gratefully. She *really* didn't want to try to extract that data from a comprehensive listing that included non-aviation incidents.

"Okay, tell you what, Captain. How 'bout you look through this file, and we meet up tomorrow at ten. That work for you?"

"That'll be terrific, Major. Thanks for being so organized. You found that file in twelve seconds—I counted."

"That's why they pay me the big bucks," Matt grinned tiredly. Then, more seriously, he added, "I'm tired of flying this big brown desk. But I owe it to those Marines to find out exactly how this all came down. And, from a selfish point of view, I'm gonna be back in the left seat of a Frog in another year and I want to know all the details of this mess."

"See you at ten tomorrow, right here, Major."

"Roger, Captain, see you then. Find something for me."

"I'll try," she uttered as she started back down the hall. Christine was pleased to have some hard data to pore over to look for patterns or deviations—anything that suggested other than random occurrences.

The Iraq War was now into its third year, but the insurgency was widespread, well equipped and funded, progressively more sophisticated in tactics, and horribly lethal. Christine could understand Sunni Muslims fighting US forces early on. They'd been on the gravy train with Saddam for years—no need to work, Saddam would provide for them—since they were his brand of Islam and a minority in Iraq, constituting only 20% of Iraq's population of twenty-six million. But one purpose of this war —beyond the suspicion that Saddam was developing weapons of mass destruction—was to bring Iraq into the family of nations that value their citizens and treat them with respect. Saddam the brutal tyrant was paying off the Sunni's to keep them happy, while persecuting the Kurds and Shia mercilessly.

But what kind of morons blow up their own country's oil infrastructure, destroy its government buildings, and murder their intelligentsia? After three long years, you'd think that they'd have figured out that 20% isn't going to rule 80%. They would figure it out, Christine knew, *but would the American people understand what was going on here? Societies that are increasing their populations faster than their economies, can't absorb their young into their work force, resulting in underutilized youth – a recipe for catastrophe. Arab economies – all of them – are practically nonexistent other than oil export, and the revenue from oil is shared by a diminutive minority of citizens.*

Christine kicked a stone as she walked along River Road, lost in thought but periodically greeting young rifle-slung Marines with "Rah" as she contemplated. *We've got to get this economy going – it's not poverty that makes suicide bombers, and it's not ignorance – the 9/11 bombers were mostly middle class and educated. It's hopelessness for the societies that breed them, arising out of incompetent governance – and we've gotta fix that. Iraq is just a start, but we've got to make it successful, and that means controlling the insurgency. And I need to determine if this helo crash is related to the insurgency.*

CHAPTER FIVE

FOLLOW THE MONEY

Wednesday, March 9, 2005

"Victory is sweet, my friend, isn't it? And so special a prize—a three-star American general—who would have thought?" Prince Mustapha Alquieri smiled broadly as he whispered into his cell phone, confident that the Saudi intelligence services wouldn't dare listen in on the line of a Royal.

"Ah, my Prince, we have succeeded so wildly, we will be richly received by The Forum," replied Prince Abdul Saad. "Allah is smiling upon us more than ever before, and over all the Muslim world. We have rid the world of sixteen more Americans, and dealt a blow to their morale that will be received poorly by the weepy American people. Who knows, maybe the *New York Times* will join hands with us as it proclaims the unlawfulness and miserable failure the occupation of Iraq has become. The Caliphate is one step closer."

"You think so far ahead, Prince Saad. But it is right to anticipate. All the mighty Arabic peoples finally united under one Caliph, who will demand absolute adherence to Sharia. The dissenters will be put to the sword. And then, with the fatwa Islam has waited for for a thousand years, we fulfill the Prophet's call to attack the infidels everywhere they work, live, play, and sleep. And we will, with Allah's blessed hand, slay them all and repopulate their lands with The Faithful. Oh, my heart throbs for the day!"

"Slow down, slow down, my brother," chuckled Saad. "Now *you* are way too far ahead. But it is good to look at the prize at the end of the journey. Allah will rule his earth from Mecca eastward, and back to Mecca from the west!"

"Now both of us are getting ahead of ourselves, my Prince. But let us savor the moment, and prepare to be received like the mighty victorious warriors we are, at the Forum of The Avengers in Riyadh next week. The entire leadership of the Sacred Sword of The Avenger will be there to revere us."

"You are right, my friend, there is much to be done yet, but we can certainly rightfully claim our respect from the brothers. And perhaps, my brother, we should begin planning our next operation – the momentum is with us now. I will contact our source within the camp of the occupiers in Iraq this very night. I will share with you tomorrow the intelligence I have extracted, and we can work on a new operation without delay."

"Until then, my Prince," said Saad.

"Go in peace, my brother," replied Alquieri as he disconnected the call. He punched up his address book, and verified the number for his contact at Camp Blue Diamond. They would have an elated conversation that very night. "Ah, death to seventeen more infidels," he whispered to himself. "May I live to see death to seventeen million, and then one hundred and seventeen million," he murmured.

CHAPTER SIX

THE EVIDENCE MOUNTS

Wednesday, March 9, 2005

Christine flipped through the log of aviation mishaps. Considering that the Marines were flying the Vietnam-era H-46, all at night, through hostile territory, usually with no visual references out over the black desert, the mishap log showed superb performance of the pilots, as well as the devoted legions of smart, highly trained young Marines who swarmed over the helo's every morning to do the preventive maintenance that averted in-flight emergencies. But helicopters are complex machines, and even with the best maintenance, some parts will fail unexpectedly. Then the prescience of the original design engineers comes to the fore, with the amazing duplication of so many systems, such that if one fails (or is shot away), another will prevent loss of control or an emergency landing in enemy territory. That's the reason military aircraft cost so much more than civilian versions, and it's worth every penny to keep the mission going forward, to not lose your expensively-trained people, to avoid the demoralization that occurs whenever people and materiel are lost, and to minimize the misery and compromises required when your own are captured by the enemy.

A hydraulic line burst in the mid fuselage, severely scalding two passengers, but the flight proceeded safely to its planned landing zone. An engine failed in flight, but was successfully shut down, and the careful design of the aircraft allowed it to continue flight on the remaining engine, albeit more slowly, to its destination. A tire blew due to a hard landing in the dark. Thankfully, failure of the rotors is exceedingly rare, because the helicopter would shake itself to bits within minutes if a chunk of either rotor separated. Again, brilliant design and manufacturing, and frequent inspections with routine replacement, rendered such catastrophic failures extremely rare. Christine was proud of her nation for producing such superb design engineers, factory workers, and supply people, disciplined

33

young mechanics, and superior pilots to guide these noisy, vibrating, but splendidly effective aircraft through their missions.

These traits are diametrically different from our militant adversaries, who can't seem to do anything right. They manufacture little. They don't author much science or literature, they don't craft art, they don't innovate commerce. Their societies are harsh, corrupt, repressive. They're nearly all failed societies. The insurgency's answer to this dismal state of affairs is to preserve their ignorant, backward status quo. And the goal of Al Qaeda is to force the rest of the world to capitulate to these stagnant societies and to a religion which, in their deviant interpretation of it, devalues human life. Their Islamist theology, in stark contrast with mainstream Islam, finds no fault with vicious brutality perpetrated against innocent civilians. Go figure.

"Hmm," she muttered, "the last severe mishap was a 46 taking ground fire shortly after departing Camp Fallujah. That's only forty miles from here. Coincidence?" she wondered aloud. "No one was suspicious of that event. One passenger dead, two injured, and the aircraft was shot up a bit, but landed safely back at Fallujah."

She flipped through the pages. Aircraft had taken ground fire at a number of airports, including a big commercial jet departing Baghdad International. It was hit by a shoulder-fired missile that destroyed an engine, but still landed safely.

Uh oh, here's another one en route to Al Asad, out of none other than Blue Diamond. So out of twenty-seven episodes of ground fire striking aircraft in Iraq over the six months, five of them have been departing from or en route to Blue Diamond. There are some forty-five USMC landing sites in Iraq. That's way too many to be disregarded. I wonder, she thought, as she peered through the window of her office, not really noticing the sparrows fluttering around the clusters of dates crowning rich and ripe just outside her window. It was latesummer, and although it still reached 110 degrees during the day, it dropped to a merciful 70 at night, far better than the perpetually-above-100-degrees oven that western Iraq becomes during the peak of summer, similar to the western hemisphere's seasons. *I need to run this by Matt,* she thought, *he's the Airdale. Maybe there's an explanation for this grouping. Maybe there are more flights around Blue Diamond than other bases. Who knows? I need an air guy for this one.*

CHAPTER SEVEN

THE SNAKE IN HIS LAIR

Wednesday, March 9, 2005

The cell phone that Samir had smuggled on base vibrated silently at precisely 9:45 PM, as planned. Samir had casually left his quarters at "TCN Village" [TCN = Third Country National] aboard Camp Blue Diamond and strode to the spot he had carefully selected for good reception, invisibility in the shadows, and privacy so no one could hear his whispering. Along the Euphrates, but not out toward the line of reeds where the sentries could see him with their night vision goggles, he stood one hundred feet from the powerful current carrying Iraq's lifeblood from the mountains in Turkey where the Euphrates originated, through Syria, and through all of Iraq, emptying into the Persian Gulf near Basra.

"God is great," the voice tersely stated.

"Allah will reign over all His earth," Samir offered his coded response.

"You have served Allah well, my friend," purred Prince Alquieri. "All of Islam salutes you today. There will be a handsome reward for your service in this operation."

"You are generous beyond need, my Prince," responded Samir, hoping it wouldn't dissuade the Prince from the reward. "Anything to serve my people and my God."

"Islamic warriors will triumph over all the infidels, my brother. But we must be clever and patient. We are interested in planning a new operation. I need you to monitor events carefully, and report back to me in seven days. I need to know about convoys, flights, especially important visitors, new tactics or weapons, new campaigns—it is all of value to us. Can you do it?"

"They trust me with all their secrets, my Prince. I can do it."

"I have deposited twenty-five thousand dollars in your account here in the Land of the Prophet. Go in peace, my brother. I will call you in seven days at the same time. Be sure your phone is charged. Notify me through your father if phone service there in Ramadi is disturbed."

"Good night, my prince. And congratulations."

"Good night, my noble warrior."

Samir clicked the phone off, slid it into the concealed inside pocket of his jacket, and slowly walked back toward his quarters. Cell phones were prohibited among TCNs for precisely this reason – to prevent the leakage of intelligence from inside the base. The most obvious harm would be calling to mortar or rocket teams where their rounds had landed, so that they could adjust their aim and hit specific targets on base. Because of the 12-foot walls surrounding the base, mortar teams could not assess where there rounds landed, so as to adjust their aim to hit targets of choice. But this approach was weak, because the U.S. Army's massive 155 mm Palladin cannon could, with its counter battery radar, pinpoint the precise location of origin of incoming rounds, and within two minutes rain hundred-pound projectiles of high explosive on any site of origin within fifteen miles. So the rogue Saudi's had decided to avoid risking discovery of their embedded agent. Samir Hashimi was far too valuable to be lost over a few mortar shell placements. He was a "terp" – an interpreter for the Marines. Hired from Pakistan by Titan Corporation, which supplies most of the Arabic linguists to all the US military services, Titan's cursory review didn't reveal any of Samir's fundamentalist furor, his childhood indoctrination into hate and violent jihad via a Saudi-sponsored madrassah, or his trips to the Al Qaeda training camps in Afghanistan, or his swearing to the murderous mission of Osama bin Laden, of ridding the Islamic world of all vestiges of the modern world, and imposing the iron rule of fundamentalist Islam, Sharia, over all the lands of Islam, and, eventually, all the lands of the earth. Because of his excellent English, which he picked up from watching American movies, followed by Al-Qaeda-sponsored travel in the US and England, he was ordered by his Al Qaeda handlers to apply for the position. They had provided him with fraudulent documents so that his travels could not be associated with his new identity. Samir was a smooth character, reassuring everyone with his quick smile, his excellent English, his ability to handle complex dialogue expertly in translation, his counseling of his American superiors on nuances of speech and gesture, and his outspoken condemnation of militant Islam. Having begun in the dangerous role of terp with field teams outside the wire, he had moved upward through the ranks till he was the Commanding General's personal linguist. It was hard to do better than this. He was privy to top secret conversations the one-star General conductedwith Iraqi government officials. Since his office was next to the General's, his exquisite hearing allowed him to surreptitiously listen in on the General's conversations with American leaders as well. Al Qaeda had done this one just right.

The money will be helpful, Samir thought, as he strolled down River Road, illuminated only by moonlight in the blacked-out base. *But I would do this work for the sheer pleasure of seeing the infidels' blood flowing like this mighty river, into the recesses of our blessed desert.* He was pumped to look for an even bigger score than the one he had just accomplished.

CHAPTER EIGHT

SUSPICION NOT CONFIRMED

Thursday, March 10, 2005

"I don't know, Captain," Matt said tentatively. "Blue Diamond is kind of in the middle of the Marine flight corridors. I wonder if these stats don't just fit in with the number of flights passing through and over it." Matt Baxter was a 737 pilot for Southwest Airlines, but a veteran Marine with 17 years' service—the first six active duty, including flight school and the Persian Gulf War, a year at Camp Futema on Okinawa, and 10 subsequent years in the Marine Corps Reserve. Strikingly handsome, back home the dark green trousers/khaki shirt with khaki tie and ribbons of his "Charlie" uniform on his chiseled body left women gawking. Here in theatre, only suggestions of his perfect physique were revealed by his loose-fitting digital desert cammie uniform. With a total of 4,000 flight hours, he was an elite aviation professional, with broad experience on both the military and civilian sides. Smart, disciplined, handsome, successful, but kind and cheerful, he was as eligible a bachelor as ever there was. And this fact wasn't lost on Christine.

A native of rural Oklahoma, where his extended family still resided, Matt grew up a dirt-poor share-cropper's son. The first of his family to attend college, he now lived in St. Louis, so as to enjoy a short commute to the airport. He kept his apartment during this deployment, and had neighbors check in on it during this 7-month tour abroad. Never married, he dated extensively. There was a constant influx of lovely young women in the airline business, and he availed himself generously of this particular professional perk. For the 8 months prior to this mobilization, however, he had been exclusively seeing a certain shapely and bright young corporative executive, Washington U MBA type, and was actively communicating with her by e-mail several times per week. "I know it's not much, Major Baxter, but I think it's enough to warrant closer examination," Christine retorted. "If there's something here," she went on, "missing it could cost Marine lives."

"Yeah, but at the same time, we're busy as hell, with the RIP/TOA of 3/6 Marines. We don't have time for wild geese." [Relief In Place/ Transfer of Authority to 3rd Marine Battalion, 6th Marine Regiment, part of the 2nd Marine Division. RIP/TOA is the process of replacing one deployed Marine Corps unit with its follow-on sister unit].

"I'll take the heat if nothing comes of it," Christine replied, determined at this point to carry on the inquiry. "I'll see to it that everyone knows you had reservations, but that I pushed the issue."

"Aw, c'mon, Major, I don't need that. I'm concerned about distracting both of us from issues that we *know* exist and warrant our attention." Matt paused. "Okay, tell you what – you collect more data, and we'll meet— what do you think—three days? Does that give you enough time?"

"I'll make it enough," Christine quipped, with a smile. "Thank you, Major Baxter. I'll see you here on Saturday morning at 10—good to go?"

"Good to go. See ya then," nodded Major Baxter, turning back to the schedules on his cluttered desk.

Christine gathered her papers into the folder and turned to leave. Her eyes met those of Captain Stella Rogers, the assistant air officer. At age twenty-seven, Captain Rogers was a black-haired, brown-eyed knockout. In her civilian life, she was an up-and-coming corporate executive, or shark, as Christine preferred to think of her. Captain Rogers was smart, accomplished, beautiful, and single. And with seven hundred hours of flying Hueys under her belt, she was an authentic aviation pro. Striding out of the COC (Combat Operations Center), Christine thought she detected a touch of territoriality in those lovely brown eyes, but she broke the eye contact without expression and walked away.

Christine was lost in thought. *Could she put her other cases on a back burner for a while without harming them? Would Major Azaz allow it?* She'd need to convince him as well as Major Baxter about the validity of the trend. With work hours of 0800 to 2100 hours six days a week and noon to 2100 on Sundays, she simply couldn't work on this project in her "spare time" – there wasn't any. 'Til she got home, bathed, and read a novel for a half hour to unwind, she needed to be sleep by 1030 to be fresh at 0600 when she customarily arose. And then it was go-go all day again. She sighed. Weekends were such a joy at home, with time to do anything you wanted – sleep late, travel, drink, go on a date – all prized activities that are forbidden or impossible in the combat zone.

But this mission prevails over all other pleasures, she reasoned. *America was attacked, and will continue to be attacked by the forces of hopelessness from the 'disconnected world.' We've got to connect up that world, or we'll never have peace. And I'm happy to do my share, despite deprivation of some of my most prized pleasures.*

As she walked along River Road, with its towering eucalyptus trees and swaying palms, she reflected on her life history. Born to privilege, her great-grandfather had been a principal shipper on the Erie Canal in its heyday, before the St. Lawrence Seaway put it out of business in the 1920s. All the agricultural and industrial output of the Midwest had passed through the Erie Canal to the population centers of the northeast, and the international ports of Boston and New York. Great-grandpa Curtis had accumulated millions, which grew over time to over $200 million. Wisely invested in generation-skipping trusts, her own share, as one of twenty-five living descendants, was $8 million when she was born, but had ballooned into some $20 million now. She had studied at swank private schools, culminating in her BS at Elizabethtown at age twenty-one.

That's when Christine joined The Corps. She had witnessed the shallow lives of some of her family who had allowed the money to ruin them, to make them obsessed with luxury and privilege, and the emptiness that comes from such self-centeredness. She wanted nothing to do with that, and had accordingly lived on a minimal stipend of $500 a month during her student days, allowing the trust to pay only her tuition, room & board, books, and fees. And to grow.

Finishing her Marine Corps officer training at Quantico, VA at age twenty-two, Christine followed in her Daddy's footsteps and chose Communications School—the rigorous four-month training to become a communications officer. Her Dad had parlayed his inheritance into building a business empire in the communications world, with cutting-edge products, computers and servers. Though capable of living a life of leisure, he chose to push himself into the impossible hours of a young entrepreneur, and succeeded wildly. At this point in his life, at age fifty-five, and with a net worth of a half billion dollars, he was turning over more and more of his business duties to his vice-presidents, and was devoting most of his time to mentoring young businessmen, funding talented entrepreneurs, leading charity fundraising, engaging in personal philanthropy, and enjoying his family.

Christine's first assignment as a buff, newly minted 2nd Lieutenant Communications Officer was as a company commander in a communications battalion. She and her Dad chatted regularly about the military's hardware and capabilities, which became yet another bond of their inseparable relationship.

Christine progressively learned more about radios, satellites, cryptography, internet protocols, and systems engineering than she ever knew existed. She received superior fitness reports for her leadership, with her company receiving awards for its high level of readiness. Her Marines loved her, because she was, first of all, tough as nails, which is what Marines expect in each other. Always scoring "outstanding" on the physical fitness tests, she was in perfect physical condition, and looked it in every way; her military bearing was exemplary.

Christine also learned to exhibit the confidence expected of a Marine officer. Her competence at communications allowed her to supervise her Marines that much more. But it was also clear to them that she cared about them as individuals, and that goes a long way, even with the iron men and women of The Corps. She pushed them to achieve personally, to aspire to higher rank and knowledge, to take the college courses available to them online wherever in the world The Corps sent them. And, although never stated by her subordinates, she was physically stunning, a beautiful woman by any standard, and a beautiful military officer to boot.

Finishing her three-year active-duty commitment to The Corps, Christine looked to a career in law. Just as she saw her participation in The Corps as enforcing the rules of the world, she felt called to a career as state's attorney in criminal law to enforce the laws of her country. So out of the twelve law schools she applied to, she shot for the moon with three "big names," and nine okay-but-not-elite schools. Somewhat to her surprise, based on her superior academics, athleticism, and compelling life history and personality, she was accepted into Harvard and Stanford, two of her three elites, and seven of the nine second-tier schools. With proximity to her family in mind. she chose Harvard Law School. She had kept her financial status from the Harvard admissions office—she didn't want to have preferential treatment by the admissions committee because of her family's resources. Besides, Harvard had an endowment at the time of some $12 billion, and if they needed to, could provide full scholarships for every student they accepted.

But as a committed Marine officer, Christine couldn't quite separate herself from The Corps. So during law school she remained a drilling member of the Marine Corps Reserve, reporting for duty one weekend a month, and two weeks per year, for continued training. Her drills were at Fort Devens Reserve Training Center, just an hour from Cambridge, in Ayer, Massachusetts, and she loved the atmosphere of courageous, committed young Americans in which she was immersed there. Away from the gaggle of specious-reasoning peaceniks, fortunately only a minority at the University, but who were content, in their personal comfort, to let the disconnected world writhe in its poverty, political deprivation, and incessant violence. Even when the towers fell and three thousand Americans were murdered in a few hours, some of the peaceniks were muttering how we had it coming, that it was all our fault. Ludicrous self-loathing, Christine believed, mixed in some of them with a certain amount of cowardice—even when their own were murdered for the crime of going to work to support their families, these self-proclaimed peace worshippers were unwilling to defend their country, even verbally. Had Americans grown that weak, that complacent, that shallow, that myopic, that narcissistic? *There is a stupidity penalty in life*, she thought. *I don't want all Americans to pay it, because of the incompetence of a few.*

So two years into her three-year J.D. program in 2005, the aftermath of the Iraq War summoned her call-up. She had expected the Marines to recall her in 2003 but the call never came. Regardless, she had been mobilized out of Devens Reserve Center, and reported to Camp Lejeune, NC, where she was ordered to HQ Bn, 2nd Marine Regiment, 2nd Marine Division. After the usual rifle and pistol range refreshers, where she re-qualified as expert marksman in both weapons, re-qualified in grenade-throwing and grenade launcher, re-qualified in 5.56 mm SAW (Squad Automatic Weapon) machine gun, as well as 240G 7.62 mm machine gun, as well as refresher in martial arts, she shipped out to Iraq with her unit. Christine thought she would be assigned to the Naval Investigative Service (NIS) in Washington, D.C., but instead she was assigned as a Judge Advocate General, a legal officer to a combat unit. Never one to shrink from danger, she accepted this new role with relish, proud to be among the courageous young men and women on the front lines of the war against terror.

CHAPTER NINE

A GRACEFUL LATERAL ARABESQUE

Thursday, March 10, 2005

"Anything new, Corporal Carbone?" Christine asked as she strode past his desk toward hers.

"The lance corporal who got ripped off by an internet scam was by, asking if there were any new developments."

"Oh gosh, I forgot about him. Did anything come in the mail or e-mail from the FBI? I was hoping that they'd take a look at this case since the lance corporal is over here".

"No, nothing yet, Captain, but the snail mail has been even slower the last couple weeks than usual—up to 4 weeks for some stuff. "

"Thanks. Is Major Azaz here?"

"Yes, he's in his office. Not having such a good day. The guys getting court-martialed for trying to sneak those AK-47s home are putting up a stink—have a Congressional. That's going to require mucho hours to pull the facts together for the beloved congressman."

"Oh boy, that's exactly what I didn't want to hear. Thanks."

Christine walked to Major Azaz's door and tapped lightly.

"Come in," the voice inside responded, sounding irritated.

"I heard. This is the third congressional this year. Why don't the congressmen wait 'til things settle out before wasting our time with these busy-work reports? Seventy-two hour response, huh?"

"Yeah, and I need you to take care of it, Captain. I'm swamped with some questions from the General about the legality of our financing the

43

Al Jamboori Clinic renovation. You know the General—announces in the morning that he wants a preliminary answer by the evening. He's killing me."

"Yeah, Major, I know. He's as good as they come in coordinating the battle space, but he sure puts the screws on his staff." Christine paused to sit down on the rickety folding chair facing his desk. "I've got an issue too, and it's equally as time-sensitive."

"Whaddaya have?" he asked, shaking his head from side to side and sighing.

"The crash three days ago, General Sienkewicz's crash. I've got some preliminary stats that are bothering me. There's a bit of a clustering of air incidents surrounding us here at Blue Diamond. I showed it to Major Baxter at the air office, and he thinks it's worth looking into. If there's something there, there's an immediate impact on flight safety—*all* flights. We've got a lot of Marines and others up there counting on us."

"Uh oh, Captain, not what I wanted to hear today. You know, you're not a prosecutor yet. You're a JAG officer in a combat unit. I'm sorry, but you need to either postpone that issue or hand it off. I need you here, on the battalion's business. Our stuff isn't very flashy, but the Marines involved don't think it's trivial, and keeping them content that we're working for them has an immediate impact on their morale. And that, I need not remind you, is *everything* in combat."

"I know, Major, I know. I'm not blowing off the importance of our Regiment work. But I have a feeling there's something here, that we owe it to all those pilots and passengers to rule out a preventable catastrophe."

"We can't do everything, Captain. I need that report."

"Okay, tell you what, Major. Corporal Carbone has just been super lately. And he's talked about law school himself. Let me get him to work on the congressional. Lance Corporals Polanski and Hernandez can pull together the documents, Corporal Carbone can write it up, and I'll review and modify it. Can you give me that?"

"I've gotta have something for the 1800 briefing. If you can get me something substantial by 1745 that gets the General off my back, you're on."

"Thanks a million, Major," she purred with a smile. "We'll have the General grinning," she assured him as she walked out the door. "Corporal Carbone..."

Chapter Ten

Enter The State Department

Thursday, March 10, 2005

Ring, ring! The phone clattered its distinctive ring sound on Christine's desk, under piles of papers. She searched for it, scattering documents onto the floor. She inadvertently pushed the phone to the edge of the desk, and it crashed to the floor as well, but Marine field phones are built for that. Retrieving the handset she shouted, "Hello, Major Curtis."

"Majah, it's Renee. How 'bout lunch? Lots to catch up with. Ah been in Baghdad the past fav days, and that embassy crowd is fah the bahds. I need to talk to a Mah-reen to get mah head screwed back on straight."

"Oh hi, Renee, I'd love to see you, but I'm really consumed with something. How 'bout next week?"

"No way, Babeh, I'm hungry and ya-all er eatin' with me. I thought you Marines knew you got to stoke the furnace if you want that fahr to keep burnin'."

Renee Booker was the State Department representative on base. Smart as a whip and Phi Beta Kappa at Vanderbilt, she was an authentic southern belle with American roots back to the Mayflower. Her lovely southern drawl concealed a razor-sharp mind, enhanced by her master's from the UCLA School of Government, and she was half way through her PhD at UNC in Chapel Hill. The "Staties" are the third wave of America's storm-troopers to hit the shores of the "disconnected world," after America's combat troops knock out the enemy's formal military forces, and the follow-on troops combat the insurgency. To build a nation that can take care of itself, skills other than combat-arms are required: governance,

45

commerce, public services, a legal system, and education that matches that of the new world its children are then privileged to compete in.

Laughing, Christine capitulated. "Okay, okay, I gotta eat, you're right. Meet you at the Chow Hall in ten minutes?"

"I'm a-walkin'!"

Eight minutes later, Christine strolled across the dusty access to the Chow Hall. The diners' access lane is surrounded by eight-foot-high, four-foot deep and wide earthen barriers called "Hesco's": cardboard/fiber fabric inside wire mesh frames—dirt cheap, like the dirt inside them, and totally effective at stopping shrapnel from incoming mortar or rocket rounds. Drawing her Beretta 9 mm pistol without thinking, she pointed it into the sand-filled barrel mounted at a forty-five degree angle, and cycled the slide—standard practice to prove no round is chambered. This maneuver verifies that a weapon is at the required "Condition Three": no magazine is kept in the weapon while inside the wire of Blue Diamond. But two magazines filled with fifteen rounds each were mounted on her holster, and Christine could have the magazine slapped in, the slide cycled, the safety off, and the first round on its way downrange within five seconds.

Christine flashed her ID at the sentry, whose weapons were in "Condition One;" he *did* have a round chambered in his M-16, the banana-shaped magazine of thirty rounds projecting from its underside. She greeted him, "Afternoon, Devil Dog," and washed her hands at the row of outdoor but roof-covered wash basins, always well stocked with liquid soap and rolls of paper towels. Falling in line with twenty other Marines lining up at the door, she saw Renee entering the washing area and fell back with her.

"So what is it with these Embassy people, Rains? They *are* Staties, aren't they?" Christine prodded.

"They're clueless 'bout what's goin' on out heah, Chris. The Green Zone is lak New York City, but with bunkahs and machine guns and 'casional rockets landin' and blowin' somebody up. They got bars, clubs, stores, Saddam's marble swimmin' pool—they forget there's people dyin' outside that wire. It bothers me. They good people. Smart, care 'bout the mission. But livin' in the Green Zone, it's easy to lose yer bearin's."

"Well, welcome back to the real Iraq, Rains. I missed you. C'mon, lets get some chow."

They strolled over to the main serving line. Renee went for the T-bone steak and a lobster tail. The front line troops eat well. Christine felt like being a teenager, so she headed for the short-order line. A big burger served up off the griddle by a smiling, uniformed, white-paper-hatted Indian cook. And fries that would do McDonald's proud. A brush by the ample salad bar, a short stop at the Baskin-Robbins fresh-dip counter, featuring a full four flavors today, and they were headed into the catacombs of the reinforced dining area. One of the minority of buildings on base built by the Marines that featured a reinforced roof to protect inhabitants from indirect fire from above (rockets and mortars), the dining area felt fortress-like because of the many heavy supports of the low ceiling, which featured a three-foot-thick earth-filled roof.

"So what's the big project, Chris? You don't get Marines drivin' drunk over heeyah. What's up?"

"Nothing certain, Rains, just something suspicious."

"So out with it, girl, what is it?"

"It's classified at this point, Rains."

"Oh c'mon girl, you know I got a Top Secret clearance. You only got Secret. 'Sides, I might be able to help. Could you use a soundin' board?"

Looking around, Christine saw that there were Marines in the booths on both sides of them. Not knowing their security clearances, she gathered her cups on the tray and told Renee to do the same. They walked to the empty tables at the far end of the seating area and set up again.

"Okay, out with it, girl. Whacha got?"

"Remember the helo crash last week, the one that killed General Sienkewicz?"

"Yeah, I read 'bout it in Stahs and Stripes" [the high-quality tabloid daily newspaper published by the U.S. military for its deployed troops all over the world]. Horrble. Twelve mreens and some civilians lost, wasn't it? One mreen made it?"

"Yeah, that's exactly right."

"So what?"

"So there may be more to it."

"Uh-oh, you startin' to sound nasty. What?"

"I'm reviewing the air incident statistics for the Euphrates Valley region, and comparing it to other parts of the theatre. There've been more incidents around here than elsewhere. It could be coincidence, but something tells me it's not."

"How many more, Chris?"

"Five incidents in the past six months around here, vice three west of here, and two to the east. There's also a cluster coming out of the Green Zone, but the Green Zone LZ is surrounded by hostile urban territory, so it's not suspicious that their launches frequently take fire."

"That's certainly in the realm of noise. Not a clear signal. What can you do to look furtha?"

"Not sure yet, but I'm working with Major Baxter over at Air. I need to finish reviewing more documents. We're meeting again Saturday morning. If there *is* something, we can't miss it."

"Ah flah in and out of here too, Chris. Now you got *me* intersted. How can Ah help?"

"I don't think you can, Renee. This is strictly military stuff."

"Need a hand with the record r'views? With concoctin' a strategy? I got a good sense for these things".

"Well, let me finish the reports I have here, and if I'm hitting a wall, I'll ring you up and ask you to review the big picture. Fair enough?"

"Sounds good, Chris. Now what's fer dessert?" Renee stood up and headed back to the serving area and its five different offerings for the sweet-of-tooth, ranging from cookies to chocolate pudding to Jell-O to cherry pie and, best of all, the hand-dipped Baskin-Robbins counter.

CHAPTER ELEVEN

SOLEMNITY

Friday, March 11, 2005

The memorial service for General Sienkewicz and the others lost on Legacy 23 was held two days after their passing. Conducted in the handsome masonry base chapel, which reportedly was once the brothel for Uday Hussein, the event was dignified and beautifully crafted. At the front of the room sat twelve pairs of boots with M-16s standing upright between them, supported by coarse wood frames built for the occasion by the SeaBees. A Kevlar helmet with digital cammie cloth cover perched on every rifle. The room was choked with more than a hundred Marines, some sitting, but most standing at parade rest in silent tribute to their fallen brothers and sisters.

Tears streamed down Christine's cheeks during the moving verses of the 23rd Psalm:

The Lord is my shepherd, I shall not want.
He maketh me to lie down in green pastures.
He leadeth me beside the still waters.
He restoreth my soul.
He leadeth me in paths of righteousness for his name's sake.
Yea, though I walk through the valley of the shadow of death,
I will fear no evil, for thou art with me.
Thy rod and thy staff, they comfort me.
Thou preparest a table before me, in the presence of mine
enemies.
Thou annointest my head with oil.
My cup runneth over.

Surely, goodness and mercy shall follow me all the days of my life.

And I shall dwell in the house of the Lord forever.

He maketh me to lie down in green pastures: how fitting for a funeral, she reflected.

The two Navy chaplains conducting the service were a Roman Catholic priest, LCDR Donohoe, and a Jewish rabbi, CDR Stiebel. They read the names of each of the departed, and made a few comments about each person. They reflected on the integration of life and death, and the nature of devotion to duty, honor, and country. Chaplain Donohoe commented on the everlasting life thesis of Christianity, and CDR Stiebel on the dignity of a life well lived. Prayers were offered to the welfare of the deceased, and that of their grieving survivors.

Toward the conclusion of the service, the group launched into the moving dirge of The Navy Hymn:

Eternal Father Strong To Save,
Whose arm doth bound the restless wave.
Who bidd'st the mighty ocean deep,
Its own appointed limits keep.
O hear us when we cry to thee
For those in peril on the sea.

The red-covered hymnal used by the US military around the world, the "Book of Worship For United States Forces," contains sixteen verses of the Navy Hymn and includes verses for eight different groups of the military. They next sang verse five:

Eternal Father, grant, we pray,
To all Marines, both night and day,
The courage, honor, strength, and skill,
Their land to serve, thy law fulfill;
Be thou the shield forevermore,
From every peril to the Corps.

At the conclusion of the hymn, red-eyed Marines filed silently out of the chapel and back to their workspaces, resolved to carry the battle to the enemy in an equally personal way. And the service cemented Christine's resolve that, despite her other professional commitments to the Marines of the battalion, she wouldn't allow any more services like this to result from an oversight by her on a lethal flaw in their operational security.

Seated in the row behind Matt, and a few seats to his side, Christine saw his head bowed and his face contorted with emotion during the prayers. Here was a man of powerful devotion, she reflected. A good man. A man to be trusted to come through. Seeing his muscular arms grasping the hymnal, she was comforted by his quiet strength. *This thing is being handled by the right people,* she thought, *We'll see it through.*

CHAPTER TWELVE

DANCE OF THE SNAKES

Friday, March 11, 2005

"God Is Great."

"Allah will reign over all His earth. Yes, my Prince, it is I. All is well here, and I have important tactical news for you."

"God is great, my son. He will bless us as we vanquish the occupiers, spill their blood on our sacred ground, and restore His law among His people. I am still celebrating our glorious victory over the 3-star general. I hope you are thinking of plans for an attack producing the same devastation to the enemy."

"Yes, my Prince, I am. You know the Crusaders maintain a CMOC in Ramadi at the Governate Center. [CMOC = Military Operations Center, a fortified, hardened building in the heart of a city, where citizens and Iraqi officials could converse with, and do business with, the Coalition Forces]. It is where they conduct the business of the devil with the weak members of our faith. I have learned that General Brier is to travel there by convoy in two days' time. The convoy will leave the east gate at ten in the morning and take the usual route, across the bridge and down what they call Route Milwaukee. I am certain that with the proper preparations, this General can be sent to the same fate as the other."

"You are right, my son. You have given me just enough time to make the proper preparations with our brothers in Ramadi. We will send the General a message straight from Allah. You have done well."

"Thank you, my Prince"

"Be sure you do nothing that could bring suspicion upon yourself. You are far too valuable to lose. But continue to gather the intelligence that will allow us to slaughter these devils."

"I shall, my Prince. When shall we speak again?"

"In a day's time, my son. I will call as usual. Until then."

"Until then, my Prince." The line went dead.

Samir concealed the phone in his inner pocket, and slowly walked back to his quarters.

CHAPTER THIRTEEN

A NETWORK OF WRITHING SERPENTS

Friday, March 11, 2005

"Hello, my brother," Prince Alquieri responded to the sleepy answer of his cousin, Prince Saad. "The news is good. We have an operation for the day after tomorrow. That is why I have disturbed your rest. I wish for you to coordinate this operation."

Groggily, Saad replied "Yes, my brother, that *is* good news." He rubbed his eyes and sat up. "Tell me about it."

"It is from our agent in Blue Diamond Camp in Ramadi. A general is traveling to the Government Center there. We know precisely when and what route he will take.

"Two generals in a row! Allah is truly smiling upon us. How do you think we should plan the operation?"

"I believe this one requires more than our few contacts among the faithful resistance in Ramadi. We should involve our brother Khalid in Damascus. He is constantly moving mujahadeen down the Euphrates Valley, and commands the resources this operation will require."

"Yes, my brother, you are right. I will contact him immediately to begin the plans. Tell me the details of the general's convoy."

Alquieri passed on the intel.

"When will we speak again?" queried Saad.

"Let us talk at noon on Monday—there should be news of the operation's success available by then."

"Noon on Monday it is," said Saad confidently. "Oh, and brother, we will need to assist Khalid with funds. Do you believe $50,000 will be sufficient?"

"We wish to keep his operations well oiled. Let us give him $75,000 immediately, and more after this operation. Use our Sacred Sword account."

"It will be done in the morning. 'Till Monday, my friend," said Saad.

"Monday noon, brother." The line went dead.

CHAPTER FOURTEEN

THE DIE IS CAST

Friday, March 11, 2005

"As salaam alikum, wa rehmat Allah." [Peace be upon you, and the mercy of God].

"Wa alikum as salaam, wa rehmat Allah, Brother Khalid." [Peace be upon you, *also*, and the mercy of God].

This is Prince Jabr calling. How are the faithful in the land of Assad?"

"My prince, I have torrents of devoted young jihadists pouring into Damascus, eager to shed their blood for Allah in the destruction of the crusaders. They come from everywhere. And many are already with Him, being serviced by the Virgins promised in The Hadith [Islamic writings attributed to the words of Mohammad, but not included in the Koran].

"We recently were blessed with a splendid victory, in the slaying of the crusader General near Ramadi. And now I am pleased to tell you that we have a similar ambitious operation planned for the day after tomorrow, Enshala" [God willing].

"I was hoping for such a call, my friend. My jihadists grow weary of simply exterminating collaborating government leaders and teachers, and imams who fail to preach the true word of Allah. We show no mercy in dealing with those who choose to be tools of the occupiers, and killing their families is necessary but unchallenging work. Tell me how my jihadists can strike a sacred blow at the infidels."

"The one-star general at the occupiers' base outside Ramadi will be traveling by vehicle to the Government Center in Ramadi on the morning of Sunday. The convoy will depart the Blue Diamond Camp at 10:00. We believe that the morale blow of two lost generals in short succession may sway the peace demanders of the occupiers' country to push even harder to withdraw the infidel soldiers. We will then be much closer to our sacred dream—a caliphate over all the Arab world, with Sharia law and no other. And then, gathering our forces under a modern Saladin, we can carry the battle to the very homes of the infidels. It is our sacred mission—Allah must be the one God of every land. And all those who resist must be put to the sword!"

"Slow down, my Prince. We have much to do before then. But I agree that we must keep our eye on the ultimate prize."

"Brother Khalid, we want you to position your fighters just after the traffic circle on the east side of the steel bridge south of the Blue Diamond Camp. The infidels maintain a strongpoint at the circle, but two hundred meters further toward the Government Center, we can overcome them all. The street will run crimson with invader blood."

"My Prince, I know the area, and I believe it is a sound plan. I will place 20 fighters on each side of the road. And I will place a bomb to stop them in our kill zone. I feel Allah is with us in this noble venture."

"I will leave further planning in your capable hands, Khalid. And The Council of The Sacred Sword will advance you more than enough funds to support this and future operations."

"Your kindness is like the sunshine, my Prince. I shall begin preparations. We will speak again after the victory."

"Allah be with you and your brave young mujahadeen."

CHAPTER FIFTEEN

THE SQUEEZE IS ON

Saturday, March 12, 2005

"Well, Captain, you're driving a legitimate argument. There clearly is an increased rate of firings on aircraft surrounding Ramadi, although there's a cluster in and out of LZ Washington in the IZ." [The International Zone, or Green Zone, is the diplomatic and government area in Baghdad, Saddam's former seat of government. As with all of Saddam's "palaces," it is surrounded by tall masonry walls.]

"I'm pretty sure there's something here, Major. But I'm not sure what to do next."

"I think you've done enough homework to take this to the next level, Captain. Let's see what Colonel Burdine, the CG's Chief of Staff, makes of it."

"Wow, Major, do you think we should jump right up to the general's staff? Do we have enough to convince him to go further?"

"I think the findings are suspicious, and I think he will too. Let's find out." Picking up the phone, Matt dialed the COS's number.

"Colonel Burdine's office, Corporal Prejean speaking."

"Morning, Corporal. Major Baxter from the Air Department calling. Is the Colonel available?"

"He's in a meeting right now, Major. May I ask to what your call relates?"

"General Sienkewicz's crash, Corporal. Does he have a short slot today when Captain Curtis and I could meet with him? We only need ten minutes."

"Let's see, he's lunching with the General after this meeting, and has another meeting at 1400. How about 1345? Would that fit?"

"We'll be there, Corporal Prejean. Thanks for making it happen. Out."

"Out."

Turning to Christine, Matt said, "Well, Captain, your question will be answered in three hours. Meet you outside the colonel's office at 1340?"

"Oh boy, Major, I'll brush my teeth and comb my hair."

Smiling, Matt responded, "Whatever it takes, Captain. See ya then." He sat down at his desk and began sifting through flight schedules.

Christine headed back to her office, trying to use every spare minute to keep her casework going, lest Major Azaz pull her back into the office full time.

"Hello, Corporal Carbone, anything new?"

"Major Azaz wants you to see you, Captain. He's been tied up all morning with the congressional request over that negligent M-16 discharge case. Don't know what they're thinking—that we give medals rather than reduction in rank for the dumbest mistake in the book?"

"Thank Heaven no casualties from this one. Not like that one in January that killed one Marine and crippled another. But the timing here is terrible—the Major's going to be even busier, and want more from me. Well, thanks for the heads up."

Tapping lightly at Major Azaz's door, she was greeted with a grumpy "It's open." As she entered, Major Azaz looked up with no attempt to conceal his irritation with the file before him.

"God I hate congressionals. But I hate *stupid* congressionals even more. All of this paperwork for a kid who made a dumb mistake and received fair punishment for it. And, of course, now everyone will hate the Marine, since his family is jumping the chain of command."

"I bet the Marine knows nothing about the congressional. But he's the one who's gonna be stigmatized because of his idiot parents. If they had disciplined him properly in the first place, he might not have made this mistake. But now they want to say he didn't make one at all. I sure hope parents like this are the minority in America. The country wasn't founded by whiners who didn't accept responsibility for their screw-ups. Where do they come from?"

"Beats me. But I'm stuck, and I'm gonna need more help from you with the mast I was preparing for the Lance Corporal with the repetitive lateness. Wants to get this out of the way, and get that kid shaped up. Wants to do the mast in the morning. So we've got to have all the documents drawn up today." [Mast is short for "Captain's Mast," a punitive legal proceeding conducted by a ship's Captain beside the mast of the ship. Formally called Non-Judicial Punishment, or NJP, the accused has no right to an attorney. If the military member accepts the punishment meted out by the Captain, the matter is closed, and no entry is made in the member's service record. If he believes he is being treated unfairly, however, he has the right to request a court-martial. This could either clear his name or result in much more severe punishment, and will absolutely be entered into his service record.]

"Bad timing, Major—I've got a meeting with Col Burdine at 1345. But I'll get right back and get the mast ready."

"How are you doing on your other cases, Captain?"

"I'm okay, Major. Corporal Carbone has been a godsend. He's gonna make a terrific lawyer if he sticks with it. He's smart, industrious, and a good creative thinker. And he's been helping me immeasurably while I've been distracted with this air incident work—look how carefully he assembled the data for that congressional yesterday. I won't let you down —promise. You've been terrific in supporting me. I owe you big league."

"Just keep my nose out of the dirt, and I'll be happy, Captain. I'll need those mast documents by eight tonight. I wanna review them tonight, and explain the procedures to the CO in the morning before he sees the Lance Corporal."

"I'll have it to you before eight, Major. Thank you."

As Christine turned around to leave, Major Azaz inquired, "So what do you have for Colonel Burdine?"

Christine walked close to him and leaned down, speaking softly in his ear: "Some crude data that suggest that General Sienkewicz wasn't attacked randomly. That we may have a serious security breach somewhere."

"Damned, that's heavy stuff," Major Azaz whispered back. "How convinced are you?"

Standing up, Christine responded, "Enough to risk looking like a nincompoop in front of the CG's chief of staff."

"Good luck, Captain," he said reassuringly, then returned to the distasteful file.

"See ya after 1400, Major." Christine exited his office with a sigh, picking up her case files to make room for the mast issues. *Should I be doing this?* she thought, as she scanned the new documents. *I have an obligation to the battalion, to my Marines, to look after their legal affairs. And it's my fault if Major Azaz ends up looking unprepared to our CO.* She sat down, elbows on her desk, leaned over and put her head in her hands. *Lots going on here, Christine. Whaddaya want to do? I'm putting my boss at risk, and risking shortchanging my Marines. But so many people fly – I can't exactly shirk my responsibility there either. What to do?* She prayed briefly, asking for Divine guidance. Then, sitting up, eyes wide open, she stared straight ahead and said aloud, "I can do it all. I've **got** to do it all. I can do it." Sliding open her right desk drawer, she extracted a blank yellow legal pad and began to pull the mast case together.

Forty-five minutes later, Christine bounded out of the office, giving herself seven minutes to reach the COC at a brisk pace. People may commonly be late for appointments in the civilian world, but not in the world of The Corps. But Christine had always been punctual—both her Mom and Dad sought to cultivate self-discipline in all of their kids, knowing that as extremely privileged children they could easily degrade into an lifelong orgy of self-indulgence. And the Curtis family instruction took root—out of her two brothers and two sisters, only her oldest brother was a bit of a slouch early on, dropping out of high school to join the Air Force. But he came around, and eventually became a first-rate electrical engineer, now working in Dad's company. The other brother was abroad in the Peace Corps, with an eye toward a career in academia in the classics. Her older sister was a high school science teacher and tennis coach. Li'l sis Roberta was a brand new M.D., doing her internship. All productive. All relatively happy. And all loaded. Their family gatherings tended to nestle around a tennis court, where all of them could hold their own, including Christine's mother, who at 46 was very well preserved, as was her ferocious backhand. A diverse, contributing, and happy group. Even the in-laws liked them.

CHAPTER SIXTEEN

THE BRASS WEIGHS IN

Saturday, March 12, 2005

"It's a bit of a stretch, Major. We do a lot of flying, and all of it's over hostile territory. I'm not sure I see a trend here. Do you have anything else?" Colonel Burdine was fair but tough, and very, very busy as a one-star's chief of staff in a combat zone with five thousand Marines in the command. He stared into Matt's eyes, paying no attention to Christine.

"No sir, this is what we've got. But we thought it was suspicious enough to bring it to you. Do you think it's a dead end? Shall we leave it?"

"I think so, Major. We're so incredibly busy, and we've had no other suggestion of a security leak. How 'bout I just keep an eye out for anything suspicious, and I'll ring you up if I see anything?" The colonel wrinkled his chin, and was nodding at Matt, having made his decision. "I haven't seen the flight schedules for tonight. Do you have them out yet?"

Sheepishly grimacing, Matt confessed he didn't, accepting the implication that if he weren't wasting his time on phantoms, the schedule would be out by now. "I'll have it to you within an hour, Colonel. Thanks for seeing us."

Colonel Burdine nodded at Matt, and briefly at Christine, and then turned his attention to the overflowing inbox on his desk.

Outside, Christine spoke first. "He blew it off in a second, Major. He didn't even think about it."

"That's what he's paid to do, Captain. He makes decisions—lots of 'em. And he's been right most of the time, or he wouldn't be sitting in that office."

"I don't buy it, Major. There's something there, I know it." Hesitating, then proceeding more gently, Christine continued, "I watched you at

General Sienkewicz's memorial service. You were very emotional. You cared as much about him as I did. We owe it to him to press on, Colonel Burdine or no Colonel Burdine."

"OK, Captain, that's sort of dirty pool, but you're right—I resolved that day to search for a leak that might have led to his death. So whaddaya think—where do we go from here?"

"I think we have a security leak, and that we need to make a list of the locations and people who have access to flight schedules and manifests. That's what I think."

"Okay, Captain, I'm with you. I've got to get that flight schedule out, and I'm overwhelmed with other administrative chores, but let's meet Monday at the end of the day—how 'bout over chow at 1730. Meet you at the wash basins?"

"Washbasins at 1730 Monday, Major. Let's see if we can't flush out a dirty rat."

"See ya, Captain." Matt turned to go, then stopped and turned back. Looking Christine deep in the eyes, he said, "Thank you, Captain. We're doing the right thing."

Christine smiled gently, and repeated, "We're doing the right thing." Holding each others' gaze for a long moment, they both then turned and walked briskly away.

CHAPTER SEVENTEEN

ATTACK!

Sunday, March 13, 2005

General Phil Brier's Personal Security Detachment, his PSD, formed up the convoy formed outside the COC to wait for the General and his chief of staff. Three minutes after the appointed time, the two most senior Marines on the base strode briskly out of the COC wearing their helmets, armored vests, holstered pistols, and carrying their M-16s. Not all senior officers took their rifles along with them outside the wire, but these two were outspoken advocates of the Corps' policy, "Every Marine a rifleman." The men climbed into separate armored Humvees, spreading the leadership in case of action. The six turret gunners each nimbly climbed onto the hood of their Humvees, stepped over the windshield onto the roof, and adeptly lowered themselves into the turret behind their machine guns. Doors slammed with the heavy clunk of steel armor, and the Humvees were promptly rolling slowly down River Road toward the East Gate.

Stopping along the side of the road near the gate, the ritual called for going from weapons Condition 3 to Condition 1, ready to fire after flipping the safe off. The turret gunners stayed with their mounted weapons, but all others clambered out of the vehicles, went to the designated side of the road where the standard tilted sand-filled barrels were positioned to accept misfired rounds. The air filled with the staccato clacking of weapons' actions as rounds were instantly and precisely driven home to the firing chambers of the weapons, with magazines locked in to reload the chamber as fast as the trigger could be pulled.

The firepower of the convoy was awesome. The lead and last vehicles featured .50 cal machine guns, which will penetrate brick walls. Three of the other vehicles featured .30 cal or .223 cal machine guns. The General's vehicle featured a 40 mm grenade launcher, which can accurately place a volley of bursting shrapnel grenades up to 100 yards away. Additionally, all the gunners kept a second weapon, either an M-16 rifle, or a 12-gauge shotgun loaded with double-O buckshot, should their primary weapon jam. And they all wore 9 mm pistols. A force not to be tangled with lightly.

On signal, the gate guards walked open the 16-foot high steel gates, and the convoy moved slowly through the gate, under observation by the machine gunners twenty feet above them in the cammie-net covered guard tower. While the towers featured similar armament to the convoy, they enjoyed the huge tactical advantage of height. With their heavy topside armor, the vehicles leaned precariously as they navigated each sharp turn around the staggered Jersey barriers.

At the end of the two hundred yard approach to the gate lay the Barrage Bridge, a dam-like structure built in 1950 by the British during their Iraq occupation. It functioned as a two-lane traffic bridge across the Euphrates, but also featured flood gates to control the river's flow. The heavy civilian traffic was stopped at the bridge's edge by Iraqi police, as the Humvees traversed the span, then accelerated into the traffic circle just beyond. For convoys in hostile territory, speed is life, so they travel as fast as they can without capsizing on the turns.

Emerging from the traffic circle, the heavily fortified Joint Communication Center [the security phone bank as well as Iraqi police fire-support base] on the right, was comforting to all eyes as the vehicles accelerated. Moving down Route Milwaukee, the first vehicle passed through the ambush unmolested. As the second Humvee approached, now moving at 45 mph, a massive explosion consisting of two 155 mm Iraqi artillery shells on the sidewalk concealed in a pile of rubble, sent shrapnel and blast effect cascading into the side of the vehicle. Instantly, both right tires were flattened, and the vehicle lifted up 30 degrees, nearly capsizing, but then slammed back down. The turret gunner's helmet was blown off, his eardrums ruptured, and his exposed skin beneath his helmet and above his Kevlar vest collar was instantly penetrated by a spray of bits of concrete, wood, and metal. Dropping down inside the vehicle, he landed with his head on Colonel Burdine lap, bleeding profusely from the neck. Meanwhile the front of the vehicle was blown laterally, putting its back toward the source of the blast. The four occupants were dazed, their helmeted heads having been knocked by the interior of the vehicle as it swung. As Colonel Burdine recovered his senses, he applied his gloved hand over the briskly bleeding neck of the turret gunner. He watched as three separate insurgents ran forward and knelt thirty yards away, aiming the tube of RPGs at the stricken vehicle. Dozens of AK-47 rifle rounds impacted the armor of the vehicle, each producing a deafening *crack*. All four windows instantly cracked under the onslaught of the rifle fire, but the expensive 15-ply armored glass held. Pushing the turret gunner to the right rear passenger for care, the Colonel wriggled up into the turret, and tried to swivel the 240G machine gun toward the grenade threat. An AK round struck the back of his helmet and pitched his head forward; the Kevlar held, but he was knocked unconscious and slid back down into the vehicle.

Suddenly rapid-fire erupted from the USMC 240G .30 cal machine gun on the fourth vehicle. Two of the three would-be grenade launchers flinched as their torsos were penetrated by three rounds each, their weapons spilling onto the ground beside their twitching bodies. The third launcher wasn't hit, but lost his aim in the fusillade, and fired his rocket high. It impacted the now-empty turret guard with a huge flash and crack. Flame shot down through the open turret, burning the exposed skin of all four Marines inside. The shrapnel was deflected outward, however, and never entered the vehicle.

Realizing that the stricken vehicle was stopped in the kill zone, the vehicles behind it advanced to the fray, accepting the risk that more IEDs could be waiting for them. The turret gunners of all four vehicles began to rake the surrounding buildings. General Brier, in the third vehicle, directed his driver to come alongside the stricken vehicle and take a look at its occupants. Two more RPGs flashed into the street. The first overshot the vehicles and detonated on the far side of the street. The other blew off the entire right front wheel of General Brier's vehicle, but did not penetrate the cabin. General Brier's turret gunner still manned his 40 mm belt-fed automatic grenade launcher, and was alternating firing bursts, then rotating his turret toward the other side, killing insurgents on both sides of the street. His 1.5 inch grenades penetrated windows the insurgents were firing from and detonated inside the rooms. With each round bearing a kill radius of five yards and a wound radius of fifteen yards, this weapon is superbly suited to urban warfare when the enemy is hiding inside buildings.

The other vehicles now positioned themselves thirty yards apart, while the radio operators tried to raise the second and third vehicles to see if they could exit the kill zone on their own power. Just then a 12.7 mm [.50 cal] machine gun opened up from the insurgents on the left; the second Humvee's armor was no match for it. The first volley ripped into the engine compartment and penetrated the cylinders, instantly jamming the engine. The second volley ripped through the windshield, and caught the driver in the face. The rounds splattered his brains over those in the back seats, then pierced the neck of Colonel Burdine's aide in the right rear seat, severing his cervical spine and spinal cord.

An RPG slammed into the fourth Humvee, penetrating the armor of the right rear door and detonating inside. It instantly shredded the body of the Marine in the right rear seat, peppered the lower legs of the turret gunner, and sprayed shrapnel on the three other occupants. Though wounded and experiencing severe pain in both legs, the turret gunner continued raking the buildings where he saw muzzle flashes. Another RPG militant ran to the sidewalk facing the right side of the General's Humvee. As he began to kneel with the tube over his right shoulder, the injured turret gunner caught him with a full burst in his left chest, splintering four ribs and shredding his heart and lungs. He was knocked aside like a bowling pin, instantly unconscious.

Colonel Burdine had recovered consciousness just in time to be splattered with the scalp, skull, and cranial contents of the driver in front of him, and to witness the violent death of his aide in the seat to his right. Recognizing the threat of the insurgent's heavy machine gun, which could readily penetrate the armor of all of the vehicles, he grabbed the twenty-five pound AT-4. This anti-tank weapon, the modern version of the bazooka, is a self-contained use-and-discard weapon. It fires a four pound projectile at three hundred yards per second, and is capable of defeating sixteen inches of armor. Climbing out of the Humvee and kneeling with the launcher on this right shoulder, he spotted the heavy machine gun in the third floor window of a building on the left side, now firing at the other Humvees. The Colonel flipped up the plastic sight and threw the arming lever to fire. He took aim at the wall just below the machine gun, and squeezed the trigger. With a whoosh, the rocket launched and traversed the sixty yards to the building in a fifth of a second. The detonation sparked a huge fireball and resounding *ka-boom*. The smoke wafted away, revealing that the wall below the window was now absent for six feet in each direction, and the flooring behind it was blown away for several feet. The machine gun was gone.

Having jettisoned the launcher, Colonel Burdine was climbing back into the Humvee when an AK round slammed into the middle of the armor plating in the back of his flak vest, hurling his body forward into the steel door and bruising his skin under the entire plate – but the plate held. Painfully pushing himself upright and hoisting his leg into the vehicle

(Humvees are notoriously difficult to climb in and out of), the Colonel was struck again. The second round winged the same plate near its edge and ricocheted into the Humvee, penetrating his right arm just above the elbow. He finished climbing in and slamming the door.

Realizing that the enemy force was large and well-fortified in the surrounding buildings, the convoy commander in the lead vehicle ordered the fifth and sixth Humvees to pull up to the second and third and push them out of the kill zone. Meanwhile, in vehicle two, the alternative or A driver, Sgt Ernesto Moreno, manhandled the dead driver out of the seat, pushed his body back to the turret gunner's stand-plate, and took the controls. At first distraught when the engine was frozen still, even with activating the starter, Sgt Moreno was elated when he felt the bump of vehicle four contacting his aft bumper. Hauling the wheel to the right, the vehicle turned to face down the street, and together the two vehicles advanced away from the ambush. Humvee tires have a rubber core that will roll even when the tire is flat.

As the fifth Humvee touched the General's, another IED exploded with a roar just aft of both. Shrapnel pelted both vehicles; the turret gunners received minor shrapnel injuries, but most of it was repelled by their Kevlar suits. [All turret gunners wear a brown Kevlar garment covering their neck, shoulders, and arms, fondly referred to as "the monkey suit," which will stop small shrapnel, but not a rifle round or shrapnel larger than splinters.] With machine guns blazing, and the whomp-whomp of the grenade launcher lobbing grenades through the windows of the buildings on both sides, fires were now blazing behind 20 windows, and screams of men on fire reached out to the street. The .50 cal machine gun on vehicle five walked through the windows of the insurgents, and reached right through the brick walls beside the windows where they were hiding, shredding six enemy bodies. The .50 cal gunner took an AK round through his Kevlar suit, penetrating his left shoulder, but he continued firing with his right arm.

Humvee Six, commanded by Gunnery Sergeant Luis Reyes, pulled up behind General Brier's wounded vehicle, but none of the participants had a clue if they would be able to move a vehicle missing its right front wheel. Fortunately, the road surface was paved, such that the bare wheel hub didn't dig into the surface much. Miraculously, with the 7 drive wheels of the 2 vehicles churning at full power, the two vehicles limped out of the kill zone as they were pelted with AK rounds from both sides., but none penetrated it's thick up-armored skin. GySgt Reyes's powerful Humvee had saved the life of General Brier and his crew.

And then it was over. All firing ceased as the vehicles exited the kill zone, and the smoke slowly drifted away. Now the Quick Reaction Force from Blue Diamond was racing around the traffic circle, bringing fresh gunners and infantry. The whop-whop of two Cobra helicopter gunships flooded the scene, rallied from fueling at Ar Ramadi base just across the river. Spotting insurgents with weapons on the rooves of buildings on both sides of the street, the Cobras trained their awesome 20 mm cannon and commenced a withering firestorm of cannon and rocket fire, killing four insurgents on the right side and five on the left. And the rounds penetrated the roof and all three floors, killing three more insurgents and wounding four. The Cobras then launched four 2.75 inch rockets each, which detonated on the rooftops, showered shrapnel in all directions, and set the rooves on fire.

An insurgent with an RPG dashed into the street and took aim at the nearest Cobra. His rocket narrowly missed the Cobra by forty feet, but the Cobra didn't miss the insurgent, literally cutting his body in half with a fusillade of 20 mm rounds.

The QRF force dismounted and scattered into adjacent buildings on all four sides of the ambush site. Two insurgents on the right side abandoned their weapons and ran out the back door, reaching the alley just as two Marines approached in battle stance. Hands up, they feigned innocence. Pushing them into a courtyard for protection, two other Marines appeared. The Marines swabbed the fingers of the insurgents with nitrate-sensitive paper. Both were positive, and they were PUC'd (placed under custody), with plastic handcuffs securing their wrists behind them.

Another two insurgents chose to fight it out, and opened fire on the Marines from their third floor window. Twenty-five Marines subsequently turned on them with their M-16s, two grenade launchers, and two SAWs. A Squad Automatic Weapon is a light machine gun which shoots the same round as the M-16, but at the increased rate of two hundred rounds per minute. Within thirty seconds, both insurgents had sustained lethal head and chest wounds from a combination of M-16 rounds and grenade shrapnel. Three more insurgents raised their hands and walked slowly from the buildings on the left, toward the Marines. They were similarly PUC'd. Knowing what these fighters had done to their brothers, the Marines desperately wanted to kill them. But the disciplined Marines recognized that their yearning to send every insurgent to his perverse version of Paradise was trumped by the potentially inestimable intel value of live POW's , which could save many more Marine lives.

The five vehicles limped ahead toward the CMOC. The General's vehicle was barely moving because of its right front "anchor," but it was nevertheless moving.   Finally a massive 7-ton truck appeared, placed a tow chain to the right front hackle of the General's Humvee, and pulled it like a feather to the PCMOC's protected parking lot. The 7-ton is named for its payload capacity in off-road use—its actual empty weight is 13 tons, and it has beastly power.

In the parking lot, Marines and Navy Corpsmen were running out of the building to assist the injured. In vehicle one, the turret gunner had some minor wounds where ricochets off his turret tore at him. In Colonel Burdine's Humvee, the driver and the right rear passenger were dead. The driver lay face down across the gunner's footplate, his legs grotesquely draped over the radios in the front. In the right rear seat, the colonel's aide sat where he died, his head hanging forward one hundred and twenty degrees, cervical spine shattered. The turret gunner was barely conscious as dark venous blood continually flowed from his neck wound.   Colonel Burdine and the A-driver had skin burns and both had ringing in their ears from the RPG in the turret, and the Colonel's right upper arm had suffered a gunshot wound. He also suffered a concussion from the helmet strike, which had transiently knocked him out cold.

In the General's vehicle, the turret gunner LPCL Jesse Stout had multiple shrapnel injuries to his upper body. Dozens of tiny wounds peppered his face, and the lenses of his protective goggles contained several more embedded particles of shrapnel, but the ballistic eyewear functioned as designed and prevented wounds that would have resulted in certain blindness. The other occupants were shaken up, with bumps and bruises from the RPG impact at the right front, but none suffered wounds.

Vehicle four was a mess. The right rear passenger's body had absorbed the bulk of the RPG explosion, leaving blood and tissue splattered all about the cabin. The turret gunner had extensive shrapnel damage to both legs. The left rear passenger had minor wounds, and the driver and A-driver both took shrapnel through the back of their seats. Their ballistic vests saved their lives, as extensive particles penetrated the fabric but were stopped by the heavy ceramic plates inside, protecting the vital organs in their chests.

Vehicle five had several cracked windows, but the occupants were uninjured. The turret gunner had multiple shrapnel wounds from nearby exploding RPG's as well as deflected and fragmented AK rounds.

And Vehicle Six had fractured windows, but no injuries to its crew, even its charmed turret gunner.

The USMC tally was three dead, two seriously injured, and eight minor injured. General Brier was uninjured. And his Chief Of Staff, Colonel Burdine, was beat up but alive. He kissed his helmet multiple times—had the Kevlar not held so valiantly, the bullet which dented its hard shell would have instead caused his skull and brain to explode. *God bless the smart chemists at Dupont who came up with this stuff,* he thought.

The insurgents were left with eighteen dead, fourteen wounded in custody, five uninjured in custody, and five believed escaped.

It was not the kind of swap the Marines will readily accept. But more importantly, that the General's convoy should be attacked with such force suggested to Colonel Burdine that he was likely dealing with a glaring security leak. Colonel Burdine was now reflecting on his conversation with Major Baxter and Captain Curtis. He would be speaking with them that same night.

CHAPTER EIGHTEEN

THE HOME FIRES

Sunday, March 13, 2005

Christine was immersed in the mast documents when Corporal Carbone knocked and entered with her mail, dropping it gently on the corner of her desk.

"Thanks, Carbone. I haven't done a mast in a while, and I'm a little rusty on the verbiage. Anything interesting in the mail?"

"Couple bills, Captain, but one hand-written envelope for you."

"Thanks. That should brighten my day," she said as she looked up smiling. She recognized her mother's elegantly printed ivory stationery envelope immediately. Running her fingers over the elevated ink of the return address, she reveled in the warm thoughts of her mother. Carefully slicing open the envelope with the sword-shaped letter opener on her desk, she extracted the richly textured paper, and absorbed herself in her Mama's words.

My dearest Christine,

How is my little girl? We're all thinking of you continually, and hope you're taking good care of yourself. You are surely as strong as your father, but neither of you is impervious to the weapons of war. So please don't take any unnecessary chances, but get the job done. We're all hoping the need for American forces there is winding down, and you can all come home soon with your mission accomplished.

Your brother Keith is home from Tanzania for 2 weeks. The Peace Corps wants him there for another 6 months. He's enthused with his work, and believes he's making a difference. We certainly hope he is.

Your sister Zita got a new job at the high school teaching math, and she likes the faculty quite a lot. She thinks the principal is much more attuned to taking care of the teachers than the fellow at Eastern High. We're hoping it turns out to be as good as it seems on first impressions. She and Daniel just celebrated their 2nd anniversary.

Roberta is doing well in her internship at Cambridge Hospital. She says the cardiology teaching there is amazing, but doesn't think it will help much for the babies she treats as a neonatologist. She's dating a handsome young engineer named Bubba.

Brother Nick is happily working out clever new designs for the latest gizmo's he and your father have concocted. He and Mary Ann are expecting! They're looking at October 15 - isn't that exhilarating? Mary Ann looks radiant — we're all so excited!

Your father is running hither and fro, happiest, as you know, when he has a whole slew of balls in the air. But he's happy, and he's raising scads of money for the United Way. The business seems to be perking along without his nurse-maiding it. He chose his vice-presidents wisely - you remember Mr. Tyler Hydelbracht and Ms. Kristen MacKee - they're a formidable team, and are making the company grow while taking care of all the old accounts very well.

Sweetheart, I have a problem. I felt a lump in my breast two weeks ago. I saw my GYN, and he was concerned, so I went for a mammogram and ultrasound, which were both worrisome. So we did a needle biopsy, and it's positive for cancer. It's small, and Dr. Kwoun can't feel any lymph nodes in my armpit, so he thinks they can get it all. I've had some other tests, and I'm going for a full excision on Thursday the 24th. Dr. Saleem Khan, the chief of the breast service at Memorial Sloan-Kettering Hospital, is doing the procedure. The risk of this procedure is minimal. It's what else they might find that's frightening

Honey, I don't know how important your work is right now, but I'd love to have you around after the surgery, if it's possible. I know it may not be. But if you can, please come. I need you.

All my love,
Mother

Christine allowed the tears to stream down her cheeks and drip onto the mast documents. She had always been exceedingly close to her mother. Her mom was one of her heroes—smart, elegant, loyal, strong, and as loving as any human could possibly be. The thought of losing her, of her being disfigured, in pain, losing her mobility and independence, unable to take care of her family in the loving way she always had, was nearly too much to bear. *I'll be there for her, of course,* Christine thought, as her Mother's illness pushed all other thoughts out of her mind. *I have eleven days—with emergency leave, I get head-of-the-line privileges for a seat out-of-theatre. I could be in Watertown in two days after I leave here. But I should arrive early—I need to leave here in eight days. I have two weeks of leave accumulated. I'll use them all to stay with Mama until she's up and around and cheerful again.*

Christine got up and closed her office door. Then she knelt down on her knees, brought her hands to the praying position, and begged God to spare her mother, to reach out and caress her, to reassure her, and to heal her. She prayed for strength for her Dad, her brothers and sisters, and herself. And she ended with her usual, "Not my will but thine be done, Lord. If granting my request is not possible, please help me, Lord, through the disappointment and turbulence that will follow. Amen."

Christine stood up and stared out the window, the tears beginning to dry in her reddened eyes as she mopped her face with tissue. She heard the phone ring and Corporal Carbone answer.

"Captain, it's Major Baxter. Can you take it?"

"Uh, yes, Corporal, of course, thank you," she said as she tried to conceal the emotion in her voice.

"Hello, Captain Curtis speaking."

"Captain, have you heard about the General's convoy?"

"Heard what, Major? Is there a problem?"

"Huge, Captain, huge. They were attacked by a large enemy force. Three KIA, nine WIA. Just out past the JCC. Hell of a mess. Anyway, Colonel Burdine was injured, but he refused Medevac, and wants to see us right away. Can you cut loose?"

"Oh boy, Major, I wasn't expecting this. I've got a personal situation going here. But... Okay, you're right, this is critical. I'll be there in ten minutes."

"Thank you, Captain. See you in ten. Out."

"Out," Christine said, and hung up. The distress over her mother was now displaced by a much closer drama of life and death. *Good Lord*, she thought, *three of our Marines dead, and ten wounded. These are guys I eat with in the chow hall every day.* Closing her eyes, she said softly, "Oh, God, take them to your bosom, and be with their families. And help me find out what's wrong here. Amen."

Grabbing her cover from the hook by the door, she walked across the hall and rapped gently on Major Azaz's door.

"Come in," came the fatigued voice from inside.

Pushing open the door and stepping in, Christine said, "Major, General Brier's convoy was ambushed just past the JCC, and there are extensive casualties. Colonel Burdine wants to see Major Baxter and me right away. I'll be back as soon as I can. Okay?"

"Holy Jesus, this place is getting way too hot. Is General Brier okay?"

"I think so. Colonel Burdine was injured, but he refused to be Medevac'd. There were three KIA and ten WIA. I don't know how bad they are."

"The mast can wait, Captain. Get on down there. Thanks for telling me."

"Okay, I'll report back, Sir, as soon as I can."

"Thank you, Captain."

With that, Christine whirled and strode out the door and out of the office, informing Corporal Carbone where she could be reached as she briskly passed his desk. She squinted as she stepped outside into the brilliant Iraqi sun. Slipping her sunglasses out of her right breast patch pocket and onto her nose, she marched down River Road double time.

CHAPTER NINETEEN

A CHANGE IN HEART

Sunday, March 13, 2005

Matt was standing outside Colonel Burdine's office when Christine arrived. The aide's desk was unmanned. Matt wondered if his friend, 1st Lieutenant Colby, was among the casualties.

"Thanks for coming, Captain. I hear him on the phone in there. We'll knock when we hear him hang up."

"Yes sir. Why do you think he wants to see us?"

"He's probably thinking that this attack was no lucky guess." Looking around, Matt lowered his voice and continued, "Let's not talk out here. We may be speaking for the enemy right now."

Somewhat embarrassed, Christine realized she shouldn't have asked about such a confidential issue in a hallway. "Yes, of course, Major."

They heard the receiver being replaced inside, and Matt gently rapped on the door.

"Come in," a tired voice replied.

Opening the door and walking in, Matt and Christine stood side by side and went to attention. "You asked us to come by, sir," said Matt.

"Yes, of course, Major, thank you. And thank you for coming Captain—" he squinted to see the name on her blouse, "Curtis. Please sit down." As the Colonel sat, he winced as he moved his right arm.

"Are you all right, sir?" asked Matt. "I heard you were injured."

"I took a ricochet off my armor into the back of my right arm. My back hurts like hell where the armor got slammed into it by an AK round. My ears are ringing like a church bell, and I have the worst headache of my life after an AK round whacked my helmet. I've still got some blood and brains on me from my Marines getting shot up. But I got in a shot with an AT-4, and took out their heavy machine gun."

"Yes sir, thank Heaven you had an AT-4 in your vehicle." Matt paused. "What can we do to help, sir?"

"I didn't think you two had anything with your review of General Sienkewicz's crash. But today, this ambush was in force, bigger than any other we've faced before. And General Brier hasn't made that trip in three weeks, yet we have two or three convoys past that site every day. I smell a rat."

"Yes sir, that's a long one to ring up to coincidence. Thank Heaven they didn't get the General. So where do we go from here?"

"I want you two to review who had access to the data on both generals' movements. Everyone, no holds barred: Marines, US civilians, TCNs— everyone. I want to know them all. Meet me here tomorrow morning at eight. Can you do that?"

"We can and we will, sir. Captain, anything to add?"

"No sirs, I'm on board. Thank you," Christine murmured.

"Okay, tomorrow, here at—no wait a minute, let's change venue. Major Baxter, your office is right around the corner, and we're concerned that your data may have been compromised. And I don't know if my office is a problem. Captain Curtis, your office hasn't been involved in any of this. Can we meet there tomorrow?"

"Yes sir, I'm in the JAG office just across from J-DAM Palace. [Uday Hussein's former palace, partly demolished by a couple USAF 1,000 lb Joint Designated Air Missile, a "smart bomb"]. There at eight?"

"Yes, eight." The Colonel watched them turn to go and then added, "And, thank you, both of you, for being on top of this. I'm really glad you're on board. Let's get this problem fixed."

"That's a go, Colonel. We're gonna get to the bottom of it. Promise," Matt nodded, and the two of them exited the office. When they were in the hall, Matt said, "Captain, let's walk outside and talk in the street. No one will be able to hear us out there."

"Good by me," Christine agreed, as they headed for the door. They blinked as they stepped into the sunshine, and simultaneously reached for their sunshades.

"Okay, Captain, where should we start?"

"We're going to need to write this down, Major. Let's walk down to my office as we talk. We can start to list the people with access to the flight schedule and manifest."

"Okay, it's my office people, Captain Rogers, Lance Corporal Adams, and Corporal Kumler. Then there's the ops people, Lieutenant Colonel Rider and his staff of five: Majors Sizemore, Wheeler, Dubble, Corporal Goetteman, and Lance Corporal Thatai. I don't think the people over in the LZ office are an issue, because they never see any of the manifests until just before the flight. And the manifests aren't published on the net or circulated on paper. So where else do we need to consider?"

"Well," Christine began thoughtfully, suppressing her instant suspicion of Captain Stella Rogers, recognizing in herself an enmity based on competition for Matt's attention rather than any evidence. "Anyone who works closely with the General's staff would know that General Sienkewicz was going flying, and that General Brier was going on that convoy. So who does that include?"

"Oh man, that's a slew of people. Probably twenty people in the COC might have known what time General Sienkewicz was flying out. And ditto for General Brier's convoy. That's a long list of Marines."

"Yes sir, it is. And some civilians fit into that as well. Who are the terps that work in the COC?"

"Well," Matt went on, "there's three different ones that rotate on the Tips Line." [Citizens can call in reports (tips) about enemy activities to an Iraqi civilian phone line, manned eighteen hours a day by an Arabic speaker].

"Then there are terps for General Brier, and General Sienkewicz had one, but he was assigned just that day and has been working back at Camp Fallujah since then. Who interprets for General Brier?"

"That terrific guy, Samir something or other. He's General Brier's favorite, because he interprets non-verbal as well as verbal communications to the General. Very smart guy."

"Okay, well let's add him," Christine went on, "and all of the General Staff Marines, and the air office people. That's about twenty-five people."

"Boy, that's a lot of people to propose monitoring. I don't think we can do them all at once. Let's narrow it down to a few, say five at a time. And how are we going to monitor them? You're a communications officer— what kind of widgets do you have for spying on people?"

They arrived at her office and entered, greeting Corporal Carbone and his two Lance Corporals as they passed into her office and shut the door. They sat in the two chairs in front of her desk, turning them to face each other.

Lowering her voice, Christine replied, "We have some USMC gear, but it's dated—kind of big and clunky, with fuzzy transmitters. It takes forever to order some up-to-date electronics through supply, and half the time they swap in something *they* like rather than what you ordered." Pausing in thought, Christine went on, "You know, my Dad is in the comm equipment business. I think he bought out a company with this kind of surveillance gear. Let me get in touch with him, and see what he can do for us. Oh—Oh my Lord, I almost forgot. I have a personal situation—big one. It's my mother, she wrote to me, and..." Christine's voice quivered. She looked down as tears welled up in her eyes. "She's got breast cancer, and wants me to come home next week to be with her for her surgery."

"Oh, Chris, I'm so sorry. Is she okay right now?" Matt asked, as he laid his hand on her shoulder. It was the first time Matt had ever addressed her by her first name. And the first time he had touched her.

"Yes," Christine choked back a sob, "there's no evidence it's spread. But with breast cancer, it can metastasize early without any sign of it." She recovered her composure and looked up. "I forgot she wants me to come home. I don't know what to do." Fresh tears now streamed down her cheeks.

Matt leaned forward and took her hands into his, looking deep into her eyes. "Family comes first, Captain. We all know that."

"Thank you, Sir," she responded, gently withdrawing her hands and placing them in her lap. But the Corps is family, too. A lot of Marines have been lost. And a lot more may be in jeopardy. Oh, Lord, why did Mom have to get sick *now*?"

"We'll get along here, Captain. You're gonna have to go home. We can still work on this 'til you leave. When do you think you'll go?"

"I postulated a Monday night departure would get me there by Wednesday or Thursday, the day of her surgery."

"Okay, that's a week from tomorrow. Let's get cookin'. How can we monitor the five we select?"

"We have a cell phone monitor on base, but it's tough to use because there are so many phones around here. If you know which number you want to monitor, it's vastly more effective."

"We can scratch around and try to learn if these five have cell phones, and get the numbers if they do."

"Good," Christine replied. "And I'll get some nano-mikes from my Dad, if he has them. We can spot them around. But it's gonna take a lot of manpower to listen to these things."

"I think Colonel Burdine will give us what we want. But he may need to bring in people from off base, since we're not sure who we can trust here."

"Okay, I'll leave that up to you. Why don't we do the three people in your air office, the general's terp Samir, and one of the ops guys. Let's go right to the top and do Lieutenant Colonel Rider. That's five. That's already a whale of a lot of listening."

"Okay, but we can't let on that we're suspicious. I'll get Colonel Burdine out of his office and tell him what we're planning. I'll advise him to spread the word that the insurgency is getting stronger locally, and this was a lucky punch. That our response will be more gun trucks on our convoys, and beefing up the perimeter defense of all the bases around here. That should keep from telegraphing the rat that we're on to him."

"Good. I've got eight days. I'll call Dad."

"We need to come up with a cover for why Colonel Burdine's coming to the JAG office tomorrow morning. Let's say a Marine had a negligent discharge, and shot another Marine. Dead. Yeah, that's a big-time offense that would involve Colonel Burdine. Okay, that's the story. Let's see, it's 1900 now—that's 11 in the morning for your Dad. Keep track of your phone expenses and I'll see to it you're reimbursed. And be circumspect on the phone. We don't know yet who's involved or what their capabilities are. See you here at eight, Captain." And with that, Matt was up and out of the room.

Christine sat at her desk, elbows down, with her chin propped up on both hands. *How am I going to explain this to Dad in a way that doesn't give away our plans,* she thought. *Hmmm. I'll tell Dad I'm doing an investigation on a Marine that we think is stealing from the base exchange's accounts. That will deflect suspicion. And if he asks for more, I'll try to talk in code to him, that only our family will understand.*

And with that she picked up the phone and dialed the Defense Service Network, or DSN, at Stewart AFB, not too far from home. She asked the operator there to give her a commercial line. Pulling a phone card out of her breast pocket, she waited for the prompts and punched in the card's PIN. Following the instructions, she dialed her Dad.

CHAPTER TWENTY

CONSULTING THE CAVALRY

Sunday, March 13, 2005

George Curtis's business inner phone line was known to but a few. His four business lines went through the bank of secretaries in the room outside his expansive, thirty-seventh floor office on 8th Avenue near Times Square. Facing south, it overlooked the blanket-like expanse of the Hudson River and the southwest side of Manhattan. He had watched the Trade Towers topple from this office, and missed their majestic, gleaming shapes. But this was Sunday, and Christine's call was electronically forwarded to her parents' home.

"Hello," Mr. Curtis's voice boomed.

"Daddy, it's Christine, in Iraq. How're you doing?"

"Whoa, Christine," he replied sitting forward and smiling. "Wonderful to hear your voice. How are you, sweetheart? Is everything okay?"

"Well, Dad, pretty much. How's Mom?"

"Oh, so you got her letter. Well, she's holding up pretty well. You know her, always looking out for the rest of us. So she's keeping herself busy taking care of us all. The surgery is next Thursday. Do you think you can make it?"

"I'm planning on it, Daddy, but it's a long way, and things can come up. Unless there's a huge problem here or with the airlines, I'll be coming."

"That's good to hear, honey. Mom needs you, and I'd feel better if you were here with us as well. When will you leave there?"

"I'm looking at next Monday night, Dad. That should get me home Wednesday or Thursday at the latest."

"Terrific, honey. I know Mom will be immensely comforted by your presence. Anything I can do for you?"

"Well, Dad, actually there is. Didn't you buy a company that makes micro-surveillance devices? For spying on people?"

"Sure, Honey, SPI Inc., we bought it last year. They're doing great, too, 30% annual growth. We got it at just the right time."

"I need a favor, Dad. I need some surveillance gear, enough to monitor five people at a time, and all of them at multiple locations. And for their cell phones, too. Does SPI make gear like that?"

"Absolutely, honey, the best on the market. Cutting edge. Every time I say these mike/transmitters can't get smaller, our guys do it. And the crazy thing is, they make the fidelity and the range better, even as they make them smaller!" He paused, then continued, "What's the issue?"

"We have money missing from the BX, the retail store on base, and we can't figure out who's taking it. We want to check up on the five guys who have access."

"I have just what you need, honey. How many different locations do you need to bug?"

"I figure one for their work, one for their quarters, and one more for wherever else they spend time."

"No problem, sweetie. The cell phone monitors go right inside the phone, it takes about five minutes to install. Unless the target is expert at cell phones, he'll never know that he's transmitting to you as well as to whomever he called."

"That's perfect, Daddy. When can you send them?"

"I'll call the shipping department right now, honey. They're in Kansas City. I'll have 'em Fedex the gear to our contact in Kuwait, and then let the military postal service take it from there. I'll send you thirty-five mike/transmitters, ten cell phone monitors, and eight listening/recording units for your people."

"Dad, this sounds expensive. I don't know if I can get the military to pay for it."

"My contribution to the national mission there, sweetie. It's a privilege to help." Pausing, he went on, "This shipment should get to you just about the time you're leaving. What else can I do for you, honey?"

"Dad, you're such a dear. Thanks so much, Daddy. I love you. And see you soon."

"You've brightened my day immensely, sweetie. Looking forward to seeing you next week."

"Okay Dad, see you then. Bye."

"Good-bye, sweetheart."

CHAPTER TWENTY-ONE

RETRENCHMENT

Monday, March 14, 2005

"Hello my Prince. Allah smiled upon us today with a blessed battle. Have you heard?"

"I have, and well done, brother Samir. Infidel blood is flowing into the gutters of Ramadi as we speak. But most important, do you know if were successful in slaying the General?"

"Regrettably, my Prince, I believe that the leader of the invaders survived our attack. We must plan again to rid this land of him."

"No, my brother, not for now. These two attacks in a brief period may make the infidels suspicious that we have knowledge of their plans. I wish you to have a period of quiet, to reduce suspicion. Continue gathering information, of course, but not for launching any attacks immediately. You are far too valuable to our quest to have you lost over some minor victory."

"Very well, my Prince, I shall go about my duties in a humble way, mimicking the ways of The Prophet. Like Him, I shall deceive them into trusting me even further. Then we shall rise up and have our vengeance, slaying all of the occupiers."

"We remain steadfast in our goal, brother Samir. But for now we must be still. I wish to speak to you again tomorrow. Please be prepared for that time."

"It will be so, my Prince. Until then." And the two phones disconnected.

Turning to his cousin, Alquieri announced, "So, Prince Saad, we have failed in our mission. A few Marines were killed and their vehicles damaged, but I fear that our own losses may have been substantial. The General came through unmolested. We must do better in our battle with the Godless ones."

"Yes, Prince Alquieri, we have risked exposing Samir, and yet gained very little. He is so valuable. Do you ever worry about his loyalty to Allah and our noble cause?"

"Of course, my Prince, we always worry that any of us can lose sight of the truth and the way. And this is why I have placed a second loyal one inside the camp of the occupiers."

"You did? That's amazing! But why wasn't I informed? This is not a small matter."

"It never came up, my Prince. I forgot that you did not know. But it is not important."

"Who is it, my Prince? How did you do it?"

"He is Massoud al-Jaffari, a faithful one from India. He is working in the kitchen of the devils. I have provided him with photographs of the wife, children, parents, and brothers and sisters of Samir. Should Samir wish to discontinue his activities on our behalf before we are ready, the photographs should convince him that we know where his dear ones are. And he would know that, for the greater good of Allah's plan, we would not hesitate to kill every single one of them. So I am confident that Samir will remain helpful to us for as long as we find him necessary."

"My Prince, you are as cunning as the jackal. I rest better knowing that your mind is constantly searching for new ways to serve our blessed mission."

"And so it is, my Prince. Samir is far too valuable to risk losing his service to temptation from the infidels. Let us meet in one week's time, to determine if Samir has any news of use to us."

"So it will be, my Prince. Good night. And Allah's blessing upon you."

"Good night, my good friend. *Allah Akhbar.*"

Chapter Twenty-Two

A Change In Heart

Tuesday, March 15, 2005

"I've decided to bring in some support from the outside," Colonel Burdine began. "We don't know who we can trust here, so we need some fresh, clean blood. I have my old terp from Al Asad, Mr. Waleed Mansour, coming. He can help review the tapes we're going to produce from the Arabic speakers. Captain Curtis, I've spoken to Major Azaz about your time. I'm bringing in a substitute JAG officer from Camp Fallujah to assume your duties. Major Dwayne Gertz is extremely capable, and will carry the ball for you with a seamless transition. Now, who have you two identified as being in a position to betray us?"

"We were comprehensive, Sir, in our review. We came up with a lot of people, twenty-five to be precise. The list includes your aide—oh, I'm sorry, Sir—is it true that Lieutenant Colby was KIA?"

"God rest his soul, Major, yes. Lieutenant Colby was a superb Marine, and the best aide anyone could hope for. I'm going to miss him dearly."

"My condolences, Colonel. So we have the two Lance Corporals in your office, General Brier's terp Samir, the three staff in my office, and the entire ops department, which is nineteen people. We think that, realistically, we can only monitor five at a time. So we've chosen to go with my office three, Samir, and—let's see, without Lieutenant Colby, we'll do ops. Might as well start at the top with Lieutenant Colonel Rider. What do you think?"

"Sounds very reasonable, Major. How long do you think we should monitor this group before moving on?"

"I'm guessing, so we don't stretch this out too long, maybe three or four days. We can always come back to people. That's already a ton of work to listen to everything they say for that long."

"That's for sure, Major. Well, I'll give you Waleed, and I'm bringing in three other junior members from the intel group at Taqaddum, to review the tapes of the English speakers."

"That should do it, Colonel. We're hoping to receive the monitors in the next couple days."

"Where did you get the gear?"

"Captain Curtis's father is in the business, Sir, and he's donating his latest and greatest to the cause."

Looking at Captain Curtis, Colonel Burdine nodded and thanked her. "And please give your Dad my personal thanks. Let's see, this is so important, we need to keep the loop closed on who knows about this investigation. Did you bring your father on board, Captain?"

"No Sir," Christine replied, looking straight into the Colonel's eyes. "I told him we had a crook in the BX, embezzling, Sir."

"Good for you, Captain." Smiling, he went on, "God will forgive you for deceiving your own father. We'll bring him up to speed if and when we get this all figured out."

"Thank you, Sir."

"Okay, I'm going back to my office. Please let me know when the gear arrives. And remember, we don't know who to trust, so don't reveal any of our discussions. We've concocted a story about a Marine from a VIP family with a negligent M-16 discharge yesterday, killing another Marine, that will require me to work closely with the JAG office for a while."

"Yes Sir," responded Matt and Christine simultaneously.

Colonel Burdine arose and took his leave.

After they were clearly alone, Matt took Christine's hands in his, leaned forward, and planted a kiss on her forehead. "You're terrific, Chris," he said. "Classy family, classy Captain. I'm really pleased to be working with *you* on this project. Gimme a shout when you hear anything about the gear, okay? You might wanna check with the post office every morning, and additionally if you see any shipments arrive."

"Yes Sir," Christine replied, smiling both inwardly and outwardly. "We make a good team."

"We sure do, Captain," and with that he bounded out the door, smiling over a productive meeting, and the privilege of working with a beautiful woman.

Christine sat down at her desk smiling, placed her chin in her hands, and reflected on the rugged good looks and flawless physique of Major Matthew Baxter, USMC.

CHAPTER TWENTY-THREE

THE INFRASTRUCTURE HUMS

Wednesday, March 16, 2005

FedEx worked its magic, and the package arrived in Kuwait City thirty hours after George Curtis's call to his Kansas City warehouse. Seeing that the package was authorized by the President of Curtis Technologies himself, Mohammed Hadi, the manager of the Curtis outlet, personally drove the package over to the military facility at Kuwait International Airport. Seeking out the military postal service, Mr. Hadi found the facility manager, Gunnery Sergeant Anton Witkoff, and conveyed the importance of the package. GySgt Witkoff noted that the destination was a JAG office, that the parcel came from an industrial electronics company, and concluded that it indeed merited priority handling. Walking the parcel to a truck preparing for departure, GySgt Witkoff spoke briefly to the A driver, Cpl George Danielsen, and handed him the package. Cpl Danielsen in turn stowed it in a corner of the truck's bed where he could retrieve it on arrival at Taqaddum Air Base, which he did some ten hours later. After personally carrying the parcel to the convoy forming up en route to Blue Diamond, the A-driver saw the package was inserted into one of the large orange bags marked CBD, and was rolling again within minutes. Consequently the package appeared at the Blue Diamond postal facility fifty hours after Christine had spoken with her Dad, he later learned with astonishment. Not expecting anything so soon, Chris nonetheless dutifully dropped by the Blue Diamond postal facility, and was astonished to find that a package had arrived for her. Sure enough, the box was from Baxter Technologies. She hustled it back to her office, not waiting to explain the package to her staff as she crossed their workspace en route to her private space.

Before exploring the contents of her package, she opted to bring Matt on board with the new arrival.

"Air office," the mellifluous female voice said. Christine recognized Captain Rogers' voice immediately, and felt a little twist in her gut.

"Good morning, this is Captain Curtis calling for Major Baxter. Is he available?" Christine intoned, striving to conceal the resentment in her voice.

"I'll see if he can talk right now," came the response. Christine was sure Captain Rogers was putting her off, and might even not alert him to the call.

"Major Baxter," came Matt's resonant voice.

Forgetting her suspicions, Christine proceeded warmly, "Hello Major Baxter, it's Captain Curtis. I have some mail I'd like to show you."

"Oh, yes Captain, sure, that would be fine. I'm really tied up with our air ops, but I know Colonel Burdine wants me to sit in on the case of that fatal negligent discharge. Sure, I'll be by shortly. Thank you, Captain." Matt hung up.

Christine immediately remembered the ploy suggested by Colonel Burdine, and noted Matt's skill in handling the issue so adeptly.

Lifting the corner of her cammie blouse to her waist, she exposed the canvas sheath on her belt containing the ubiquitous Gerber "Leatherman", a combination pliers/screwdriver/knife widget that has almost religious significance among Marines.

Popping out the knife, she deftly incised the packing tape of the box, pulled back the flaps, and peered in at the fancy color design of the shrink-wrapped cartons inside. Extracting them, Christine counted twenty microphone/transmitters, the best current technology could produce. Measuring only a half inch square and a quarter inch thick, they could be hidden in innumerable places and be totally undetectable without a careful search. Transmission capability was cited as a hundred meters, less through masonry walls.

Cutting open one package, she realized that these were high-end product, worth hundreds of dollars each. Then she found the cell phone bugs. Incredibly tiny, these devices labeled the transmission of the phone to which it was wired so that it could be picked out of a crowd, and monitored continuously. Next were the monitoring stations, nicely designed, pastel-colored molded plastic with electronic controls, LED read-outs for frequency and signal strength, and a built-in high-fidelity electronic recorder. The cell phones transmitters had separate monitors with wide band capability. She was elated; her Dad had come through when she really needed him, and unbelievably fast. *No wonder he's been so successful in business,* she thought. *And God bless the good men and women that designed and fabricated these amazing devices, and all the good people who transported them here so quickly.*

Knowing that the circle of insiders aware of the monitoring needed to be minimized, Christine emptied a file drawer and inserted the devices. The office Marines knew not to enter the file cabinet in her inner office, so that site should be relatively secure. But even if they were discovered, a JAG office with investigative tools wouldn't necessarily raise eyebrows. As Christine carried the box out of her office, Corporal Carbone greeted her with a smile.

"So what was in the big box, Captain?"

"A gift from my Dad, Corporal," she responded in good cheer. "Dads are fantastic. I hope you're being as thoughtful of your own daughter, Corporal Carbone."

"I sure think of her often, Captain, but at two years I don't think she knows if I'm being nice or not. I'm sure looking forward to seeing how she's changed. Three more months."

"I'm with you. This combat-zone life is oppressive, isn't it?"

Supporting the empty box with one leg and one hand, Christine pulled her cover from her pocket and popped it on her head, as she stepped outside and headed for the dumpster. She was lifting the lid when Matt walked up behind her.

"Take on a second job, Captain?" Matt joked.

"I just can't seem to make ends meet on this military pay," Christine smiled as she turned around to face him. "At least *some* of the evidence of our project has been jettisoned," she said as she nodded toward the dumpster.

"Ah, so that's what you're up to," he smiled. Lifting the dumpster lid, he peered at the box. "Curtis Technologies, huh? Any relation?"

"I told you it was my Dad who was gonna help us."

"I know. Just teasing. Ain't no Baxter Technologies in *my* family."

"Well, let's hope the Dad connection proves useful. Come on in. My office staff is *not* going to be in on the project. I've told them that the negligent discharge case involves a Marine with VIP connections, so we're keeping the handling restricted, with some senior officer involvement."

"Good, we can maintain the same cover on all sides, then." They walked inside.

"Attention on deck!" Corporal Carbone announced loudly as he immediately rose and snapped to attention, as did the two lance corporals.

"As you were, Marines," said Matt. "Good morning. I'm going to be in and out frequently over the next couple weeks, working with Captain Curtis. So no need to come to attention when I enter in the future, okay?"

"Thank you, sir. Yes sir, that will be fine, Sir," replied Corporal Carbone, as the three enlisted men sat down and returned to their work.

Proceeding into Christine's office, they closed the door and Christine withdrew a box each of the two types of transmitters, and the monitoring stations. Gently extracting the devices, they marveled at the miniature dimensions containing such a robust transmission capability. They plugged in the monitors, and listened to the remarkable clarity of sound from the transmitters. Twice Matt's hands brushed Christine's on the desk as they faced each other and manipulated the gadgets. The first time was coincidence; the second time they both knew was intentional, but neither acknowledged it.

"So how will we get these babies planted?" inquired Matt.

"Well, the office will be easy. Some midnight visits by us, and we're all set there. Getting into their hooches is another issue. And it means we'll definitely need to get someone else in on this. How shall we do it?"

"Oh boy, let's see... Let's arrange for an electrical inspection, and smoke alarm check. That should do it. So we'll have the S-4 [Logistics/ Supply Department, takes care of quarters issues] send out an e-mail that the cans will be serviced on thus-and-so date. We'll use one of the intel guys coming in from Taqaddum as the inspector. After he's done that, he'll have to leave again—can't have an apparent electrical inspector working in our office with us. Same thing with the terp, we'll have KBR [Kellogg, Brown, & Root, the massive DOD contractor that runs support functions on US military bases all over the Middle East, and services the quarters of the TCN's] do the same thing. We'll enter the other trailers to provide cover, but obviously won't plant anything there. Whaddaya think?"

"Sounds like a plan, Major," Christine smiled.

"Colonel Burdine wanted to know when the hardware arrived. I'll drop by his office and let him know. And I'll ask him to have the TQ guys sent over immediately. They might even be able to fly in tonight."

"Terrific, Major. Do you wanna plant the office bugs tonight?"

"How long will those batteries last, Captain?"

"It looks like they're good for at least a week of continuous monitoring. They don't transmit if it's quiet."

"Great, then no harm in getting started right away, even if we don't have comprehensive monitoring of the signals just yet. Whaddaya think—midnight?"

"Should be pretty quiet up there about then, Major. Everyone is used to seeing you cruising around there at all hours of the day and night, so I don't think they'll pay any mind in seeing me as well."

"Midnight," Matt nodded.

"Midnight," Christine echoed with a smile, and extended her hand, which Matt received with a firm squeeze and barely detectable shake.

CHAPTER TWENTY-FOUR

ALL QUIET...

Wednesday, March 16, 2005

"God is great".

"Allah will reign over all His earth."

"Good evening, my Prince. It is good to hear your voice."

"Ah, Samir, I hope Allah's blessing has been upon you."

"Thank you, My Prince. I am well. I have not much to report. I have not taken any chances that my function would be identified. The occupiers mourned their dead, and have resolved to increase the strength of their convoys. But they can never increase them enough for Allah's *mujahadeen* to be thwarted. We will strike them regardless of what they do. Because Allah is with us, but rejected by them."

"You are right, Samir. So there is little new to report?"

"It appears that no important missions or travelers are anticipated, my Prince. But I shall be vigilant—I am certain that Allah will reveal to me new methods of punishing the aggressor. And when he does, we shall lunge for their necks!"

"Your spirit finds favor with Allah, Samir, and with us. Your blessed work will be revealed to The Forum this very night. And I have deposited an additional $20,000 in your account. Let us talk again in three days' time, Samir. Perhaps there will be something for you to report at that time."

"I will do my utmost, my Prince. I wish you a glorious meeting of the Sacred Sword of the Avengers."

"Thank you, Samir. Good night."

"Good night, my lord."

CHAPTER TWENTY-FIVE

MONEY FROM A DEN OF JACKALS

Wednesday, March 16, 2005

The Regis Hotel in Riyadh featured resplendent architecture and decor. Such is possible with the wealth available when some of the world's richest oil reserves are controlled by a single family. The Saudi royal family has amassed a staggering fortune, and, in some cases, engages in a lifestyle of indulgence and in western luxuries, despite preaching personal austerity and hate of the infidels to the masses. While engaged in convivial conversation with Western leaders, some Saudi's sponsor a massive array worldwide of indoctrination centers (madrassas) preaching hate and intolerance. Their intolerant brand of Islam might have remained the lunatic fringe it started out as, were it not for the discovery of oil in the land controlled by fanatics. But oil *was* discovered, and a worldwide Muslim generation seething with hate was created in the graduates of these schools of intolerance.

And here was a gathering of rogue ideologues, thoroughly indoctrinated to those passages of the Koran that can be interpreted to advocate the violent spread of Islam throughout the world, with virtually no restraint on the barbarism that can be exercised on innocent Muslims and non-Muslims in the pursuit of the spread of their virus-like murderous ideology. And their evil was particularly pernicious because of their enormous wealth. All of it was pilfered from their countrymen, of course, but it was the wealth of Midas nonetheless, with huge revenue streams siphoned off by this minority group to fund the merchants and practitioners of hate and violence around the world.

"Muslim brothers," began Prince Adnan Ghalib al Hassani, chair of *The Forum*, the twelve member board of directors of the hundred-and-fifty

96

member *The Sacred Sword of the Avengers*. 'Welcome to our monthly colloquium. There is much to discuss. Our sacred mission is being fulfilled around the world, thanks to your generosity, and the courage of our legions of *mujahedeen* from every continent. In Palestine, the latest generation rockets that you have funded to destroy the Zionists can now reach their cities, killing them where they work, and killing their families at home. For this blessing, we can all be grateful."

"Allah-Akbar!" The summoning of their deity to celebrate the murder of children in their homes was murmured throughout the room, by every tongue.

"In Indonesia's Bali, the killing of two hundred and maiming of hundreds more of the degenerate Australian youth has been a rallying cry for more such operations against these enemies of Islam. Would that tomorrow we could exterminate them all, and replace them with honorable, ethical, peaceful disciples of the Prophet, like ourselves. Ah, but that will take time.

"In Europe, our brothers lament, 'So many trains, so few bombs.' We can help them with their problem!" and he laughed boisterously, and the entire room erupted in vitriolic mirth. We will replicate the culling of the herd of infidels in Madrid and London, with similar but hopefully more lethal operations in Dublin, Glasgow, Brussels, Amsterdam, Paris, Stockholm, Oslo, Rome, Berlin, and Vienna. And the cartoonists of Denmark—yes, those who violate that most sacred tenet of the beloved Prophet that he not be imaged—we will show those apostates the vengeance of the practitioners of the Religion of Peace. We will find the cartoonists, and chop them into as many pieces as newspapers they printed. We will burn down the publishers of the desecration. And we will bomb their trains as well. We will teach them what it is to meddle with the People of Peace.

"Now with regard to operations in our beloved but besieged neighbor, I will ask Prince Alquieri to describe his activities in Mesopotamia. Prince Alquieri, you have the floor."

Rising from his chair at the middle of the conference table, Alquieri was resplendent in his finest flowing white silk robe with eighteen-karat gold thread crochet, and red checkered *kiffiyeh*, or head scarf, secured by a stunning gold-braided *agal*. "Thank you, Prince al Hassani. And my warmest greeting to all of my blessed brothers in peace. It gives me extraordinary pleasure to relate to you certain maneuvers we have conducted in the beleaguered city of Ramadi, in Anbar Province, approximately seventy kilometers west of Baghdad, on the Euphrates. Approximately three weeks ago, we had the good fortune to learn that the commander of all Marines in Iraq would be flying out of the Marine base there, and the direction of his flight. Our *mujahedeen* were in place and waiting. They successfully destroyed the General and all save one of his crew. The cost was substantial, with the loss of all but one of our courageous avengers, but the prize was worth this cost ten thousand fold."

The room erupted in applause, and every member rose to his feet. "Allah akhbar!" was shouted over and over, and some of the princes danced in place with joy.

When the audience was reseated and the room quiet, Alquieri continued, "Last week we learned of the travel of another Marine General, and again led the attack. We successfully disabled a number of their vehicles, and killed a number of the Marines, but their General escaped. Yet I have reason to believe that I will have another opportunity to slay this devil, so I hope to have much to report to you at our next meeting."

The Forum again applauded loudly and shouted praise and thanksgiving over the spilling of more infidel blood. But they would have been equally as joyous over the spilling of Muslim blood; any form of violence meted out to anyone remotely considered antagonistic to their goals was an event worthy of celebration by them, the self-declared guardians but in fact the perverters of The Religion Of Peace.

Arising from his seat, al Hassani reassumed the floor, and proceeded, "Brothers, *jihad* is our cause, and the most worthy of all possible causes. But Brothers, the work of the Prophet is not inexpensive. To prosecute the battle, we must raise our budget dramatically. From each of us, I will assess a minimum of three million dollars per year, and more for the more senior members. And I need your consent to increase the assessment for the entire membership of the *Sacred Sword Of The Avengers*, to one million dollars each. And, of course, we may periodically require additional contributions for special operations. I realize that the price of oil is vacillating, which makes financial planning difficult, but be aware that as China industrializes, the demand for our oil will rise progressively, and the price must respond accordingly. So I believe this request does not pose excessive burden on our members. The floor is now open to discussion."

Standing at his seat, Abdul Mahari spoke, "Beloved leader, there are so many demands for our resources. Some of us have teams of *mujahedeen* that we fund entirely by ourselves. Could an agreement be worked out that such members deduct the cost of such personal jihad groups from our assessments to The Servants?"

"Ah, brother Abdul, a reasonable question. Needless to say, we, and all Muslims, are grateful to our brothers who seek to slay the infidels. But the work of *The Avengers* must not be compromised for any reason. So I say to you, step down from *The Forum*, where the assessment is higher, and simply be a member of the *The Sacred Sword*."

"Thank you, my Prince, but I prize my service to *The Forum* above all else. I will find a way."

"Very well, Abdul, it will be for the best, for the Prophet."

Standing in place, Said al-Hasshani spoke up, "Beloved leader, some of us have many children. Four wives can produce so many!" Ripples of laughter circled the room. "Perhaps those of us blessed with more than ten children could receive some small credit for our providing so many more *mujahedeen* for The Cause."

"Ah, brother Said, well stated. We do need to repopulate this earth with The Faithful. But as with brother Abdul, we cannot allow this. I offer you the same alternative: step down from *The Forum*, or pay the full assessment. Allah's work is costly. And perhaps you should seek other entertainment in the evenings." Boisterous laughter followed.

Said blushed and replied, "I, too, value my contributions to *The Forum* above all else. I will find a way," and sat down.

Very well, my brothers, is there any new business to be brought before us?" There was silence. "So be it, brothers, let us recess to the salon, where we will be entertained with music and dance."

And with that, the group stood and wandered off in small groups towards the ballroom emanating exotic music, entranced by the sinuous movement of the already-gyrating nubile double-jointed belly dancers.

CHAPTER TWENTY-SIX

STEALTHY APPROACH

Wednesday, March 16, 2005

The COC was only a black silhouette on a nearly black sky as Christine approached it. Because there are gentle stairs at its entrance, anyone approaching without flashing a hand light would be injured, so the ubiquitous glow-sticks are used, one on every other stair and one at the curb. Christine had never liked the dark. Although throughout her childhood bedtime was associated with stories, songs, and kisses from her parents, she never took to lights-out. Now as an adult, she always kept some sort of night-light going. She padded along, periodically shining for a half second the tiny light clipped to her holster.

As Christine passed the pitch-black sentry stand, she volunteered, "Rah," and a baritone voice responded gently from the blackness, "Rah." Night sentries wear NVGs, so she had been under surveillance for the entire hundred meters before she reached the sentry.

Pushing open the huge wooden door at this former palace, she entered the pitch black vestibule. She felt the hairs standing up on the back of her neck. But she flashed her light and pressed on, passing through the door on her left that led to the former ballroom, now divided up by unpainted plywood partitions into offices. Here, a few dim lights glowed over desks, where some of the offices were manned twenty-four hours a day. Stepping over the myriad of wires that connected up all the computers and telephones with the General's area, she advanced to the last office, where Matt sat alone, staring at his computer screen.

Nearly whispering, Christine greeted him. "Good evening, Major."

Glancing at his watch, Matt smiled and said, "Wow, midnight already. I thought it was about ten. Guess I got involved here. Pausing, he went on, "I see you've brought goodies," as he pointed at her shoulder bag.

"Yes sir," she whispered, moving closer. "Five mikes and a spare, just in case. Are you ready?"

"Sure," he whispered, and stood up quietly, avoiding grating his chair on the floor. "I checked ops earlier, there was only one guy left, and he was leaving shortly. I think we're good to go there, we have three desks here to fix, and Samir's desk is over in General's country. Let's check out ops first, okay?"

"Ready," whispered Christine, as she extracted one mike/transmitter from the bag. Concealing the bag under his desk, the two silently walked the three partitions down to the ops area, where they approached Lieutenant Colonel Rider's desk. The big clunky green tactical phone would be an ideal hiding place, because it's big enough to hide something, and heavy enough that it rarely gets lifted up where its underside comes into view. Looking around to verify they were alone, they upended it and found that the spot they had pre-selected for bugging was available on this phone. The green "tac" phones have a bulky plastic case, with a number of ledges on the sides and underneath. Christine and Matt picked the ledge on the left, partially obscured by the cord and handset intakes. They quickly applied some double-stick tape to the mike, and slid it inside the groove. Checking once more for any unwanted observers, they silently returned to the corridor and headed for Samir's desk, in the northern portion of the building. If seen there, they would be placed on report. Colonel Burdine would rescue them, but their cover might be blown.

Passing through double doors reading "Restricted Area – General's Staff Only," they entered the vestibule of General Brier's office. Samir's desk sat just outside the plywood partition, such that voices inside the General's office passed right over the plywood edge and down to his ears. Finding a similar tac phone, they duplicated their maneuver, and had the bug planted within two minutes. Retracing their steps, they returned to Matt's office, where they found concealment spots for all three desks of Matt's Air Office colleagues.   Finished, they retreated to Matt's desk, and chatted softly.

"We've got to get the monitors set up tomorrow," Christine ventured. "I hope the intel guys from TQ arrive tonight."

"They should, Captain. They're manifested on the 0100 bird, which will be arriving any minute. We'll let them sleep in tomorrow morning, and try to meet up with them after lunch. Wanna meet for chow at noon?"

"That'd by great, Major," Christine smiled. Holding out her hand, Matt took it in both of his, and gently rubbed his thumb over the back of her hand.

"We're making progress here."

The double-entendre was recognized by Christine, although she wasn't certain he meant it. Withdrawing her hand, she muttered, "See you at noon, Sir," and was gone.

Matt returned to his computer for a few minutes, as Christine ambled down River Road in the cool of the evening, pleased with the mike deployment, and pleased that she had been with Matt.

CHAPTER TWENTY-SEVEN

REINFORCEMENTS

Thursday, March 17

Colonel Burdine called first thing in the morning. Matt had already been at his desk for three quarters of an hour. He had arrived at 0645, knowing that the investigation would consume time usually devoted to his air ops duties. At 0730 the phone rang.

"Air Ops, Major Baxter."

"Mornin', Major, Colonel Burdine here. The staff from TQ came in last night, and I want a meeting this morning with all of us. 1100 hours, in the JAG office. Any problem?"

"None, Sir. New developments to relate to you, so 1100 will be good, Sir."

"Good. 1100. Out." And the line clicked.

Matt immediately dialed Christine's number, and the Lance Corporal informed him that she was in.

"Good morning, Captain Curtis."

"Good morning, Captain. Major Baxter. Can we meet in your office at 1100? The TQ staff are in."

"Uh, let me think, uh... Sergeant Carbone, do I have any conflict with an 1100 meeting?" She paused. "Fine, Major, 1100 here. How many attending, Sir?"

"Not sure, Cap'n, but at least six including yourself."

"All right, Sir, I'll reserve the battalion library/conference room. It's relatively soundproof."

"Great, Cap'n, see ya at 1100. Out."

Matt arrived at 1050 hours. Colonel Burdine and Lieutenant Colonel Hiroon Amanee, the regional NCIS (Naval Criminal Investigative Service) commander, arrived at 1055, along with three intelligence enlisted men— two lance corporals and a corporal. The interpreter that Colonel Burdine had worked with in the past, but had been transferred to Baghdad, was with them as well. Blessed with an exceptionally agile mind, Waleed Mansour was Lebanese, but had lived in Iraq when his father was in the diplomatic corps during the Saddam era. Consequently, he was skilled in both the dialect and cultural nuance of Iraq. Still more importantly, Colonel Burdine had known Waleed and his family for decades, and trusted them unquestionably. And on top of all that, Waleed was Sunni Muslim. A perfect fit.

Lieutenant Colonel Amanee was an extraordinary spook. An Ethiopian Muslim, he had immigrated to the US via Algiers, Rome, Marseilles, and Canada. He was fluent in Ethiopian, English, Italian, French, and Arabic. With a jet-black complexion, he was a classic of the American melting pot. Top-secret clearances don't come easily to naturalized citizens, but as a 1st Lieutenant, Lieutenant Colonel Amanee had proven his patriotism in combat, heroically leading his Marine company into intense enemy fire during the Gulf War, culminating in the defeat of a numerically superior force. He possessed an exquisite intellect, not to mention his linguistic and cultural insight.

Entering the Comm Bn JAG office, Christine offered the cover story, which she had previously briefed to Major Azaz, to the office staff, explaining that the negligent discharge case with the VIP family would receive premiere command attention. She then escorted the visitors out of the office, leading them next door to the battalion offices, where the conference room was more soundproof than most in a combat zone. Additionally, the conference table and chairs were first rate—possible spoils of war, found on base when it was occupied by U.S. troops in 2003. *The Iraqi's will get it all back before too long*, Christine thought. *But we'll put this furniture to good use until then.*

"Let's introduce ourselves around the table," Colonel Burdine began. "And keep your voices low. I'm Colonel Burdine, Chief of Staff to General Brier." He looked to his right.

"Corporal Stacey Dunbar, G-2, Taqaddum." [G-2 = General's staff, Intelligence Section].

"Lance Corporal David Kimmel, G-2 Taqaddum."

"Lance Corporal Joao Mattos, G-2 Taqaddum."

"Lieutenant Colonel Amanee, NCIS Commander, Western Iraq."

"Waleed Mansour, linguist."

"Captain Curtis, Assistant JAG Officer, 3rd Comm Battalion"

"Major Baxter, Air Officer, Blue Diamond."

"All right, then," Colonel Burdine led, "Major Baxter, what 's the status of our hardware?"

"Very happy to tell you, Colonel, that the gear arrived and it's first rate." Nodding to Christine, he went on, "Last night Captain Curtis and I deployed mike/transmitters to the first five targets we selected: my three air office personnel, Lieutenant Colonel Rider, the ops officer, and Samir, General Brier's interpreter."

"Wow, that's moving, Major." Acknowledging Christine, "Superb work, both of you. Can you show us some of the hardware?"

Standing up, Christine hoisted her duffel bag off the floor, and set it on the table. She extracted two mikes and passed them around in opposite directions. Then she pulled out a base monitor, and explained its functions. The group was mesmerized.

"Okay, Corporal Dunbar, you and your people are going to run this gear, so when the meeting ends, I want you to take this monitor and a mike to the can opposite the COC that I've established as your monitoring station. Pick up the keys from the base headquarters duty station. If anyone asks what you're doing, you go with the same story about assisting me with the VIP negligent discharge case. Work with the gear until you can listen and record with the mike you have. Then tune in the five mikes already in place, and begin recording and listening. Obviously, every word must be recorded, and listened to either live or off the memory circuit." Looking back at Matt, he went on, "Major, what's next?"

"We need to place mikes in their trailers and cell phones, sir. For that we need an announcement that KBR electricians are doing safety inspections of wiring and smoke alarms in the cans, and then we need the keys. I think I need to bring the base commandant on board with the investigation, to get him to make this happen. Is that approved, Sir?"

"I guess there's no choice, Major, so yes, that's approved," responded Colonel Burdine.

Matt went on, "If their cell phones are in the hooch, we'll bug them then. But they probably won't be, so we'll need to recall cell phones from headquarters to allegedly change their programming. It only takes five minutes to bug them."

"Okay, Major, let's proceed with bugging the quarters, and we'll go with the phone recall if we don't get the phones that way."

"Yes Sir. That's all I have."

"Thank you, again, Captain Curtis and Major Baxter," and Colonel Burdine smiled at each of them. Looking at Waleed, he said, " Waleed, I'd like you to go with the S-2 folks so you can monitor Samir when he's speaking Arabic."

Waleed nodded, "Yes Sir."

"Lieutenant Colonel Amanee, comments?" Colonel Burdine queried.

"I believe I have the big picture now, Colonel. I'm very impressed with the quality of this gear. Where did you get it?"

"We have Captain Curtis to thank for that, Colonel. Or her father. Apparently he's in this business, and lent them to us. He got them here in three days, if you can believe that."

Nodding to Christine, Lieutenant Colonel Amanee said, "Please convey my thanks to your Dad as well. Then looking around the room he went on, "Marines, I want to remind you that the person we're looking for is responsible for the death of at least nineteen Marines and civilians, and probably a lot more. So if he feels cornered, he's likely to react violently. Be prepared. Any time you're out of the crowd on base, I want you to have a round chambered in your weapon. No magazines inserted, or you'd be accosted by base security. Any questions?"

The room was quiet. Looking at Colonel Burdine, Lieutenant Colonel Amanee continued, "Colonel Burdine, I propose that we move immediately—today—with the notification that the cans will be serviced tomorrow. And that we all meet tomorrow at this time, 1100 hours."

"That'll be fine, Colonel. Thank you." Looking around the table, Colonel Burdine went on, "Any saved rounds?" Greeted by silence, he stood up and said, "Very well, break now, go about your duties, see you at 1100 tomorrow."

"Attention on deck!" announced Corporal Dunbar, and the sound of chair legs grating on the plywood floor suddenly jarred the room as all stood and assumed the position of attention.

"Carry on," quipped Colonel Burdine, as he strode briskly from the room.

CHAPTER TWENTY-EIGHT

THINGS AREN'T ALWAYS WHAT THEY SEEM

Wednesday, March 16, 2005

Sitting at her desk in the U.S. Embassy building in the Green Zone, Renee was reviewing her email inbox. Husband Don, kids Jackie, seven, and Sammy, five—fantastic—she loved reading their notes so much. She always answered her drudgery mail first, and savored the thought of reading the notes from her VVVIP's last, work done, able to read slowly, rapturously, and repeatedly. But there it was, crammed between State Department employee notes, Green Zone security alerts, and business from her array of acquaintances throughout Iraq . An email from the Yahoo account, peace235@yahoo.com. She recoiled when she saw it, shuddering. She had never regretted anything in her life like she did her involvement with the owner of that address.

It had begun so innocently. Four months before, Renee had been grabbing a quick soup and sandwich in the elegant lobby of the embassy. There weren't enough tables, so a Middle-Eastern-looking middle-aged man asked if he could share her table. She wasn't pleased, but graciously welcomed him. He wanted to engage in light conversation, so she indulged him. He worked on the support staff of the Embassy as a KBR employee, coordinating minor construction projects. Trained as a civil engineer, he was highly competent, and enjoyed considerable respect from his workers as well as his employers.

Introducing himself as Hamid Amin, he spoke impeccable English with a thick Arabic accent, and conversed articulately about a wide variety of topics. They talked briefly about his construction projects, his wife and four children back in Egypt, his hopes for Iraq and the entire Middle East. But most of the personal history, and all of the philosophy that he related, was bogus. He was actually Palestinian by birth, and he hadn't seen or communicated with his family in nine months. He was a radical Islamist who sought the overthrow of all Middle Eastern governments in favor of a caliphate who would violently demand compliance with the most radical form of Sharia. And his hope, expressed every day in his prayers, was that radical Islam would replace all religions and peoples of the world either willingly or by the sword—preferably in his lifetime.

Renee found him so interesting that she agreed to meet him for lunch the following day. Because her family was back home in North Carolina, her evenings were open, and she agreed to have dinner with him a week later. Several dinners later, during which he violated his principles and consumed distilled spirits while promoting Renee's liberal ingestion, Hamid found his way to her bed. He was not a great lover, but Renee was lonely, and he seemed to be unusually sensitive and supportive.

During pillow talk, they spoke of their work. Gradually, the topic of her travel by Marine helicopter came up. Renee discussed in detail the difficulty of getting an Assault Support Request, or ASR—a seat reservation aboard a USMC helicopter. So she frequently ended up flying "Space A," finding seats on available basis. She described how she could look up on her SIPR computer the schedules of Marine Air on any given day. Since she came to know the air ops people as well as the junior enlisted staff running the large LZ [Landing Zone] at the Green Zone, known as LZ Washington, she also commonly was aware if any notables were flying in those aircraft.

Without realizing it was happening, Hamid convinced Renee that they were not merely bedmates, but soul mates, who just happened to have origins on different ends of the world. That they both saw the US invasion of Iraq as destructive, and that the sooner US troops withdrew, the better for everyone. And ever so gradually, he got around to persuading her that should additional helicopters be shot up—not downed, no injuries of course—the American public may demand a cessation of hostilities and US withdrawal. And so it came to pass that Renee was feeding Hamid information regarding helo departures times and destinations, which would allow easy prediction of flight routes—and readily permit insurgents to conceal anti-aircraft batteries in precisely the right places. The US tried to minimize predictable routine and times, of course, but there were only so many ways to fly from Baghdad to Mosul. Mobile batteries could readily be temporarily positioned in the open desert in a number of places where routing was likely, without discovery by Iraqis or Americans.

109

And after the first few helo's had taken fire, with the inevitable casualties that Hamid promised would not happen, Renee couldn't be sure if her own perfidy had been a factor in those mishaps. But she suspected that it was.

At first the sex was just missionary position, ordinary. But gradually Hamid wanted more positions: woman on top, side-by-side, front to back, doggie, and even taboo sex that Renee didn't even allow Don to do. Hamid became aggressive and seemed to want to demean her during sex. Eventually Renee realized that Hamid's idea of lovemaking was to desecrate the woman, have his way, and then abruptly stop when he came. No thought of the woman, it was all about him. It wasn't lovemaking at all—it was sex-making. And Renee wanted no further part of it. She cut him off.

Renee had stopped seeing Hamid, but at this point he threatened to expose her infidelity if she betrayed him. She hadn't heard from him in two weeks, and had hoped that she had seen the last of him. His email glared at her from her screen, invading her space, haunting her thoughts.

Summoning all her strength, she clicked on the message. Hamid's macabre voice figuratively spoke from the screen: "Meet me tomorrow at noon at the old parade field, by the Crossed Swords Monument." *The lying monster knows he can't be seen with me without arousing suspicion, and he doesn't know who might be in my apartment, so he's shrewd enough to demand a meeting in an isolated place.* As much as she dreaded the thought, she believed that she had to see him, but she was searching for the right course. Should she just accept her fate, and report to the military authorities what happened? Her marriage might be sacrificed, her relationship with her children forever blemished, her job lost forever. And likely she would be prosecuted and incarcerated for treason. Maybe even executed—treason during wartime was a capital crime. Her self-respect was already gone. *What's the right answer?* She decided she had to meet with him no matter what.

He chose a fitting place for their meeting. The deserted, dusty parade grounds once saw legions of glittering troops goose-stepping to Saddam's delight, in a bizarre mockery of what military power constitutes. Expert at dressing up and dancing for Saddam's whim, Iraq's military was a paper tiger, gutted by his hopelessly foolish 1990 decision to invade Kuwait despite the stern warning of a combat-vet US President Bush, commander-in-chief of the most powerful military force the world had ever known. But at this site, the evil one was entertained by controlling his pawns, watching them dance to his music, just as Hamid planned to manipulate and be amused by Renee.

So she typed back, "I'll be there. This needs to stop."

CHAPTER TWENTY-NINE

SURVEILLANCE

Wednesday, March 16, 2005

The trailer opposite the COC was silent. All three intel technicians and Waleed Mansour were sitting at desks in front of their monitor stations, intently listening to their headphones, laptops open for rapid transcription, and all input being recorded on electronic memory built into the monitors. Periodically, one of them would widen his eyes and begin typing intently, while the others stared into the wall, or doodled on their scratch paper. No one heard anything worth compelling the others to listen in.

Lieutenant Colonel Rider's mike was continually hot, because the ops boss needs to speak to so many different factions, both by phone and in person. Corporal Stacey Dunbar, the only African-American of the four TQ Intel enlisted Marines, assigned to Col Rider's monitor, was forced to listen with all of her wits. The conversations were rapid, terse, and full of acronyms, but Corporal Dunbar's highly trained ears were savvy, picking out every nuance.

Due to a planned combat operation near the Syrian border, Lieutenant Colonel Rider's desk was unusually busy. Completely unknown to him, the tone of his voice changed based on the rank of the person he was addressing. When he was conversing with a general officer, his voice was sonorous and soothing. To subordinates, his voice was raspier, leaving no question as to who was boss. The gentle tapping of his computer keys was nearly continuous, even during voice conversations. The periodic exasperated expletives, cursing the computer as well as its mother, father, aunts, uncles, and cousins, were typical of all of those who spend their work lives in front of one. At least he wasn't into mouse slamming to retaliate against the computer, as so many people are. It would have deafened Corporal Dunbar, listening so intently across the street from him. Despite the verbal excess, nothing remotely suspicious came up.

Captain Stella Rogers' desk was intermittently active. Her duties required her to walk between ops, intel, logistics, and the LZ, so her mike was silent half the time. Lance Corporal Kimmel kept a textbook of mathematics with him, to keep his mind from going blank during periods of silence. Five semesters into the pursuit of his BS in math, he aspired to a career of teaching high school math. So when Captain Rogers' chair grated on the floor as she stood up to walk to another office, his textbook came up to the desk and popped open to the section of advanced geometry he was working on. The only interesting issue was when she called her beau back home—a flashy young salesman with her company. Because of the eight hour difference between Iraq and Central US time, most such conversations must wait till late afternoon/evening Iraq time. Apparently Captain Rogers' boyfriend keeps weird hours, because she was chatting with him at 0230 hours Chicago time.

Lying through her teeth, but sensing the power of her feminine mystique, she would tell him she was alone in her hooch, in her underwear. She would describe loosening her bra and touching her nipples till they erected. Then she'd describe spreading her thighs and stroking her panties at the moist region overlying her vulva. She'd relate sliding her hand into her panties, and gently massaging her clitoris, intermittently sliding two fingers deep into her vagina.

Sometimes she'd not only excite her boyfriend, but herself as well. At those times, Stella would strive to actually touch her groin, but could only do so for a few seconds at a time, her groin partially concealed by her desk.

Intel work can be rather boring, so listening in on the lascivious conversation was Lance Corporal Kimmel's reward for the hours of drab observation Captain Rogers had provided him for the rest of the day. The very proper-looking Captain Rogers astonished him with her fabulous dirty talk to her young stallion. But these conversations, no matter how prurient or raunchy, are protected. Intel people are *very* discreet, so the amusement stops there. Although the conversations are recorded, only summary transcripts are made of non-suspicious conversations.

The two lance corporals in the Air Department spent most of their time mute at their computers, with only the gentle tapping of their keyboards audible on their bugs. Lance Corporals Kip Adams and Doug Kumler's conversations were all business, except for some light banter between them, centering on sports and women. Again, nothing remotely suspicious transpired. Corporals Kimmel and Dunbar were bored but diligently listening.

Samir was in and out of his office that day. He was called into General Brier's office a few times, where the conversation was inaudible. His phone conversations were all innocent enough, speaking with the base exchange and the base laundry about trivial matters. A very drab day for Waleed Mansour, listening in to what was mostly a mike transmitting silence.

CHAPTER THIRTY

WEAVING THE WEB

Wednesday, March 16, 2005

"Captain Kalopolis," answered the highly competent twenty-eight year-old manager of the teams that protected all the staff of Blue Diamond by maintaining "the wire" – preventing the enemy storming over the walls.

"Captain, it's Major Baxter, from the Air Office. I need to meet with you. Are you free now?"

"Yes, now is good, Major. What's it about?"

"Can't say on an unsecured line, Captain. Is your office fit for a secret discussion?"

"Yes, Major, if we close the door, it's secure."

"Great, be right over. Out." And the line went dead. Major Baxter arrived in the base security office in eight minutes. Sweating a bit, he was nonetheless grateful it wasn't the peak of summer, when that walk would have drenched his uniform in sweat.

"Major Baxter to see Captain Kalopolis," he said to the private first class at the reception desk.

"Yes Sir," the PFC responded promptly, and stood up to walk back to Captain Kalopolis's office, where he was advised to send the Major right in.

Strolling back to the office, Matt met Captain Kalopolis at the door, The Captain extended his hand, motioning Matt to the chair facing his desk and shutting the door.

Sitting behind his desk and leaning forward to speak more softly, Captain Kalopolis got down to business. "What can I do for you, Major?"

"Captain, this is a privileged communication. You are to discuss this with no one. Is that clear?"

"Yes Sir." Captain Kalopolis was accustomed to secrets in his line of work. Perceived weaknesses in base defense were topics of which he should be aware, but certainly never transmit to anyone else.

"Captain, we believe we have an insurgent informer on base, and that they've been reporting out activities that put Marines in the line of fire. We suspect that this plant could have been involved in the loss of General Sienkewicz."

Shaking his head, the Captain responded "Wow, Major, that's horrendous. Any idea who it is?"

"We've think we've narrowed it down to twenty-five people. We're bugging their desks, but we need to bug their cans and cell phones, if they have them."

"Yes Sir, I get it. You need access to their cans."

"Precisely. But we need to do it in a non-threatening way. We don't dare enter the cans surreptitiously and run the risk of discovery and frightening off the rat. We need a cover. That's where you come in. We want you to get the keys from KBR on the basis that you need to carry out electrical and fire checks. We're bugging five people at a time, so I think you should ask KBR for twenty can keys at a time, to make it look authentic and not narrowed down to our suspect list."

"Okay, Major, I can do that. When do you want me to proceed?"

"Today, if possible. Do you have a relationship with the KBR key guy —can you can pull it off without raising suspicion?"

"I believe so, yes, Major. I've been working with Tony Raad for some time. He won't question me, and he can keep his mouth shut anyway."

"Good, Captain. I want you to get on this right away. Are you able?"

"Yes Sir. I had a meeting scheduled with my guys, but I can postpone it. I'll have the keys for you tonight."

"Terrific, Captain. Tentatively we'll enter the cans tomorrow about 1000 when they're all at work. And we'll need to put our people in KBR uniforms so nothing looks suspicious. Can you get me some of those coveralls the KBR workers wear?"

"Yes Sir, I'll have them tonight with the keys. How many?"

"Five, just in case. One size fits all?"

"Yes Sir, they're baggy, but they wear like iron."

"I'll drop by here tonight at, what, 2000?"

"I'll be here with the keys and coveralls, Sir."

"Great, Captain, thanks a million. See ya at 2000." And with that, Matt stood and left the room. Captain Kalopolis lifted his phone and dialed Tony Raad, manager of KBR services at Blue Diamond.

CHAPTER THIRTY-ONE

PREPARING THE NOOSE

Wednesday, March 16, 2005

"What did you find?" asked Colonel Burdine leaning forward.

"Not much to report, Colonel," responded Corporal Dunbar. "Lots of legitimate business, Sir, and a smattering of the usual chit-chat. But nothing of interest."

"How 'bout Samir? Anything there?"

"He wasn't in the office much, Sir," responded Waleed. "It was a pretty quiet day. We really need monitors in their hooches."

"Yes, yes, that's in the works. Major Baxter, how are we doing on monitoring their quarters?" Colonel Burdine inquired.

"Sir, the TQ Intel boss has three more junior enlisted arriving tonight, in civilian clothes so that they can impersonate KBR technicians. I've already arranged for Captain Kalopolis to get us the keys to the five people we're monitoring, plus fifteen others to distract attention. We should be able to start monitoring the quarters by tomorrow afternoon."

"Excellent, Major, thank you." Looking at Christine, Colonel Burdine went on, "And thanks to Curtis Electronics."

Christine blushed and looked down.

"OK, we'll meet again here on Wednesday morning at 10. Any saved rounds, Marines?" asked Colonel Burdine.

"Sir, we'll need a few hours to review the recordings from tomorrow night. Can we meet on Wednesday afternoon rather than morning, so we'll have time to rest and review the tapes in the morning?" asked Corporal Dunbar.

"Yes, good point, Corporal. Sure, let's go for 1400 hours. Does that work for your team?"

"Yes Sir, 1400 will be fine. Thank you, Sir."

"All right, see you all here at 1400 hours on Wednesday. TQ Marines, sorry, but I need you to stay away from the Blue Diamond Marines, so no one is asking who you are. Please stay around your hooch. Major Baxter, can you arrange for them to have a DVD player and a couple movies?"

"Yes Sir, I'll drop by MWR and pick up some stuff for them."

"Fine. 1400 Wednesday." Colonel Burdine smiled at the group, who jumped to attention as he stood up. "Carry on," he said as he left the room, still moving his right arm gingerly.

When the Colonel was gone, the group began animated conversation among each other. The TQ intel team bid farewell and walked out with Waleed, leaving Matt and Chris alone in the conference room.

"Moving right along, Captain," said Matt, smiling.

"We're certainly making progress, Major," Chris smiled, "but we don't have anything to show for it yet. I hope we're on the right track."

"I think we are, Captain," Matt smiled as he extended his hand. Chris extended hers, and Matt held it gently in both hands. Then, looking around to be sure no one could see them, he leaned down and kissed the back of her hand. "How 'bout you and I meet tomorrow at 10, just to keep the ball rolling?"

"I'd like that," Chris agreed.

"Okay, I'm outta here, see you at 10. Give me a shout if anything comes up," said Matt as he walked toward the door.

"I sure will, Major," said Chris as she trailed him, en route back to her desk. As Matt walked in front of her, she couldn't help but admire his broad shoulders, muscular arms nearly stretching the fabric of his ordinarily loose-fitting desert cammie blouse. And she could just make out the meaty curves of his butt as he walked. She smiled at herself for looking.

CHAPTER THIRTY-TWO

THE SHE-BEAR AND HER CUBS

Thursday, March 17, 2005

Renee had a difficult morning. She had slept poorly, torn by thoughts of her horrible predicament. She had been weak, she knew, and consorted with the enemy. But it wasn't her intent. It was never a conscious decision to betray her country and her countrymen. Hamid had ever-so-cunningly manipulated her into a position where she felt she was *being* patriotic in striving to end hostilities, and the US occupation. But now in the cold light of rational thinking, she realized that she had in fact committed treason. That she had almost certainly contributed to injuries and probably deaths of her American brothers and sisters.

Renee had strayed quite a long way from her proud membership in the Daughters of The American Revolution back in Nashville. She would certainly not feed Hamid any more information. No matter what. Exposure of her infidelity would be horribly embarrassing, and exposure of her inadvertent complicity in insurgent attacks was almost certain. What to do? She would have had no difficulty killing herself, except for her children: she had no right to convert each of them into a motherless child, regardless of the humiliation. She needed to come clean, no matter the price. She would simply tell Hamid that their communication was ceasing, that he could do what he had to do, but that she was shutting him out permanently. She didn't want to tell him she was turning him in, although he had to suspect that she would. Easy enough for him to disappear, though, after she announced her firm decision to withdraw from him no matter what the cost. He could simply fade into the six million people in Baghdad without a trace. The Iraqi police were still rudimentary, and couldn't possibly track him down.

Nearly worthless at work that morning, she couldn't concentrate on her computer. During phone conversations, her mind wandered, and the callers were irritated with having to repeat themselves, then still finding she hadn't processed what they said. A wasted morning, and noon was approaching. She was going to make the leap. Her life would change irrevocably. She would be known as an adulterer, and probably as a traitor, but her mind was made up. This was it. She couldn't continue to be the puppet of some violent, hypocritical sociopath, preaching peace, love, and godliness, but practicing deceit, hate, and violence.

Striving to be unobtrusive, Renee grabbed her purse and headed for the door, hoping her coworkers would think she was simply going to the rest room. She didn't want any lunch invitations—there would be no lunch today. Instead, a massive catharsis, a confession, a resolve to repent, an acceptance of punishment earned, and status lost. It *had* to be.

Leaving the embassy building by a side door to minimize encounters, Renee strode down the driveway and out through the heavily fortified entry point. She passed through the bulletproof glass barriers, into the blast-proof guard building, through the one-way whole-body turnstile, and out into the busy street. She immediately headed southwest, toward the desolate area of the Crossed Swords Monument. It was only a mile's walk, and the spring morning was crisp and pleasant, warming from the 60s during the night to the 80s now. The traffic thinned as she moved away from the embassy area, and the bombed-out Baath Party Headquarters Building. She could hear intermittent helicopters coming and going to LZ Washington across the street from the embassy. They reminded her of her guilt. Tears began to stream down her cheeks, but fortunately there was no one around to see them.

Only a rare car or bus passed her now on the street. She could see the monument ahead, rising high into the air. Now dusty and abandoned, the entire area had gone to seed, including the Tomb of The Unknown Soldier beside the parade grounds. The souvenir vendor, who sometimes set up shop at the base of the huge hand on the left holding the sword, wasn't there today. Business was exceedingly slow there, and he must have decided to try the bustling road along the river, where the seat of government produced a vibrant street life.

Arriving opposite the site, she looked down the parade road, with its massive crossed swords towering over each end. Each sword was held up by a wrist and hand, positioning them forty feet high, with the top of the swords towering to one hundred and fifty feet. At the base of each hand, in a macabre gesture to Saddam's dark side, the helmets of thousands of fallen Iranian soldiers were poured right into the concrete, projecting them upwards in bizarre angles.

Standing directly under the near swords, she looked down the three hundred yard blacktop expanse of the parade ground. Off to her right was a massive semicircular colonnade that extended from the near swords to the distant ones. The grandstands that had seated thousands of cheering toadies were gone now. The squared legions of Saddam's flawlessly uniformed and beribboned troops that had goose-stepped down this plaza had borne witness to the perfidy of the entire regime.

Like most dictators, Saddam had been persuaded by his sycophants that his wishing something could make it come to be. So when he wished that, despite having purged his best and brightest generals, he could defy the President of the United States, even after having convinced the world that he was in possession of dangerous offensive weapons, Saddam believed that the prettily decorated dancers prancing around in front of him here could mount a significant response to the most powerful integrated military force in the world. And his fatuous wishful thinking resulted in the current state of decay of this formerly majestic place.

Surveying the desolate scene, Renee gazed at the four-story building off to the left. From the fourth floor balcony, the grinning dictator routinely hoisted a rifle in tribute to the charlatans before him. At the base of the building, barely visible through the brush, was a bench. She could just make out the shape of a man sitting there. The hairs on the back of her neck stood up, but she began a measured gait toward him.

As she approached, she confirmed that it was indeed Hamid seated, reading a newspaper. He heard her approaching and put down the paper.

"Renee, how nice of you to come." Hamid was wearing dark trousers and a white shirt open at the collar. Unlike all lower class and many middle class Iraqis, he wore shoes rather than flip-flops. He also sported the fashionable two days' beard growth.

"How dare you talk to me that way, you lying bastard. This is over, Mister, OVER!"

"Oh, Renee, Renee, you're upset, please...sit down," Hamid intoned soothingly as he lifted the paper.

"Forget it, Hamid. This is over, I'm out. OUT, do you understand," she shouted.

"Oh please, Renee, we have much too much in common to have such difficulties. We have much to do together still."

"Hamid, I was your sucker. You deceived me with all your lies about stopping the war. Everyone winning. Getting the troops to go home. And you said no one would get hurt. You knew there would be deaths. And there were. I don't know how I'm gonna resolve this in my mind, but one thing's for certain – I don't want to ever see or hear from you again. Do you get it? Can you get that through your thick Arab skull?"

"Renee, Renee," Hamid cajoled, standing up, "please sit down. We're going to work this out." He gestured to the far end of the bench.

Renee sat down at the far end, clutching her purse. "Hamid, I don't know how to tell you this, but I've my lost my self-respect, and I'll live with guilt for the rest of my life over what I did with you and to our Marines. But one thing is certain—this is the last time I'm ever going to see you, hear your voice, or even think of your name."

"Renee, Renee, you don't want that. We've been through too much together. There's no need for anyone to know what we've been through together. Your husband, your children, your employer, your colleagues... the General. There's no need for any of them to know about us."

"Don't even try it, you bastard. I'm prepared to accept the consequences of my bad decisions. Beginning with the decision to let you share my lunch table. And all the other times over these months that I saw you. And let you touch me. Oooooooh," she shuddered. "You're even a lousy lay. A ten-dollar vibrator would do any woman better than your pitiful excuse for lovemaking. You and that pathetic little cock of yours."

"But now I know what slime you are, how you manipulated me. That's behind me now. I'm ready to accept whatever follows. But the first step is to get you out of my life." Renee's eyes were moist, and she was sniffling a little. She reached into her woven-rope bag, and extracted some Kleenex.

"Oh Renee," Hamid shook his head, "there's no need for it to come to this." He reached into his brief case and withdrew a business-sized yellow envelope. He slid out contents and stared at the top paper, holding it so that she couldn't see it. Then, setting the paper on the bench between them, he showed it to her clearly. It was a photograph of her husband, Don. The tears started silently streaming down her cheeks.

"My God, what have I done?" she whispered, and began to softly sob, hands to her face.

Hamid took the second paper and placed it on the bench beside the photo of Bill. The photo showed her children, Jackie and Sammy, sitting on a bench side-by-side, eating ice cream cones. When Renee saw it, she started wailing, and rocking back and forth.

"Oh my God, my children, my children."

"There, there, Renee," Hamid purred. "There's no reason for these tears. And there's no reason why anything should happen to your family. No reason at all. They are beautiful children. And you'll be back to them in no time at all. I just need your help for a short while longer." Then Hamid turned his head and stared out over the parade grounds. He heard her sobbing slowly subside.

Turning back to her, Hamid found himself staring into the muzzle of a .32 caliber automatic pistol.

Everyone—military and civilian—carries arms in Iraq, even in the Green Zone. Hamid forgot that he was dealing with an American girl from the south. Southern girls grow up around guns. And they learn how to shoot them.

"Renee, Renee, what's this? There's no need for this."

"You're threatening my family, you son of a bitch," Renee spat out, as she wiped at her tears with her free hand. "You're threatening them."

"No, no, Renee, not at all, not at all. I wouldn't do that. Please, put down the gun."

"You're threatening my family, you lying son of a bitch. Nobody threatens my family."

Once again misjudging Renee, Hamid decided that he could bully her, the way many Arab men bully their women. "I am not afraid, Renee. Allah will protect me. And your weak Christian religion prohibits you from harming me. Now give me the gun!" And he reached forcefully for it.

The gun barked, and the first round passed between his outstretched fingers then penetrated his chest four inches to the right of his third button. It ripped through his right upper lung, and lodged in the muscles of his back.

Hamid's mouth dropped open, and his outstretched right hand retracted and touched the hole in his shirt, now sprouting a red halo. The gun barked again. And again and again.

The second round entered his upper abdomen, penetrating the abdominal wall, three loops of gut, ripped along the wall of the aorta, and lodged in his thoracic spine. The torn aorta began pumping a thick jet of pulsating blood into his abdominal cavity. And the gun kept barking.

The third round hit him square in the sternum. The force knocked him backwards, but the round tore through the thin bone, and penetrated all three walls of his heart. Hamid felt an odd sensation deep in his chest, which he had never felt before—but he had never been shot in the heart before. He began to get dizzy, as his heart's output dropped precipitously. The fourth round went wild because he had flopped backward, and penetrated the muscles of his left arm. As he began to sit up again, the fifth round entered just below his left eyebrow. Penetrating the thin bone of his orbit, it ripped into his left cerebral cortex and snuffed out his consciousness instantly. He fell backward again, as Renee stood up and emptied the remaining four rounds into his chest. After the ninth round, the slide of the automatic pistol remained in the back position, indicating depletion of all rounds in the magazine.

Renee dropped her arms to her sides, then threw the gun on to her handbag. Then she sat down and sobbed, hands on her face, shoulders convulsing. After a few minutes she stopped crying, dried her tears, and stared straight ahead, deciding what to do.

Plan concluded, Renee stood up and went behind the bench, behind Hamid's slumped body, his neck bent backward awkwardly, leaving his open but unseeing eyes staring into the sun. Blood was silently dripping from the many fresh holes in his body, onto the beige dust under the bench. Careful to avoid getting his blood on her clothes, Renee pushed on his shoulders until his body rolled forward and fell on the ground, face down. Walking around the bench to him, she latched her hands under his arms and pulled him a few feet from the bench. Then standing up and walking to his feet, she grasped both ankles and began dragging him into the bush. After about thirty feet, he was in low scrub and palm trees. Gathering dead brown palm branches, she laid them over him until he was concealed. Returning to the bench, she noted that the blood was already drying into brown goo in the bright sun. She knew that within twenty-four hours, the blood would simply look like brown stains. Gathering dust and sand in her hands, she threw it on the blood on the bench, as well as the pool under the bench. Using a palm branch, she smoothed the sand where she had dragged him.

Looking around and seeing no one, Renee picked up the photographs and Hamid's envelope as well as her bag and walked at a leisurely pace directly across the parade road, and then turned right toward the swords and the main road. She was reflecting on what she had just done. She felt no remorse for killing Hamid, nor did she feel any compulsion to dignify the treatment of his corpse. Left where it was, it would be consumed by feral dogs, cats, and insects within a day or two. *A fitting end for that lying murderous monster.*

Reaching the main road, Renee walked briskly toward the Embassy. While an occasional vehicle passed, her appearance was entirely unremarkable. Reaching the security gates in fifteen minutes, her sweaty appearance was normal for this time of day, and she crossed into the grounds uneventfully. Relieved to enter the air conditioned atmosphere of the building, she passed the lobby café where she had first met Hamid, and entered the black marbled ladies' room. Washing her hands and face with soap, she felt enormously refreshed. Then she headed for her office, to proceed with her plans. Once again she reflected on the morality of what she had just done. He had been a predator, threatening the she-bear's cubs. And he had seen the wrath of the maternal instinct where her young are endangered, first hand, lethally. She found no ethical dilemma in his killing. *Nobody threatens my kids.*

CHAPTER THIRTY-THREE

NOT SO ROUTINE AN INSPECTION

Thursday, March 17, 2005

The additional intel staff flew in, in civilian attire, from their base at Taqaddum on the evening of the 16th. Reporting in the next morning to Christine's office by telephone only, they remained in the KBR tent to which they were assigned to fulfill the role of visiting KBR technicians.

"Air Office, Lance Corporal Pratt speaking."

"Captain Curtis for Major Baxter, please."

"Stand by one."

"Major Baxter. Good morning," Matt's voice came on.

"Good morning, Major, this is Captain Curtis. I wanted to let you know that the KBR techs are in, and ready to get to work. Are you able to accommodate?"

"Oh, yes, of course, Captain. I'll take care of it. Thanks for calling." And with that, Matt finished the email he was writing, logged off his computer, and advised Corporal Kumler that he'd be out for an hour or so.

Arriving at the KBR tents, Major Baxter had already picked up the transceivers from his can, and brought them to the techs, along with the keys to the cans for the day, and a map of the can lay-out. Passing out the materials, Matt instructed, "You're going to 'inspect' twelve cans today, but you're only bugging five. I know you men have done this kind of work before. Do you have any questions of me?"

"No sir, looks pretty straightforward," replied Corporal Pratt, who was in charge of the crew. "We'll get right to it, and get back to Captain Curtis when we're done. Do the monitoring staff have the frequencies for these devices?"

"Good point, Corporal. Yes, that team went through all the hardware, and set up their base stations to receive all the transceivers we have."

"Very well, Sir, we're ready to start. We brought KBR uniforms with us. So we'll jump into those, and get to work right away."

"Terrific, Corporal. Thank you." Shifting his gaze to the other two men, lance corporals, he thanked them as well. "And I need to say it, sorry —this project is absolutely top secret. Don't speak to anyone on base you don't need to. And when your work today is finished, I want you flying out tonight. We'll bring you back every three days as we move on to other suspects."

"Loud and clear, Sir. We'll be on our way this evening. We already have an ASR for a 0130 flight, show time 2330. We'll await your call to come back in three days."

"So be it," responded Matt. "And thank you again." He saluted the men, all of whom, though in civilian garb, returned the salute smartly.

CHAPTER THIRTY-FOUR

REVERIE

Thursday, March 17, 2005

Matt returned to his office and sat at his desk. He was cooling off from walking briskly, as he had heated up despite the cool morning temperature. He leaned back in his desk chair, and put his hands behind his head. A good time to reflect.

The investigation was going well. It was a frightful time, with a spy in their system—probably sitting within two hundred feet of him right now. But at least they were organized, had a plan, the right equipment and people, and were on the move.

Having Lieutenant Colonel Hiroon Amanee here was a different matter. Matt had worked with then-Captain Amanee many years earlier, when he himself was 1st Lieutenant Baxter, and a flight instructor in the training command at Pensacola. Matt had a superb student—a natural flyer, who undoubtedly would be selected for fighters—but who had a personal problem. Sam Bowey had allowed himself to get caught up in excessive gambling, and at one point had knowingly written a couple bad checks to keep his head above water financially. Matt learned about the issue, and believed he could salvage Ensign Bowey's career. He believed that saving Bowey was the right course for the Navy, which had already invested heavily in Sam, a supremely talented pilot.

But Captain Amanee, assigned to the case by NCIS, was unexpectedly hard-nosed about the issue, despite Matt's requests to be allowed to intervene, and bring Sam back into the fold. Captain Amanee insisted that he had worked with compulsive gamblers before, and that until they were abstinent for two years, they were very high risk for recurrence, which always resulted in compromise of their professional duties. No matter where or what Sam ended up flying for the Navy, people's lives were dependent on his being undistracted. Captain Amanee was unwilling to

129

take that gamble himself. So Ensign Sam Bowey was booted out of flight school and sent to a ship, where he was prohibited from gambling. They told him he could reapply for flight training after two years, but the fact is that, once washed out, he was extremely unlikely to be picked up again by the flight program.

Matt never quite forgave Lieutenant Colonel Amanee for that situation. And the fact that Amanee had shortly thereafter eaten Matt's lunch in the Iron Man Triathlon at Camp Lejeune did nothing to assuage Matt's irritation with him. Matt was proud of his superior conditioning, and was accustomed to winning most military competitions he entered. But Captain Amanee proved to be, while less muscular than Matt, lithe and powerful with phenomenal endurance, leaving Matt in his dust on both the half-mile swim and the five-mile run portions. Matt was considerably faster than Hiroon on the fifteen-mile bicycle portion, but not nearly enough to make up for the difference in the other portions. So Matt had several reasons to resent Lieutenant Colonel Hiroon Amanee.

Captain Rogers walked by while he was thinking—his eyes trailed her shapely form as it passed. What a treat to have such a handsome woman in the same office! Matt had known her when she passed through the flight training command as a student. He had even instructed her on a couple flights, some six years earlier. He had wanted to date her then, but both he and she had several relationships during that period, and it never happened. He would love to develop a relationship here, but since she was subordinate to him in the same command, fraternization rules absolutely prohibited such an evolution. He even considered establishing a clandestine rendezvous with her during their R&Rs, [Rest & Relaxation period mid-way through a deployment], but because it was against the rules, he immediately dismissed it as pleasant fantasy.

Damned, I almost forgot – my R&R's on the twentieth, and it's extremely unlikely this investigation will be wrapped up by then. And with Christine gone home to be with her Mama, there's no way I can leave then. Damned!

Thinking about R&R, Matt remembered that he had plans to meet up with his girlfriend of eight months prior to deployment, corporate executive Sarah Coughlin. A fitness buff, she was an accomplished rower, taking regional championships when she was at Temple U in Philadelphia. Sliding along the Missouri River beside her in a rowing shell, he was no match for her. Between strength and technique, she flew past him like he was dragging an anchor. When running, he could outdistance her quickly —but he did so rarely, because she was such good company.

He recalled how she had planned his send-off. She wanted to make it particularly memorable, to give him something to fight for, and something for him to want desperately to come home for. *Oh boy did she ever!*

First it was a gourmet dinner at St. Louis's finest, the Candlelight Inn. Then it was dancing at the Renoir Club. Back to her apartment for brandy snifters full of the clear pungent beverage—she said it allowed her to remember where her esophagus was—pleasantly burning all the way down.

Sitting on the couch sipping from their bulbous glasses, Sarah got up and put on a CD of gentle music, starting with The Girl From Ipanema. Standing in front of him, she began to sway rhythmically with the music, dancing for him. Silently moving about the room as she danced, she then returned to stand right in front of him, facing away. Then she slowly bent forward at the waist, keeping her knees straight, and slowly lifted her black satin dress. First he saw black stockings. Then milky white thighs adorned with garters, and then silky black bikini panties. Sarah had a supremely beautiful body, and he was getting to see it decorated, at its most voluptuous. Her magnificently rounded butt was just inches from his face.

As Matt leaned forward to encircle her thighs with his arms, Sarah danced forward, smiling, and turned to face him. Slender, graceful arms over her head, she lifted her shining auburn hair and let it drop into place several times. He was always astonished at how much her appearance changed with the location of her hair.

Then one arm snaked behind her, and slowly slid down the dress's zipper. Turning her back, he was treated to the sight of her graceful shoulders and a seductive slender black bra strap across her back. Now facing him again, she slowly slid the dress straps down her arms, revealing the black brassiere holding breasts into a cleavage that seemed to be begging for release. She jiggled her breasts for him, and then reached back and unhooked her brassiere.

Slowly lowering the bra, her flawless full breasts were freed from constraint, and stood straight out at him. With the firmness of youth, her breasts pointed to the ceiling, and were exquisite. Matt could feel his trousers growing tight in the groin. Then Sarah bent over and gently rubbed her nipples across his lips, driving him mad.

Sarah gently writhed her way out of the dress altogether, and it slid to the floor. Slowly, she unhooked the garters, and unsnapped the garter belt, dropping it on the dress. Then she danced around the room again, wearing only her black heels, black stockings, and black bikini panties.

Now returning to him, Sarah slid her panties down her long silky thighs, finally stepping out of them. Her auburn muff matched her flowing mane. Swaying gracefully, Sarah again turned her back, and again slowly bent over with her knees straight. This time, with her perineum inches from his face, she didn't evade his encircling arms. The pungency of her lady parts was mesmerizing. Matt pulled her to him, and embraced her passionately. Sarah didn't realize she had begun softly moaning.

Gently sliding her off his lap and on to the couch beside him, Matt stood up and kicked off his shoes. Pulling off both his trousers and skivvies in a single motion, he yanked off his socks, and his shirt.

Kissing her aggressively, Matt proceeded to make love to her with the passion available only to the young. After 15 minutes of steamy and semi-acrobatic union, he gently kissed her, and they rested silently.

The rest of the night was devoted to alternating periods of violent lovemaking, followed by the peerless pleasure of post-coital lovers' rest. They explored most of the secrets of the Kama Sutra. It was the best sex Matt had ever known. *Hell yes I wanna go home and see Sarah!*

His reverie was interrupted by the phone ringing on Lance Corporal Adams' desk. Sitting forward, and putting his arms on his desk, he willed his rigid erection to subside, so he could get back to work.

CHAPTER THIRTY-FIVE

KBR CALLING

Friday, March 18, 2005

The crew was into the KBR uniforms by 1100. They arose later than most of the Marines, so as not to mix with the BD Marines in the latrine and shower trailers. Matt had already dropped off their gear, as well as a map of the cans of the 4 Marines and one terp to be bugged. He pointed out which additional 15 trailers were to be "inspected", and provided keys for all of them. And, of course, the monitors themselves, which had already been tuned to the receiving stations opposite the COC. They had tested the mikes outside the trailers, and found transmission to their base station to be quite good.

Walking the three hundred yards to the chow hall, they ate separate from others, but carried on an animated conversation among themselves, coming across as American technicians working for KBR. They needed to return to their quarters to get their tools and monitors, because no bags of any kind are allowed in the chow hall. But they had all day, so they didn't mind. It was a cool, sunny morning—a lovely day to be out and about.

Arriving at the berthing area, they found the hooch that Lance Corporal Kumler and Lance Corporal Adams shared. The keys were well marked, and after receiving no response to their gentle knock, they were inside in a second. Rather disorderly, clothes were strewn about, and the beds unmade. The crew lingered over the splendid pin-ups on most of the walls. No "don't ask-don't tell" types here. The monitors were quickly attached to the battleship-gray angle-iron bunkbed-capable bedposts facing the walls. Negligible chance of discovery in the three days they'd be there. A search of their lockers uncovered clothes, frisbees and a football. And, of course, even raunchier pin-ups. No booze, they were pleased to see—it was prohibited, and they wouldn't have reported it anyway, but always good to know the boys were behaving well. The crew searched under the beds and up under the mattresses, looking behind the lockers, and a quick run through the drawers of the bed tables – no evidence of cell phones. Five minutes after arriving, they were relocking the door from the outside.

On to a couple hooches that were the "cover", not to be bugged. A few minutes of walking around inside, flicking the switches and shamming an inspection, they were outside again in five minutes, and on to Captain Rogers' room, which she shared with another female Marine officer. The room smelled feminine. It was decorated with rugs, wall hangings, posters —very personalized. Neat as a pin. The same inspection—no pinups here. A little embarrassed to be looking through her frilly things, they did their duty efficiently. As men, of course, they couldn't control the fact that their minds wandered to what the nubile bodies looked like that fit into these ever-so-feminine panties and bras, but they didn't linger. And, ever professional, they didn't sniff. The monitor went to the same place, on the concealed side of the bedpost. No cell phone found. And they were outside within the same five

Next to Lieutenant Colonel Rider's hooch, which he shared with another Marine Lieutenant Colonel. Both of them had "big" jobs, resulting in their working fourteen to eighteen hours a day, returning to the hooch only to sleep and change. Bare walls, military gear in and on top of the lockers. Nothing remotely personal, other than their names sewn into their uniform blouses and trousers. No cell phone.

Out the door, locking up, and moving on to a few more "cover" inspections, they then headed over to Samir's quarters, which were in "TCN Village," where all the non-US workers resided [TCN =Third Country National citizen]. As a relatively senior person, Samir rated his own room. First "inspecting" three other quarters, the team was seen by a number of TCN's, but their cover was effective, and no one gave them a second glance. Then it was on to Samir's quarters. As they rounded the corner of the hooch two trailers down, they saw his door opening. Quickly turning to the door in front of them, they produced its key, knocked, and then let themselves into the room, gently announcing, "KBR electrical inspectors, coming in." Out of the corner of his eye, Corporal Sammel saw Samir glance their way, but showed no interest in them. Samir locked his door and strode away.

Waiting a full ten minutes in the trailer of the Filipino kitchen workers that they had entered, the team opened the door without hesitation, stepped out, and locked the door while Lance Corporal Reid made phony notations on his clipboard.   Then they walked to Samir's door, unlocked it, and entered.

The room was cozy, with carpets made from remnants, sold at the BX for ten dollars each. A brightly colored prayer rug was draped over the baseboard of the bed. A Koran sat on the desk. The closet revealed a dishdasha (Arab "man-dress"), a pair of sandals, and a few sports shirts and slacks. His bedside table featured an alarm clock, tissue box, and a radio. Inside the drawer were a paperback book in Arabic, dental floss, his Afghan passport, an Arabic magazine and newspaper, and a few coins.

Corporal Sammel closed the drawer, but as he stood up, he wondered what kind of coins they were. Reopening the drawer, he picked up five of them and, squinting, read the country of origin. Two were Iraqi, two were Afghan, but the smallest one was in Arabic only. Showing it to Lance Corporal Reid, who was studying Arabic, they concluded it was Saudi. *Hmm, Samir is Afghan, and he's made the Haji (pilgrimage to Mecca in Saudi Arabia), but there's no report that he's been to Saudi recently.* Checking the passport, which was four years old, they found no stamp from Saudi Arabia. *He could have received this from any number of sources, but it's a little odd, regardless.*

Replacing the coin in the drawer and closing it slowly, Corporal Sammel resolved to look around a bit more closely. Opening the locker again, he patted down the clothes. Looking under and behind it, there was nothing. He patted down the bedclothes again. Looked at all the bed poles and under the mattresses again. Nothing. Looking around, Corporal Sammel thought, *Now if I wanted to conceal a cell phone here, where would I put it?* The walls and ceiling were hardboard with no loose seams. They had examined all of the floor and furniture. Then his eyes cast on the air conditioner projecting through the wall. Walking to it, he ran his hands over the top, opened the grates, looked at the seal with the wall achieved with urethane foam. The foam seemed to be disturbed on top, in a place invisible unless standing on a two-foot high ladder or table. Pulling on the foam, a chunk of it came away easily. *It was just setting there – not attached at all.*

Peering through the inch-thick crevice between the wall and the air con, he saw something shiny. Squeezing his fingers into the crevice, he could feel something smooth that pushed back, but he couldn't grasp it. *If that's a phone, it's clearly contraband, and he's working hard to conceal it. He must have some kind of long needle-nosed pliers to reach in there and retrieve it. Time to look outside.*

The team exited and locked the door. Lance Corporal Reid dutifully played his part of writing sham findings on his clipboard. They walked around the back of the trailer, and stared at the air con. Nothing definite came into view. Standing up the stepladder, Lance Corporal Reid climbed up and looked at the urethane foam seal, which was undisturbed. Reaching over and tugging at it, it was secure. Extracting his pocketknife, he slid it down the wall of the trailer, slicing through the foam and hitting the air con, cutting a section six inches long. Then he cut into the foam perpendicular to the trailer, and readily extracted the block of foam. And there, in a pocket extending through the wall of the trailer, was a Toshiba cell phone.

Because this was the first air con they had touched during the trip, they knew they must get away from it quickly to avoid arousing suspicion. Lance Corporal Reid passed it down to Corporal Sammel, who extracted the battery cover and deftly slid the tiny radio marker into the crevice between the battery and the phone housing. Snapping the cover back on, he carefully replaced the phone in the precise location, and slid the urethane chunk back into place. *Wish I had some urethane foam to seal it up again, but I'm gonna need to get to it again in three days anyway.*

Because rain is uncommon even in March in Iraq, he was willing to leave the urethane unsealed. He did tape it on with some electrical tape, which was conveniently dull yellow and blended with the urethane, and couldn't be seen without a ladder anyway. Then he was down, the ladder collapsed, and they were walking to the adjacent trailer for a sham inspection. *I wonder if Samir is the one. Guess we're gonna find out. Hope he uses that phone soon.*

CHAPTER THIRTY-SIX

SOUNDS OF LIFE

Friday, March 18, 2005

After retreating to their guest quarters, the TQ crew that planted the hooch monitors did what young military guys and gals worldwide do during their down time. One did college coursework, one paged through a magazine before launching into a novel, and the third lay on his bunk, earplugs in place, listening to his iPod. Then they all watched a DVD together on the tiny DVD player that Lance Corporal Reid had brought with him. At 2300 hours, they walked over to the LZ, checking in two hours before their flight time of 0130 h, and again tried to avoid mixing with any of the Marines waiting there in the windowless unfinished plywood hut that was the passenger terminal. The Marines in the hut were mesmerized by a showing of "Dirty Harry" on the TV placed for waiting passengers, so nobody wanted to talk anyway.

CHAPTER THIRTY-SEVEN

CLEARING THE AIR

Friday, March 18, 2005

"The General will see you now," said Lieutenant Wiggin, aide to General Jacques Jabbour, gesturing for Renee to follow him. Lieutenant Wiggin had been the aide to General Sienkewicz, but had not taken that fateful trip to Blue Diamond, when General Sienkewicz rode the mortally wounded Legacy 23 down into the insurgent-filled desert. Wiggin and Jabbour were still getting to know one another.

"Thank you," Renee replied meekly as she stood and followed him, clutching her purse. She entered the General's substantial office. Some of General Sienkewicz's memorabilia was still there, as General Jabbour gradually took over the office.

General Jabbour was seated behind a large mahogany desk signing documents. He looked up as she entered, then stood and extended his hand. "You wanted to see me, Mrs. Booker. Please sit down," and he motioned for her to sit in one of the handsome leather chairs facing the desk.

"Yes, General, thank you for seeing me." Sitting, she went on, looking down, "I don't know where to start. I, I'm so ashamed. I didn't... I would never have chosen what's happened. It just developed, slowly and I thought innocently, and then... then I was betraying you and all those brave men and women out there in uniform. And betraying my husband and children. And my parents, and my employer and coworkers, and, and, and all those who have trusted me." And she began to sob, her hands to her face, her shoulders heaving. The General was silent, and allowed her to cry.

Renee recovered in a minute, and looked up at the General. He raised his eyebrows and nodded, inviting her to proceed.

"General Jabbour, I have provided information about helicopter flights and manifests to, to, to the insurgency. I know now it was wrong, but at the time I thought I was doing the right thing."

"Tell me more, Mrs. Booker," the General replied softly, shifting his seating and leaning forward toward her, hands clasped together on his desk.

"His name was Hamid Amin. I met him in the embassy lobby café, when he asked permission to join me for lunch because there were no open tables. He was a supervisor for KBR."

"You're saying 'was,' Mrs. Booker. Where is he now?"

Renee hesitated, then swallowed and said, "He's lying under some palm fronds at the Crossed Swords Memorial. I killed him."

"I see," the General said, his eyebrows rising. "When was that?"

"Yesterday, sir. He wrote to me and demanded to meet with me. I had terminated all contact with him, but he wanted to blackmail me about our... relationship. I was unfaithful to my husband, General. I was lonely, and... well, that doesn't matter. Most Americans around here are lonely. Anyway, I was going to break off with him, accepting that he would publicize my infidelity. I was prepared to accept the consequences of my behavior. But then he pulled out recent pictures of my husband and two children." Leaning forward, Renee's eyes moistened once more. "He threatened them, General. He *threatened* my husband and my children. He shouldn't have done that. At that point, it was him or me. And I made it him."

"How did you dispatch him, Mrs. Booker?"

"32 automatic, Sir. I emptied the entire magazine into him, Sir, and I don't feel one bit of remorse. He couldn't be permitted to live, or my children would be in perpetual danger. I decided that in a second there on the bench – I had no plans to kill him when I went there. I've been carrying that automatic around with me for the entire eight months I've been in Iraq. But once he threatened my family, the gloves came off, and I was ready to instantly do whatever it took to protect my home. And I did."

" Okay, Mrs. Booker. Tell me about the helicopters."

"Hamid moved into my life, and I trusted him. After our relationship progressed to intimacy, he gradually brought our conversations over to the war. I've always believed that this war was a mistake, and that the best thing the U.S. could do is bring the troops home, and let Iraqis sort out

Iraqi problems. That they would evolve a representative government, that wouldn't threaten its neighbors. He said he felt the same way, but it turns out he didn't. He was Al Qaeda. He wanted a new kind of dictatorship foisted on the people, and he was willing to kill mercilessly to accomplish his goal—including my family."

"Go on, please."

"Yes Sir, well, because my official duties require a considerable amount of nocturnal flights on Marine helos, I got to know the military crews that staff the passenger terminal and the flight line. Gradually I learned what flights were going where and when. And, most saliently, I knew many times if a VIP was flying. And I passed that along to Hamid." Pausing, she went on, "He promised me there would be no deaths, that his people would shoot out the engines of the helicopters, which could auto-rotate down and save the lives of the passengers and crew. That the loss of the aircraft would encourage the American public to withdraw support for this war. I never intended to hurt anyone. I thought I was doing the right thing." Pausing, "But now I know that I was wrong. Dead wrong." She lowered her head – "and I'm prepared to accept the consequences of my acts."

General Jabbour sat quietly, nodding, staring across the room to the empty corner.

"Well, General, what do you want to do with me? Are you going to arrest me?"

Pensive for a minute, General Jabbour said, "I'm not sure, Mrs. Booker. I need to think about this." Standing up and pacing silently, hands clasped behind him, he asked, "It's possible that we can turn this situation on the insurgents. Who else knows that Hamid is dead?"

"No one, Sir. I've told no one. I haven't had the nerve to call my family yet."

"Good. Then the insurgents don't know that you've turned to us. That might be helpful. But we need to explain Hamid's death. I think we can cook up a story that we arrested him and he resisted violently, resulting in his death." Sitting up erect and staring into Renee's eyes, he went on, "Which means that his group will come to you with a replacement for Hamid."

"Oh, God, I thought I was through with them!"

"I don't blame you, Mrs. Booker. But you're into this up to your neck, now. They obviously know about your family, both who they are, and *where* they are. So you're still involved, with or without us. But you're a lot better off *with* us."

"General, I'll do anything to help. *Anything*. I've done serious harm, and I want to make up for it. And I'm not looking for penance. Inside, from myself, I am. But not from you, or the military, or from America. I'll accept whatever punishment is meted out to me. But if I can help first, I want to—desperately. What can I do?"

"Well, first we need to take care of Hamid. Where is he again?"

"At the Crossed Swords Memorial. You know the building on the left where Saddam used to shake his rifle? There's a bench about twenty-five yards in front of the main entrance. He's about thirty feet to the left of there, in a palm grove, covered by palm branches."

"I hope he's still there. With the feral dogs and cats around here, they might have dragged him around."

Lowering her head, Renee replied, "I realized that, but I was so angry at him that I didn't care."

"Well, I don't want to make a scene. We'll need to retrieve his body at night with minimal fanfare. I'll take care of it. Tomorrow we'll mention in a news conference that he was being arrested, and was killed trying to escape."

"What will you do with his body?"

"We'll have a dignified Muslim burial for him."

"Good." Renee responded with comfort. Then uncomfortably, "Am I going to be arrested now?"

"No, Mrs. Booker, I don't think that's necessary right now. And the fewer people who know about this, the better. I want you to return to work, and return to your normal routines. I'm sure Hamid's collaborators are going to contact you. When they do, call me. Do not tell anyone about this, without my permission. Is that clear?"

"Yes Sir."

"I'll be in contact with you by tomorrow noon. Did you have any immediate plans for travel outside the Green Zone?"

"No Sir, none."

"Good. Please don't go anywhere. I need you to be available to me. I need your email address, your office phone, and your Iraqna number." [Local civilian cell phone network].

"Sir, I'll write them down for you. And I'll email you as soon as I get to my office for backup." She extracted a notepad from her purse, leaned on the corner of his desk, and jotted down the info in her graceful script. Then she stood up, gave a crooked half smile, and said, "Thank you, General," as he handed her his card.

"Thank you for coming to me, Mrs. Booker. You did the right thing. We're going to work closely together to get your family out of this mess, and bring these criminals who threaten families to justice. I'll get back to you by noon tomorrow."

"Yes Sir. Thank you again." With that, Renee turned and walked briskly out of the General's office, nodding at Lieutenant Wiggin as she passed.

General Jabbour called out for Lieutenant Wiggin, who promptly entered the office and stood straight, saying, "Yes Sir?"

"Lieutenant, we have a very unusual situation here. Please close the door." Lieutenant Wiggin shut the door, and turned to see the General indicate that he should sit where Renee had been seated three minutes before. The seat was still warm as he slid into it.

"Lieutenant, we have just received a traitor into this noble office." He saw Lieutenant Wiggin's jaw drop and brows furrow, as he expected. "Mrs. Booker has been consorting with the enemy, and has conferred secret information about helo flights that may well have resulted in combat losses."

"My God, General," he uttered as he reached for the telephone, "Shall I have her detained?"

"No, no, I don't think so, Lieutenant. That's why I'm talking to you. I want to think out loud with you, and come to a decision. As you know, every cloud has a silver lining. We might be looking at that lining."

"How so, Sir?" asked Lieutenant Wiggin, scratching the back of his neck.

"She was dealing with an insurgent named Hamid, who was working here in the embassy as a maintenance supervisor. She killed him yesterday."

Lieutenant Wiggin did a doubletake. "*She* killed him? Lord, General, she didn't like the type who could kill a man, much less a violent man."

"Yes, I know, Lieutenant. But never underestimate the viciousness of a woman whose children are threatened. That's what Hamid did – that son of a bitch threatened her husband and children. Fortunately, he was stupid enough to wrong a strong American woman, and a strong Southern woman at that. And now he's lying in the weeds, probably being torn apart by feral animals."

"My Heavens, General, what should we do?"

"I want you to call Lieutenant Colonel Singleton, director of base security for the Green Zone. Get him to come up here as soon as he can. I don't want to talk over the phone if I can avoid it."

"Yes Sir, I'll get right on it," he said as he stood up. "Anything else for now, Sir?

"No, thank you, Lieutenant, we need LTC Singleton to get a team out there tonight and retrieve the body. I'll fill you in further when LTC Singleton arrives [Army Lieutenant Colonels are abbreviated LTC; Marines use LtCol].

"Yes, Sir, I'll get right back to you, Sir," the Lieutenant said, backing up, then turning around and walking briskly to his desk and picking up the phone.

CHAPTER THIRTY-EIGHT

CLEANING UP

Friday, March 17, 2005

"**G**ood morning, Sir. What can I do for you?"

Lieutenant Colonel Singleton greeted General Jabbour, having been escorted into the office by Lieutenant Wiggin."

"Thank you for coming, Lieutenant Colonel Singleton. Lieutenant Wiggin, please close the door and join us," said the General, motioning to the two leather armchairs facing his desk. After they were both seated, he proceeded. "I had a visit today from a GS-14 level woman in the Department of State, who works here in the embassy building. She's killed an insurgent, and I need your help in cleaning up the mess."

"Whoa, General, this is an odd one," LTC Singleton expressed, holding up both palms. "What happened?" he asked, as he unconsciously leaned forward.

"She had an affair with a maintenance supervisor for the grounds here, and he turned out to be an insurgent. He was pumping her for info on our helo flights, especially when VIP's were flying, so he could have the flights attacked. She kind of got sucked into it slowly, and it appears that she didn't really appreciate that she was aiding and abetting the enemy. When she realized what she was into, he extorted her with threats to reveal their affair. She was prepare for that, but then he made a big mistake. He threatened her family. Dumb bastard pulled out recent photographs of her husband and kids taken near their home. She went bananas, blew him away with her .32 automatic. Guess he thought he was pushing around a submissive Arab woman. There's a price for stupidity, and he paid it. She pumped the entire magazine into him."

"Anyway, he's lying on the Crossed Swords parade grounds. Or whatever's left of him after the feral dogs and cats have had at him. I

144

want you to retrieve his remains tonight, under cover of darkness, and with minimal fanfare. Leave no evidence behind. Give him a simple Muslim burial here on the grounds. And keep this all top secret. Do you have enough men with clearances?"

"No Sir, I don't. But I can get some guys out of intel. I have a good relationship with LTC Acosta, who runs the 2-shop here. [USMC and US Army command organization 1, 2, 3, 4, 5, 6 = Admin, Intelligence, Operations, Supply, Plans, Communications]. He'll give me three privates. That should be enough." Looking down sideways to think, he went on, "Where exactly is the body, Sir?"

"When you enter the grounds from the south, the entrance to Saddam's building is 150 meters in, to the west. About thirty yards in front of the entrance is a bench. She shot him on that bench, and dragged him south from there about thirty feet into the palm grove, and covered him with palm branches."

"All right, Sir, I can find that. Is there anything else, Sir?"

"No Colonel, thank you. Please get back to me when you've completed the mission."

"Yes Sir. Thank you, Sir. By your leave, Sir," and he moved toward the door.

"Good day, Colonel." The General waved a half-salute and sat down at his desk and turned to his inbox.

CHAPTER THIRTY-NINE

GUMSHOE WORK CAN BE BLAND

Friday, March 18, 2005

The transmitters were live when the TQ crew planted them, but no one was in the hooches but for a drop-by at lunch by Captain Rogers, and a one-hour visit in mid-afternoon by Samir. Except for Captain Rogers talking to herself softly about her work planned for the afternoon, the monitors only revealed the sound of knees and chairs creaking, and occasional flatus from both of them. The only difference was that Captain Rogers giggled after hers.

The desk monitors revealed the same semi-chaotic scene as the first day, with endless telephone calls in and out, conversations among the staff and with their many visitors, and the perpetual acoustic backdrop of gentle tapping on computer keys.

"I got a whole lot o' nothin' here," whispered Waleed. "He's in there, but he's not moving around much, and not talking at all. He's certainly not used the concealed cell, either."

"Thank you, Waleed," replied Corporal Stacey Dunbar. "Lance Corporal Seidenstucker, what say you?"

"Ma'am, my two subjects are in their room, and they're talkin' plenty, but I haven't heard anything remotely suspicious. Corporal Kimmel is monitoring the far bed. Kimmel, anything?"

"Nothin', Stacey. He periodically hits the bed frame with something metallic, probably his holstered pistol when he moves around. It kills my ears. He ought to take the damned thing off when he's in his hooch, the idiot. But nothin' suspicious."

"Good, Dave. Hang in there. We haven't nailed down our perp yet, so be attentive. I've got the Captain, and she must be reading or sleeping, 'cause it's really quiet in there. But occasionally I hear the bed springs creak, and her clearing her throat, so I think she's reading. That interference we had earlier is much less frequent than an hour ago – maybe the perimeter defense team's handhelds. We're lucky there isn't more EM noise out there." [ElectroMagnetic Noise such as radar, radio, TV, etc].

With that, the room became silent again, the three Marines and interpreter wearing their headphones, peering intently at the acoustic monitors in front of them, occasionally reaching forward to adjust the controls. All was in order.

CHAPTER FORTY

THE RAT REVEALED

Friday, March 18

"Asalaam alaykum, Brother Samir," said Prince Alquieri, with the benefit of his caller ID function. "Good to hear from you. How are things in the Occupied Land?"

"Good evening, my Prince. It is a joy to hear your voice. I am calling with routine news."

"Yes, Samir, I am here. Please advise me what is transpiring in the Crusaders' camp of Blue Diamond."

"Ah, my Prince, there is talk of an offensive in the upper Euphrates Valley, near the Syrian border. But that is far from here, and is unlikely to affect this base greatly."

"Yes, Samir, well, even ordinary news is important to our cause. At least we are reassured that we are not missing opportunity. How is your relationship with your general officer—is it Breer?"

"Ah, my prince, his name is Brier, and our relationship is strong. He trusts me implicitly, and I can usually overhear even those conversations which do not involve me or require my linguistic services. The situation is calm. But I am positioned to report to you the moment opportunity arises to strike the Occupier with a blazing fist."

"That is good, Samir, very good. Your presence there is vital to our future, and I need you to protect your secret at all costs. Sometimes the American devils can tempt you to abandon your principles. Do you find that their ways sometimes make you think of drawing away from us and our sacred mission?"

"Oh no, my Prince. Without reservation, I am committed to our goal, an omnipotent Caliphate over all the Arab peoples. For that Caliphate to then rise to have dominion over all the lands of the earth. For every man, woman, and child to accept The Prophet as the only true word of God. And all who reject the true word, even when offered to them in peace – for these, death is the only answer. To this Holy mission I submit myself with every breath."

"That is good, Samir. Our mission must not fail. And it shall not. Your work is crucial to us all. Remember to answer the call to prayer – the Crusaders are foolish enough to not look askance at your practicing The Faith. So be devout—your spiritual health and commitment must be nurtured all five times each day. This I command you."

"And so it shall be, my Prince. I shall be resolute in my support. And now I should be going. I will call you in four days, but sooner if there is opportunity here. Good night, my Prince."

"Good night, my faithful Samir. May Allah walk with you every step, and may Allah assist you in maintaining your integrity, as you deceive the Invader devils. I will speak to you in four days' time." The line went dead.

CHAPTER FORTY-ONE

HARD PROOF

Friday, March 18

"**C**orporal Dunbar, he's on the cell!" Waleed whispered excitedly. "I'm switching from the room to the cell. This could be it!"

"Fantastic. David, Joao, leave your stations on record, and let's put Waleed on speaker, just in case the recorder screws up, we'll all listen in. Waleed, switch to speaker!"

Waleed turned the knob from phones to speaker, and it crackled to life. Samir's resonant baritone was unmistakable, speaking in Arabic, some of which the intel staff could comprehend.

"...from here, and is unlikely to affect this base greatly."

"Ah, yes, Samir, well, even ordinary news is important to our cause."

The electronic recorder preserved every detail of the voices. Just as important, the tracker was identifying the phone number Samir had dialed.

Hmm, international code 293. Let's see – Corporal Dunbar pulled out her Palm and punched in "Intl" to his search function, and selected "Intl Phone Codes" from the list presented. *293, 293, let's see – no huge surprise – it's Saudi Arabia.*

The entire conversation was recorded. When the cell went dead, Waleed left it on monitor, but returned to Samir's room mike. Five minutes after the cellular conversation ended, Waleed heard Samir re-enter his room.

"He must have bad reception in his trailer, so he goes outside to use it," whispered Waleed. "Sounds like we've got a perp."

"Fabulous work, Waleed! But let's keep going with the monitoring. We'll present the findings in the morning. Fabulous work!" Corporal Dunbar sat down and initiated a play-back of the cell conversation.

Waleed would transcribe it word-for-word tonight, and make copies for all the members of the task group. The meeting in the morning would be triumphant!

CHAPTER FORTY-TWO

ANALYSIS

Saturday, March 19, 2005

The members of the meeting were all smiles as they filed into the room in the morning. Corporal Dunbar had alerted Matt of the finding, who had in turn notified Christine, Colonel Burdine, and Lieutenant Colonel Amanee. All of them were elated at this monumental breakthrough, and had to contain themselves to keep from telling all of their staff and acquaintances about their spectacular good luck. But they were all professional military officers, accustomed to dealing with state secrets, so the news remained confined to the group. They sat down, and all eyes looked to Colonel Burdine.

"Task group, Murphy screwed up, and gave us one hell of a break. Captain Curtis, is this room acceptably soundproofed for us to play back the recorder?"

"Yes Sir, I think it's okay. My staff are busy, and it's pretty noisy out there. I believe it's safe."

"Good." Looking to Corporal Dunbar, he went on, "Corporal Dunbar, turn the volume down to just enough for us to hear, and let's hear it, please."

"Yes Sir." Corporal Dunbar circulated copies of his transcript of the recording, then produced a hand-held mini-recorder and player, on to which he had loaded the recording. He switched it on.

"A salaam alaykum, Brother Samir..." The tape was played in completion. Corporal Dunbar switched off the player, and said, "No other findings on any of the recorders last night, Sir. And as you know, the call was placed to a cell in Saudi Arabia. Because of the hour last night, I didn't initiate an inquiry to determine the owner of the line. Would you like me to pursue that via the intel system, Sir?"

"Lieutenant Colonel Amanee, what do you recommend?"

"Yes Sir. Intel isn't really structured for that sort of inquiry. But it's right in our NCIS lane, Sir. I'll take care of it. We'll status it as Top Secret, of course, Sir."

"Good, Lieutenant Colonel, thank you." Then looking around the group, he continued, "So, what do we do next? Arresting him now will leave us with just this telephone contact to trace. There might be a whole lot more intel on the insurgency support system if we keep him around for a while. What do you think, Major Baxter?"

"Sir, I fully agree that we may have a real gold mine here, and we'd be crazy to shut it down. I think we should go on with business as usual, just being excruciatingly careful that we not give him any useful intel."

"Good, thank you, Major. Colonel Amanee, what do you think?"

"Sir, I'm with Major Baxter. He shouldn't be able to do us any harm if we're very careful to control what he hears. But it's going to take some very fine acting on the part of General Brier, to limit what Samir hears without letting on that we're on to him."

"Right, Colonel, I'll meet with General Brier today and run this by him. The final decision of how to proceed is up to him, of course. And we'll have to figure out how to communicate all this to General Jabbour. I don't think our SIPR is compromised, but I don't want General Jabbour's aides or other staff to know. Too many people, too much hazard of inadvertent compromise. I may even fly there and discuss it with him in person. This whole thing may turn out to be a huge positive, despite our losses thus far.

"Captain Curtis", Col Burdine went on, "What do you think? After all, you brought us the gear that enabled this ID. And, now that I think of it, it was you that initiated the entire inquiry, was it not?"

"Yes, Sir. Major Baxter and I kind of became suspicious that we had a mole, almost at the same time," she said, as she glanced at Matt. "So now, what to do. We certainly can exploit Samir's contacts, and it looks like there may be some very rich rewards. We might find a major money trail. It's long been suspected there was Saudi money flowing into the insurgency, and now it looks like we're gonna prove it."

Matt leaned forward over the table and interjected, "Sir, after we follow Samir for a while and ID his contacts, maybe we could use him to… set up some sort of sting. You know, feed him false intel, and set up his forces for a fall. Maybe we could even engineer something big."

"Well, Major, that's thinking outside the box. What kind of event do you think we might be able to stage?"

"Sir, as you know, insurgencies don't commit large forces to single battles, because they really don't have much depth in personnel and weaponry. But they might be tempted to commit in force, if we set the stage for a ringing victory for them, something that they would see as a huge propaganda windfall, maybe even enough to turn American public opinion sufficiently against the war as to force the President to withdraw."

"Intriguing, Major. So you're proposing that we might extract not only critical intel from this situation, but perhaps extend on to a tactical or even strategic battle victory."

"It's just a thought, Sir."

Rubbing his hands together, the Colonel mused, "But a tantalizing one, Major. All the troops are disgruntled that they're usually attacked by IED's with no visible enemy. And when they do have someone to shoot at, it's usually one-sies and two-sies. A major battle would be a gargantuan morale builder for our troops all over Iraq. Not to mention public opinion." Nodding at Matt, he went on, "Super idea, Major. I want you and Captain Curtis to develop it and report back to me. How 'bout we meet tomorrow?" Looking at Matt, he asked, "Can you two come up with a rough plan by tomorrow?"

Glancing at Christine, Matt responded, "Yes Sir, I'm confident we can flesh out some sort of preliminary plan by then. Ten o'clock here good by you, Sir?"

Eyeing the pair of them, Colonel Burdine responded, "Yes, that'll be fine."

Turning his attention to Lieutenant Colonel Amanee, Colonel Burdine asked, "Colonel, do you think it's worth surveilling any others, or shall we confine ourselves to Samir?"

"Sir, I think we should concentrate our efforts on Samir. It's unlikely there's a second agent here, and even if there is, we'll probably learn about him by monitoring Samir."

"Good, Colonel, I agree." Smiling at Corporal Dunbar, Corporal Kimmel, and Lance Corporal Mattos, he went on, "So, we're going to cut loose our ace intel team from TQ? Who have been so wonderfully helpful? Okay, team, on behalf of General Brier and all of us, and for the Marines' lives you have surely saved with your good work, thank you."

Pausing, he went on, "You're professional intel agents, so I'm sure I need not say it, but we could be on the verge of a massively important intel source. That can't be compromised in even the slightest way. So I can't overemphasize how carefully all three of you need to monitor your own speech. No mention of this whatsoever. Not even to your coworkers at TQ, even those with top secret clearances. There is no need for *anyone* to know about this activity, except perhaps General Brier. Do I make myself clear?"

"Absolutely, Sir," responded Corporal Dunbar firmly.

"Yes Sir," agreed Corporal Kimmel and Lance Corporal Mattos.

"All right, team," Colonel Burdine concluded, standing, "You're dismissed. I'll be in touch with your command regarding the good work you've done here." Shaking hands with each one in turn, he said, "Thank you," to each, staring into each Marine's eyes for a few seconds. Then, "TQ team, you're dismissed. Safe flight home, and Semper Fi."

"Semper Fi, Sir," they all chimed in, and filed out of the room.

Turning back to the remaining 3 officers, Burdine, still standing, asked, "Any saved rounds, Marines?"

"No Sir, responded Lieutenant Colonel Amanee as he stood up. "I'll get on the phone number, and get back to you as soon as I have something. But with your permission, I'll see what we can do to begin monitoring that phone once we find it, as well as the phones that it's used to call. Is that approved, Sir?"

"Terrific, Colonel. Please proceed."

Looking at Matt and Christine as they stood up, "Major, Captain, anything else?"

"Nothing, Sir," said Matt, "We'll meet you here at ten hundred tomorrow."

"Nothing, Sir," chimed in Christine. "I don't know how much, but we'll have *something* for you tomorrow."

"Good. See you both then. Oh, Major Baxter, would you be so kind as to write up NAM's for all three of the TQ Marines? Be evasive about the operation, of course." [NAM = Navy and Marine Corps Achievement Medal, a personal award worn as a ribbon on the working uniform, and a medal on the formal dress uniform].

"They've certainly earned it, Sir. And I love honoring our Marines. I'll have a rough for your review at our meeting tomorrow, Sir."

"Super. Thank you." He turned and strode out of the room, leaving the door open.

Matt looked at Christine. They were both elated. "Permission to approach the Captain?" he asked softly.

"Hmm, close-order drill, huh?" smiled Christine. "Permission granted."

Matt walked over and shut the door. Then he walked back to Christine, took both her hands in his, and said softly, "This is so good, Chris. I'm beside myself."

"It's unbelievable, isn't it, Matt," she rewarded him with a glowing smile.

"Chris, it isn't just the investigation. It's you. I – I'm incredibly attracted to you. You are so smart, so beautiful, so – so perfect..." Matt interrupted himself and curled his left arm around her waist, pulling her against him. With his right hand, he cradled the back of her neck, and guided her lips to his. She didn't resist. Their lips met, gently, sinuously moving against one another. Then his mouth opened, and his tongue gently probed at her lips. Her lips slowly parted, allowing his tongue to probe cautiously into her mouth, caressing her tongue and her teeth. The kiss lasted a full minute. Matt held her tightly against himself, compressing her firm breasts against his chest. Christine could feel a progressive prominence where his groin pressed against her lower abdomen.

Their lips separated, and Matt whispered, "I really care about you, Chris. Big league."

Smiling, she whispered, "Major, you've become my favorite flyboy."

Pleased with her acceptance of the kiss and the subsequent banter, Matt was encouraged to proceed. "Okay, Captain, we've got to celebrate. Not that much we can do here – the chow hall doesn't serve champagne, and last time I checked, there wasn't an O'Club – but – how 'bout a movie in my hooch tonight?" [O'Club = Officers' Club, a restaurant/bar on every non-combat-zone base].

"Won't your roomie find that a little tight?"

"He's out of town this whole week. We've got the place to ourselves."

"The JAG respectfully accepts the gracious invitation of the Air Department to a celebratory special event. What shall the JAG bring?"

"How 'bout coming by at 1930? We'll have chow on our own. Just bring yourself." Smiling again, Matt gently intoned, "That's all I want. I just bought some new DVD's. You can pick which one we watch. Deal?"

"Deal, Flyboy. See ya at 1930." She punched him gently in the belly.

Stealing another quick kiss on the lips, Matt responded, "'Til then, sweetie." With that, he opened the door and strode out.

Chapter Forty-Three

Rendezvous – Splendor In The Lass

Saturday, March 19, 2005

It had been hot during the day, but air cools fast in the desert, so Chris was not sweating much as she strolled to Matt's hooch. She had worked at her desk for most of the afternoon, had chow with Major Azaz, and then retreated to her quarters for PT followed by a shower. It was all she could do to keep from telling Major Azaz about Samir, but she had the right stuff to avoid the issue, and he never asked. As an attorney, he would have understood her need to enforce the rules of confiding only in those with need to know, but it was always uncomfortable when that policy was invoked, regardless.

Chris recognized how strongly she was attracted to Matt. Beyond his handsome face and taut muscular body, he was smart, disciplined, and had a certain *joie de vivre* about him that made her feel good in his presence. But she felt the tugs of her old distrust of men, reaching right back to her preadolescent experiences with Uncle Hilary. Although he had never overtly assaulted her, she had gradually become uncomfortable around him. Seemingly innocent behaviors, like wanting her to sit on his lap, or occasional touching of her chest or butt, could have been inadvertent, but happened repetitively enough that she was sure the touching was calculated. Her relationships with men became tainted with suspicion. Even the eminently wholesome and profoundly loving relationships she enjoyed with her brothers and father, couldn't totally compensate for the dark thoughts she had evolved about Uncle Hilary.

Christine had never confided her suspicions about her uncle to anyone. She loved her immediate family with her every pore, and was fearful that an ugly accusation of an inappropriate uncle-niece contact could damage the family in unpredictable ways. And her Dad was proud of his family; Chris didn't want to take that from him. Of course, there was always the possibility that she had imagined it all—that Uncle Hilary really *was* innocent, and it was her sinister mind that had created the entire affair.

As with many victims of sexual abuse, part of the power of the crime is the guilt felt by the victim, for knowing that they were partly aroused by the abuse. Although Christine had never reflected on this fact, defensively burying such memories deep in her subconscious, this guilt arose without explanation when she felt arousal by a potential lover. And she was feeling it now – a vague sense of trepidation – precisely because she was *extremely* attracted to Matt. For a moment, she debated turning around and going back to her can, reneging on her date. But she pressed on, the vague uneasiness being successfully challenged by the euphoria of detecting Samir, and the prospect of spending the evening with an exceedingly attractive man with whom she had become unusually enamored.

Continuing on, Christine turned off River Road on to the last left, which led to the firing range, the auxiliary LZ, and the hooches of the senior staff of the COC. The paved road gave way to gravel, and she ambled down the hill to the forty trailers nestled below. It was already dark, but there was just enough moonlight to let her walk without use of the tiny flashlight she always wore clipped to her blouse.

Down the narrow lane between the cans, paved with stepping stones, between the chin-high sand bags, she came to the one he had drawn on a map for her. "Major Kierce/Major Baxter" was secured to the door under a clear plastic cover. Stepping up the two metal stairs, she knocked gently, then drew back as the door swung outward after a few seconds. Like her, Matt was attired in his desert digital cammie uniform. And like her, he was freshly showered, and wearing all fresh clothes.

"Welcome to the Air Department's auxiliary landing field, Captain," smiled Matt, as he gestured her inward.

"Thank you, Air," she smiled. "Request permission to enter your airspace."

"Permission granted," Matt grinned as he motioned her into his room. "Please keep airspeed up—you have following traffic."

Entering the tiny vestibule with the bath dead ahead and Major Kierce's room on the right, Chris passed through the door on the left opening into Matt's warmly lit but cramped room. His desk and chair were facing her. His bed was in the right forward corner, his closet in the right rear corner, and the bookcase supporting his TV and DVD player was on her left. To the left of the bookcase was a thigh-high refrigerator. Matt positioned the chair for her in the crook where the desk met the bed, retrieved two O'Doule's near-beers from the fridge, and sat on the bed beside her. Popping the cans open and handing Chris hers, Matt raised his in the air, whispered ceremoniously, "To the intrepid investigators of Blue Diamond, who have cracked The Case Of The Insolent Insurgent," and took a swig.

"Hear, hear," responded Chris, and she tipped her can back for a mouthful of the refreshing and surprisingly beer-like taste of the non-alcoholic beer.

"Hey JAG, doesn't the law state that we can't drink to a toast about *us*?" Matt queried fake-seriously.

"The letter of the law, aye. The spirit of the law, who cares?" Christine laughed.

"Okay, Captain, your turn. What are we toasting?"

Christine smiled and lifted her can, "To the fly, who had the courage to drop by the spider's web, and to the spider, for inviting her." Both laughed as they enjoyed another swig.

"Oh man, Chris, this is some amazing situation, huh? We've got ourselves an international spy ring here. And we're the ones who found it. Can't beat that, huh?"

Looking him squarely in the eye, Chris responded, "Matt, I'm incredibly psyched to exploit this situation to the fullest. It's pay-back time for General Sienkiewic and all those Marines who died with him. And for the other helos that took fire, and our Marines shot up here in Ramadi, thanks to that bastard Samir."

"Hear, hear," chimed in Matt, "to revenge!" They held their cans high before grabbing another swig.

"Hey, maybe we should think about your plan, Matt, the sting. What do you have in mind? After all, I'm the JAG. You're the warrior. Come up with something!"

"Orders, orders, that's all I get from you. I outrank you! And we're not even married!"

"Easy does it, big fella, easy there. I haven't even proposed yet," laughed Chris, leaning over to kiss him on the cheek.

"Ya know, Captain, I don't think I wanna be serious tonight. We've been a good little boy and girl for a long time with this project. Maybe tonight we should just relax and be naughty."

Chris put her hand to the side of her face and said, "But I *am* a good little girl. What would Mother think?"

"The good news of it all, good little girl, is that Mother ain't here. And I have no intention of telling her. Do you?"

Chris pressed her index finger perpendicular to her pursed lips.

"Fantastic, no witnesses. Okay, JAG, what do you wanna watch? Maybe we have a movie here about sharks. To make you feel at home."

"How 'bout something about airline pilots who are pinching the stews, when they're supposed to be flying?"

"Uh-oh, I have no knowledge of such events." Matt held up a plastic jacket: "Ah, how 'bout a fine action film? Here's Jackie Chan and Chris Tucker in "Rush Hour Two.""

"Sounds good, Captain," Chris said playfully. "Pass it here to the nice stew, and she'll get it fired up, and quiet down the passengers."

"If there's one thing I like, it's quiet passengers. *Paying* passengers, but quiet," Matt said solemnly.

Chris inserted the DVD, adjusted the volume, and sat down. Matt clicked off the lamp in the corner, such that the room was illuminated only by the flashes of the TV screen. He verified that her beer was still alive, and then snaked his arm around her waist as the movie started.

Five minutes into the movie, Matt reached down to untie his boots, pulled them off, and removed the blousing strap from his trouser legs. "JAG is cordially invited to unfetter the feet, as desired," he said.

"A winning idea," said Chris, and she reached down and likewise removed her boots. Then she sat back on the bed and sighed.

"Hey JAG, 'fore we get into this movie, we gotta plan on comin' up with somethin' for Colonel Burdine in the morning. How 'bout we relax tonight, and meet at 0800 to sketch something out. Deal?"

"JAG is on board, Air."

Matt reached for her head and gently guided it to his, as he again planted his lips firmly on hers. Chris felt some of the tugs of discomfort from Uncle Hilary, but fought to ignore them, and allowed Matt's tongue again to penetrate her lips and explore her mouth. She felt her heart rate rise, as she enjoyed his touch and smell. She detected a hint of Old Spice on his neck, as she removed her lips from his, and gentle kissed his ears, and then his neck.

Matt reached to the back of Chris head, where her light brown hair was precisely gathered in a tight bun, per Marine Corps standards. Gingerly tugging at it, he released her shining mane, which fell down about her head, rendering her even more beautiful in the dim light. Then he stood up, and pulled her up to stand against him. He returned to kissing her lips, but now began firmly massaging her back. Her silky hair brushed across his lips, and smelled of vanilla.

Matt felt his breath increasing, with forceful beating of his heart. And he was pleased to feel Chris's chest rising and falling at a faster rate than two minutes earlier. Matt's hand went between them, and began to slowly unbutton her blouse. Chris continued to kiss him, and didn't impede his advance.

With her blouse hanging open, exposing her lacy white brassiere, Matt gently caressed her breasts still encased in the bra. He inserted a finger into the right cup, and felt her shudder as he touched the nipple, softly massaging it as he kissed her even more passionately.

Reaching around her back, Matt unhooked her bra, and then smoothly guided both her blouse and bra off her shoulders and on to the floor. Massaging each firm breast, he then lowered his head and tasted the sweat between them. Then his lips moved on…

Chris's hands massaged his head and back as he petted her. Matt then guided her smoothly to the bed, and laid her down softly. Kissing and licking, he slowly moved downward toward her bellybutton, which he explored with his tongue. Her taut abdomen was rising and falling with her breathing. He began to massage her thighs and lower legs, moving slowly up and down, slowly prying apart her thighs. He felt no resistance as they opened, and his hand gently massaged her. Her breath was becoming fast and hissing, and she massaged his hair as he opened her belt buckle and unbuttoned her uniform slacks. Standing up, he went to her feet and pulled on her pant legs. She lifted her pelvis, allowing slacks to slide off her legs. Her white bikini panties accentuated the graceful curves of her waist and pelvis. He was being driven wild by the swarthy aroma of her womanhood.

Matt hastily removed his uniform, and climbed onto the bed between her knees, and the two lovers intertwined with the rigor of two very healthy and athletic young warriors.

After ten minutes of unspeakably pleasurable lovemaking, Matt shuddered and plunged deeply, hoping that she was protected, and convinced that she would not have allowed him to enter her if she were not. Sex on deployment is one thing, but pregnancy is another entirely.

Matt rolled off her torso, settling on his back beside her on her left breathing deeply. She lay her head on his right muscular arm as his right hand reached around and gently caressed her breast. Lying silently, glowing in the ultimate pleasure they had both experienced, their breathing slowly returned to normal, and their skin gradually dried.

"Christine, that was unbelievable. I really care about you."

Whispering, she replied, "And I really care about you, Matt." And she kissed him full on the lips, her tongue provocatively probing his mouth as she reached up and held his head with both hands.

"I certainly didn't plan this, sweetie, but I've been feeling more and more attracted to you over the past week. I can't tell you how good I feel lying here holding you," Matt confided.

"It feels like it was meant to be, Matthew. But I'm not done with you tonight." She began to stroke his inner thigh with her right hand, and he closed his eyes to concentrate on the new waves of pleasure it was producing, as Chris took charge and began to massage his entire body with her lips, giving him ecstatic pleasure. After they climaxed, Christine laid her head on his chest, and they drifted off to the perfect sleep of lovers, as their sweat and heavy breathing once again subsided together.

CHAPTER FORTY-FOUR

RETREAT

Saturday, March 19, 2005

Christine awoke after an hour, having rolled beside Matt during their sleep. She watched his chest rise and fall in the distinctive breathing of deep sleep. She lightly kissed the side of his muscled chest, and couldn't resist running her hand along the contours of his pectoral muscles, lightly kissing them over and over. Then slowly, to avoid awakening him, she slipped out of the bed and gathered her clothes. Sliding on her bikini panties, she looked down at him and wanted him all over again. But she didn't want to scare him off, so she angled her arms into her bra and snapped it on. Her cammie trousers rustled gently as she pulled them up, secured the belt buckle, and sat on the chair to pull on her boots, tie them, and blouse the pant legs. Standing up to slide into her cammie blouse, button it up, and don her cover, she slipped out the door of his trailer, silently latching it behind her, and walked in the cool evening air back to her quarters. Her thoughts were all about Matt and the electrifying lovemaking they had just shared. She felt his seed silently draining out of her as she walked. She sniffed her hands, and could detect his cologne on them. In the darkness, she gently kissed her fingertips, wanting to embrace him again.

Arriving at her trailer, she slipped quietly inside the unlocked door, trying to avoid awakening her roomie, whose deep breathing revealed her sound sleep. Quickly and silently undressing to just her panties, she slipped into her rack, and promptly lapsed into a glowing sleep, with euphoric thoughts of her lover and her love.

CHAPTER FORTY-FIVE

MORE THAN A
WORLD AWAY

Monday, March 21 , 2005

Ring-a-ling-a-ling-a-ling. All the kids leaped to their feet and poured out the doors. Twenty seconds earlier the school had stood motionless and lifeless. Now jubilant young life was flowing exuberantly out of its doors, spilling onto the sidewalks in all directions.

The crocuses were just beginning to bloom, even though it was technically still winter in Nashville, Tennessee. It had been a mild one, and the temperature on this Monday, March 21, 2005, was 60 degrees. A bright and sunny nearly-spring day.

The two young men in the nondescript blue Ford sedan sat quietly across the street, one reading the newspaper, the other a magazine. Both wearing sports coats and neckties, they looked like ordinary businessmen. Of course, most businessmen don't have a bulge under the breast pocket of their sports coats, faintly suggesting their shoulder-holstered, FBI-issue, 9 mm Glock automatic pistols   Subtly, they glanced past their reading material, searching for the Booker children. They had watched them walk to school that morning, so they knew what clothes to look for in the teeming diminutive humanity now streaming home.

"There they are, just passing that oak tree, lined up with the third window from the left of the school," said Inspector Nick Splane. "The boy's thumping the baseball glove."

"Got 'em," responded Agent Hiram Peterson, still holding his newspaper up. At ages twenty-six and twenty-five, the two FBI agents were not so interested in seeing the children, but rather in who else was interested in watching these children. Their trained eyes had scanned

165

the street on both sides, looking for anything out of the ordinary. The task was rendered considerably more difficult by the fact that a number of stationary cars nearby contained parents of children, and those children were now opening car doors and hopping in, swapping kisses with their drivers. So the goal was to see which occupied cars did *not* draw any kids.

Nothing suspicious yet. Maybe we ought to recruit a kid to jump in our car, so we blend in with the parents, thought Inspector Splane.

A separate team was following Don Booker through his day. Two separate surveillance teams were an expensive undertaking for the FBI Nashville branch office, but if they paid off, the yield might be more than just protecting one family. They might identify a terror cell, and perhaps track it to its command structure. Now *that* would be quite a reward.

It was only the first day of observing, and the agents were busy trying to identify patterns in behavior of their subjects, allowing them to predict the Bookers' next move, rendering the surveillance infinitely easier. The station chief had been willing to invest two weeks of continuous daytime surveillance. Nighttime was just too expensive to add, and the yield would be extremely low. It was unlikely that anyone would actually harm the family just yet – they were the bargaining chip the insurgency was using to extort more tactical information from Renee.

Jackie and Sammy were walking home together, each wearing a Peanuts backpack. Jackie, of course, had Lucy Brown, and Sammy sported Linus. The portrait of innocence, Agent Peterson wondered what kind of animal would threaten children. *The kind that lives right here in this community – that kind,* he realized.

The kids arrived at their house, and entered. The sitter was in there, the agents knew, because they had seen her arrive a half hour earlier. The blue Ford parked four houses before the Booker house, having followed the children all the way. No suspicious persons identified to this point. They'd keep an eye on things for another three hours, and bug out at 1800 for their own dinner and evening. But they'd be back "at the office," sitting right on this street in this car, tomorrow morning at 0700. The front door of the Booker home would burst open promptly at 0730 with the kids hustling out, Dad shouting well wishes from the door. Then Don Booker would be out by 0740. The other team would pick him up as he passed the first intersection on the way to his own office.

CHAPTER FORTY-SIX

SETTING PRIORITIES

Monday, March 21, 2005

"Good morning, Captain. How's the negligent discharge case coming along," greeted Corporal Carbone.

"Morning, Corporal, Chris responded cheerfully, as she walked across the office toward her door. "We're making progress. How's the court-martial coming?"

"It's a pain, Ma'am, but it's coming together. The trial is set for next Monday. Not soon enough for me."

"I'm with you all in spirit," she responded cheerfully. She entered her office and was organizing her desk when Matt arrived, with his warmest possible smile.

"Good morning, JAG. Sleep well?"

Glancing to verify that he had pulled the door closed behind him, she responded with a similar broad smile, "Like I'd been ravaged."

Matt approached her, took both her hands in his, and said, now serious, "Chris, last night was one-of-a kind, but it wasn't a flash in the pan. I really care about you. Like *major league*. Alarmingly."

Chris squeezed his hands and responded, also in earnest, "Matt, this Judge finds you worthy of her affection. Equally alarmingly."

Matt stared at her silently for a full ten seconds, hands squeezing tight, 'til he broke the spell with a smile. "Much more to come. But for now, how 'bout these two alarmists get to work?"

"So long as there's more to follow, I'm on board, Major."

"Okay, Captain," and he gestured her toward her chair behind the desk, as he pulled the other chair over beside hers. "Let's get cookin'. We need a set-up that'll make the insurgents commit their forces. We need to raise the ante dramatically, where their potential gains aren't tactical but strategic, affecting the entire conflict – maybe even being the blow that so energizes the war opposition back home, that they could force the President to withdraw the troops immediately. It's got to be that big a prize for them. So our task is to figure out what would constitute such a prize. Gotta be a VIP kill—someone big—very senior military or SECDEF [Secretary of Defense], civilian, like an entertainment celebrity, or political, like Secretary Rice, or VP Cheney, or even the President himself."

"Wow, Matt, you think big. But I understand what you're saying; the prize must be so dazzling that they'll be willing to commit the largest force they can muster. Making them violate their own doctrine. The scenario we create will need to smack of authenticity through and through. What do you think—shall we go with the blue ribbon, POTUS himself?" [President Of The United States].

"It will require some very intricate dance steps, Chris, but I think we should go with the President. An opportunity like this doesn't come along very often—we need to milk this to the absolute max. And POTUS is clearly the most desired target on earth for the insurgents."

"Oh man, Matt we're thinking *really* big here." Suddenly looking down at the date on her watch, she exclaimed. "Oh my heavens, my Mother's surgery is in ten days, and I'm supposed to be leaving either tonight or tomorrow morning! Oh no, the timing couldn't be worse. Oh, what am I gonna do? My Mom asked me to come home, and I'm really close to her. But this situation is, is, so critical, maybe with historic implications. And I'm right square in the middle of it." Turning to Matt, Christine extended her fingers over her chin and mouth, "Matt, what do you think I oughta do?" She repetitively cupped her nose with a praying hands configuration.

"Oh, that's right Chris, I forgot too—I'm supposed to go on R & R on the twenty-eighth. Can't happen. I need to be here. And, I hate to say it, Chris, but I need you here as well. I didn't foresee this getting so large, but it is, and you're a key player. Is there any way you can beg off? As I understand it, this is relatively minor surgery, even though the findings may have weighty implications. It's extremely unlikely she would be in danger of dying with this surgery, isn't it?"

"Yes Matt, it's only an excision biopsy. Very low risk. Oh my, Mama." She stared out the window, "I don't want to desert you, but I believe you'd want me to stay, if you knew the stakes here." Then she looked at Matt and said, "All right, Matt, I'll work it out with Mama, I'm staying here." Looking up at the ceiling, she said, "Forgive me, Mama."

"Thank you, Chris. I believe it's the right decision. And when I get to meet her, I'll take the hit as my idea. It was, you know."

Stepping forward and embracing him with both arms, looking up into his face, she replied "You're loyal and protective, Matt, but it's my decision, and I'll take my licks for it." She kissed him briefly on the lips, then stepped back, sat down, and said, "Now let's flesh it out. I think we're really on to something."

Matt sat down beside her again. "Okay, Captain, I think we should be a little obscure in naming POTUS as the visiting VIP, but if we drop enough hints, it will be clear who we're alluding to. That should make the case more convincing."

"I like it, Matt. But how long do you think we need to wait, collecting intel on his calls, until we spring the trap? We certainly want to milk this case for all it's worth."

"I would think one week would be enough. Because we can trace the Saudi party, and let the net expand from there. It's likely that he has only that one insurgent contact."

"Okay, today's the twenty-first. Shall we spring the trap on the twenty-eighth? Think there's time to do all the prep?"

"I do, Captain. And the fact is, you never know when something might botch up the opportunity—some other agency get a whiff of him, or the Saudi government get on to his contacts there, who knows – any number of snafu's could come up and kill this opportunity. So yes, I think a week from today is right on the money. Let's do it!"

"What kind of scenario shall we have? What will cause them to mass their forces?" Asked Chris.

"An airplane doesn't require a large force. How 'bout we do this – let's create a script that says Blue Diamond's base security is severely compromised—we'll say it's been gutted by sending off most of its guys —and the best guys—off to kinetic ops on the Syrian border. We can embellish it with all kinds of other stuff – we'll say morale is low, maybe because of a bad CO. That the base security force has an unusually large number of weak players – that the best weapons were taken out west, and the ones left here jam all the time. Let's try and get them to go for a take-over of the base. *That* would be a hell of a prize. Throw in POTUS, and you've got something worth risking all their forces at once."

"Do you think they'll buy POTUS? Why would he be coming to Blue Diamond?" asked Chris.

"Blue Diamond is in Ramadi, the Provincial capital of Al Anbar Province. Al Anbar's population is near-totally Sunni, an the heart of the insurgency. If we win Anbar, we win Iraq. So POTUS has a cogent interest in instituting representative government here. If he succeeds, the insurgency is doomed. Yes, I think most observers—and especially the insurgents—could find it credible that the President was planning a clandestine visit here, to meet with Governor Mehdi."

"Okay, so we have a prize, and a time. Where shall we set up the President for their attack?"

"Same as General Brier's convoy attack. They learned from their attack that day what worked and what didn't. Mostly, they learned that they need a larger force. Just what we want them to do."

"How can we know where they'll plan their attack?" asked Chris.

"We won't necessarily know. We might, if they discuss it on their phone call, but they probably won't. But it's only two miles from Blue Diamond to Ramadi Government Center. We have a number of bases along those two miles, so we should be able to cover all the conceivable ambush sites."

"Sounds like a plan. What time is it, Major?"

"Zero nine forty-five, Captain. Colonel Burdine arrives in fifteen. What else do we need to discuss before the conference?"

"Us, but that can wait," Chris responded sincerely.

"Okay, Babe, later on today for that one. We've both got to cancel our travel plans with those we were gonna meet. How 'bout we meet for lunch?"

"Oh, you had someone you were gonna meet on R & R, Major?" Chris asked, smiling.

"*Were*, Captain, *were*," he responded with a smile.

"Okay, Flyboy, so long as she stays past tense."

Matt winked at her with a smile, and they walked to the meeting room side-by-side, but not touching. The military has no problem with romance of roughly equal ranks and from different commands, but amorous activity in view of others is considered "conduct unbecoming an officer," and is punished substantially.

CHAPTER FORTY-SEVEN

RESURRECTION OF THE DEVIL

Monday, March 21, 2005

"Good morning, General Jabbour's office. Lieutenant Wiggin speaking."

"Hello, this is Mrs. Booker. It's imperative that I speak with the General immediately."

"Yes, Mrs. Booker, the General is on another line. Stand by one moment, please."

Renee tapped her fingers nervously on her desk, blinking back the tears. She had begun to hope that the worst was over, that with Hamid's death, she and her family would be off the insurgents' radar screen, and she would need deal only with the repercussions of her errant conduct with American authorities. And, of course, with her beloved Don. But those hopes had been shattered several minutes earlier, when she logged on to her computer for her routine scanning of overnight e-mail messages and found one from an unknown but clearly Middle Eastern source: ibrahim. fawaz594@yahoo.com. Her skin prickled and broke into a light sweat, a feeling of constriction growing in her chest as she began to tremble. She recognized the numbness and tingling around her mouth and in her fingers as symptoms of hyperventilation, and tried consciously to make her breathing slower and shallower.

She had glanced around, to see if any of her coworkers noted her distress. Fortunately, they were all engrossed with their computer screens, and oblivious to her overwhelming waves of anxiety. She used her tried-and-true relaxation technique, repeating her mantra, the twenty-third Psalm:

The Lord is my shepherd, I shall not want,
He maketh me to lie down in green pastures.
He leadeth me beside the still waters.
He restoreth my soul.
He leadeth me in the paths of righteousness for His
    Name's sake.
Yea, though I walk through the valley of the shadow
    of death,
I will fear no evil, for Thou art with me.
Thy rod and thy staff they comfort.
Thou preparest a table before me,
    in the presence of mine enemies.
Thou annointest my head with oil,
    my cup runneth over.
Surely, goodness and mercy shall follow me,
    All the days of my life.
And I shall dwell in the House of the Lord forever.

By the third time through, Renee felt her terror ebbing, the tingling subsiding, and rational thought returning. The message was simple but dreadfully telling; she wasn't off the hook with the devil with whom she had chosen to dance.

I am friend with Hamid. What happen him? He betrayed? I need you answer now. Ibrahim.

"Hello Mrs. Booker, this is General Jabbour. What can I do for you?"

"General, thank Heaven you're there. I'm frightened, terribly frightened. I received an e-mail..."

General Jabbour interrupted her, "Let's not talk by phone. Can you come to my office? I can see you right now. Bring your computer, or download whatever we're discussing on to a thumb drive. Can you do that?"

"Yes, General, thank you... thank you. I'm leaving right now."

"Good, Renee, I'll be here." And the line went dead.

Chapter Forty-Eight

Plan Approved

Monday, March 21, 2005

"Attention on deck," shouted Corporal Carbone, and Lance Corporals Hernandez and Pride abruptly leapt to their feet and assumed the position of attention.

"Good morning, Marines. Carry on," boomed General Brier as he strode through the outer office toward Christine's inner office, accompanied by Colonel Burdine. Matt and Chris were still working at her desk, when they heard the call to attention outside, and the somewhat unfamiliar voice responding. Both recognized General Brier's resonant tenor voice at the same time, and immediately stood up. Matt opened the door, just as General Brier arrived outside. Snapping to attention, Matt greeted him, "Good morning, General Brier."

The General admired the flawless uniforms, physiques, grooming, and posture of the two officers inside the room, then responded, "Good morning, Marines. At ease. I hope you don't mind if I attend today's meeting."

Matt immediately responded, "No Sir. We're honored you're here. We're making considerable progress."

"I know we're a little early, but I had a break in my schedule, and thought we might start a little early. Can you do that?"

"Yes Sir, we can." Looking back at Chris, Matt went on, "Captain, shall we move over to the conference room?"

"Yes Sir, of course," Chris demurred, and began moving toward the door. "Good morning, Colonel Burdine," she beamed as she stepped out into the outer office. "This way please, General." And she led the way out of the office, and next door to the conference room. She glanced at her watch as they walked, and saw that the General was only ten minutes early. She knew that Lieutenant Colonel Amanee always reported early for meetings, such that he'd probably already be at the conference room.

Arriving at the room, Chris and Matt stepped back and allowed General Brier and Colonel Burdine to enter first. Sure enough, Lieutenant Colonel Amanee was already seated inside, and he snapped to attention when he saw General Brier. "As you were, Colonel Amanee," said the General. "Good to see you."

"Thank you, Sir. Your presence is an unexpected but welcome pleasure, Sir," said the always polite Colonel Amanee. As an elite athlete, he always demonstrated superb military bearing, with a trim physique, erect posture, perfect grooming, and graceful movement. Seeing him move reminded Matt of his resentment over his loss to Colonel Amanee at the Triathlon, of his wrestling with the notion of not being the best of his group. And then Sam Bowey's face appeared in his memory, adding to his negative reaction to Colonel Amanee. Matt sought to suppress his anger, knowing that the mission took precedence over all else, and that Colonel Amanee, despite his irritating qualities, was unexcelled at what he did.

All seated, Colonel Burdine spoke first. "The intel folks should be here shortly. I've been keeping the General informed of our status. And I think it's time he was hands-on with this planning. Looking at Matt, he went on, Major Baxter, what do you have for us?"

"Sir," Matt began, "to persuade the insurgents to violate their own doctrine, to encourage them to field all the forces they can muster in a single attack, we propose a scenario that might convince our adversaries' leaders that the prize is worth the gamble. That their victory here might be so earthshaking that this single battle could end the war, raise so much political heat back home that the President would be forced to capitulate. So we needed a suitable prize. And we propose a double prize: a successful attack on Blue Diamond which would destroy the base, and the assassination of a premiere target. For this, we propose that the target be no less than the President himself."

Matt and Chris saw what they expected from the others with this announcement—eyes widening, shifting in their chairs, clearing of their throats.

"We propose, General, that we never overtly confirm that the President is coming to Ramadi, but that we imply it sufficiently often that the message is received and believed. And we believe the scenario makes sense – that if the President can win Al Anbar Province, he can win Iraq, and he needs to go to Ramadi to speak to the Anbar leadership, and demonstrate his support of the Anbar government to the world."

The session was interrupted at that point with the arrival of the intel crew, Corporal Dunbar and Lance Corporals Kimmel and Mattos. All three snapped to attention when they saw General Brier, but he gave them a quick "At Ease" and waved them in. Matt gave them a three-sentence overview of what he'd already covered.

Looking at Corporal Dunbar, General Brier asked, "Corporal, any new findings from the monitoring?"

"No Sir, General. Routine dialogue only. And nothing else suspicious from Samir."

The General shifted his attention. "Lieutenant Colonel Amanee, anything on the Saudi phone number?"

"Nothing back from higher intel headquarters either, Sir, regarding the Saudi phone contact. But I'll expect something during the next 24 hours."

"Good, Colonel, please come to my office to report the Saudi findings when you receive them. We'll meet somewhere out of Samir's range, to discuss."

"Yes, Sir, I certainly will."

"Major Baxter, I like your ideas," General Brier went on. "What did you have in mind to convince the enemy he could successfully attack Blue Diamond?"

"General, we've come up with sundry bits of misinformation that make Blue Diamond look extremely vulnerable. First, we'll let on that most of the troops here, and the best members of the Base Security force, have been deployed to Operation Iron Fist up at the Syrian border. We'll also say that the best weapons went with them, leaving us with weaker Marines and weapons prone to jamming. Next, we'll report that we received a bad load of ammo, with many duds, which obviously disable the machine guns for up to a half minute at a time. We'll put out gouge that what's left of the Base Defense unit is demoralized from bad leadership, resulting in a pervasive drug problem. And finally, Sir, we'll plant a rumor that our base defense units' radios can be jammed with a certain frequency such that no coordinated defense can be mounted in response to an attack. We've also toyed with the idea of suggesting that a single well-placed grenade or cell phone-triggered explosive charge, by someone inside the wire – and we're talking Samir here – could cause a diversionary explosion in an ammo dump that would further distract us from a coordinated defense."

Nodding, Gen Brier approved, "Well, Major, you've certainly thought this one through. I like your ideas. If I were our adversary, I think I'd take that bait. How do you want to set up the President for an attack?"

"Sir, we propose that the President be scheduled to meet with Governor Mehdi at Government Center. We think the insurgents would probably use the same location to attack as they did against your convoy, Sir. Only in much greater force. But we'd cover the other three likely attack locations as well. That is, assuming Samir's phone calls didn't tell us what they were planning."

"Okay, Major, this sounds very good." Then looking at Lieutenant Colonel Amanee, he went on, "Lieutenant Colonel, I'm very interested in pursuing this sting operation, but I don't want to shortchange intel collection from Samir prematurely. How long do you think we should hold off pulling the trigger on this one?"

"Sir, I believe that Samir probably has only a single telephone contact with the insurgency. So I doubt that we'll get much else out of him, other than that one critical connection, which we are already exploiting. So I think a week would be fine."

"All right, Marines, a week works for me. Anyone have a reason why we can't schedule the sting for Monday, March twenty-eighth?" Everyone looked around the table, but no one spoke up. "All right then. One week from today a vigorous attempt will be made to assassinate the President, and to overrun Camp Blue Diamond. Major Baxter, Captain Curtis, you two have had the lead on this project all along. I want you to coordinate the plan. The immediate need is to get the ball rolling with Samir. I've always wondered if Samir was listening to my conversations even when he was outside at his desk. So, Major Baxter, I want you to come to my office this afternoon at three and tell me about this planned visit from the Commander In Chief. We'll just have to hope that Samir is at his desk. If he's not, we'll have you keep coming back until he is. Then I'll get Governor Mehdi on the phone, and imply that something momentous is going to happen at Government Center on the twenty-eighth. Samir will need to interpret that call, so it will augment whatever he hears from you, Major.

"Captain Curtis, I want you to work out full details of the weakness of Blue Diamond, and coach Captain Kalopolis. Then schedule him to come to me with his concerns, and, just as with Major Baxter, we'll keep him coming back 'til Samir gets to overhear what he has to say. I'll drop a few clues to Samir as well, regarding both aspects of the bait.

"I'm going to bring in Colonel Lou Servi, a senior infantry officer, to plan the springing of the trap. So don't be surprised if he comes to you to coordinate.

"Okay, any saved rounds?" There was silence, as all the members looked at one another. "Very well, Major Baxter, I think you can shut down the monitoring operation. Is it worth trying to retrieve the transceivers right now?"

"No sir, I think it can only raise suspicion that something's going on, Sir. I advise that we leave the monitors in place till after the sting operation," said Major Baxter.

"Okay, done. Well folks, this is a momentous time. Be certain to practice the utmost operational security, and let's set up the sting-heard-round-the-world. Try to maintain your normal work rituals, so nothing looks out of the ordinary."

CHAPTER FORTY-NINE

RESPONDING TO SATAN

Monday, March 21, 2005

General Jabbour inserted Renee's thumb drive in his laptop and called up the email. "Hmm, Ibrahim Fawaz. I don't recognize the name. And we can't track him down via Yahoo—they can only say where he registered, but he could use any computer in the world to write to you and service his account."

Looking at Renee, he went on, "The animals had gotten to Hamid's remains a bit, but we recovered what we could, and buried him with appropriate Muslim ritual. The next day we mentioned in a press conference that routine COIN measures [counter-insurgency] identified him as a person of interest, but that when we sought to arrest him, he resisted and was killed in the interchange. So I think we deflected suspicion from you, Mrs. Booker."

"Thank you, General. But I was hoping they'd let me alone. That Hamid would just turn into a bad dream, and that I'd only need to make my peace with you and my family." Putting her hands to her face, she began to sob, "But they're not going to let me alone. My God, my God, what have I done?" She began to rock forward and backward.

"Mrs. Booker, there's no way they were going to leave you alone. Nor your family. These are violent, unprincipled people. Just like all the other power-hungry barbaric tyrants of history—Atila, the Crusaders and the Inquisitionists, Stalin, Hitler. Murder and mayhem is a way of life for them. They chant religion, even while violating its most sacred precepts. No, you're stuck with them until we eliminate them."

Looking up, with tears still streaming down her cheeks, Renee asked pathetically, "But how, General, how can we get rid of them?"

"We have pretty extensive resources here, Mrs. Booker. You didn't take advantage of them before when Hamid was extorting you, but now I'm going to press them into action. You're going to meet this Ibrahim character, and we'll be monitoring it all. Then we'll follow him and initiate a complex surveillance, trying to find the social rot wherever it is. And then we'll move in and clean house. Only then will you be free of them. But you're going to need to work with us. This will take courage, Mrs. Booker. But we've already seen what you're capable of doing when your family is threatened, and your family is still at risk. Are you up to it?"

Drying her eyes and cheeks with tissue, Renee stiffened at the mention of her family. She nodded and replied, "Yes General, I'll do whatever I need to do."

"Good, Mrs. Booker, then here's what I want you to do. Don't come here any more—if not already, you'll be watched. An occasional visit here isn't bad, because your work requires you to come here periodically. You have SIPRnet, don't you?"

"Yes Sir, I do."

"Okay, I'm sure that the insurgents can't get into it, so let's communicate exclusively by SIPR. No telephones, no public internet or NIPR, I want you to write back to Ibrahim. Tell him you have no idea what happened with Hamid, that you hadn't seen him in weeks, and want nothing to do with him. That won't stop Ibrahim, of course, from picking up where Hamid left off in extorting you. You'll feed him false info that my office will provide you, and in the meantime we'll track down his entire network, and then arrest them all in one fell swoop. Okay?"

"Yes, General," Renee said as she stood up. "I'll write back to him today, and try not to be too upset when he won't let me alone. And I'll write to you on SIPR with progress."

"Good, Mrs. Booker," said the General, as he walked her to the door, arm around her with his hand on her right shoulder. "Some good may come of all this, if we clean out a full cell of the insurgency. I'll look for your note."

Turning to face him at the door, beside Lieutenant Wiggin's desk, Renee said, "Thank you for everything, General Jabbour." And before he could resist, she reached around him and hugged him. Then she turned and walked out of the office.

The General looked down at Lieutenant Wiggin, who wiggled his eyebrows.

"That's enough of that, Lieutenant," the General asserted, smiling. "She executed a sneak attack."

"I saw nothing, Sir," lied Lieutenant Wiggin.

CHAPTER FIFTY

PLACATING THE 2ND PRIORITY

Tuesday, March 22, 2005

"Christine! What a wonderful surprise, sweetheart. Are you home early? Are you in New York?"

"Ah, no Mama, I'm not. But how are you, Mama? Are you feeling alright?"

"Yes, Honey, and even better knowing you're going to be here with me. Where are you, anyway? You're not stranded, are you? My surgery is in two days."

"I know, Mama. I know." Hesitating, Chris went on, "Mama, I can't come home."

"What's that, Honey, you haven't left yet? Dear, are you cutting this kind of close?"

"No, Mama, I said, I can't come home at all. Mama, I'm so sorry, but I'm overwhelmed here. We're extremely short-staffed, and I just can't leave my fellow Marines in this condition. We're in a combat zone, Mama."

"Oh, dear... Chris... you can't come home at all?"

"No Mama, this is hurting me deeply, but I just can't. The Marine Corps sent me here to do a job, and right now they need me more than you do, Mama. I know that sounds heartless, but you know I love you more than anyone in the world except for Dad, so the last thing I want to do is disappoint you. But I just don't have any choice. Can you forgive me, Mama?"

"Oh, gosh, Chris, dear, I, I...I was so looking forward to your being with me." Pausing, "But I'll be all right, Honey. Dad's here, as well as Nick & Zita, and the surgery really isn't dangerous. I'm just worried about what they'll find. You know. But I understand, Chris. I raised you to take on challenges, and stick with them 'til they're completed. That's what's happening here. If you weren't busy, I wouldn't take "no" for an answer. But you are, and I know you wouldn't stay away if it weren't really important. So, yes, Sweetie, I'll be okay. What's the work that's keeping you so busy?"

"Mama, we have a thief who works at the Exchange. Daddy sent me some electronic gear to try to catch him. And we have a court martial, and a congressional—and there's a major offensive underway out on the Syrian border—a lot of important issues, Mama, so I just can't leave right now. How 'bout if I promise to talk to you each day from now until two days post op. Is that a fair compromise, Mama?"

"Certainly, Honey, that'll be fine. That'll be just fine."

"Mama, I love you so much. I've been praying for you every night, and I'm gonna pray twice a day for you from here on."

"I love you too, Christine, ever so much. You'll always be my little girl. Even when you're a Marine Corps officer in a war zone, defending our nation, you're my little girl. You stay safe. And don't work too hard."

"I won't, Mama. And Mama, this was a really tough call for me to make. Thank you for being so understanding, Mama, thank you. I hope you've built your qualities of character into me."

"Sweetheart, love conquers all, and I love you unconditionally. I'll look forward to your call tomorrow, Honey. And please keep praying for me."

"I will, Mama, God knows, I will. I love you. Good-bye, Mama."

"Good-bye, my dearest."

CHAPTER FIFTY-ONE

BAITING THE HOOK

Tuesday, March 22, 2005

"The General will see you now, Major."

"Thank you, Lieutenant," Matt said to Lieutenant Wiggin as he strode into General Brier's office. This was his third trip to the General's office, but Samir wasn't at his desk the first two times, so he simply waved off and came back later.

General Brier remained seated at his desk. "Good morning, Major, what can I do for you?"

"Hello General Brier," Matt said, trying to be sure his voice was loud enough to be heard by Samir, but not so loud that the intent was revealed. "Something big coming up, Sir. Something very big."

"Sounds provocative, Major, What do you have?"

"Sir, we are to receive a distinguished visitor. A *very* distinguished visitor. The visitor is coming to meet with Governor Mehdi and his Directors General at Government Center. We're providing security back-up. In the face of this level of prominence, Sir, we need to do some intense planning."

"Very reasonable, Major. But for Heaven's sake, who *is* this mystery visitor?"

"I'm not sure, Sir, although I have my suspicions. All I was told was that this was an exceedingly high level person, and that we should expend our energies accordingly."

"Do you think it's ambassador Zhaikav, perhaps with Prime Minister Allawi?"

"Could be, Sir, but I suspect higher. *Much* higher."

"Oh. Oh boy. That high. Okay, you're right, we have work to do. I know that air security is your bailiwick, but as you know, Blue Diamond has had a tremendous drawdown of combat troops over the past two weeks, to support Operation Iron Fist out on the Syrian border. They even took our best Base Security people. We're practically running on fumes here, in the Base Security realm."

"Yes Sir, I'm aware of the drawdown. Furthermore, apparently they took the best weapons from the armory as well, leaving us with the old clunkers that jam. And to make matters worse, the current shipment of machine gun ammo has about a five percent dud rate, putting the guns out of commission every 20 rounds, 'til the gunner can clear it. That lousy ammo is turning our machine guns practically into bolt-action Springfields."

"Oh, boy, I didn't know that, Major," said the General, scratching his temple. "When's the replacement ammo due in?"

"Sir, everything's diverted to Iron Fist. We won't get re-supplied for at least another two weeks. But our visitor arrives next Monday."

"Oh boy, terrible timing. Well, we'll just have to make do. Can you work with the Base Security acting chief? Captain Kalopolis is NPQ [Not Physically Qualified] and is pretty much bedridden. I thought malaria, but they tell me there's no malaria in western Iraq. Some kind of flu I guess. His XO is Second Lieutenant Britt. Unfortunately, I've heard that Lieutenant Britt not only is fresh out of OCS but that he lacks fundamental leadership skills. To the point that morale of the Base Security force is at an all-time low. There are even rumors of an extensive drug problem in what's left of the force. Can you work with Lieutenant Britt to try to bring his unit up to snuff?"

"Sir, that's a tall order for results needed in six days. But I'll certainly try, Sir. The distinguished visitor will bring with him a professional security force, but we're supposed to supply the heavy-lift combat backup. Not sure we're gonna be able to do that so well. We can *look* like we're doing it, but with the material we have to work with, I'm afraid we're going to be paper tigers 'til our people get back from Iron Fist."

"Well, Major, we'll just have to make do. Like The Man said, 'You don't go to war with the force you *want*. You go with the force you *have*.'"

"Yes Sir. We'll make it do. I'll go look up Lieutenant Britt. Anything else I can do for you, Sir?"

"Yes, Major, you can pray that next Monday goes smoothly."

"Yes Sir, I can and I will. Thank you, Sir." Major Baxter did a curt about-face and marched out of the office.

"Oh Samir," General Brier called, "are you free to assist with a phone call?"

"Yes Sir," came Samir's immediate response. So quickly that Gen Brier was sure he had been listening in all along. *Perfect.*

"Samir, would you get Governor Mehdi on the phone for me? I need to chat with him."

"Certainly, Sir. I'll inform you when I have him, Sir."

"Thank you, Samir." And General Brier turned his attention to his inbox, although he could barely focus on any of the documents, over anticipation of further baiting the trap for Samir.

Four minutes later, after General Brier heard Samir speaking Arabic on the phone, Samir buzzed Gen Brier's phone and said, "General, Governor Mehdi is on line one."

General Brier punched line 1 and said, "Wa asalaam alaykum, Governor Mehdi."

"Wa alaykum asalaam, General Brier," responded Governor Mehdi in his thick accent."

"Governor Mehdi, we are bringing a very senior government official to meet with you next Monday afternoon. Rather late in the day, about 1800 hours. Would you and your staff be available to meet with him then at Government Center?" Samir translated.

"That's a little late, General. My DGs [directorate generals = department heads] like to be home for dinner with their families, and their security detachments are not paid for night work, when, of course, the roads are more dangerous for all of us. Could we meet earlier?"

"I'd much prefer that myself, Governor, but this is an extremely prominent dignitary, and we're stuck with the time his staff allots us. Governor, this may be the most distinguished visitor you can imagine, if you get my drift. Can you make an exception with your DGs, and get them to stay into the evening?"

"At your request, General, it will be done. We will look forward to meeting your official at 1800 hours next Monday."

"Thank you, Governor. I appreciate your working with me on this. I look forward to seeing you next Monday at 1800 hours, with my very distinguished visitor."

"*Enshala*, General Brier. Good bye."

"Will there be anything else, General?" asked Samir.

"No,ō Samir, that was extremely productive. I may well have floundered without your special skills. Thank you. That will be all."

"It was my privilege, General," responded Samir, as he touched his right fist to his left chest and bowed his head, the Arabic sign of respect, and returned to his desk.

CHAPTER FIFTY-TWO

THE CRAB SNAGS THE BAIT

Tuesday, March 22, 2005

"God is great."

"And Allah shall rule over all His earth."

"Good evening, my Prince."

"Good evening, Brother Samir. How are conditions in the occupied land?"

"The news is good, my Prince. Extremely good. In fact, it may be the best news I could possibly bring you!"

"What is it, Samir? Do not keep me waiting after such exciting words!"

"My Prince, next Monday, a distinguished visitor is coming to Blue Diamond. I do not know how or when he arrives, but I know that he will travel by convoy at 1800 hours to the Government Center of Ramadi. Prince, this visitor was described as 'the most distinguished visitor you can imagine.' I believe that makes him higher than the Prime Minister Allawi, or Ambassador Zhaikov. Higher than a senior US senator or Congressman, or Secretary Rumsfeld or Secretary Rice. Prince, I believe this visitor is to be the Vice President Cheney or, even more likely, the crusader Bush himself. Prince, I am so excited I am trembling."

"Oh Samir, this is good news beyond belief—the most wonderful news imaginable. Eliminating the crusader Bush could result in a strategic victory for us. The Americans could even be forced to pull out after such a blow. When can you confirm the identity of the visitor?"

"I will try, my Prince, but I may not be able to derive any more certainty without arousing suspicion upon myself. I believe we should proceed as if the identity is certain."

"Yes, I believe you are right, Samir. Is there anything else you can tell me?"

"Yes, my Prince, there is. Imagine if we were to both slay the leader of the crusaders, *and* overrun one of their bases, killing all of its invaders. I cannot imagine a more resounding blow to the warmongers in America."

"Certainly true, Brother, but why would you think such a thing is possible?"

"My Prince, I have learned that the base is severely weakened. The Crusaders are concentrating their forces in the western Euphrates region, and have severely depleted their forces at Blue Diamond. They have even taken the best weapons, and the ammunition here is defective. Even better, they took the best members of the Base Security force. Their usual leader is ill, and has been replaced by an incompetent, allowing the occupiers to resort to their immoral drug use. Their morale is extremely low. I believe that with proper planning we could overwhelm their perimeter defense, enter the base, and destroy everyone and everything there. Coupled with the slaying of Bush, the repercussions could be everything we have prayed for. Oh my Prince, Allah is presenting us with such an opportunity!"

"Yes, Samir, Allah is being more than merciful and benevolent. But to properly approach these tasks, we would need to assemble an unprecedented force. As you know, our strategy calls for small groups of fighters only, such that, even in a disastrous defeat, our losses will be limited. This engagement would demand a different strategy. We would be severely exposed. If favor were not with us, we might suffer a blow from which we could not recover."

"I understand, my Prince. And I will, of course, defer to your judgment in the matter. But from these eyes, I see the opportunity we could only have prayed for—a victory so historic, that the fate of the world could be determined by us with a single blow!"

"You are right, Samir. Now I must decide how to proceed. You have performed beyond my hopes for you, my Brother. I shall see to it that another $20,000 is placed within your account by tomorrow. I will be back in touch with you regarding my decision, and how you can help. Listen carefully to the invaders, to extract as much more information about next Monday as you can."

"I am always at your service, my Prince. And I am grateful for your generosity."

"Good-bye, Brother Samir. Call me tomorrow night at the same time."

"It shall be done, my Prince."

CHAPTER FIFTY-THREE

THE DOMESTIC FACE OF TERROR

Wednesday, March 23, 2005

The usual ritual of end-of-school-day jubilation was being manifest all over the sidewalks, as it had been at this hour for the prior two days of monitoring for FBI Inspector Nick Splane and Agent Hiram Peterson. From their unadorned dark blue Ford Taurus, they followed the flowing stream of kids, readily identifying Jackie and Sammy Booker, having seen their clothes on the way in to school that day.

It was only three blocks to their house, and once again the agents had confirmed the arrival of the sitter at the Booker house, a half hour earlier. During the school day, the agents had driven over to Don Booker's office, even though a separate team was covering him as well.

Nothing remarkable had transpired over the entire three days thus far. It was enough to make the two agents wonder if the Iraq insurgency truly had talons long enough to reach across the globe to this quiet little town of cheerful children, families, churches, and Friday night high school football. Not to mention the current local and national obsession, basketball's March Madness. The agents had not seen the face of Satan incarnate in Hamid Amin when he thrust the pictures of the Booker children and their father at Renee, with the implicit threat of their murder, should Renee not assist the insurgency. So, in this town of peace, harmony, and tolerance, it strained credulity to believe that such hideous beasts lurked here to spread their message of hate and control-by-terror. Yet their professionalism prevailed, and they continued their disciplined scan of the scene.

"Hey Nick, that green Chrysler over there—opposite side of the street, to the right about fifty yards—looks familiar for some reason. Thirty-something woman in the driver's seat, whaddaya think?"

"Doesn't ring any bells, Hiram. Why, what strikes you about it?"

"Not sure…can't put my finger on it…just seems familiar."

"Maybe she's been here each day to pick up kids."

"Yeah, maybe, but she doesn't have any in there yet. Let's keep an eye on her and see if she gets any."

"Sure. Still a lot of kids haven't gotten to where she is yet."

"Roger. Lots of parents here, mostly Moms, sittin' in their cars, waitin' for their weeners."

"Wonder if the Dads sittin' here are going off to work on the evening shift, after they get the kids home."

"Seems likely. Life ain't all that easy, is it?"

"No, but it's good anyway,"

"Nick, you're married two years now, when are you gonna start a family? You're not gettin' any younger, ya know."

"Hey, easy does it, guy. I still have more hair than you!"

"Oh man, you're a street fighter. Going for the jugular with the first blow. Don't ya know I'm very sensitive about this pink pate?" Hiram smiled as he lightly stroked his bald spot.

"Course I know, Hi, why'd ya think I went for it?"

"Used to be, the Bureau only hired *sensitive* agents. Now look what we got. Callous brutes like you."

Squinting forward, Agent Krazan now suddenly spoke softly and seriously, "Hey Hi, those kids are about all past your thirty-somethin', and she didn't get any. Maybe you're on to something."

"Nick, you're reminding me—think I may have seen her over at Mr. Booker's office building. Yeah, yeah, I think it was her. She was walking on the sidewalk to her car and got in when we drove by. That's why the car was familiar, and now she is too."

"Check her out with the binocs, Hi. What's she look like up close?"

"Kind of bronze complexion, man. Could be Hispanic, but could be Middle Eastern. Hey, we may really have something here."

"What's the plate?"

"Can't read it – blocked by the car on this side of it. But if we drive, I can get it. Let's do it."

"Okay, Hi," Nick said tersely, as he started the engine. Slowly pulling out of their space, they drove at twenty miles per hour down the block while Hiram trained his glasses on the car.

"Tennessee 836-24P."

"Got it," Nick said softly as he scratched the number down on the tablet on the seat beside him, eyes swiveling while he drove.

Nick turned left at the next intersection, drove a half block further, turned around in a driveway, and drove back to the intersection. Glancing a hundred and fifty yards up the block, he could see the green Chrysler beginning to move out. Keeping the full hundred and fifty yards behind it, he followed the vehicle, which obeyed all traffic laws, and took the cloverleaf onto the freeway into Nashville. Meanwhile Hiram called in the license number and asked for a trace. But they didn't want to lose the car, because the plate may well have been stolen.

Entering Nashville, the car took an exit into the seedy section of town. It then drove eight blocks to a four-story city-run tenement, where it parallel parked with some difficulty, as is the case with those who learned to drive as adults as opposed to most Americans, who learn at age sixteen. The agents pulled over, still maintaining their distance, and watched as the approximately thirty-five year old woman got out and locked the car. She had black hair which she wore in a bun. Her clothes were western but ordinary—a blouse and long skirt in drab colors. She was carrying a camera. The woman walked briskly towards the main entrance of the building, past the graffiti-covered walls and trash strewn about on the front yard.

"Welcome to the hand-out society," quipped Nick. "People who don't own things, don't take care of 'em. This place is disgusting."

"Entitlements breed a sense of deserving more entitlements," responded Hiram, who was appalled by people who choose to live in trash rather than cleaning it up.

The woman entered the front door, and disappeared behind the inner door. They had no way of knowing where she was going. But they certainly weren't going anywhere. They were on to something, and they knew it.

There were some forty windows across each of the four floors, and this was only the front—the same forty windows were present on the rear-facing apartments. And ten across each end of the building—one hundred windows per floor, and four hundred altogether. The likelihood of seeing anything useful through a window, sitting there at the south end, looking at only the front-facing apartments, approached zero. But their three uneventful days of surveillance had now produced an unexpected hot lead, and the FBI has tremendous depth in its investigative capacity. Despite the formidable size of the task, the resources existed within The Agency to act on what they had.

Hiram dialed his office on his cell, and asked to speak to his supervisor. "Mel, Hiram here. We've got something. A thirtyish Middle Eastern-looking woman was watching the kids at the Booker children's school, carrying a camera. We've got her license number, and the apartment building she went to. We need some look-ups."

"Terrific break," exclaimed Special Agent Supervisor Melvin Nankov excitedly. "This could get interesting. Glad we devoted the resources to this case that we did. Whaddaya have?"

"Tennessee eight-three-six, twenty-four Papa. Late-model green Chrysler. We're looking at 6236 Blackbird Road in Nashville. It's a four-story tenement. No idea where she went in there, but it's city-owned. We thought we'd stay here and watch. Get back to us?"

"Will do, Hiram. Superb work. Out."

"Out." Turning to Nick, Hi went on, "Mel's on the numbers. He'll call us when he's got something. I think we should sit it out here. Agree?"

"Yeah, Hi, we've got hard data to work on. And she's not spooked, so if she comes out, she'll walk right past us, and we'll be on her." Glancing at his watch, he remarked, "It's only four, but I don't care if we stay all night. I'm pumped. If those slimeballs are here in Nashville threatening kids, I'm ready to go the distance, no matter what. You in?"

"You bet. I wanna see this one through. Like you said, I'm thinking of starting a family. Anybody who threatens kids is gonna have to deal with me. And my thumbs long for their tracheas. I'll personally squeeze the life outta the sonsabitches."

"Okay, buddy, we're good to go. You can read the paper for a while if ya like, and I'll watch the street."

"Cool, Nick, we'll switch off every half hour." With that, Hiram raised his Nashville Gazette, and opened to the sports section.

CHAPTER FIFTY-FOUR

THE SNAKES PLAN
THEIR ATTACK

Wednesday, March 23

"Good morning, my Prince," greeted Prince Alquieri. "God is great. How are you and your families today?"

"Allah is merciful, my Prince," responded Prince Saad. "The wives are busying themselves shopping, and the brood is in school learning the words of The Prophet. What is on your mind this day?"

"Saad, you won't believe this, but the mercy of Allah has been without parallel this day. We are presented with the most auspicious opportunity for victory since Saladin freed Jerusalem."

"Whoa, Alquieri, slow down, this is too good to rush. What do you have?"

"No less than the opportunity for two spectacular victories on the same day. Earthshaking!"

"Go on, my friend, go on!"

"An extremely senior American is to visit the government center in Ramadi next Monday. We're not certain who it is, but we believe it may be their Vice President Cheney, or, more likely, the crusader Bush himself."

"God is great," rejoiced Saad. We must hit them harder than ever before. We must *annihilate* them. We shall muster a larger force than ever before. This is the opportunity we prayed for but never dared believe could come to be! We could win the entire war in a single battle! We will become the greatest Arab heroes in six hundred years!"

"Yes, my Prince, it can all come to be. And there's more—the base of the crusader Marines in Ramadi, Blue Diamond Camp, is severely weakened. We believe we could overrun the base and kill all inside. So there is a possibility of a double massive victory! "

"How could we receive so many blessings at once? We must act quickly and decisively!"

"But these attacks are not without hazard. We have never assembled a large force, because we could not risk its loss. If somehow the invaders learned of our plans, we could lose virtually everything we have worked for."

"Then they must *not* find out!" pronounced Saad. "We must not lose this opportunity. Victory is the prize of the bold! We must commit everything to this battle!"

"All right, my Prince. I feel the same way, but wanted to consult you before preparing strategic plans. I will proceed as you say. All resources will be mobilized."

"Perfect, Alquieri, perfect. I am dancing with anticipation. What a gift we have been given! The Americans will be seized by the Arab viper as never before! All of them will perish, or be driven from our sacred Arab land. Oh, Allah, your gift is received with such jubilation!"

"I will report back to you, Prince Saad. There isn't time to involve the rest of The Forum. But I am certain they will be supportive of our decision to lash out at the invaders with all of our strength in a single blow."

"Let us speak again soon, Prince Alquieri. And I shall call you should I conceive additional suggestions for victory."

"'Til then, my Prince."

"'Til then, my brother."

CHAPTER FIFTY-FIVE

EMBELLISHING THE BAIT

Wednesday, March 23, 2005

"Hello Mrs. Booker," read the SIPR email from General Jabbour. "I know you're meeting with Ibrahim tomorrow. I have the first bit of misinformation for you to feed him. Do your usual 'I want out' routine, and be prepared for him to threaten your family, because I'm certain that he will. Act upset, but don't lose control. Make him ask for it a couple times, but then advise him that you've heard a rumor that an extremely senior political figure is going to visit Ramadi next Monday—a person either at the top or next-to-top level. That you don't know details, except that it's probably in the late afternoon, but you don't know how or when he's getting to Ramadi. Please write back to confirm that you've received this message. With best regards, Gen Jabbour."

Renee stiffened when she saw that the message was from Gen Jabbour. She was already on edge, knowing that she had scheduled a visit with Hamid's insurgent replacement that evening. Now being asked to plant false info with him was imposing that much more strain on her. But then she remembered the threats to Jackie and Sammy, and she felt vitriol suddenly rising up in her. She sat up straight, clenched her fists, and resolved that she could do anything to undo monsters who threaten families for political gain. *I'll meet with that son of a bitch. And I'll lie to him like Delilah to Samson. I'll walk that pig right into the trap that will destroy him and all his murderous cronies.* She was ready. And it wouldn't go so well for Hamid's successor, nor for those who sponsored him. Not well at all. She keyed in her reply to Gen Jabbour: "Booker on board, Sir. I'm going snake-hunting."

CHAPTER FIFTY-SIX

BLUE DIAMOND CHARADE

Thursday, March 24, 2005

"All right gents, let's get started. We've got four and a half days," Colonel Servi looked across the table at the intent eyes of Matt and Captain Kalopolis. "We've planted the seed, and we know that Samir took the bait and ran. We've got people monitoring his Saudi contacts and tracking down all of their networks. But we've got one hell of a battle to plan. With luck, the battle that breaks the back of the insurgency."

Captain Kalopolis began, "Colonel, I want the insurgents to take out our guard towers. They've never tried a coordinated assault of Blue Diamond, because they knew they didn't stand a prayer of breaking through the perimeter. Their snipers *have* shot a few of my guards in the towers, but that's been the extent of it."

"Why are you so eager to lose your guard stations, Captain?" queried Colonel Servi.

"Sir, to get the insurgents to commit themselves out in the open, we've got to convince them that they've silenced our automatic weapons coverage of the approaches to the perimeter walls. So I propose letting them *have* the towers. I think they'll use RPGs, and I might even assist them a little with some munitions to blow the towers if they get even close with an RPG round. Of course, my guards won't be *in* those towers –I'll come up with some alternate, concealed site for them, so they'll be ready with one hell of a surprise after the insurgents rush the walls. I may even have some kind of motorized guard silhouettes up in the towers, to make them look occupied. Even with good field glasses, through the cammie netting, the enemy wouldn't be able to discern that the motion isn't that of live Marines."

"Okay, Captain, that's a bit expensive. You're going to blow up all your towers, but I guess rebuilding them is a small price to pay for this opportunity. What else do you propose?"

"Sir, I want to have Marines dug in outside the wall about a hundred meters, positioned so that the insurgents run right by them, and then be subjected to fire from their rear and flanks."

"Won't those Marines be subject to friendly fire, Captain?"

"It's clearly a dangerous maneuver, Sir, but if I brief my Marines on the wall that they're to fire only laterally or down, with no rounds landing more than fifty meters from the wall, I think they'll be okay. They'll be able to engage those insurgents who escape fire from the walls, and are retreating."

"Sounds good, Captain, but you'll lose the capacity to use mortar fire, won't you? You can't fire mortars with friendlies so close to the kill zone."

"Right, Sir. What I propose is turning the insurgents' tactics against them with their IEDs, which they allow us to approach before detonating them remotely. Under cover of darkness and infrared shields, to blind any night vision surveillance, I proposed burying anti-personnel mines in the region, which will detonate on my command."

"Very well, Captain. You seem to have some exceedingly unpleasant surprises in store for our adversaries. And to complete the circle, what do you propose to do to engage any reserves they may keep outside the battle zone?"

"Oh boy, Colonel, I hadn't gotten to that one yet. Let me think about that."

"Well, Colonel," Matt broke in, "I think my specialty could be useful there. What if we had an aerial drone watching that area, able to localize any massed troops, so we could engage them with mortars and artillery? We could also arrange to deliver fresh troops from Fallujah or Taqaddum to the battle, once we know where the enemy force is. With the right intel, we could encircle and annihilate them. The drone we use here on Blue Diamond is the Dragon Eye, which is low altitude and noisy, so it'd spook the whole operation. I think we ought to bring in a Prowler from the Air Force, which flies too high to hear, but can see right through any clouds with its infrared. We could have them start learning the area now, so they'd know the scene, and be able to pinpoint any new concentrations of people during the battle. We'll make sure they'll be flying high enough that we won't hit them with any of our mortars or arty."

"Terrific, Major. Collateral damage is always an issue with those weapons, of course, so you'll need to figure out where the enemy reserves are likely to concentrate, and figure out how to minimize collateral damage from our fire."

"Yes Sir, I'll be all over that," Matt agreed, nodding.

"So what do we do if the perimeter *is* breached, gents. That's always a possibility."

"Yes Sir, I've considered that, and concluded it's a real possibility. I propose having fire teams on the ground inside the small concrete bunkers to minimize injury from incoming mortars, with coverage of the entire perimeter. And should anyone get past *them,* we'll have our usual mobile rapid response force."

"Sounds good, Captain. Now how are we going to keep Samir from seeing our preparations?"

"Sir, I propose establishing a restricted zone for the TCN's for the next week. We'll say that it's because of new construction at the south gate, with sensitive features to the construction. And we'll see to it that Samir doesn't get a look at that end of camp, where we'll concentrate additional forces and gun trucks. Furthermore, we'll have tanks, LARs, Strykers, and gun trucks concentrated at Ar Ramadi right across the river, to back up the force responding to the attack on the 'President's' convoy."

"Good, but what if the insurgents take out the bridges? Your tanks can't swim across the Euphrates."

"Right, Sir. The enemy hasn't blown those bridges because he uses them as well as us. But I agree, he might be willing to drop them for this battle, if he perceives the stakes to be high enough. And, of course, if he believes that the President is gonna be on that convoy, he's gonna want no reinforcements coming from Ramadi. So yes, Sir, we're going to need to protect the bridges."

"How are you going to accomplish that, Captain?"

"Well Sir, we'll have gunboats deployed both upstream and downstream from the bridge to block all navigation. And I'll put several .50 cal stations both upstream and downstream from the bridge, to take out any boats that evade the blockade.

"To counter the car or truck bomb technique, I propose closing the bridges for emergency repairs. We can close Barrage Bridge at least two days in advance, and hope they don't blow it before then. However, this would be a huge blow to civilian commerce here, and we're striving to *build* their economy, not trash it. Even so, I think those two days are unavoidable. We'll leave Steel Bridge open until the day of the sting, and close it around noon. We can put some work teams out there, looking like they're doing something important."

"Very well, Captain, sounds like you have a sound plan." Pausing, and looking at Matt as well as Captain Kalopolis, Colonel Servi went on: "All right, 'gents, your preliminary plans for the defense of Blue Diamond are sound, and I want you to proceed with implementing those measures. Don't tell anyone what you're up to, of course – not even your officers. Just tell them it's a hush-hush operation, and to follow orders without question.

"Now, how are we going to defend the convoy? It sounds to me like we're going to need to put a number of our people in serious harm's way. How are we going to protect them?"

"This is a work in progress, Sir," Matt volunteered. "We don't think we can really put Humvees into that kill zone. Their armor is equal to the threat of AKs, but that's about it. RPGs and heavy machine guns will rip right through 'em. On the other hand, if we *don't* have Humvees show up, the enemy may hold fire, and we may lose the chance to engage them."

"There isn't much time, Major, but since you've got such refined unmanned *aerial* vehicles, how 'bout cookin' up a couple remote-controlled *ground* vehicles? Doesn't seem like it should be all that hard."

"Oh, wow Sir, well… it's a terrific idea, but we have so little time to execute."

"Well, Major, I have good news. This issue has come up in the past, and a system has been devised for Humvees. It's been tested pretty extensively in Kuwait, and I believe they could get us a bunch of those babies up here in twenty-four hours. How many do you think we'd need?"

"Well, Sir, we'd need at least four. And how are we going to ruse the turret gunners? And any chance we could get an armored Suburban or similar diplomatic vehicle, since that's what Distinguished Visitors usually ride around in."

"Oh, now that's a toughie, Major," replied Colonel Servi. "You're right—no one would ever believe an extremely senior diplomat would be carted around in a cramped, noisy, dirty Humvee. But if the team in Kuwait could rig a Humvee, they should be able to do a Suburban as well. It'll take a day to transport them here, so that gives them forty-eight hours to come up with a fit. We'll bring the operators of the vehicles here, rather than try to learn that skill ourselves in a couple days. What do you think?"

"I think it sounds like a go, Colonel," Matt asserted. "Will you take care of getting the vehicles and operators sent here?"

"Yes, gents, I'll take care of that. They won't be very pleased when they find out our plan was to let their creations be blown to smithereens, but this mission trumps any and all concerns about preserving hardware. This is an unprecedented opportunity to deal a profound, and possibly lethal, blow to the insurgency.

"I advise that we break now and get after our plans, but meet tomorrow to iron out further plans. In agreement?"

"Yes Sir, but with the caveat that you back me up when I put the tanks at Ar Ramadi on call for that day. They have two squadrons over there, with about a dozen tanks each. Do you think we need all twenty-four?"

"Yes, if we're to surround the enemy in this urban landscape, we're going to need a lot of tanks. So you have my authority to cite General Brier as the approving authority. And their people are to maintain absolute silence about their orders. Clear?"

"Clear, Sir," responded Matt and Captain Kalopolis simultaneously.

"Okay, men, see you here tomorrow at 1000. Good day."

The two more junior officers sprang to their feet, and stood at attention as Colonel Servi strode out of the room. After he was gone, Matt looked at Captain Kalopolis and said, "Okay, Steve. Are we squared away with our assignments?"

"Let's run through it, Matt," Steve replied. You're doing Prowler, and interfacing with our Kuwait people re transport of the vehicles. I'm working up my ground forces, getting motorized mannequins for the guard towers, laying some land mines, and plotting where my guys are gonna dig in outside the wire. I'm also calling 3rd Tanks and putting them on alert for Monday. And I've got gunboats to set up, and planned bridge closures. Tell you what, Matt—I've got too much—will you take care of bridge defense?

Cocking his head and raising one brow, Matt acquiesced, "I've get it covered, Steve." Pausing and looking down, Matt then went on, "Hey, if you can get motorized mannequins, can we get four for the gun turrets on the convoy to simulate the gunners: I don't want to expose real Marines to the ambush."

Wrinkling his brow and grimacing, Steve responded, "Not sure how many I can get, but I'll make it a flash priority request.

"We've got to set up with Taqaddum and Fallujah to have combat troops delivered at the onset of the battle, so we can surround the attack forces of both the convoy and Blue Diamond. I think we should engage in overkill—2 full battalions—sixteen hundred troops. The H-53's can carry fifty guys each, but we'll never get sixteen of 'em for each base. And we can't put them in much danger of being shot down – they're too valuable to be lost to ground fire. So we're going to need troop surface convoys instead. If we convoy in from both Taqaddam *and* Camp Fallujah, their departure from those bases won't be as noticeable. Although you're the air guy, I'm going to give the entire battalion reinforcement issue to you – you're a smart guy."

"Every Marine's a rifleman, Steve," Matt smiled. "I'll take care of those reinforcements."

"Good, Major. Because our forces will have the huge advantage of surprise and tactical positioning, those two batallions will almost certainly be enough to destroy the enemy forces. But just in case, I think we need to have back-up reinforcements. You've got all the available Marines engaged already. I think we need to set up some Army backup on standby."

"I agree that we should, Colonel, but the more people involved, the greater chance of leakage of the plan."

"Absolutely, Major, so I wouldn't promulgate the true reason for the Army preparation for battle, but rather explain that it's for a new push in the Korean Village area."

"Sounds good, Sir."

"Okay, Matt, lets get cookin'. We have some fish to fry." Both strode out of the room.

CHAPTER FIFTY-SEVEN

RENEE ATONES

Thursday, March 24

Renee arrived at the entrance of the 357th Combat Surgical Hospital, the former Ibn Sina Hospital, one of the few places in Iraq during the Saddam regime where world-class health care was available. At that time, of course, such care was extended only to Friends of Saddam, while the remainder of the Iraqi people coped with a second-world, under-funded, under-equipped, and undersupplied public healthcare system in which the few existing resources were further pilfered by rampant corruption at every level of the system.

The insurgent chose this location because of its bustling activity, with both vehicle and foot traffic moving briskly in all directions. As directed, Renee sat on the bench across the street from the entrance. Reading a fresh copy of *Stars And Stripes*, she was easy to spot for Ibrahim Fawaz, leader of a particularly vicious group of insurgents. His cell took great pride in the body count of innocent men, women, and children, blown to bits by their suicide car bombers in marketplaces and cafés all around Baghdad.

"Hello Meessis Boooker," Ibrahim said as he walked up to her. "I am Ibrahim. Perhaps we walk together," he said stoically, and gestured down the sidewalk. Renee folded her paper, inserted it into her purse, and stood, mounting the purse on her shoulder. They walked south on the road, away from the Embassy, where the crowd thinned gradually. "What happened Hamid, Meessis Boooker?" Ibrahim said.

"I have no idea, Ibrahim," Renee responded coldly. "I thought he had honored my wishes to get out of my life, but then I heard that he was killed in a gunfight. Our Bible says, 'Those who live by the sword, die by the sword.' Maybe he should have reflected on that wisdom."

"You betray him," Ibrahim countered.

"Are you out of your mind, Ibrahim? That son of a bitch threatened my family. Are you simple enough to think that I'd jeopardize them, for *anything*?" Renee said, slightly agitated. "Whatever happened to him was *his* doing, not mine."

"Why I should believe you?" he retorted.

Stopping and turning to face him, Renee spoke, progressively more angrily. "I don't really care what you believe, Ibrahim. In fact, the last place on earth I want to be right now is here with you. I didn't initiate this contact—you did. I want nothing to do with you. Why did you contact me? What do you want with me? I want nothing to do with you, or any of the vermin you work with. Hamid had his fun with me. That's over. And so is my relationship with your crowd of hypocritical Koran-thumping liars who murder their beloved Muslim brothers and sisters wholesale, while piously praying to your supposedly merciful God. You're the most dishonest, back-stabbing, treacherous, treasonous, anti-Muslim butchers the world has ever known. Does that offer you some sense of why I don't wish to have a relationship with you and your herd of swine?"

"You no understand us. We serve Allah."

"You bloodthirsty moron! What kind of idiot do you mistake me for? I have dozens of Muslim friends, and you have nothing remotely in common with them—ordinary, kind, industrious, family-devoted, peaceful people. You're the same two-bit power-hungry, incompetent unprincipled pig that's plagued humankind since its inception. You're nothing more than a common criminal, with a mind just slightly smaller than an earthworm. You and your ilk have never built a business, met a payroll, invented anything, manufactured anything, composed music or written books, made scientific discoveries, or pursued a just society. You crave power, pure and simple. Somehow your mothers screwed up and never taught you that other people may think differently than you, and to get over it. No, you and your nest of venomous spiders, never having accomplished anything yourselves, have now appointed yourselves the dictators of how other people should dress, should socialize, should vote, should worship, should... form relationships, should... study, travel, speak—you're like two-year olds waddling around with your thumbs in your mouths and loads in your pants. Don't kid yourself, bud—you ain't servin' Allah—you're lookin' out for Number One. You're as stupid as the assholes who murdered for Jesus. And you've industrialized it, like the slimeball Nazi's—you need cars to haul around the massive bombs you use to murder women and children—yes your innocent Muslim brothers and sisters. Gimme a break. You're running your own private Jack-Ass show here."

Ibrahim's face grew cherry-red as Renee ranted. His face and neck muscles grew taut and he developed a twitch of his left eyelid. He stared at her with a riveting gaze, trembling. His hands flexed open and closed, itching for her throat—his solution to any form of frustration, regardless how trivial. But he was bright enough to know that he'd never escape if he assaulted her, and besides, he still needed her alive. So he spoke slowly, virtually spitting out the words, "You talk that way to me again, I kill your children myself."

Renee jerked upright and stiffened, pupils dilated, suddenly realizing that she'd indulged herself with her vituperative attack on Ibrahim. Her rational side kicked into overdrive. Lifting her hands, palms forward, she sought to lower the tension, "Okay, okay, I went overboard. I'm not sorry, but now you know where I stand. You're ruthless enough to get your way threatening children—I hear you. What do you want?"

"You help us serve people of Iraq, and all Arab world. You tell us when occupiers fly special passengers. What you know now?"

"Oh shit, *that* again," she said, shaking her head, shrugging her shoulders and sighing. Then running her palms down her face, from eyes to chin, tears streaming down her cheeks, she said softly, "All right, all right, I'll hate myself for it, but I don't have any choice. I'll do it."

"Good. What you know now?"

Renee didn't answer. She sat back, crossed her arms, and stared into the sky, sighing. Then she leaned forward, placing her right palm under her chin, left hand under her right elbow, and thought.

"What you know?" Ibrahim demanded.

"All right," Renee said softly. "Nothing for certain, but I heard something." She stopped, biting her lip.

"You tell me," Ibrahim commanded. "You tell me *now*."

"I heard that a very senior American diplomat may be coming. Next week. Monday. To Ramadi."

"Who this person?"

"I don't know. No one is saying. They might not even know themselves. Just that's it's a *very* senior person. Maybe even the *most* senior person."

"You mean the crusader Bush?" Ibrahim asked, now softly, incredulously.

"I really don't know. I don't think any of the people at the flight line know."

"When?"

"Monday. Sometime in the afternoon. To Ramadi. I don't know how he's getting there."

"How sure you are?"

"I'm not sure at all. How could I be? I'm just a fly on the wall over at the flight line. I don't have any formal access to this information. That's why you should leave me alone. I can't really help you."

"You leave now. I write when need you," Ibrahim said as he stood up, already planning his communiqué with his superior about this tantalizing new development.

"Why don't you leave me alone?" asked Renee, as she stood up. "I've done all that I could."

"I write when need you," Ibrahim repeated, and he walked briskly down the street.

Looking downward and dejected, Renee slowly walked back toward her office in the embassy. She was pleased with how the encounter had gone. She had gotten to vent her spleen with the enemy, and she fulfilled the mission assigned her by General Jabbour. At least she had done something to begin to atone for her prior misdeeds.

CHAPTER FIFTY-EIGHT

THE FBI FOCUSES ON A RAT'S NEST

Thursday, March 24, 2005

"Agent Splane, Supervisor Nenkov here, over."

"Splane here, Mel, over."

"Nick, we've got a make on the Chrysler. Tennessee 836-24P is registered to a Rania al-Shaykh, a thirty-seven year-old Egyptian woman here in a refugee status. Claimed she was a Coptic, being persecuted by the Muslim Egyptian state. Here for two years, collecting welfare, food stamps, Medicaid, and housing. Claimed she had six kids, still in Egypt with her parents, and she's filed to let them come here. Came here with what she claimed was a husband, but we don't know if he's still in the picture. No known Muslim or terror connections, over."

"Okay, Mel, which is her unit?"

"She's in 318, Nick. Why?"

"I think we have plenty of reasonable suspicion to get a search warrant, Mel."

"I'm sure we do, Nick, but it's way too soon for that. We could have an exquisitely valuable lead here, and don't wanna spook her. We'll tap her land line and her cell—we're working on that now. And you guys are gonna follow her—see if you find something or someone that the phone doesn't tell us."

Glancing at Hiram, Nick replied, "Got it, Mel. This is one surveillance we're taking personally. We wanna run these lazy, lying, stupid, murderous sonsabitches out of our city, our state, and the country."

"Good, Nick, stay on her and keep me posted. Out."

"Roger, Mel, out".

"We differ a little on that last quip, Nick," Hi commented. "You wanna run 'em outta town. But for anyone who threatens, kids, I wanna kill the sonsabitches. Dead. Let 'em go screw their homely virgins in the rat-heaven that baby killers go to. I wanna send 'em there with my own hands."

"Amen, brother," Nick responded. "Let's take care of these bastards."

CHAPTER FIFTY-NINE

ENEMY BATTLE PLANS

Thursday, March 24, 2005

"Ah, good afternoon, Brother Ahmed. This is Prince Alquieri calling. And how are things in the occupied land?"

"Ah, my Prince, how good to hear from you. Here in Ramadi we are going about our usual duties of guerilla warfare against the occupiers. Not glorious, but it will prove effective over time."

"Well, Brother Ahmed, I have startling good news. But I must caution you, secrecy is of the essence. Brother Ahmed, Allah has smiled upon us. The massive victory that you dream of is at hand. We have reason to believe that a priceless target is coming to your region – perhaps the best target any of us could imagine. We believe it may be the chief crusader himself, Bush."

"Allah be praised, my Prince! How could such good fortune befall us! Tell me more."

"We believe that the enemy leader will travel from their Blue Diamond Camp to Ramadi Government Center next Monday, March 28, at 4:00 PM. We believe he will take the same route they always take, down what they call Route Milwaukee. We must strike him there, and strike him with sufficient force that there can be no doubt about the outcome. We *must* commit more fighters than ever before, Brother Ahmed. The last attack on their General Brier committed insufficient force, and their General escaped. This must not be permitted to happen with this target. Brother Ahmed, this battle could end the occupation. It could truly produce a new world order. *It must not fail!*"

"I understand, my Prince. I will be prepared."

"Believe it or not, Ahmed, there's more! We believe that the Blue Diamond Camp may be vulnerable to conquest; we have reason to believe that its defenses are so weak that it could be easily overrun."

"My Prince, no American base has been successfully assaulted by our blessed *mujahadeen*. In what way is it vulnerable?"

"Most of its base defense personnel have been transferred to their operation on the Syrian border. Their best weapons went with them. Their current weapons are unreliable, their ammunition is defective, and the infidels on the base defense team are compromised with ingestion of drugs. The time is ripe for a resounding victory. Coupled with the slaying of their leader, this could be the strategic victory we could only have dreamed of! While much of their base defense force is diverted, being attacked in their convoy, the base can be ours!"

"My Prince, this is the most joyous telephone call of my life! But the forces required—two simultaneous major battles—are without precedent. I must rally all of my forces. I should bypass my usual restraint, and bring every *mujahadeen* I command into this battle. The prize is of inestimable value! But I will need advance funding for so large an operation."

"Brother Ahmed, today I will wire to your account two million dollars, and double that when the victory is complete. This battle is one which we take special joy in funding!"

"My Prince, I will need even more: my own forces are not sufficient for two Major battles at the same time. I will need to bring in special fighters from Syria and Saudi. I will need triple that amount. And time is of the essence, I have only three days to prepare."

"As you say, brother Ahmed. It shall be done. We are counting on you to bring glory to all of the faithful, around the world, on Monday."

"*Enshala*, my Prince. It shall come to be."

"*Enshala*, brother Ahmed. Go in peace."

CHAPTER SIXTY

THE ENEMY UNVEILED

Thursday, March 24, 2005

"Mr. Arroya, Lieutenant Colonel Amanee here. This is a secure line. What do you have for me?"

"Hello Colonel Amanee, you've brought us quite a gold mine. I think you showed terrific judgment in coming to us at CIA rather than going to the Saudi authorities. No one knows if or how much their security services have been infiltrated by Al Qaeda. We were a vastly safer bet. Besides, we really don't want to tip our hand to them on how intensely we can monitor their systems."

"Thank you, Mr. Arroya. So tell me what you've got."

"There's a lot to tell, Colonel. You've really brought us the kahuna. Seems that the number you gave us belongs to a Prince Alquieri, a member of a rogue faction of the Saudi royal family. And he's a leader in a large Saudi-based organization that funds terror around the world. They call themselves the *The Forum*, and their larger organization is *The Sacred Sword of the Avengers*. We've identified ten of the twelve leaders, and sixty or so of the roughly one hundred members overall. We think we can ID every single one of 'em. And we think the Saudi government is going to be incredibly embarrassed by these bad players. Don't think I'd want to be one of 'em when the Saudi government comes to visit 'em at home."

"That's fantastic work, Mr. Arroya. I came to the right agency with this issue. When do you think you'll be ready to move on these bastards?"

"We'll be at least another week tracking them all down, and verifying. We'd like to listen in at one of their meetings as well to nail down the evidence. And I understand that you have a major operation going down next week, such that you don't want any disturbance from us before them."

213

"Absolutely right, Mr. Arroya. So let's plan to communicate next week about this time. Thanks for being there when we needed you, and your super capabilities. God bless the CIA."

"Thank you, Colonel. The nature of our work requires that we receive little credit for anything we do. Always nice to hear a little gratitude first hand."

"Your team is fabulous, Mr. Arroyo. Thanks again. Out."

"Talk to you next week, Colonel. Out here."

CHAPTER SIXTY-ONE

PREPARING THE BATTLEFIELD

Friday, March 25, 2005

It was 0100 hours, three and a half days before Time Zero. It was a black, moonless night, and the infrared jammer was aimed over the side of the wall, and twenty Marines covertly lowered ladders, silently descending to the open space on the side facing the open countryside. A hundred yards from the wall, the Marines stealthily dug fighting holes, five feet deep, such that they could stand in the holes and lean their rifles on the turf at shoulder level. To conceal their digging, they brought the earth back to the wall and lifted it over, preparing plywood lids covered with turf to conceal the holes. The lids needed to be substantial enough to support any insurgents who inadvertently stepped on them while storming the wall during the attack. When the holes were complete—one every twenty-five yards for the length of the wall, there were some thirty fighting holes for the half mile length of the wall. Every one would be manned by a Marine with a Squad Automatic Weapon, or SAW, a light machine gun firing the same round as the M-16, but at a rate of two hundred rounds per minute—a frightful fusillade of high-power bullets emanating from a rather small and lightweight weapon.

The Marines then set about implanting the Claymore mines. Each needed to be camouflaged inside the vegetation growing on the wall. They were invisible at night regardless, but these devices needed to be installed in advance, and it was vital they not be detected by insurgent surveillance during the days preceding the attack. The Claymores were rigged to detonate on electronic command, and would constitute part of the planned Insurgent Surprise. Claymores fire projectiles in an arc of sixty degrees, with a kill radius of fifteen yards, and a wound radius of thirty—a nasty opponent by any standard.

Finally, the Marines created a conventional minefield between fifteen and twenty-five yards out from the wall. Contact-triggered, they would

215

eliminate some of the insurgent threat on Monday, without further Marine intervention. Additionally, they were undetectable during the day from remote surveillance.

Captain Kalopolis got his motorized mannequins in forty-eight hours, and set about planning where he would position them, how he'd power them, and when they would replace his real watchtower machine-gun crews. He set some small explosive charges in each of the twelve machine gun nests guarding the perimeter, and rigged them such that he could detonate each one independently whenever an insurgent RPG had a near miss, confirming destruction of those machine gun positions and encouraging the insurgents to charge into the kill zone. The real machine gun crews would set up in the dark at other unconventional locations along the wall, where they'd be invisible, but would still allow fire sweeping the tops of the walls, should any insurgents succeed in scaling them.

The Humvees with radio controls arrived promptly, along with a handsome late-model armored Chevy Suburban with darkened windows. Colonel Amanee's staff practiced working the controls in the west end of camp, which had been closed off to TCNs for the past four days to allow concentration of DOD assets there. Five tanks were brought in to escort the convoy, as were four Strykers [Army eight-wheeled lightly armored troop-transport vehicles with .50 and .30 cal machine guns and a 40-mm grenade launcher], and two LARs [USMC eight-wheeled light armored vehicles with mounted 25 mm cannons].

Both battalions of tanks at Camp Ar Ramadi were assigned as backup to this mission; after the five already in the convoy, eight were left in the first battalion, and twelve in the 2nd. They'd be staged by the gate at Ar Ramadi, ready for instant deployment when summoned.

Marine Air was on board. Eight Cobra helo gunships would enter the fray when fire commenced, each featuring a 20 mm cannon projecting from its nose, and two-inch rockets on its wing stations. Furthermore, five F-18 Hornets would be fully armed and already on station, 20,000 feet above the battle as it evolved. Fast boys like Hornets aren't very useful in close air support missions like this because of the danger of fratricide, but if a building needs to be taken down in a hurry their GPS-guided JDAMS can achieve terrifying results with surgical accuracy.

Heavy artillery like the Paladin system, firing an 80-pound high-explosive bomb up to fifteen miles, isn't usually engaged in a close-up battle like this. But should enemy reinforcements be spotted in the open, this ferocious weapon system can rain havoc from the skies with no warning, decimating the ranks of unprotected troops. Accordingly, the eight massive Paladins dug in at Camp Ar Ramadi were placed on standby, and would be already precisely aimed at the likely target sites.

Because of the possibility of water-borne assault, three gunboats would be deployed both upstream and downstream of the base, and two would be secreted on the shore of the base, should enemy craft evade the perimeter forces. Each boat would mount both a .50 cal and a .30 cal machine gun. Because the Euphrates is so shallow, the gunboats were twenty-foot rigid-hull but inflatable-gunwale Zodiac craft, featuring two hundred horsepower outboards, able to race across the water at up to thirty knots. Crewed by only three sailors, a helmsman and two gunners, this agile but heavily armed craft was a formidable opponent.

An eight-hundred-man infantry battalion would be launched from each of Taqaddum Air Base and Camp Fallujah. The Fallujah battle group would depart at 1400 hours, giving them an hour to find their way to the battle for Blue Diamond. All cell phone and ground phone transmission would be jammed commencing at 1230 hours so the insurgents could not be warned of this convoy. The Taqaddum battalion would deploy at 1300 hours, so as to arrive at the Presidential convoy ambush only minutes in to the battle. The two battalions would encircle the battlefield, blocking escape for the enemy fighters.

Colonel Servi had extensive battle experience, including Vietnam, the first Persian Gulf War, and widespread operations in Iraq. He was a master planner, and a particularly skillful integrator of all aspects of his force: air, artillery, armor, and infantry. If you were going to be in a fight, you wanted his exquisite planning skills on *your* side.

CHAPTER SIXTY-TWO

ENEMY BATTLE PLANS REFINED

Friday, March 25, 2005

"Brother Ghazi, you will be in command of forces attacking the convoy. Whereas you commanded twenty fighters in the unsuccessful attack on the General two weeks ago for this battle you will have a thousand! You will place three hundred on each side of the street, leaving you four hundred fighters for the secondary attack site. After the initial explosions, when the convoy is stopped, your fighters will concentrate their fire on the turret gunners. When they are silenced, you will approach with RPGs and destroy every vehicle. When all vehicles are penetrated and on fire, your fighters will approach every vehicle, cast grenades into each one, and then apply rifle fire to any survivors. You must select the location for the attack, but I wish for you to plan a second attack site, should the target escape the first. You will complete your plans, and see me tomorrow at eleven o'clock to review those plans. You must not fail. Are there any questions at this time?"

"None, Brother Ahmed. It shall be so. We shall not fail. I will report to you tomorrow at eleven o'clock."

"Brother Hassan, you will command the assault and destruction of the Blue Diamond Base. You will have boats approach the base from both upstream and downstream, to attack the base from the east. Your main force will attack from the west. Your first requirement will be to destroy all the machine gun emplacements on the gates and towers—twelve towers in all. Your task will be easier because of the weakness of the enemy soldiers, and their defective weaponry. But those weapons must be silenced before your main attack commences, or your forces could be shredded.

"After the base perimeter defenses are neutralized, your forces will attack from both sides. The boats will land from the east. From the west, your fighters will use grappling hooks to scale the walls. When they are on top, follow-on forces carrying ladders will approach. Some of those who have scaled the walls will be assigned to open the gates at the north and south ends of the camp. A main force of fighters will then enter the camp through those gates. Each group entering the base will have a target to destroy with explosives and incendiary grenades. Every major building is to be attacked, and all inhabitants of the camp are to be killed. Do not spare the foreign workers of the occupiers—they made their choice. Kill them all.

"For this attack, you will need no fewer than three thousand fighters, and more if I can arrange it. Forces like this are unheard of in our organization—we are hastily bringing in fighters from Syria and Saudi. It is expensive, but the prize more than justifies the cost. You will commit the bulk of your forces in the initial assault, but you must hold a fourth of your force in reserve; I will show you on the map the best places I believe you can position your reserves.

"You will report back to me with detailed plans at noon tomorrow. Do you have any questions at this time?"

"None, my Prince. It is such an honor to be appointed leader of the first Arab force to destroy an American base. We shall succeed! We shall destroy every one of the enemy, and their base itself!"

"Excellent, Brother Hassan. Proceed with your planning."

CHAPTER SIXTY-THREE

PROGRESS IN NASHVILLE

Saturday, March 26, 2005

The graffiti-covered project door opened, and Fatimah emerged, dressed in drab clothes but without a head scarf; this Al Qaeda operative maintained her disguise even at night. No camera in tow this time—just a plain black pocketbook slung over her shoulder. She walked casually to her Chrysler, started it up, switched on its lights, and pulled out onto the road. It was eight at night, and Nick and Hiram were exhausted, but their hearts were thumping now—their patience had paid off.

The Chrysler drove straight ahead on Pine Tree Road for four blocks, then turned right on to Sievers for three blocks, followed by a left on Edgewood for another four blocks. Pulling into a parking spot in front of a row of run-down bungalows, she switched off the lights and climbed out. Looking about to see if anyone was watching, she turned into the walkway to 537 Edgewood Road. At her knock, to the curtains beside the door parted, and a face appeared to inspect the visitor. Then the door opened and she entered.

Following agency protocol, to avoid loss of critical data should they be neutralized, Hiram immediately called up headquarters on the radio. Working late in light of the intensity of this case, Mel Nenkov answered.

"Hello Hiram, Mel here. What's your status?"

"Mel, the target is on the move. She's driven to a run-down bungalow at 637 Edgewood about a mile from her apartment. Someone let her in, but we couldn't see who. We're in position now, parked about one hundred yards south of the house."

"Terrific, guys. I'll get a make on the house. Do you see any place where we could set up a fixed surveillance?"

"I saw a sign on a house across the street from the target, a few houses down. I couldn't see if it was for rent or for sale, but it was one of the two."

"Perfect, Hi. I'll get one of our women down there first thing in the morning, and see if we can rent it for a couple months. You guys must be worn out."

"We are, Mel. We'll give it another hour, and then call it a day."

"Way to go, guys. Talk to you tomorrow. Terrific work today—you guys have discovered a diamond mine for us. Out."

"Thanks, Mel. Out."

"So whaddaya think, Nick. Another hour?"

"Yeah, Hi, I think we've got good stuff for today. We've gotta be rested for tomorrow. One more hour."

"Gotcha, buddy."

The street was quiet with only the occasional car passing through. Two cars parked, and occupants went into other houses. Just before nine, a car parked, and the male driver with a male passenger walked to the target house, knocked, and were let in.

"Okay, Hi, our extra hour paid off. Let's wait fifteen minutes; if nothin' else happens, we'll drive slowly past that car and get its license, then keep goin' on home."

"Gotcha, Nick."

The lights remained on in the house, but no one else appeared. At a quarter past nine, Nick started the car and drove slowly down the street, striving not to pause near the car parked directly in front.. They didn't dare use a flashlight, but Hi was an experienced license reader. An old dark blue Toyota, North Carolina license 428-EP6.

"Got it," Hi said. Nick continued the slow rate down the street, turned left, and they disappeared into the night. They'd call in the plate in the morning. It was a rewarding night for the American counter-terror effort. And it was going to prove vastly more rewarding than they suspected.

CHAPTER SIXTY-FOUR

THE RUSE IS PROMOTED

Saturday, March 26, 2005

The military personnel in Iraq didn't even know it, but the sting was being facilitated back home, with counter-information. The President had a full schedule on Monday and Tuesday, including a few high-visibility appearances in Ohio and Iowa. These events were cancelled, in case Al Qaeda had operatives looking for the President's plans, and reporting back to those planning the attack in Ramadi. In fact it was the CIA folks, whose skills didn't stop at electronic wizardry, but extended to political connections and insight as well. A low-key call from a CIA operative to a personal contact on the White House staff resulted in the President being briefed, and his consenting to lose a few political points by canceling those appearances to augment the likelihood of success in Ramadi. To complete the ruse, arrangements were made for Marine One, the President's helicopter, to land at the White House Sunday afternoon for all to see, and Presidential and First Lady look-alikes boarded the plane. Marine One then took off for Andrews AFB, where the decoys boarded Air Force One, which dutifully took off and flew to Kuwait City. When it arrived, who knows how many Al Qaeda operatives working near the airport saw it. The look-alikes then boarded an Air Force C-17 transport, which flew to Baghdad Airport, where it could likewise be seen by any number of covert enemy agents. They spent the night in the VIP Quarters at Camp Victory, adjacent to Baghdad International Airport, and then dutifully flew in a USMC H-46 to Camp Blue Diamond Monday morning the 28th, arriving at 1300 hours.

The most senior executive in the most powerful nation on earth had now played his part in promoting the sting operation. As had hundreds of discreet, loyal, honorable Americans, executing their duties to perfection. While maintaining the utmost secrecy in all they did. Professionalism.

Personal restraint. Duty. Honor. Fortunately, America has legions of such superb citizens.

And their diligence was about to pay off for the nation, and for the world.

CHAPTER SIXTY-FIVE

THE ENEMY FINALIZES HIS BATTLE PLANS

Saturday, March 26, 2005

"Brother Ahmed, I am prepared to present my plan of attack on the Crusaders' convoy."

"Good, Brother Ghazi. Go on."

Producing a map of the route from Blue Diamond to Government Center via Route Milwaukee and its environs, Ghazi pointed out the path of the convoy on the map.

"The convoys leave Blue Diamond by their south gate. They do a two hundred and seventy degree passage of the traffic circle outside the gate, and then pass over the river via the Barrage Bridge. They then do a one hundred and eighty degree passage of the traffic circle on the east side of the bridge, and enter Milwaukee directly in front of their communications and police center, what they call JCC. Two hundred meters further to the east is where the attack on their general was launched, and I believe that to be the best location for this attack as well, with 750 fighters. This time we will position a second smaller force of 250 fighters, three hundred meters to east of that site, should the target escape the first assault."

"Very good, brother Ghazi, continue."

"We are tunneling under the road to position 2 large bombs, which we will detonate when the target's vehicle is over it. We are planning for 100 kg devices, which will destroy virtually any type of vehicle, many times over, but hopefully not demolish the nearby buildings. The tunnel is required, because surveillance from their JCC facility could detect any excavation performed from the middle of the street.

"We will strive to also disable the first and last vehicles in the convoy, hopefully blocking escape for the remaining ones. We will use RPGs to disable and penetrate all vehicles, and we will be prepared with anti-armor missiles as well, should heavy armored vehicles be included in the convoy.

"As you suggested, all fire will be directed on turret gunners. When they are neutralized, RPG launchers will be deployed into the street for relatively close-up attacks on the vehicles. When the vehicles' armor has been penetrated, hand grenades will be hurled into the vehicles. Follow-up gunfire will be used to kill any surviving occupants. Maximum attention will be devoted to the vehicle which appears most likely to be carrying diplomats, but we are prepared for the crusaders to engage in deception, and perhaps place their most precious personnel into an ordinary Humvee, and perhaps even attire them in military uniforms. Accordingly, all vehicles must be destroyed, and all personnel killed, to be sure we have neutralized the target."

"Wonderful, brother Ghazi. And what is the back-up plan, should the first attack fail?"

"Brother Ahmed, I will allot an additional 250 fighters to the second attack zone. We will not be able to dig in an explosive there, for time and manpower reasons. But we will have explosive devices on the sides of the street, directed into the street. And we will have no fewer than fifty RPG launchers ready to fire simultaneously. The approach will be the same, once the vehicles are stopped. This is my plan."

"Your plan is good, Brother Ghazi. I believe that the explosives in your secondary attack zone must be at least 500 kg each, to be effective."

"Sire, such large explosives from the side of the street would collapse the buildings there, where my fighters will be positioned on multiple floors. I must limit those explosions to 100 kg each, which still jeopardizes the stability of those buildings. But I am confident that these resources will be adequate to kill the target, and hopefully all other members of the convoy as well."

"Very well, brother Ghazi. But your fighters must be prepared to be martyrs for the cause; the target must *not* escape, regardless of the cost."

"Sire, all of my fighters are prepared, and indeed wish, to become martyrs for our cause. Their skill and bravery will prevail in the battle. We will kill the chief crusader and his entire escort force. I am confident of this."

"Very well, brother Ghazi. Please return to your forces, and make plans to surreptitiously insert them into the battle zone. The excavation for the primary explosive must be commenced without delay."

"That task is well under way, Sire. The earth there is soft and porous; we should have no difficulty in completing the tunnel and explosive placement in plenty of time."

"Excellent, Brother Ghazi. I have clearly called on the right man for this task."

"Thank you, Sire. To victory!"

"To victory, Brother. Go in peace."

"*Enshala*, Sire."

Then Ahmed turned his attention to Hassan, responsible for the assault on Blue Diamond.

"And so, brother Hassan, what do you have for me?"

"Brother Ahmed, I am confident that my plan will lead to a resounding victory. We will overwhelm their defenses, open the gates, kill every living thing, destroy all their equipment, and video the most grotesque images we can devise, especially of ourselves lording over the severed heads of their leaders. By killing the foreign workers, we may succeed in ending their international recruitment of such traitors. If we have time, we will video their torture and killing as well; the internet will be teeming with such terrifying evidence of the consequences of opposing the true sons of Islam, Allah's chosen agents of The Religion of Peace. Finally, by collecting the personal effects of the foreign workers, we can identify and attack their families back in their home countries. We will teach them a lesson they won't soon forget, for siding with the enemies of peace."

Laughing, Ahmed responded, "Oh brother Hassan, you've clearly gotten into the spirit of this attack, and I like your ideas. But give me details of the assault."

"Yes, Ahmed. I will send five boats from the north and five from the south. Each boat will carry ten fighters. As you know, we cannot attack directly from the eastern shore because that riverbank is part of the infidel base Ar Ramadi. Those naval forces will eliminate the watchtowers facing the water with RPGs and rifle fire. They will then land, and immediately detonate explosives in five buildings I have selected near the water, to divert the enemy from the next assault, coming from the west.

"From the west, as soon as the explosions in the buildings near the river occur, we will launch RPG attacks of all the remaining watch towers. Fortunately, it is easy to see where these sentry stations are, and we have probed them many times. While all of those efforts have resulted in the martyring of the attackers, we have gained vital intelligence of the location and nature of their defenses. The towers contain machine guns of various calibers, and grenade launchers. I am confident that we can silence them all.

"As soon as the towers are neutralized, I will send five hundred men with grappling hooks against the four meter concrete wall that runs the thousand meter length of the camp. Most of them should successfully scale the wall. They will neutralize the infidels' Quick Reaction Force, clearing the way for 500 more men with ladders. The combined forces of up to 1,000 men inside the camp will then advance to the iron gates that close the north and south entrances to the camp. They will open those gates, blowing them up if necessary. I will have car bombs in reserve in the civilian areas within one kilometer of the camp, to move in to blow the gates should they not be opened from the inside.

"Once the gates are opened, my primary force will be divided into two, with seven hundred fifty men entering from the north and seven hundred and fifty from the south. They will enter via the gates, and commence the slaughter of the camp inhabitants. I have maps from the Saddam Government of the camp, and I have assigned teams of fifty men each to attack the larger buildings, and two hundred to destroy the area housing the foreign workers. If time allows, they will record the torture and killing of both the foreigners and the Marines. We especially want images of ourselves holding and laughing over the severed heads of their most senior leaders.

"For the women captives, we will reserve special treatment. We will strip them of their clothes, tie them down, torture them, and then rape them, all on video. In ancient fashion, we will then disembowel them. And finally, we will cut their heads. The propaganda value of the sons of The Prophet defiling the infidel women is inestimable.

"Very good, Hassan. And what of your reserves?"

"Yes, Sire, I will keep one thousand fighters in reserve. I will deploy them to four separate vacant areas within two kilometers of Blue Diamond, so that they can be summoned quickly if needed. I will keep them away from populated areas to reduce the risk of discovery by infidel spies in the town."

"Very good, Hassan. And what of your retrograde?"

"Yes, Ahmed, that is crucial to preserve this unprecedented mass of fighters, so they can live to kill the infidel yet another day. I will destroy the bridges that would allow reinforcements from Camp Ar Ramadi to reach Blue Diamond, allowing our forces to fall back into the city of Ramadi. They will enter houses in groups of three, and pretend to be residents of those houses. All who resist will be slain. They will then slowly withdraw, fading into routine city traffic, and return to their homes in other cities and countries. I will pay them in advance in cash, but they all know that, after being paid, any hesitancy in proceeding to the battle will result in instant death. I don't believe we will have a problem with cowards. I almost hope a few do try to desert—their immediate execution will be memorable to any others considering a similar course."

"Yes, Hassan. And how will you sever the bridges?"

At the beginning of the battle, I will have boats approach the western end of both bridges, because the supports are most vulnerable at those sites. The boats will each carry 1,000 kg of explosives. The drivers of the boats will martyr themselves. As backup, truck bombs driven by martyrs will attack the bridges immediately after the boats explode. They will detonate their charges anyplace they can once on the spans.

"Good, Hassan, very good. The bridges are helpful to our cause, but this operation takes precedence; I agree fully that the bridges must be sacrificed. The Camp Ar Ramadi Marines cannot swim their tanks and gun trucks across the Euphrates."

"It shall be, Ahmed. We shall achieve a spectacular victory, which will be remembered throughout Arab history. I can taste the sweetness already."

"Go in peace, dear Hassan. Assemble your forces. Time is short."

"So shall it be, Ahmed. *Insha'Allah*. When I see you again, we shall both be mythic heroes!"

"It shall be, Hassan. Go now."

Hassan turned and abruptly departed. *The complex plan was being passed down through the troops of fighters. Spirits were high. The killing would be so sweet. Not to mention the rapes...*

CHAPTER SIXTY-SIX

HOUSE FOR RENT

Sunday, March 27

The house on Edgewood was for sale, but the agent assigned to acquire it discovered from the realtor's website that it had been sitting vacant for eight months. She correctly surmised that the owner might rent it out for a reasonable rate, and besides, houses sell better when they're furnished, and the owner had removed all his furniture. When she requested a three-month lease, the owner countered with twelve months, and they settled on six. He wanted $1200 a month, which was a little high but reasonable, could readily be met by the Agency. But for the sake of realism, she quibbled it down to $1150. She insisted on immediate occupancy, explaining that she was in town with her family, and needed a place that same day. So within hours, keys in hand, she was strolling up the front walk.

The Agency provided her with a dented-up jalopy with lots of rust, to let her blend into the neighborhood. They rented some beat-up old furniture, and had it delivered the same day. Then the real work began; the technicians, dressed in scruffy old clothes and posing as the furniture delivery people, opened up their plain, battered cardboard boxes of gear and got to work.

A side window and the two front windows allowed a view of the target house, about eighty yards away. On the inside of the windows, innocuous-looking but high-tech panels that allowed only one-way viewing were installed. One pane had a small hold cut into it, through which a remote listening device was aimed. Plans for round-the-clock manning were devised, with most agents sleeping over to avoid too much foot traffic in and out. Groceries and cooking materials were brought in, and the place was livable. A conventional phone line was placed, and it was monitored with a device that could detect if it were tapped.

229

The agents didn't need to wait long. They had stumbled onto a dormant Al Qaeda cell, and its three members were confident in their anonymity, such that visitors made no effort to conceal their appearances or license plates. The phone was tapped, and a special device was brought in to identify the phone numbers of cell phones being used in the house. Subsequently, those cell lines were monitored as well.

The three Arab men residing there kept a low profile. They dressed in drab American work clothes, were clean-shaven, and kept to themselves, never interfacing with neighbors. Anwar Azizah was a twenty-six year old Egyptian, with a bachelor's degree in engineering, but who found no jobs in Egypt. Regrettably, all of the Arabic countries have flat or contracting economies, yet they continue to produce millions of young men yearning for useful activity. So they make perfect recruiting grounds for extremist groups, which promise them all the things they long for. What idle young man wouldn't be attracted by promises of money, purpose, travel, and the prospect of unlimited sex in the next life? The only drawback was the minor matter of dying for the ludicrous cause of forcing a 9th-century lifestyle on everyone. A lifestyle which was quite reasonable when it was dictated by its prophet some 1300 years ago. And which can be and is allegorically interpreted to guide a productive, harmonious, and fulfilling lifestyle in modern times, as most 21st century Muslims practice. But when interpreted by fundamentalists, every detail of ancient life needed to be replicated, regardless how impractical or superfluous to the spiritual content of the faith. Nevertheless, young men need to be busy, and Al Qaeda provided that outlet.

Mohammed Haneef, the second cell member, was an upper-class Yemeni, whose parents were technocrats in that otherwise primitive country. Having completed three years of study in political science, he was foolish enough to be recruited away from college and into the clutches of the extremists.

The third member was every bit as bright as his partners, but arose from much less auspicious means. A poor Algerian, son of a street vendor in Algiers, he had witnessed the brutal slaughter of fellow Algerians by militant Islam. But with no other future apparent for him, he was readily recruited by the flashy money and excitement of an international organization like Al Qaeda. Feiz Hadba was somewhat troubled by the barbarism and carnage routinely practiced by Islamists, but his concerns were overridden by the possibility of a ticket out of the poverty and drabness that was his life otherwise. He was willing to do *anything* to get anyway from that life.

Al Qaeda paid the three to live quietly together, and report in weekly on any obvious opportunities to wreak mayhem. But as a sleeper cell, the primary function of the group was to be available on a moment's notice, should a special target of opportunity appear. Reserve troops, as it were, paid to *be*, not to *do*. Since they ate well, got along with each other, loved American TV, and had access to all the porn they wanted, they were content with their lot. And, of course, the sense of mission, that they were achieving something beyond themselves. They didn't have women, but they each longed for the dozens of luscious virgins promised them when they died for the cause. Their brand of Islam is a puritanical religion for the living, but not for the dead.

Sleeper cells weren't supposed to know about each other, and certainly weren't supposed to consort, but living in an alien culture that you're taught to hate, and that you're required to remain aloof from, breeds loneliness. So these three had discovered the nearest two cells and, contrary to explicit orders, occasionally visited them or received visits. Fortunately for the Americans, these were not the most disciplined people on earth, and they were willing to break the rules for comfort. Those infractions led to their undoing.

The visiting cell that Nick and Hiram observed was from the other side of Nashville. But that group, likewise, occasionally violated the taboo, and visited its neighboring cell. Now that the agency had fingered two cells, they were to lead to seventy-two more cells across the east coast, and one hundred and fifty-six others spread throughout America. The manpower involved in tracing these monstrous people was staggering, but it was a virtual platinum mine to counter-terror efforts across America. The trigger for these momentous discoveries was the ill-advised threat made on the family of a lonely and unfaithful but otherwise strong-willed American woman living halfway around the globe. If the conflict of militant Islam with western values was one of ideas, it appears that the idea of threatening a mother with the murder of her children was a bad one.

CHAPTER SIXTY-SEVEN

PROLOGUE TO THE MOTHER OF ALL BATTLES: THE TRAP IS BAITED

Monday, March 28, 2005

The Marine Corps H-46 carrying the Bush Family look-alikes lifted off Baghdad International Airport at 1300h, as planned. Three identical aircraft took off together, to confuse any antiaircraft gunners as to which of the three held the VIP. The ruse called for escorting it with three Army Apache attack helicopters, and three USMC Cobra gunships. In addition, six USMC F-18s scrambled out of Al Asad Air Base about one hundred miles west of Blue Diamond. The jet jocks were elated over their orders to do what every fighter pilot's machismo motivates him to do: make a hell of a racket over the entire flight route, making frequent high-speed low passes over the flight route, impressing everyone with their bone-shaking roar. The gun ships frequently fired off brightly colored decoy flares, designed to deflect heat-seeking missiles. None of these features were SOP, so it was clear to even casual observers that something was up.

The flight to Blue Diamond was more erratic than normal, again emphasizing that this was not the usual Blue Diamond run. Besides, USMC helicopters don't usually fly during daylight hours, such that seeing them flying at all during the day was in itself unusual.

On landing at Blue Diamond, the decoys were hustled into a waiting van, and transported to General Brier's office. They camped out there, thankful that their duties were completed, and that robots rather than them would be inside the doomed gleaming black suburban sitting expectantly at the other end of camp.

Captain Kalopolis had his motorized mannequins carried up to the machine gun emplacements in plain military duffel bags. At each site, technicians were rigging them, being careful to keep the cammie netting tighter than usual, so enemy surveillance could not detect the ruse. Every attempt was made to make camp routines look normal, except for the VIP arrival. It wasn't usual for tanks to be inside Blue Diamond, because they were stationed across the river at Camp Ar Ramadi, but the five tanks had been secreted over five days earlier, before surveillance of the camp was likely to be intense. The presence of LARs and Strykers was routine, so the presence of those was unremarkable.

Captain Kalopolis's new machine-gun emplacements were unmarked, and thereby the plans for relocations of the .30 cal machine guns were undetectable. The .50 cals were too big and heavy for temporary placement, but they were removed from the towers to preserve them. Only light SAW machine guns were kept up in the towers; their loss would be trivial. All of them would be fired remotely, with their tracers assuring the enemy that the emplacements were active. What the enemy would *not* know is that the emplacements were unmanned.

The Marines manning the fighting holes were all in place, having slipped over the wall the prior night under the cover of dark, with flashing lights used to blind any enemy observers with NVGs. Then those Marines spent the entire day in their fighting holes, preparing for the most important battle of their lives. On the prior day, they had cleaned their weapons meticulously, deftly disassembling, thoroughly cleaning, lubricating, and reassembling the moving parts. All thirty of the selected men knew that they would be behind enemy lines, in great danger. But they trusted their weapons, their training, themselves, their buddies on the wall, their back-ups, and their leaders. If you had a warrior's spirit, this was the fight you wanted to be in. The misery of spending an entire day crouched upright in a small dark hole was trivial to these gallant warriors. They knew they were to remain in the protection of the cool earth, until they heard the Claymores fire. Then they would lift their sod-covered roofs, set them aside, lift their light machine guns onto the turf, barrels supported by the unfolded bipods, and open fire on the backs of the insurgents striving to scale the walls. Each man had four boxes of ammunition, each box containing one thousand, seven hundred and fifty rounds. So each Marine was prepared to launch seven thousand rounds of high-velocity bullets at the enemy. Each man wore a 9mm pistol as well, to facilitate his escape if he needed to abandon his fighting position too quickly to bring along his SAW. The plan was for the backs of those Marines to be protected by fire from the wall, shooting over their heads into any other insurgents approaching their positions.

The gunboats were being held behind cammie netting on both sides of the Euphrates, between Blue Diamond and Camp Ar Ramadi. They would launch at 1400 hours in their missions of protecting the bridges, and blocking any naval forces launched by the insurgents. The crews entered the boats at noon, doing last-minute checks of their vessels and their weapons.

Traffic to Barrage Bridge, at the south end of Blue Diamond, had been shut off three days earlier, under the guise of repairs. Iraqi traffic was confined to Steel Bridge on the north side of camp, and the plans allowed for its possible destruction by the insurgency some time prior to the assault. That it was still intact a few hours prior to the battle was simply good luck. All traffic was stopped at 1400h, with an announcement that it would be reopened at 1800h after completion of a structural inspection. Access to both ends was then blocked with the lateral parking of Amtraks fifty feet from each end; those vehicles weighed 29 tons each, and could not be pushed out of the way by an approaching suicide vehicle.

The Blue Diamond infantry force was reinforced by five hundred additional combat troops. And the five hundred Blue-Diamond-based military support personnel, from typists to truck mechanics, were all in battle positions, weapons loaded and in Condition One, ready for action at 1500 hours, more than an hour prior to the anticipated assault. Every U.S. Marine is, of course, highly trained and competent in combat arms, and all are excellent marksmen.

Matt and Christine were wearing their helmets and flak vests, pistols loaded, with their M-16s in their hands, and assigned to provide additional rifle support to the approach to the large palace used as the Combat Operations Center, housing Gen Brier's office as well as Matt's air office, as well as some twenty-five other offices, conference rooms, and communications centers. Matt and Christine were crouched inside a sandbagged bunker, rifles poking out over the top.

Furthermore, all Blue Diamond military personnel on board had been ordered the day before to check the fit of their gas masks and verify that the filtration canisters were current. So they all now had their masks bobbing at their sides, suspended by dedicated belts. Night vision goggles were mounted on top of their helmets, should the battle last into the night. At night, the goggles are rotated down in front of the eyes, the battery switched on, and night becomes an eerie green-tinted day to the wearer.

The advantage to the wearer over an adversary without similar capability is literally the difference between night and day.

The supporting aircraft were being fueled and armed. The Cobras were verifying the firing wires were attached to their rockets on both weapons stations, which look like mini-wings on each side. The F-18s were attaching two hundred and fifty pound bombs, eight on each wing. The F-18 can carry one thousand pound bombs, but smaller bombs are required in urban warfare, to minimize collateral damage. Two hundred and fifty pounds of high explosive is extremely destructive; some commanders wanted hundred pound bombs for that reason, but the U.S. inventory doesn't carry them.

The tankers were loading rounds in the chambers of their main guns, and assuring that their .50 cal and .30 cal machine guns were in combat readiness. The crews would be wearing their helmets and flak jackets, in case the enemy proved to have anti-armor capability. The Stryker and LAR crews were likewise verifying their weaponry was in perfect condition, and fully loaded. No Humvees would be manned for this event; all four would be operated by remote control, as would the black Suburban in the middle of the convoy. Uniformed mannequins were positioned in the turrets, with motorized arms moving about—the ruse didn't need to last for long. Spare ammo was carefully stowed aboard all manned vehicles.

At 1500 hours, all cell phone and ground line phone service in eastern Anbar Province was jammed. The huge battalion of 800 Marines of 1st Bn, 25th Marines, based in Devens, Massachusetts, moved out through the gates of Camp Fallujah, clambering on to the freeway toward Ramadi, and accelerating toward destiny. 2nd Battalion, 24th Marines, was already underway from Taqaddum Airbase, 100 miles west of Ramadi. The huge procession from Fallujah consisted of two M1A1 tanks in the lead, followed by four LARs, followed by twenty-five Amphibious tracked vehicles (Amtraks), which are lightly armored floatable troop carriers with two propellers poking out their aft ends, and each containing a dozen Marines in full battle load. Then came 20 seven-ton trucks loaded with Marines, sixteen in the bed and two in the cab, carrying a total of three hundred and sixty Marines. Throughout the convoy were scattered twenty-five gun-truck Humvees, each containing four Marines seated, and one standing in the machine-gun turret.

Finally at the back of the column were two more LARs, and two more tanks. Both columns had similar composition.

Overhead, the columns were each protected by four Cobra attack helos, as well as six high-flying USAF F-16s. Silently, ten thousand feet up, the columns were further protected by EA6 electronic countermeasures aircraft, equipped with massively powerful radio transmitters designed to jam radio signals in the region of the convoy which could otherwise be used to detonate IEDs in their paths.

An hour ahead of the convoys, three-vehicle convoys of Explosive Ordnance Disposal, or EOD Buffaloes, scoured the highway for IEDs, and were prepared to detonate any that threatened the convoy.

At 1530h, the VIP convoy began to form up on the main road inside Blue Diamond; two M1A1 Abrams main battle tanks in the lead, then a Stryker and an LAR, then two Humvee gun trucks, then the shiny black Suburban with black-tinted windows. Then the lead was repeated in reverse order: two more Humvees, a Stryker and an LAR, and finally three tanks bringing up the rear. A formidable array of power, although slightly less than it looked like: manned only by dummies, the gun trucks could not fire a shot .

At ten minutes to four, all guard towers at Blue Diamond were evacuated, and the mannequins were set in motion. Machine gunners and their weapons were positioned on platforms just under the crest of the wall on all sides, giving nearly the same protection as the abandoned facilities. However, they had somewhat decreased vision due to their lowered height, and were without their heavy .50 cals. The new stations could nonetheless see three hundred yards out, plenty to levy a withering fire on assaulting forces. From outside the wall, they were undetectable. And they had been constructed in such a way that they looked to Samir and any other spies in camp, like masonry work stations for routine wall maintenance.

At the stroke of 1600h, the south gates of Blue Diamond swung open, and the convoy slowly passed through the gates, weaving the requisite zig-zag through the Jersey barriers. The tanks inadvertently pushed a few of the barriers back while turning; the barriers were placed for tight-turning wheeled vehicles, not the much larger tracked armor, but no harm was done.

The aircraft hung back, wanting the insurgents to commit themselves, and hopefully putting many of them into the open.

CHAPTER SIXTY-EIGHT

THE NAVAL BATTLE OF THE BRIDGES

Monday, March 28, 2005

Snaking over Barrage Bridge, the convoy rounded the traffic circle in front of the JCC, and headed toward its destiny on Route Milwaukee. With the trailing three tanks still passing the mid-point of the bridge, the suicide boat just downstream commenced its high-speed run for the bridge, hoping to drop the two tanks into the Euphrates as it destroyed the bridge. A twenty-five foot whaler, it was low and fast, and not initially seen by the U.S. Navy gunboats of Boat Group One. But when its whirring engine sound drifted across the river, the Navy sprang into action. The Navy was on the west bank, and the insurgent craft running along the east, having correctly guessed where the bridge defense would be situated. The enemy craft was eight hundred yards south of the bridge, but approaching it at forty knots. Two of the three Navy craft pushed off shore and began racing to intercept. The third Navy Zodiac hit its prop on a rock as it accelerated too fast, dipping the aft end of the boat, and shredding its prop. That boat began to drift lazily downstream, although its guns were still alive. All three Navy craft opened fire with their .50 and .30 cal machine guns, hurling heavy steel slugs at three thousand feet per second at the explosive-laden speedboat. Bullets were kicking up water around the boat, and a few rounds struck its hull, but weren't stopping it. As the speedboat grew closer to the bridge, the unpowered Zodiac boat needed to cease fire, because its two sister ships were in its line of fire. Then a .50 cal slug found its way to the 300-horse outboard of the speedboat, and it immediately slowed from forty to fifteen knots, one of its six pistons having been knocked out of action when the slug fractured its piston arm, and decompressing a second cylinder.

With the speedboat slowed, the Navy boats were clearly going to be able to intercept the path of the crippled speedboat. They continued to lay withering fire on the enemy craft, which now yielded fragments of wood and fiberglass splattering into the air as the rounds found their mark. Of the two insurgents on board, one was at the helm and the other was standing at the bow, returning fire with an AK-47. Then one of the 240G .30 caliber gunners angled his course of tracers toward that man, and two bullets ripped through his right thigh, blasting bone fragments out the back of his leg, and causing him to collapse in the bow. But the insurgent was made of tough stuff, and got up on his knees and continued firing. Then one of the .50 cal gunners concentrated his tracers on the gunwale just below the man's head. The gunwale began to disintegrate as the fired walked from aft forward, toward the man, till the stream of bullets found their mark, and ripped his chest apart. The gunner was hurled backward, dead before he dropped his weapon.

Realizing that his crippled boat now could not achieve its objective of the bridge, the insurgent at the helm now turned his craft toward the Navy vessels, which took a few seconds to realize that they were now the target. The two boats separated, and concentrated their fire on the helmsman. Suddenly five rounds in succession ripped into his abdomen, and he was mortally wounded, his spinal cord severed at his waist. But as he fell, he reached forward to the trigger of his bomb, and pushed the button as he took his last breath. Instantly, every piece of his boat exploded in every direction with the massive force of one thousand kilos of dynamite. The deck above the explosion flashed on top of the fireball five hundred feet into the air. The driver's body ripped into hundreds of pieces, as did the entire boat.

Navy Zodiac One was fifty yards from the speedboat when it detonated, and Navy Two was seventy yards. The crew of Zodiac One all instantly suffered flash burns of all exposed skin in the direction of the speedboat, and all three were blown overboard, two knocked unconscious. The inflated sides of the vessel were punctured, and as the men hit the water, their boat began to settle in the water, sinking fast. Bosunmate 1st class Ronald Kinney, the skipper of Navy One, found himself dazed but awake in the water, and pulled the toggles of his lifejacket to inflate it. Looking around, he saw his vessel going down by the stern—he weight of the engine pulling it under. Then he spotted Bosunmate 2nd class Michael Glass, motionless and face down in the water. Ten yards further was Gunnersmate 3rd class Jose Virata, conscious but floundering slowly, barely keeping his head above water.

Swimming quickly to Glass, the Skipper reached underwater and pulled his toggles, immediately inflating his jacket and lifting his face up. Pulling Glass's face to his own, Kinney gave two quick breaths of mouth-to-mouth ventilation, and then swam over to Virata. Similarly inflating his gunnersmate jacket, Kinney verified that Virata was breathing, and then returned to Glass.

Checking Glass's pulse, Kinney confirmed the presence of a weak rapid pulse. And just then Navy Two was pulling up to them. Commanded by Chief Bosunmate Anita Bakeman, Navy Two crewman EM3 Eli Alexander and BN3 Audrey Howe also suffered flash burns, but they were not blown overboard, and their vessel was intact. Pulling Glass over the black rubber side, he remained unconscious. Then they noticed blood oozing out from his uniform in his right upper abdomen. They would later learn that the gunfire from the speedboat had struck Glass in the abdomen, but he never acknowledged his injury and continued firing. It was only at his autopsy that they learned he had suffered a fatal wound, with the AK slug passing through the portal section of his liver, mangling the huge blood vessels that congregate there—an untreatable injury. Glass lost his pulse en route to shore, not to regain it despite heroic CPR by his corpsman waiting on shore.

Navy Two then picked up Virata, who at this time was regaining his senses, and able to assist in his rescue. While performing recovery operations, BNC Bakeman was constantly scanning the water for a possible second saboteur boat, but none appeared.

To the north, upstream of Steel Bridge, Navy Four, Five, and Six were preparing to put to sea when they heard the high-powered engine of a boat at full throttle coming their way, headed downstream toward their bridge. The three craft accelerated to their peak speed of thirty knots, and headed to intercept the sound. They saw the speedboat after one minute, racing toward the bridge at forty knots. All three vessels opened up with their machine guns, and all three quickly found their mark. The engine of the boat took several rounds and began smoking dramatically, but was still running. Fragments of wood and fiberglass were kicking up all over the boat as slugs ripped it to pieces. The helmsman suddenly grasped his chest, where a .50 cal slug had ripped a large hold in his left side. As he fell, his body caught the ribs of the wheel, turning the boat violently to the left, causing it to flip into the air, then crash back upside down in a cacophony of white water. The insurgent on the bow firing his AK was hurled thirty feet in the air, still firing his weapon, but uselessly toward the sky. When the engine submerged, it sputtered to a stop. Suddenly the only sound was the purring of the Zodiacs' Evinrudes, and Chief Bosunmate Luis Reyes, commander of Boat Group 2, ordered all three boats to idle.

"Look around for more insurgent craft," he ordered his men.

"Aye, sir," came the response from Engineman Second Class Chad Gilbert and Gunner's Mate First Class Jimmy Wilkie, skippers of the other two boats.

Seeing and hearing nothing, Chief Reyes then realized that the explosive-laden craft was drifting in the current toward the bridge, now two hundred yards downstream.

"All boats one hundred yards to the west, flank speed," Chief Reyes commanded.

All three Zodiacs lurched forward and turned smartly away from the capsized speedboat. At one hundred and fifty yards from the target, Chief Reyes ordered all three boats to turn broadside to the target. As they did so, the sailors saw the insurgent from the suicide boat pulling himself up on to the capsized hull.

"That's a very ill-advised choice for him to make," thought Chief Reyes, even as he ordered, "Commence Firing!" This was simple target practice for the machine-gun marksmen, and Radioman Third Class Devin Jones and Aviation Ordnanceman Third Class Fernando Baez, the best sharpshooters of the lot, immediately walked their fire into the white hull of the capsized speedboat. The insurgent suddenly realized that he was in an unsafe place, and dived overboard. But his late decision was futile: after some hundred rounds had penetrated the hull, one of AO3 Baez's bullets found its mark in one of the ten huge duffle bags of explosives in the boat's hull locker. The boat exploded with the full power of its two thousand, two hundred pounds of dynamite, splintering into a million pieces, many of them hurling eight hundred feet straight up. The sailors all felt the intense heat of the explosion on their faces, and the shock waves knocked them all backward. Boat fragments began to land around the Zodiacs, and the men took cover. Then all was silent, save for the idling murmur of the three Evinrudes.

Knowing that the insurgent in the water was instantly killed by the blast wave, Chief Reyes considered not searching for his body. But since intel frequently comes from unexpected places, he directed BNC Steve Post, commander of boat 5, and Chief Gunners Mate Matt Gratton, commander of boat 6, to slowly motor toward the patch of burning gasoline and oil that marked the site of the former speedboat. EM2 Gilbert spotted the floating body of the insurgent, pulled him aboard, then looked and listened for evidence of another saboteur boat. Detecting no further threat, Chief Reyes, EM2 Gilbert, GM1 Wilkie, Chiefs Post and Gratton, as well as crewmen BN3 Ray Trentalange, Radioman 3rd class KJ Shuey, and Electrician Mate 3rd class Ayla Alexander, the victors of The Naval Battle of Steel Bridge, quietly motored their vessels back to the west shore of the Euphrates.

CHAPTER SIXTY-NINE

LAND ATTACK ON
THE BRIDGES

Insurgent Jamil Badani sat in his battered pickup truck in the civilian housing area seven hundred yards from the western entrance to Barrage Bridge. A native of Oman and a child of relative privilege, he had been recruited by Al Qaeda with the usual promises over his drab existence: money, travel, purpose, and religious zeal. And, of course, the tantalizing prospect of unlimited posthumous celestial sex with all the beautiful young women he could possibly lust for. Like virtually all militant Islamists, he also fell for the sucker line that the miserable state of affairs in his native Oman, and in fact in virtually all the twenty-two Arab nations, was not due to corruption, incompetence, and apathy of the elite over the plight of the peasantry, but rather was somehow a consequence of perfidy in the west. Not taught to engage in rational thinking, Badani never questioned why the fabulous wealth of the petro-rich Arab states never found its way to improving the lives of the millions of impoverished Arabs living in third-world conditions. He just swallowed the tired nonsensical line that all Arab problems were thrust on them from without, and that killing westerners would somehow abolish systematic official theft, greed, an interpretation of their religion that inhibits creative thought and invention, and the stunning vacuum of any sense of social covenant throughout the Arab world.

Regardless, here he was with 2500 pounds of high explosive in the bed of his pickup, covered over with tarps and some bags of flour. His duty was to get anywhere on the bridge, and blast it into oblivion. And himself, of course. He still had a few misgivings about leaving this life, just in case the virgins weren't truly waiting for him with open thighs, but now he was in what in a few minutes was likely to be an exceedingly hot seat.

Jamil watched the convoy crossing the bridge. His orders were to disable the bridge after the VIP target was en route to the kill zone, blocking reinforcements from Ar Ramadi from reaching the besieged Blue Diamond. So as the next-to-last tank was preparing to turn onto the bridge, he jammed down the accelerator and began racing toward the narrow bridge entrance, which at top speed, he could reach in about thirty seconds. Because the usual sentries were no longer atop Blue Diamond's south gate, and the new positions wouldn't peer over the wall 'til the assault began, the usual five machine guns atop South Gate remained silent, and Jamil unseen. As he drew within a hundred yards of the final tank, which was now commencing its turn, Staff Sergeant Dan Truax, tank commander and commander of the five-tank group, standing with his shoulders projecting out of the tank's turret hatch, glanced back, and saw the pickup racing toward him. There wasn't time to swing the main gun around, so he rotated his .50 cal machine gun to the side and began firing at the truck. The rounds walked their way up the road, kicking up little poofs of dust, until they entered the front of the truck. As they punctured the radiator, a cloud of steam arose, blinding Jamil from the view ahead. Continuing his fire, Staff Sergeant Truax trained his fire on the driver's location. Finding its mark, one round each shattered Jamil's left shoulder, then his chest, and then his right shoulder. Unable to see forward or to move his arms to hit his detonator, the pickup careened into the right rear side of the tank, imbedding sheet metal into the tread sprocket, but not exploding. Jamil sat motionless in the driver's seat, his head rolled back, lifeless eyes staring at the ceiling, blood streaming down from his shoulders and chest. It was a miracle that none of the .50 cal slugs detonated the bomb. The slugs had ripped through the flimsy sheet metal of the truck, but none found their way into the huge charge.

Not knowing whether the terrorist was stunned or dead, and not wanting to risk detonating any bomb present, Staff Sergeant Truax nimbly hopped out of his turret, scampered across the forward body of the tank alongside the cannon, shimmied down the front, and ran over to the truck. Unholstering his pistol as he ran to the pickup, assumed a double-hand grip with both arms extended, and fired three rounds into the side of Jamil's head.

The tank was now paralyzed, its right tread immobile, with a massive bomb that could blow the tank to oblivion embedded in its side. Staff Sergeant Truax looked back at the convoy, now proceeding across the bridge, but with his tank deleted from the rear guard. He immediately radioed Sergeant Yiro Matsushaka, tank commander of the tank in front of him, to inform him of his plight, and ordered Sergeant Matsushaka to assume command of the remaining four tanks in the convoy.

Then Staff Sergeant Truax radioed Blue Diamond to send EOD (Explosive Ordnance Disposal) to the site, and ordered his tank crew to abandon ship, opting to spare their lives should the bomb detonate. He didn't like leaving his fully armed tank unmanned, but he correctly assessed that his men were more valuable than the tank, and that, even if the tank were captured, the insurgents would be unlikely to be able to drive the tank or operate its weapons. So the crew quickly shut down the engine, abandoned the tank, and climbed on to the USMC Amphibious Troop Carrier, or AmTrak, that had pulled back to allow the convoy through. Since the tank was blocking access to the bridge, the AmTrak was no longer needed. It turned and headed back to Blue Diamond, the tankers sitting on it shouting for the gate to be opened as they approached. All the Marines escaped harm, but the bridge was out of service, blocked by the disabled tank.

On the north end of Blue Diamond, Steel Bridge glittered in the bright afternoon Iraqi sun. A nondescript gray panel truck with handwritten Arabic on its sides reading, "Zerkawa Plumbing" on the sides, pulled out from behind a house one kilometer from the east end of the bridge. Bouncing up onto the paved road, its 2500 pounds of explosives in the back caused it to ride low on its suspension. The driver, Abu Dahdah, a nineteen-year-old Tunisian, had said his prayers that morning, polished his shoes, and been videoed by his Al Qaeda handlers, a post-mortem gift for his parents. Suckered into killing himself with the usual dung-laden arguments, he was eager to do damage to those who had the temerity to believe that an Arab nation could enter the twenty-first century as a progressive, prosperous, free society. It never occurred to him that destroying the already scarce infrastructure of an Arab nation was an odd way to make progress. Instead he loved to hate, something all militant Islamists are quite good at. So here he was, ready to undo the diligent work of millions of man-hours of his beloved Muslim brothers, in destroying one of the few lovely and commercially critical architectural landmarks of this impoverished province.

Accelerating to sixty miles per hour, he knew there would be bridge defenses, but he and his handlers believed that stealth, speed, determination, and Allah's favor would allow him to slip through. He had already heard the boats detonating and seen the massive clouds of smoke from their bombs; he didn't know if the bridge was still intact. No matter: his mission was to hit the bridge, regardless of any other factor.

Two hundred and fifty yards out, Abu could see the entrance to the bridge. *DAMNED!* There was an armored vehicle sitting cross-ways at the access. And its turret gunner was staring at him, swinging his machine gun over toward him. Abu held the throttle down, thinking he might be able to get around the Amtrak and reach the entrance to the bridge.

Aboard the Amtrak, Sergeant Rich Young, vehicle commander, shouted to his crew to prepare for action. He pointed the barrel of his .30 cal machine gun at the approaching racing truck, and, per the ROE [Rules Of Engagement], fired a burst of five rounds into the road in front of it. He held down the trigger until at least one tracer round fired, so that the driver would know he was being shot at. Any innocent driver would instantly brake, and turn away. Anyone who continued toward a military vehicle shooting at him was likely an enemy, and was going to be engaged regardless.

Abu saw the Amtrak firing, but continued relentlessly on toward it, hoping to find a way to avoid it. He thought he detected a possible route around it to the right, although it looked like the road fell off sharply to the right, so it would be tight. Now the Amtrak machine gun was no longer in warning mode; it was firing directly at him. He heard the rounds penetrating the sheet metal of his hood, like a hot knife through butter. The windshield shattered to his right as four rounds passed through it, and on out the back door of the truck, shattering the rear windows.

The next burst penetrated the radiator, sending steam pouring out the front of the truck, but he was going fast enough that it didn't block his vision. The next burst shattered his half of the windshield and spattered a cloud of tiny glass fragments into his face. Instantly blinded in the right eye as a glass shard sliced through the entire eyeball into his retina, he could barely see out of his left as he began blinking uncontrollably, aware of sharp pain in that eye. Sensing a foreign body in the eye, Abu didn't know that he had four glass splinters sticking in his left cornea. Blinking through pain and blood from multiple forehead wounds, he continued toward the Amtrak, now only eighty feet away, and tried turning slightly toward the right. The next burst from Sergeant Young, at nearly point-blank range, walked four rounds upward, starting in the middle of his chest, then the base of his neck, then shattering his chin, and the fourth crashing straight through his forehead. With the driver now dead, the truck careened to the right of the Amtrak, and overturned on its right, rolling down the hill.

While the truck was rolling, Abu's lifeless shoulder by chance impacted the detonator and the massive bomb exploded. The Amtrak was lifted straight up by its nose and thrown upside down. Sergeant Young was still standing in the hatch when this happened, and tumbled out as the 10-ton vehicle was at its apex of roll. Falling straight down onto the road, Sergeant Young never saw the massive armored vehicle crashing down on him, crushing him like a bug. The driver, Corporal Larry Libby, in his tiny cubicle inside the armor of the vehicle, came down heavy on his head on the ceiling, severely spraining his neck, but his helmet protected his skull from injury.

The loader, LCpl Brendan Pecha, standing in the open compartment of the cab of the Amtrak, fractured both his forearms when the vehicle crashed upside down, but his injuries were non-lethal. The engine was still running, so Libby and Pecha opened the hydraulically activated large hatch aft, then shut down the engine, and stumbled out. They correctly identified the location and fate of Sergeant Young.

The bomb blast had discolored the superstructure of Steel Bridge, but because it was still fifty feet away, the bridge remained structurally intact. The Amtrak had catapulted off the road. Some of the road had been blown away at the approach, but the primary bomb crater was some forty feet down the hill, and enough of the road was preserved for the reinforcements from Ar Ramadi to reach Blue Diamond when they were needed.

CHAPTER SEVENTY

THE BATTLE OF ROUTE MILWAUKEE

First Lieutenant Melissa Brooke, in charge of the remote movement of the four Humvees and the Suburban, was situated in the belly of the Army Stryker in front. The Stryker's crew were all Army, but 1st Lt Brooke's four USMC crew, Sgt. Josh Elrod, Corporal Ivy Rosal, LCpl Chance Edison, and LCpl Reverie Dune, were working the joysticks for the Suburban and 2 forward Humvees. In the second Stryker, in the rear of the convoy, sat 2nd Lieutenant Jim Quinn, commanding Lance Corporals Charles Nadeau and John Harr operating the aft two Humvees. All the controls were working flawlessly, as they needed to for the ruse to work. It would be a disaster if one of the Humvees veered off the path and stopped. Marines never leave a vehicle alone, so when no Humvee came to assist the stricken one, the insurgents would know that they'd been had. *Thank God for reliable electronics*, Lt Brooke thought.

The convoy had now negotiated the deserted, rubbish-strewn traffic circle at the end of Wisconsin Avenue, and the lead vehicles were passing the JCC, with its four cammie-net covered machine gun emplacements on its roof.

"Hold steady, hold steady," whispered Kamal al-Mur in Arabic to his radioman crouched beside him. They were peering out the third-floor window of one of the buildings fifty yards past the kill zone. The radioman repeated the instructions over the air, where it was received by four different radiomen accompanying their commanders.

Kamal was chagrinned to see the tanks, but not surprised. For the chief executive of the most powerful nation on earth, such formidable escort vehicles would not be excessive. He was relieved that he had successfully procured anti-armor missiles, and whispered to his radioman to order them into action as soon as the primary bomb detonated. Kamal was relieved to see only two tanks in front, and two in the rear. He had sixteen anti-armor missilemen, twelve in Kill Zone 1 and 4 more in KZ2. each with three rounds, so he was prepared.

The tanks clanked toward him, both passing over the subterranean 220-pound bomb reserved for the Suburban. Kamal was relieved that he had found the digging so easy, that he had buried no fewer than four 220-pound bombs in the kill zone. He had four separate triggermen, and now dispatched orders for the other three bombers to take out the tanks if possible, but for nothing to blow before the Suburban.

The lead tank commander, Staff Sergeant Mark Lesavage peered through his telescope at the barren streets before him. Months before, Route Milwaukee had been ruled off-limits to all civilian traffic, which struck the death-knell for all the businesses on this street, so it became totally deserted. He saw the gaping hole in the second deck of the building on his left, where Col Burdine's AT4 missile had eradicated the heavy machine gun emplacement. *Eerie*, thought Sergeant Lesavage. *I hate this place. With luck, we'll be in the protected courtyard of the CMOC fifteen minutes from now.*

KA-BOOM! A hundred kilo's of TNT erupted under the Suburban, and the entire vehicle was thrown fifteen feet into the air. The explosion readily penetrated its armored floor, and incinerated the entire interior of the vehicle. All its windows blew simultaneously, and all six doors blew off their hinges in a microsecond, along with its hood and three of its four wheels. The flaming wreck crashed back down onto the street, right-side up, but it was clear to the insurgents that there were no survivors inside that red-hot maelstrom.

Then the street erupted into chaos, as no fewer than a hundred RPGs whooshed across the street from both sides, crashing near and into the remaining vehicles. All four Humvees were hit immediately, and all four turret mannequins blown out of position. Small arms fire began crackling from six hundred AK muzzles, and a second volley of RPGs crashed into the convoy.

KA-BOOM! The lead tank was lifted up on its right side, it's tread instantly converted into hundreds of pieces of jagged shrapnel moving outward like bullets. The tank crashed back down on what remained of its right tread. All the crewmembers were stunned, and Sergeant Lesavage was knocked unconscious. None of them could hear anything—a loud ringing sound replacing all of their hearing. While outside the battle raged around them, they didn't yet know that their tank was disabled. What they did know was that they were still alive, and that the tank's cab hadn't been penetrated by the massive explosion. Sergeant Lesavage had directed the driver to steer to the left of center of the road, and that was why they were alive—the bomb detonated some ten feet to their right; had they been directly over it, the inside of their tank would look like the inside of the Suburban.

"Good Lord," shouted Sergeant Peter Young, commander of the second tank. "They whacked Tank Alpha. Driver, steer over toward Tank Alpha—there won't be any more IEDs there." Sergeant Young pressed the button to rotate his tank's turret and point its massive 5-inch cannon at the battle ranging behind them. He immediately saw two insurgents with anti-tank missiles racing toward the tank. When they saw the turret turning toward them, they both knelt at thirty yards out and aimed their weapons. They both fired as Sergeant Young got his .30 cal machine gun aimed at them and commenced firing. BAM! The first missile struck the angulated portion of the turret and ricocheted off, exploding harmlessly in the air just above the turret. BAM! The second missile struck the angled underside of the tank, and deflected into the road below, exploding harmlessly beneath the tank's thick belly. Tat-tat-tat-tat-tat-tat-tat-tat-tat, rattled Sergeant Young's .30 cal, as he raked his fire across both of the still-kneeling missile men, killing both instantly. Driver Frank Polanowski and gunner Jack Cahn both rose to the occasion with expert maneuvering and marksmanship.

What Sergeant Young didn't see was two more missile men kneeling to shoot him from his left side, but Sergeant Lesavage had awakened from his concussion. He had a vicious throbbing headache, but he was back in the battle. Rotating his turret around toward the battle, he saw two missile men taking aim at Tank Two. With two quick bursts from his .30 cal, he dispatched both missile men. The Marines didn't know it, but that was four anti-tank missilemen down, six to go.

The tanks now began to rake the buildings on both sides of the street with their .50 cal machine guns. Sergeant Lesavage ordered the right side battery of four grenades to be launched; two were smoke grenades, and two anti-personnel fragmentation devices. They fired fifteen meters, pre-aimed in a spread, crudely aimed by rotation of the turret. When the other armored vehicles saw the smoke, they immediately launched half of their own grenades. Suddenly the roadway was filled with ferocious, razor-sharp grenade fragments and vast clouds of smoke. Everyone who wasn't inside armor was wounded or killed. Twenty-eight insurgents immediately fell dead, and thirty-five were injured, out of the fight.

Suddenly a heavy machine gun opened up from the second floor of the building to the left of the kill zone. Sgt Young rotated his turret, and ordered his gunner to fire. The front wall of the building where the machine gun was sited, erupted outward in a massive roar, the tank round having penetrated the brick, then detonated behind it. Both tanks now fired repeatedly into the buildings, extinguishing all life within the target rooms and adjacent ones, and leaving gaping holes in the facades.

The LAR's primary weapon is a 25 mm [one inch, or 1.00 caliber] cannon, capable of firing two rounds per second. The rounds can penetrate two consecutive masonry walls, so as the two LARs raked the buildings on both sides with cannon fire, they also didn't need to aim for the windows: the huge exploding 1-inch rounds made their own windows, and raised havoc inside every room they penetrated as they spread fragments throughout the rooms.

Tank three, commanded by SSgt Mohammad Haji, was driving in circles, bringing its guns to bear on multiple targets, and striving to confuse the aim of enemy missilemen. Driver Sgt Jesse Christy expertly wove figures of 8 on the battlefield as gunner Cpl Sawyer Lara and loader LCpl Terry Michele fired their .50 cal and intermittently their main cannon. But despite Sgt Christy's evasive maneuvers, two anti-armor missilemen drew beads on tank 3 from inside buildings on opposite sides of the street. The shot from the missileman on the north side struck the sloped side of the turret, and ricocheted up to the 3rd floor of the opposite building, where it detonated, killing six insurgents and wounding four. But the missile from the south side found its mark, striking just under the turret, where its shaped charge burned through the heavy armor and detonated in the cabin. Tank 3 blew up with a monstrous roar and a tower of fire ejecting its turret. Tank 3 was dead.

The forward Stryker, commanded by Staff Sergeant Jerome Goldberg, U.S. Army, was likewise engaged in strafing the buildings with its .50 cal machine gun. Furthermore, the Stryker gunners were firing their Mark-40 40 mm grenade launchers, which fire 1½-inch grenades like gunshots, accurately within a 100 yard radius. No tracers were needed, the rounds were large enough and slow enough that the gunner could watch them in trajectory, and walk his fire toward the target. Aiming for windows, the grenades were killing or disabling nearly everyone in every room they penetrated. Insurgents were spared only when a co-conspirator absorbed fragments between them and the exploding grenade. These two devastatingly effective weapons, operated by only the two Stryker gunners, Cpl Corey Teryn and SSgt Declin Griffin, accounted for 41 enemy dead, and 68 wounded.

Knowing the anti-armor risk, Staff Sergeant Goldberg's driver was driving erratically around the battlefield, confusing the enemy gunners – that is, the ones able to concentrate enough to aim, despite the smoke wafting throughout the battlefield. Explosive 1-inch rounds from the LAR chain guns were detonating everywhere, while .50 cal and .30 slugs from the tanks and Strykers zipped through the air from multiple angles, and the terrifying grenade-launching machine guns on the Strykers continued their lethal WHOMP-WHOMP-WHOMP.

Nevertheless, Stryker Two shuttered with a BAM! An RPG ripped into the right front second tire and detonated, shredding the tire. But the Stryker has seven other tires, and each tire has a hard rubber rim inside its center section that can help support the vehicle even when it's pneumatic portion is perforated and deflated. BAM! Another RPG ricocheted off the curved turret, exploding harmlessly two feet away as it careened upward. POP-POP-POP! A burst of insurgent 12.7mm machine gun fire ripped through the Stryker, virtually amputating the left arm at the elbow of its loader, Private Arun Chaudhury. Private Chaudhury pulled the CAT tourniquet from his shoulder pocket, which every military member in Iraq carried in the same place. Using his teeth, he threaded the tourniquet around his upper arm, and pulled it tight. Then twisting the binding peg, he extinguished the flow of blood, secured the peg so it couldn't unwind, and attempted to return to reloading the .50 cal machine gun – but a one-handed man was practically useless for this demanding task.

Lieutenant Quinn and his corporals, now without duties since their remote-control vehicles were all destroyed, came to his aid—all U.S. Marines are trained in Combat Life Saving.

Fifty cal magazine boxes weigh eighty pounds, and must be hoisted up to the outer surface of the vehicle, via an open hatch. The receiver of the gun must be opened, the first round in its break-away linkage must be placed in the groove, and the receiver closed and secured, before firing could recommence.

Private Chaudhury couldn't lift the box or open the gun's action, but he advised his crewmate, Corporal Raven Metzger, who was doing the heavy lifting. First they positioned the .50 cal magazine and got it firing. Then they called for the 40 mm grenade box, which weighs ninety-five pounds. Passed up to them with great difficulty because of the constant swerving of the vehicle, they were securing the gun's action when an AK round impacted the helmet of Corporal Metzger, causing him to instantly lose consciousness and fall back through the hatch he was standing in, but the Kevlar held and his skull was not penetrated. Private Chaudhury, supervising Metzger despite his injury, wasn't as lucky. The same burst that hit Corporal Metzger sent a round through the middle of his neck, and another through his upper chest. With his last conscious effort, Private Chaudhury locked down the action of the M-40, then fell back through the hatch, unconscious. He bled out through his wounds within one minute, and was gone.

Meanwhile, the driver of Stryker 2, Cpl Sam Hagadone, decided to utilize the agility of his vehicle as a weapon. Seeing missile men kneeling fifty feet ahead of him to fire at the tanks, he gunned the engine and caught the one on the right with his four-foot high wheels, running over the insurgent with all four tires, each bearing more than a ton of weight. The insurgent's body squirted blood out on both sides as he was crushed like a grape, and was left a flattened mass of flesh. The second insurgent was hit by the body of the Stryker, knocking him down and forward. He lost his missile tube, which was bent by the impact, and thought he would survive intact under the high body of the Stryker, but his left arm flailed out and was crushed mercilessly by the left third and fourth wheels, removing him from the battle.

All four Humvees had now been penetrated by RPGs and were afire. Teams of insurgents approached each one of them, lobbing grenades through the broken windows, and then raking the interior with rifle fire. In the smoke and confusion, they never realized they were shooting mannequins.

In the rear, Sergeant Matzushaka, commander of tank 4 at the back, was raking the buildings and the battlefield with his .50 cal, and his loader Sgt Chin Lo, was doing the same with the .30 cal. With the turret aimed forward, they couldn't see the two RPG missilemen running toward their rear. Knowing the vulnerable part of the M1A1 to be its radiator system, they aimed their missiles from forty feet out, and launched. One hit just to the right of the radiator screen, and detonated harmlessly on the heavy armor. But the other found its mark, readily penetrated the steel screen covering the engine cooling system. It detonated inside the engine compartment, instantly causing red caution lights to illuminate in the driver's compartment and forcing him to shut it down for fear it would come apart and kill the crew.

"Sergeant Matz, the engine's hit!" shouted the driver. "I'm shuttin' it down!"

"God help us, Sean! Okay, okay. Do it! Do it! We still got electric power?"

"Yeah, electric's okay, Sarge."

Sergeant Matzushaka rotated the tank's turret, and saw the two RPG wielders running back toward a doorway on the left side of the street. Firing his .30 cal, he walked his fire up behind them, but they disappeared inside the doorway.

"Main gun, take out that doorway," shouted the commander.

The gunner deftly aimed the gun, and confirmed, 'Main gun ready!"

"Fire, fire!" responded Sergeant Matzsushaka.

The huge cannon boomed, and the entire room inside the doorway exploded. Sergeant Matzsushaka didn't know it, but he had blasted a room full of RPG rounds, and an enormous secondary explosion followed the tank round by one second, immediately collapsing the building onto twenty-four insurgents spread across the three floors, and a third of all the RPG rounds prepositioned for the battle.

The LAR in front of the tank whirled around in time to see four more missilemen taking aim at Sergeant Matzsushaka's tank. Raking the area with his .30 cal, vehicle commander SSgt Jody Ossermen and his gunners Ian Watson and Ingridatio Neri dropped two of the insurgents. The first took two rounds to the back and dropped, but the second took a bullet into his anti-armor round, and it exploded in its tube, blowing his head clean off and killing two other insurgent riflemen nearby. But the other two launched; one impacted the sloped upper portion of the heavily armored turret, and exploded harmlessly as it richocheted upward. But the second found its mark in the crevice under the turret where the turret meets the body of the tank. Burning its way through the heavy steel, the round penetrated into the cab of the tank, showering molten steel throughout the cab, and violently overpressurizing the cabin. Sergeant Matzushaka and his loader were killed instantly, and the gunner was severely injured with shrapnel throughout his left side, from his ankle to the edge of his helmet. The driver, Cpl Sean Donovan, forward from the main cabin, was untouched, but dazed and deafened by the explosion. Calling to his crew but getting no response, either because of his impaired hearing or their incapacitation, Cpl Donovan sensed he was in big trouble, trapped in the middle of a raging battle with the crew probably dead and a tank without an engine. Looking back at the grotesquely postured bodies of his dead crewmates, he opened his driver's hatch on the forward body of the tank and clambered out. Before Donovan had even reached the edge of the tank, he was under fire by twenty insurgents sheltering in the buildings. Immediately hit by ten rounds, he was dead before his body rolled off the tank onto the road. An insurgent then jumped on top of the tank, opened the hatch, and threw two grenades inside. Jumping aside, the grenades roared with a puff of smoke followed by a huge roar and a massive cloud of smoke and flame as the main cannon rounds cooked off, and the entire turret blew 20 feet into the air. Tank Four was dead.

LAR #2's driver, Cpl Marion Briggs, was driving wildly in circles, firing at the buildings, when it drove directly over the third buried bomb. KA-BOOM! The bomb erupted, and a massive fireball penetrated the floor of the cab, incinerating the crew and initiating a series of secondary explosions as live rounds cooked off. The main hatch blew open, and fire erupted from the hatch, as the LAR blew itself apart inside.

At this point in the battle, the insurgents' primary goal was accomplished: all passenger vehicles were destroyed and all occupants killed. Two tanks were destroyed, and their crews dead. One LAR with its crew was dead. But Kamal knew that his VIP target may not have been where he expected; he might be in one of the Stryker or LARs, or even one of the surviving tanks. He needed a complete kill. He radioed his commanders to press the attack on all surviving vehicles, regardless of cost. The VIP *must* be killed!

Meanwhile, the Cobra gunships arrived overhead. Having previously divided up the battle zone into sectors to avoid mid-air collisions, Captain Slava Lesser in Cobra 1 and 1st Lieutenant Paul Gaufberg in Cobra 2 set about pouring fire into the insurgent positions. Their 20 mm cannon (.80 cal) rattled as the huge slugs arced toward the enemy. The Cobras immediately cleared the rooftops, killing twenty-three insurgents, and wounding another fifteen. Twelve other insurgents were killed, and nine disabled, on floors below the roof, as the .80 cal slugs penetrated deep into the buildings. But the Cobras couldn't shoot into the street where the missile men were still hunting the armored vehicles, who were now largely on their own.

KA-BOOM! The fourth and final buried bomb exploded as the lead LAR drove ten feet beside it. The explosion blew off all four wheels on its right, and flipped the vehicle over on its roof. The crew were battered but functional, and rushed to the aft hatch, hoping their Stryker would come for them, which it promptly did. Backing up to the upended hatch of the LAR, both vehicles opened their rear hatches at the same time, and the bruised and partially disoriented LAR crew of three hobbled into the Stryker, which immediately lurched forward to avoid RPG and anti-tank fire, raising its rear-wall steel hatch as it maneuvered.

As Stryker 1 pulled away, LAR 1 was hit by no less than seven RPG's, three of which penetrated its skin and set off multiple internal explosions. LAR 1 was dead.

At this point, the remaining vehicles knew the ruse was complete, and that they needed to get out of the kill zone. Their losses included 2 tanks and crews, and both LARs with one crew, as well as the uncrewed Humvees and Suburban. The convoy now consisted only of one intact tank, one disabled tank, and two Strykers. Knowing they couldn't extract the remains of the dead crews while under fire, SSgt Young advised Stryker 1 to streak away out of the kill zone. Sergeant Young was unable to speak to Sgt Lesavage in tank 1 because of loss of its antennae, but he directed his driver to pull up behind the right rear of tank one and begin pushing it. As soon as Sgt Lesavage felt this motion, he order his driver to drive straight ahead. With power on its left track, and a push from its right rear, both tanks exited Kill Zone 1. A shower of RPG's rained on them, with a dozen hits, but because the anti-armor missilemen and their weapons had been killed, the RPG's couldn't penetrate the Abrams' thick skin, and both tanks clanked away from the holocaust.

Kamal radioed his commanders in Kill Zone One to cease fire, and immediately begin withdrawal of his force into the town. He hoped that his VIP target had been inside one of the destroyed vehicles, as he ordered his Kill Zone Two force into action. And he had no idea that the entire region of his huge force was being surrounded that very moment from the south by 800 crack Marines of 2nd Battalion, 24th Marines.

The Cobras hadn't broken off, and continued to pepper the buildings with their .80 cal cannon, wreaking havoc on the surviving insurgents and periodically setting off caches of weapons in large secondary explosions. Even after the remains of the convoy broke off, the Cobras killed another twenty-four insurgents, and wounded sixteen more. Their losses were horrendous, but the surviving insurgents had no idea that their troubles were just beginning.

On command from Lieutenant Colonel Jack Brusch from 2/24, the Cobras broke off, to avoid fratricide. But before departure, Cobra One identified a large concentration of at least a thirty insurgents in a single building. Calling to his USMC fast-boy colleague in the F-18 15,000 feet above him, Cobra One gave the precise GPS coordinates of the building. Captain Deanna Rundell, USMC pilot of the F-18, punched in the coordinates on her #1 250 pound smart bomb, and launched the weapon. All her bombs were fitted with delay fuses, allowing them to penetrate multiple floors of the target building before detonating, enhancing the likelihood of collapse of the target building. The bomb whistled away, its electronic brain adjusting the fins on the tail of the bomb, guiding it with awesome accuracy to the roof of the three story building harboring no fewer than thirty-four insurgents on the first floor.

Easily punching through the roof and the top two floors, the bomb detonated as it entered the ground floor room where the insurgents were congregated. With a blinding flash and a terrifying BOOM, the bomb shredded the bodies of every insurgent in the room and blew out all four walls. Then the entire building collapsed in on their mangled remains. A huge cloud of dust emanated from the pile of rubble which had been the building, which Kamal could see dejectedly from his command post a hundred yards ahead.

Back on his radio, Kamal commanded his lieutenants of his Kill Zone One force, "Disband, disband, do not congregate, we are under surveillance from the air. Melt into the community! Move!"

With prodigious stealth, the Marine battalions surrounded the insurgent zone, without the insurgents realizing their dilemma. Early on, while the Marines were moving into their positions, some thirty insurgents in small groups, striving to leave the area early, encountered the Marines, and, not knowing the Marines' strength, made the mistake of opening fire on them. The Marines answered with deadly fire, killing them instantly. Those shots went unnoticed in the din of the battle still raging on the convoy route.

Now the noose was in place: the area was completely surrounded with a huge, highly trained force of disciplined, coordinated warriors, wielding the best weaponry in the world. Standing orders were to arrest, or kill anyone resisting arrest, in the target area. Every Marine carried three sets of cheap lightweight disposable plastic handcuffs to accommodate.

Of the initial force of 750 insurgents attacking the convoy at Kill Zone One, 172 were dead, and 197 were injured, of whom 102 were unable to evacuate the battlefield. That left 483 fighters in full retreat, thinking they had survived the battle, but were about to enter the belly of the beast.

Back on Route Milwaukee, the battered remains of the convoy pressed on, hoping to reaching the CMOC in 10 minutes, unaware that they were about to enter a second kill zone. They had lost one both LAR's and 3 tanks, one back at the bridge, and one of the surviving 2 was crippled, with no right tread. The limo and all 4 Humvees were gone, of course, but none of them contained defensive firepower anyway. The surviving Strykers were intact but a bit crowded with LAR2's crew aboard. 70% of each vehicle's ammo had been expended. And they had seriously wounded. They needed to get to shelter, medical care, and resupply, and fast.

Tank one was now again lead vehicle, but was being pushed from its right rear by tank 2. Stryker 1 followed. All of the crewmen's hearts sank when the massive bomb in Kill Zone 2 erupted 10 feet to the left of tank one, ripping off it's remaining tread, and lifting up its left side 5 feet, then crashing back to the road. What little gear remained on top on the left side —jerry cans, some crew packs, the grenade launch tubes, were all blown away. But the armor held. The crew inside were severely traumatized, but no skulls fractured despite all 4 heads crashing into metal inside the cabin, saved by their "cranials", or special tanker helmets. The driver, Cpl Jack Brickley, suffered a left arm fracture, and the commander, SSgt Mark Lesavage, fractured his left femur and was totally incapacitated, in early shock. The gunner, Sgt Morgan Mahn, had bilateral knee, hip, and back pain from the sudden lift of the floor, but no fractures. The loader, Cpl Ram Stevens, was knocked unconscious. And they were all suffered multiple contusions from the violent motions of their vehicle. Stunned but conscious, they peered out of their tiny viewports and saw insurgents swarming into the streets, many of them with RPG's and four anti-armor missiles.

Manning his machine gun in pain in his now-immobile tank one, Sgt Mahn began raking the battlefield in front of them with his .30 cal machine gun, dropping 23 insurgents and scattering the rest. 4 missilemen went down, but 5 more scampered out of range with their weapons intact. Tank one rotated its turret right and began engaging the buildings directly lateral to them. Stryker One immediately drove close past the bomb crater, knowing there was no bomb there, having been "cleared" by the first one and began raking the battlefield with it's .50 cal and .30 cal machine guns.

The three intact vehicles knew that tank one was in huge trouble, but it was firing it weapons, so it wasn't dead. Without comm with its antennae blown off, there was no way of knowing if the crew suffered serious injuries. Staff Sergeant Young in Tank Two decided to once again try pushing tank one out of the new kill zone. With his turret swiveled left to shoot at the buildings opposite them, Tank Two's driver was ordered to close with Tank One in its center rear and strive to push it, now on no treads at all. So with the machine guns and main cannons of all 3 vehicles raking the battlefield, the convoy sought to exit the kill zone. RPG's were arcing everywhere. They detonated on the tanks' thick skin harmlessly. Thus far they had deflated two tires on the Stryker, but the vehicle remained highly mobile. Many RPG's and a few anti-armor missiles struck the tanks and the lightly armored Stryker, but they all impacted at an angle and glanced off. The defensive fire was taking its toll. The tanks' grenade launchers were blown away, but the Stryker now launched all of its remaining grenades. Detonating in rapid succession, 22 insurgents suffered lethal injuries, and 32 were wounded and out of the fight. The one-inch guns and tank cannons were wreaking havoc on the insurgents inside the adjacent buildings, killing 42 insurgents and wounding 78.

Miraculously, tank one began to roll forward as tank two pushed it, even as its steel wheels rolled off its now-ruptured tread and began cutting into the blacktop of the road. It had gone another 10 yards, and it looked to Tank Two like salvation was at hand, when disaster struck. RPG's were bouncing off both tanks harmlessly, and at least 15 missiles missed them clean. But the law of averages caught up, and two separate anti-armor missiles crashed into Tank One just seconds apart, from opposite sides. Burning violently through the thick armor, both missiles penetrated into Tank One's cabin, killing all four crew members instantly, and detonating two stored main cannon rounds. Like Tank Four earlier, Tank One's turret blew twenty feet straight into the air, and all the other cannon rounds detonated, creating a burning inferno that became the funeral pyre of Tank One's crew.

SSgt Young ordered his driver to back up, and hastily pull around the hulk of now-dead Tank One. Gunning the engine, Tank Two exited the kill zone 10 seconds later.

An RPG struck Stryker One broadside, penetrating its one-inch armored relatively thin skin, but because it had been fitted with chain-link-fence-like outer protection, designed to cause shaped charges to detonate before they touched the armor, most of its warhead was expended before it entered the cabin. Cpl Metzner inside the cabin took much of the force into the rear ceramic chest plate of his body armor. Fragments of molten steel and shrapnel burned through his clothes below the vest, and embedded in the flesh of his buttocks and calves, but they were not lethal or even crippling injuries. Stryker One's commander suffered burns and minor shrapnel injuries, as did the driver, Cpl Patrick Mazilla. The fabric of Mazilla's vest caught fire, as did some paper and cloth items inside the cabin, but Cpl Harr manned the fire extinguisher and knocked out the fires within a minute. The other crew suffered minor shrapnel and burn wounds, but were saved by the simple chain-link fence outside the vehicle which muted the force of the RPG.

The Stryker commander saw Tank One blow up, and Tank Two racing forward, so they all immediately changed course to follow in its track, knowing there were no bombs in that path. The diminutive remains of the convoy sped out of Kill Zone Two after a frightfully lethal battle that lasted only 8 minutes.

American losses from The Battle Of Kill Zone Two included one tank and its crew, one dead in Stryker 1, with moderate injuries to 3 other crewmembers. A few .50 caliber rounds had penetrated both Strykers and LAR One, causing shrapnel injuries to every crewmen, and peppering their goggles with metal fragments, but the ballistic goggles held, and the eyes were spared, even though the periorbital region of 4 crewmen was dotted with tiny shrapnel wounds. Sgt Elrod from LAR One had a .50 caliber round penetrate his right upper arm missing the bone, and much of the velocity of the round had expended in penetrating the armor, so the arm was not laid waste. Corporal Rosal and LCpl Edison had minor shrapnel wounds. 1st Lt Brooke and LCpl Dune were unscathed.

Insurgent losses from Kill Zone Two were frightful: 44 dead and 63 wounded, of whom 38 could egress the battlefield. So of the 1,000 enemy combatants in the combined battles, 377 were uninjured, and half of the injured were able to join the retreat of the survivors of The Battle Of Kill Zone One.

At this point, the retreating enemy combatants totaled 558. 442 of their cohorts were left dead or dying on the battlefield.

Frightened, fatigued, and low on ammunition, but believing they had probably accomplished their mission, the retreating insurgents looked forward to melting into the town. They were utterly unaware that their fighting for the day was far from over. Slowly, as pockets of retreating insurgents encountered Marine ambushes, none of the insurgents had reason to believe that those Marines were part of a vastly larger force. Accordingly, all of the retreating insurgents chose to fight rather than surrender. Battles broke out in batches, but the tides were turned; this time the Marines were the ambushing force, and the insurgents were the ones marching unaware into the kill zones. On all four sides, as the insurgents strived to disappear into the community, they found themselves walking into kill zones of converging fire set up by professionals in combat arms. The Marines laid out classic ambushes, taught in every professional military school in the world. But the insurgents were largely untrained, and their retreat was not under command of those who were. Brave but now disorganized and poorly disciplined, willing to trust that the God for whom they murder would protect them, the retreating insurgents were cut down in their tracks.

Kamal was attempting to escape to the northwest, accompanied by his radioman and four of his senior leaders. As they walked into an alley, they heard an the voice of Company Commander 1st Lt Alex Reiser shout, "Halt, drop your weapons." The same was then repeated after one second in perfect Arabic by the Marines' 'terp. Kamal had run in to Kilo Company, 24th Marines, every member of whom was itching for a fight with the shadowy fighters who had killed and maimed a number of their mates on patrol. There would be no sympathy from the Marines of Kilo Company. And Lt Reiser's Marines were sensing payback time.

Kamal raised his weapon and fired a burst in the direction of the voices, simultaneously dropping to a crouch, and quickly moving over against the adjacent stone wall. He had no way of knowing that this alley was selected for ambush, and that every square inch of it was covered by the weapons of Kilo Company. Kamal's group split into two, all members crouching against the walls on either side of the alley. But they were hiding from no one.

Kilo Company's one hundred and twenty-eight Marines were divided into four platoons, each consisting of two or three squads of thirteen. Each Squad consisted of three fire teams, and each fire team had a Squad Automatic Weapon, or SAW. This light machine gun fires the same round as the M-16, but at a rate of 200 rounds per minute. So Kilo Company had forty light machine guns in this fight, as well as two heavy machine guns, the .30 cal (7.62 mm) 240G version.

Unfortunately for Kamal, he chose the precise alley that 2nd Lieutenant Del Ritchheart predicted would be a fruitful ambush site for retreating terrorists. And of Lieutenant Ritchhart's ten SAWs, three of them were covering the two spots that Kamal's group chose to "hide." Incidentally, but quite superfluously, so were one of the 240Gs and four of the Marines with M-16 grenade launchers, as well as fifteen other Marines rated expert marksmen with their M-16s. So it wasn't a fair fight; but then it's a long-standing Marine maxim that Marines *never* engage in a fair fight.

Virtually every weapon with a shot opened up simultaneously. Kamal's body was impacted by thirty-eight rounds within the first five seconds, splattering his brains, lungs, guts, and bones all over the wall behind him. His radioman received only fourteen rounds, but with similar results. On the other side of the alley, Kamal's four lieutenants were peppered with M-16 and .30 cal rounds, and didn't live to feel the exploding 40 mm grenades detonating all around them. After a total confrontation time of twenty seconds, all was silent. The smoke in the alley drifted slowly away, revealing tiny streams of bright red blood flowing from both sides of the alley toward the center. Kamal had coordinated his last attack on Americans. His radioman had made his final call. The lieutenants had issued their final orders. And the world was rid of six more scourges and impediments to democracy and peace.

And so, except for forty-two lucky insurgents who individually crept through the Marine lines while leaving their weapons behind, the terrorist force was completely eliminated. In the end, only one hundred and twenty-nine prisoners were captured, many of them grievously wounded. The remaining eight hundred and thirty-some terrorists were killed in action. The Second Battalion, 24th Marines, with eight hundred Marines, lost four dead, fourteen wounded. The convoy had lost thirteen dead and fifteen wounded, with bridge and naval losses of 2 dead and 8 wounded. With a kill ratio of roughly 47:1, the U.S. commanders were satisfied with the outcome of the battle.

CHAPTER SEVENTY-ONE

THE MOTHER OF ALL BATTLES: ASSAULT ON BLUE DIAMOND

At ten minutes to four, the machine gun emplacements were abandoned atop the guard towers of Blue Diamond. Thirty feet up on the huge masonry structures overlying the steel gates of North and South Gates, no sentry eyes now looked down on the camp perimeter. Eighty feet above mid-station, atop the massive masonry gate built by Saddam to separate the workers from the royal zone, there was silence. The five towers built into the eight hundred-yard western wall, and three towers on the eastern side to guard the Euphrates shore, all were, for the first time since conquest of the camp a year earlier, unmanned.

Staffing all these sites 24/7 with disciplined, highly trained marksmen is no inexpensive matter: security in a war zone isn't cheap. The Blue Diamond security force for perimeter defense alone consumed one hundred and thirty men, all of whom needed to be paid, housed, fed, and receive services of water and sewage, laundry, post office, recreation, gymnasium, firing range. Freedom isn't free.

The security personnel assumed their new positions on the "wall repair platforms." They remained invisible from the outside and, even if Samir saw them, his cell phone was jammed so he couldn't alert the assault forces outside the walls. The machine gunners were assisted in lifting up and positioning the sheets of Kevlar-lined plywood that would protect them from shrapnel from the expected aerial bombardment.

The assault forces were congregating in the concealed streets of Ramadi. Locals saw the huge numbers of heavily armed insurgents, and shut their doors and shutters; this wasn't their fight, and the sooner the fighters moved on, the less likely they were to draw American artillery and aerial bombs to their neighborhood.

The insurgents' orders were to wait for the sound of the convoy attack, and to then simultaneously attack every guard tower with RPGs and rifle fire. Accordingly, the RPG missile men were in the front, ready to march into position. Predicting a hit with only one of every five rockets, the insurgent planners had assembled their largest assault force ever seen in Iraq, with no fewer than fifteen missile men per guard tower, each with five rounds for his weapon. As soon as the first barrage of RPGs arced toward the towers, insurgent snipers would open fire on the Marines in the towers. Furthermore, to paralyze relief operations to the towers, and cause general confusion and destruction, rockets and mortars would be fired in quantity to cover the entire base. Nazir Hassan had assembled thirty three-inch mortar tubes, each with ten rounds, and one hundred four-inch, six-foot long rockets, each with a thirty pound explosive warhead. As the towers were being neutralized, they would launch their aerial bombardment, followed promptly by their infantry assault from the river and from the west simultaneously. The aerial bombardment would terminate when the walls were breached.

Inside the "wire," as the perimeter of U.S. bases if referred to, every military member and contractor was at General Quarters. The TCNs were herded into the chow hall, which with its 3-foot thick roof covering of earth, would provide cover from aerial bombardment, and the four-foot thick Hesco barriers surrounding it would arrest shrapnel from nearby ground hits.

Samir was distraught to hear Marines walking through TCN Village, knocking on every door, awakening the shift workers still rubbing their eyes, softly ordering all TCNs to report to the chow hall double time. Grabbing his emergency bag containing a Marine desert cammie uniform, he slipped away toward the Euphrates shore. Miraculously, he was not seen by any of the ready forces, since any one of them would have dispatched him if they saw him with his cell phone.

Hastily dialing Alquieri, he was even more distraught to find a dead phone, with the words, "no signal" appearing on the screen. After trying four times and changing his location slightly each time, Samir was beginning to understand that the smile he had been sporting throughout the afternoon in his hooch was fatuous at best. His dreams of promotion to a senior position in the insurgent hierarchy, and ultimately in the trans-national Caliphate, were now dissipating into the clear light of day. He was beginning to realize that he had become the Marines' bitch, their sucker, induced by his own narcissism into not constantly questioning his situation. He was intensely humiliated, and getting angrier by the second. Suspecting an imminent bombardment, he stole away to the huge motor pool garage, knowing it would be abandoned during combat, and would make a good hiding place with its heavy, protective masonry. Removing his civilian clothes, he slipped into the Marine uniform, complete with collar devices of a Sergeant Major and sewn-on name, "Rodriguez" above its right breast pocket, "U.S. Marines" above the left. Then he sat down to plot his revenge.

KA-BOOM! The massive 220-pound bomb that instantly destroyed the expensive armored Suburban on Route Milwaukee sent reverberations of its destruction in all directions at seven hundred and fifty miles per hour. Every member of the Blue Diamond force heard it, and it sent their hearts pounding: they knew that the defining moment of their lives was approaching. And every insurgent felt he was hearing his very own Shot-Heard-Round-The-World, and danced with anticipation of an Arab assassination of a U.S. President, and a first-ever insurgency capture of a U.S. base in Iraq. "Allah Akhbar, Allah Akhbar," was whispered throughout the throngs of thousands of assembled fighters. They would have been less joyous had they known of the rude reception that lay waiting for them, courtesy of the United States Marine Corps.

On cue, one hundred and thirty-six RPGs arced toward the guard towers; four were duds, but were quickly replaced in their tubes with live rounds. As expected, only twenty-five hit close enough to compromise the towers, but the nine successive salvos resulted in two hundred more hits. Captain Kalopolis' lieutenants fired off their pre-planted charges whenever an RPG hit his tower, confirming the kill to the insurgents' scouts.

In ten separate locations around the base, insurgent mortar and rocket stations commenced their bombardment of the base. Because much of their equipment had been destroyed in the past with counter-battery fire from the massive Paladin artillery aboard Camp Ar Ramadi, fully half of the mortar men and rocketeers were using PVC pipes for launching tubes; their accuracy suffered accordingly. The rockets whooshed away, carrying their deadly payload at six hundred miles per hour. Because of their flat trajectory and the narrowness of the base, however, fully two thirds of the rockets either impacted harmlessly on the outside of the walls, or passed over the base entirely and exploded harmlessly in the Euphrates. Portions of the perimeter wall were holed by the rockets, and a few were large enough for a man to crawl through. Some fifteen houses in Ramadi were inadvertently impacted, with the civilian occupants suffering twenty-eight dead and fifty-four wounded.

Thirty-five rockets successfully impacted the base, however, and their deafeningly loud explosions frightened even the toughest Marine. The TCNs were terrified, and hid under the dining tables in the chow hall, but they were well protected. One rocket hit a Hesco outside, showering the area harmlessly with the dirt inside it. The computer-filled huge COC, a former large palace, took four hits, two on the roof and two on the walls. Small portions of the roof collapsed, destroying the offices and computers beneath those areas. Additionally, two walls were holed, with the warheads damaging offices and starting fires inside, but the building held. Thirteen Marines concealed in bunkers were injured with shrapnel, four of them seriously.

The mortars had six rounds to every one of the hundred rockets, and the ten-pound mortar warheads began raining down on the camp like hailstones in an Oklahoma thunderstorm. TCN Village took ten hits, destroying forty of the two hundred housing units, and starting fires. Three rounds detonated on the chow hall roof, frightening even further the TCNs huddled inside, and causing great clouds of dust to spew into the dining hall from the seams of the plywood ceiling, but the sturdy roof held. The medical clinic's masonry roof was holed by two hits, and one Navy Hospital Corpsman was killed, four injured. The trailer-style officer housing area took eight rounds, destroying twenty-two units, but all the occupants were in hardened structures elsewhere on base. Some shrapnel penetrated the Kevlar/plywood shields protecting the perimeter defense force, killing one Marine and disabling eight. But there were four men to each position, and all guns remained manned. Two of the shower/toilet units prized by the Marines were destroyed, irritating the Marines but harming no one. The rec hall with its big-screen TV, ping-pong and pool tables, internet cafe , and paperback book library, was destroyed, its roof collapsed and interior devoured by fire. That *really* irritated the Marines who saw it burning.

As the last of the ten volleys launched, Zeeshan Husaini, commander of the attack, ordered his troops bearing grappling hooks forward. Five hundred men leaped from their hiding places and ran screaming toward the wall five hundred yards in front of them. Simultaneously, the river craft, five each from upstream and downstream, commenced their runs toward the base. The boatmen were distraught to see both bridges standing intact, despite water- and land-borne attacks on them.

Out in the areas devoted to the five hundred insurgent reserve forces, spirits were high. The fighters were eager to join the fray, and earn their reputation as the first Arabs to overrun a U.S. base. And they longed to be able to brag that they had personally killed Americans. But they couldn't hear the distant drone of the Prowler unmanned aircraft fifteen thousand feet above them, controlled by a USAF Sergeant Steve Cavalio in an obscure building on Camp Victory in Baghdad.

The Sgt Cavalio and his team were operating the high-definition telescopic video cameras, and had been mapping the accumulation of reserves all day. So now they called in their Army colleagues with the exquisitely accurate, massive 155 mm cannon emplaced at Ar Ramadi, and gave the coordinates. To achieve surprise, Lieutenant Colonel Brendan Carroll directed that his six huge Palladin cannon would fire on the same target simultaneously, raining their eighty pound high-explosive rounds down simultaneously. At Site One, a three-acre construction site, the reserves were standing about holding their weapons when the WHOOSH of the approaching rounds appeared. Having never faced artillery before, the fighters never knew what hit them; four of the six rounds exploded within one hundred yards of every fighter. The other two rounds were two hundred meters away, but were fused to detonate fifty feet above the ground, so their razor-sharp shrapnel ripped into some of the fighters despite the distance. Of the hundred and twenty-five insurgents at Site One, thirty-four were killed outright and forty-two injured. So half their force was removed from the fight with the Palladins' first salvo. The Army gave Site One another volley for good measure, and the rounds detonated over many insurgents leaning over their wounded comrades, killing another dozen and wounding twenty-eight. So of the force of one hundred and twenty-five at Site One, the first minute of battle resulted in forty-six dead and seventy injured, leaving eight fighters of the original one hundred and twenty-five. The insurgents hadn't yet learned that amassing troops in the open, within range of artillery and opposing an enemy with eyes in the sky, is a recipe for disaster.

The Palladins were then guided sequentially to the other three areas of reserve massing. Some of the areas were near civilian residences, but there was no choice; this was a fight for survival, so the Palladins boomed away. It was not the decision of U.S. commanders to bring residential areas into the fight; that was all insurgency doing.

Of the five hundred reserve fighters, one hundred seventy eight were killed and one hundred and twenty-nine injured. Radio communications from other sites alerted the final targets to move immediately, saving their fighters. Even so, much of their ammunition was destroyed when it was left behind in the artillery impact zone. Fortunately, the Palladin gunners were having a banner day, and negligible civilian casualties occurred.

Then Col Carroll's Palladins turned their attention to the amassed forces six hundred yards west of the Blue Diamond western wall.

Zeeshan Husaini had wanted to wait until the gates were opened for his primary force to move forward, but when artillery shells began to rain down on his forces he ordered them forward, knowing the Palladins couldn't engage targets close to Blue Diamond.

As the first wave of insurgents with grappling hooks passed the concealed Marines in the fighting holes, they began to trip the land mines, never having suspected such weapons might be there. With land mines going off the entire eight hundred yard length of the wall, Captain Kalopolis depressed the transmit button to detonate the Claymores. With a terrifying roar, the thirty Claymores fired simultaneously, hurling their ball-bearing missiles at fifteen hundred feet per second, shredding any flesh they touched, dropping forty-five insurgents in their tracks.

Then the machine gunners on the inside of the wall lifted their guns and ammo feed boxes to the crest and opened fire. The insurgents were in the open, and the fire was relentless. The wall gunners had waited until the insurgent line was within fifty yards, careful to keep their fire away from the fighting hole Marines, just one hundred yards out. Markers, visible from the base but not from the town, alerted the gunners to the 50-yard distance.

Ordered by radio to engage, the Marines in their fighting holes lifted their sod roofs, set them aside, hauled up their SAWs, and opened the bipods on their barrels. Still blinking in the daylight after twelve hours in the holes, they opened fire on the backs of the insurgents approaching the wall.

The insurgents dropped in waves, screaming as their bodies were shredded by the tiny but extremely high-velocity .223 caliber rounds of the twenty-five SAWs on top of the wall, and thirty behind them. They barely knew what hit them. Only forty-two of the five hundred managed to close the distance to the wall sufficient to hurl their grappling hooks and grasp the wall, but fifteen of these fighters were killed as they climbed up.

Twenty-seven actually made it on top of the wall, because three Marines manning the wall had been killed, and eight wounded—the insurgent snipers six hundred yards back had scored. Five of the twenty-seven that scaled the wall were killed as they shimmed down the inside of the wall, and twenty-two raced for the gates, eight for the North and fourteen for the South. All were cut down before they had scampered a hundred yards. The first wave of the siege had been annihilated. Every one of the five hundred were down, three hundred and seventy-three of them already dead.

Zeeshan could see that his plans were coming undone. But at this point he needed to either retreat or advance—the artillery was forcing a decision. He didn't know it yet, but retreat was no more viable an option than pressing the attack, because he had the entire First Battalion, 25th Marines with air, armor, and artillery support, behind him, and the un-breached wall of Blue Diamond before him. Seeking the glory of victory, he pressed forward, which, with the information available to him, was an imprudent decision. But it wouldn't have mattered anyway.

Meanwhile, the twenty tanks at Ar Ramadi were leading convoys of gun trucks and LAR's toward the battle, Half the group commenced its run across Steel Bridge on the north side, and half across Barrage Bridge on the south. First Lieutenant Jimmie Thompson, commanding Tank Group 2 to the south, peered across Barrage Bridge and winced when he saw the tank blocking the bridge exit, paralyzed on a quarter-turn posture. But he was aware of the awesome power and bulk of the steel monster encasing him, and resolved that he could deal with the obstruction. Traversing the bridge at high speed, he commanded his driver to impact the motionless tank on its aft end, pushing its butt sideways. Then rapidly executing a two hundred and seventy degree turn, he rammed the tank broadside, severing its left tread and mangling its runner wheels, but shoving the tank backward five feet, giving a small but adequate clearance for the other vehicles to pass. Miraculously, the insurgent's 1,000 kg bomb in the truck embedded in the tank's tread, did not detonate during these violent maneuvers.

Looking forward, Lieutenant Thompson observed an enormous wave, ten men deep, of insurgents charging at Blue Diamond, three hundred yards to his right. The insurgents were coming from his left and dead ahead, as far as he could see down his right to the western wall of BD. Directing his driver to charge into the insurgents on his left, knowing his armor was immune to the machine gun fire emanating from the BD walls, he ordered his other tanks to likewise charge at the insurgents, one tank per thirty yards. That formation of ten tanks engaged the left third of the wall of advancing insurgents.

Seeing several insurgents charging directly at him with anti-armor tubes on their shoulders, Lieutenant Thompson ordered both machine guns and the main cannon to engage them. Simultaneously, the two machine guns began to chatter, and BOOM, the main gun fired dead ahead into the bellicose humanity. Pointed slightly down, the tank round burst with a huge crash among the wave, knocking down thirty men, half of them permanently. The machine guns were mowing down rows of insurgents, whose return fire cracked and banged on the armor impotently. The tank was also taking friendly rounds on its rear, doing no harm, but most of the rounds from BD behind them were passing by them and knocking down insurgents.

Peering to his right, Lieutenant Thompson could see his other nine tanks rushing into the insurgent lines just as he was. The insurgents were terrified to see these massive war machines bearing down on them, but many were unable to get out of the way, and a dozen men were bowled over by each tank, many falling under the tracks, never to rise again. Then turning back toward the insurgents who had now passed them, the tanks turned and again raked them with machine gun fire.

The LARs saw the tank maneuver and joined in, alternating bulling through the lines, and turning to rake the masses with machine gun fire.

Four emplacements of grenade launchers had been positioned on the wall, and they were firing continually, arcing their 1½ inch grenades into the masses. With their kill radius of five yards and wound radius of fifteen yards, their range of a half mile, and their rapid fire of one hundred and twenty rounds per minute the Mark-19 grenade machine launcher was a ferocious weapon: lethal to enemy infantry, but irrelevant to the friendly armor in its target area.

Meanwhile, on the river side the ten boats each bearing twenty fighters, bore down on Blue Diamond, five from upstream and five from downstream. As the insurgents cleared the bridges, U.S. Navy Boat groups 1 and 2, with fresh crews, sortied from their shores, eager to join the fight yet again. Group 1 had lost two boats in the Battle Of Barrage Bridge, so one boat from Group 2 moved over to 1. The insurgents on the boats were more formidable adversaries than the speedboats had been, however, and the twenty AK-47's on each boat opened up on the Navy craft. A heavy machine gun was emplaced on the bow of each insurgent vessel, and these ten weapons engaged the Navy vessels immediately. The Navy boats were essentially matched in firepower, but vastly outnumbered, ten to four.

In Group 1, Bosunmate 1st Class John Wei was coordinating his two vessels. Respecting the heavy machine guns on the insurgent vessels, he opted to engage them and remain at a hundred yards distant, counting on the superior accuracy of his gunners over the insurgents. Bosunmate 2nd Class Ira Greene,on Boat 1's .50 cal, walked his fire into the second insurgent vessel, and saw bits of the boats frame splintering as his heavy slugs penetrated both sides of the enemy boat, and penetrating some of the insurgents' bodies as well. Greene saw the gunner on the insurgent boat slump, dead of a .30 cal burst from his shipmate BM3 Jesus Virata. Greene then concentrated his fire on the aft part of that boat, and after several bursts, he saw flames shoot up as his rounds penetrated the outboard of the boat, and its fuel caught fire. Dead in the water, that boat was out of the fight and couldn't reach Blue Diamond, so he moved his fire to the third insurgent boat.

POW-POW-POW! Greene's shield in front of his .50 cal deflected three rounds of someone's accurate fire. ZING, ZING, rounds flew by over his head. Hearing a gasp, he looked over to see Virata holding his belly, where a round had passed under his shield and through his abdomen. Boat One's .30 cal was now out of action, but the .50 cal stinger was still very much alive.

Suddenly Greene felt the boat lurch to the right, and he looked back to see BM1 Wei fall backwards overboard, blood spurting from his temple. Greene was forced to abandon his gun, run to the helm, and steer away from the insurgents. Navy Boat One was out of the fight.

Aboard Boat Two, Gunnersmate 2nd Class Butch Kranz on the .50 cal had engaged insurgent boat one, and trained his fire on the larger threat of the bow gunner. Kranz succeeded in splintering the enemy boat's bow, but didn't hit the gunner, who was directing his fire at Navy Boat One. Concentrating his fire on the bow again, Kranz saw the entire bow at the waterline disintegrate under twenty hits, and the boat pitched forward as water rushed into its hull. The bow gunner was ejected over the front, eliminating that threat. Kranz then trained his fire on the helmsman and engine. He saw several insurgents drop their weapons and clutch their bodies as they fell, victims to Navy fire from himself or his mate Engineman 3rd Class John Dawson on the .30 cal. Finally he saw the helmsmen grasp his thigh and fall to the deck, and the insurgent boat veered to its right, giving Dawson a clean shot at its engine, which he now engaged with two long bursts of ten shots each. The housing of the engine splintered, a belch of flame and smoke shot out, and the engine stopped. Insurgent Boat One was out of action.

But just as Dawson killed the insurgent boat engine, he heard a number of rounds impact his craft's rubber gunwale, and the rushing air of deflating rubber. Seeing the problem, the helmsman, Bosunmate 3rd class Virgil Post, immediately turned away from the insurgents, downstream, and prepared to abandon ship with his crew. Navy Boat Two was out of the action. The remaining three insurgent boats continued toward Blue Diamond.

From the north, both Navy boats of Boat Group Two were likewise knocked out of action, with two of the six crewmen killed and the other three wounded. Group Two had disabled only one of the insurgent craft, although they had killed five and wounded eight of the remaining forty fighters speeding toward the shore of Blue Diamond.

With the insurgent boats still pressing their attack, the Blue Diamond shore stations now opened up on them. As with the other walls of Blue Diamond, the ruse had been used on the river side, with guard towers occupied only by mannequins, who dutifully died with the early insurgent RPG bombardment. But the real perimeter guard was very much alive and in force, only at a lower level. So now the perimeter guard opened up with everything it had—five .50 cals, eight .30 cals, and three grenade launching Mark 19's. The exposed insurgent boats were negligible matches for the dug-in and battle-ready Marines on shore.

Three of the seven insurgent boats took hits from grenades, killing twenty-four fighters and wounding eighteen. The machine guns were ripping through the boats as well, and three USMC 124 mm mortar crews were now raising huge geysers of water with massive BOOMs near the boats. The lead boat took the bulk of the initial fire, and, its waterline pierced by forty .50 cal rounds, began to settle into the water while it was still one hundred and fifty yards out. Like most third-world citizens, the fighters couldn't swim, but even if they could they were weighted down with more than fifty pounds each of military hardware, so as Boat One went down, all twenty fighters on board went down with their ship, like rocks.

Boat Two was gallantly fighting back, its bow gunner firing at the source of the tracers arcing toward him. He severely wounded two Marines before a devastating fusillade from ten different machine guns riddled his body with hits, and he lay suddenly still behind his gun. The insurgents on board the boats were hiding under the gunwales, but the lightweight craft offered no protection from even the .30 cal rounds, much less the .50's. The hulls would have stopped the .22 cal rounds of SAWs or M-16s, but none of these lightweight weapons were being trained on them. Most of the insurgents aboard Boat Two were already dead or wounded by the time its engine was silenced, and it drifted slowly downstream toward the bridge. With its motion predictable, the mortar crews could walk their fire into it, which they did immediately, and Boat Two disintegrated with a direct hit after three progressive near misses.

Insurgents commonly employ less-than brilliant tactics, but they don't lack for courage; despite the withering fire facing them, and seeing their sister vessels maimed and sunk, they doggedly continued toward their objective.

On shore, the Marines followed protocol, and expertly changed out the barrels of their machine guns after every box of ammo was expended; if not changed, the barrels would melt from the intense heat generated. The barrels have wooden handles to prevent hand burns, but, as usual, two Marines in their haste grasped the barrels directly and severely burned their hands through their heavy leather gloves. But the Marine batteries continued firing, and one by one the attacking boats were ravaged, and either sank or lost power, only to be destroyed by mortars as they floated helplessly downstream. The grenade launchers continued to land murderous rounds inside the boats, causing frightful carnage aboard every boat.

Finally it was over: every attacking boat was sunk, either directly by machine gun fire, or by the violent explosions of the mortars. Every one of the two hundred fighters was dead—those who survived the gunfire abruptly thudded to the bottom of the Euphrates when their boats went down. The naval attack on Blue Diamond was history. Except for the killing and wounding of a dozen brave sailors and Marines, for the insurgency it was an abysmal failure. The shore defense stood.

Zeeshan was overwhelmed; the Marines seemed to have anticipated his every move. They seemed ready for precisely this attack. Far from being compromised, the Marines on the perimeter fought like lions, and their weapons and ammo functioned flawlessly. Zeeshan began to realize that he was the victim of a sting operation—a massive, complex, brilliantly executed sting that induced the insurgent leadership to gamble way beyond their means. The annihilation of his attack force was unfolding before him. And he suspected that the attack on the convoy had suffered a similar fate. *There never was a VIP visit,* he realized. *It was all a hoax. A perfect, irresistibly tempting hoax, that caused us to lose all our forces in a single battle.*

There was nothing Zeeshan could do at this point to win the battle. His forces were being mowed down in their assault phase. The bridges were never blown, so armor and other reinforcements poured over from Camp Ar Ramadi. Enemy artillery knew where his reinforcements were, and shredded them. All he could do was retreat, and try to salvage some of his forces.

Zeeshan ordered his radioman to transmit the order to retreat at once, and melt into the portion of Ramadi city on the west bank. Little did he know that a full battalion of battle-hardened Marines—800 of America's finest—had taken up fortified positions in the city behind him—there was no place to go. So the remains of his force, some five hundred men, reversed direction and ran for the residential areas they had come from. But his troops were still falling from the fire pursuing them from BD, as well as the armor and some twenty Humvee gun trucks now pursuing them as well. Thinking they were nearing sanctuary, the surviving insurgents were overwhelmed with grief to see concentrated fire suddenly erupt from the housing area two hundred yards in front of them. They were doomed. One hundred and thirty insurgents, realizing there was no hope of escape and not fully trusting the virgins-in-the-sky hype, lay down, abandoned their weapons, and prayed for survival. The remaining three hundred continued to advance toward the housing, shooting forward but still taking fire from their backs. Every single one was cut down by a combination of mortar, machine gun, grenade, tank cannon, and M-16 fire.

Suddenly the battlefield went quiet, except for the pathetic cries and weeping of the wounded.

CHAPTER SEVENTY-TWO

RESPONSE IN CONUS: NICK AND HI SEE ACTION

Monday, April 4, 2005 (or several weeks later) 9 AM

"Okay, Nick, this is the big one. We earned this. Good thing Mel saw it our way: we found these slimeballs, and we get to bring 'em in."

"This is gonna cancel out all the missed dates, sleepless nights, and misery of sittin' in this beat-up old Ford looking at your ugly mug. This is gonna be sweet, Hi."

"Okay, buddy, the deal is, we go to the front door to serve the warrant. This is even sweeter, because the bitch Fatima is here—we get to take down all four of 'em."

"It doesn't get any better than this, Nick. But let's stay alive, while we're at it. No sense gettin' killed taking down garbage like these pricks. These mil vests will stop most types of rounds, but they don't cover much of us. When we get to the door, we'll stand to the side, announce the arrest, and be prepared to hit the deck. We have twelve SWAT agents here—four out back, two on each side, and four on the street behind us. Hope they don't whack us in the crossfire."

"I trust these guys. They're seasoned vets. Know how to control their fire. They're the team to have playing on *your* side. And Gloria, Betty, and Waseema are as tough as any of the guys. I wouldn't want to cross any of those three.

Gloria Sanchez was a thirty-five year-old Mexican-American mother of two, in perfect physical condition, and more fun than a barrel of monkeys—she knew more jokes than the others put together, and knew how to tell them such that you were nearly incontinent with laughter, even if you're heard them before. Betty Gude was an exceedingly attractive thirty-six year-old African-American mother of three, tough as nails when dealing with perps, but soft and feminine in her personal life. Waseema Mazarraf was a 27 year-old Sunni Muslim native of Pakistan who grew up from age 8 in the U.S., and was enraged by the violation of her faith's fundamental tenets by the Islamist terrorists of the world. Tender mother of one toddler child, she was an accomplished martial arts expert, and a crack marksmen in pistol and rifle. Lighthearted most of the time, she turned deadly serious when it came to her professional life. FBI women are in a league of their own.

"The M-16 round's muzzle velocity is three thousand feet per second, whether the trigger is pulled by a big hairy finger, or a dainty little one. You're just as dead when it hits you, either way."

"Ouch, Hi. Remind me to duck if those M-16s open up. With twelve agents shooting, that's three hundred and sixty rounds before they need to change magazines. That's a lot of steel flyin' toward the house. And us."

"You don't need to convince me, bro." Checking his watch, "OK, buddy, time zero. The vans are down the street. I see the agents sneaking into position. Let's do it."

The two agents climbed out of the car, touching their 9mm pistols behind their coats to verify they were still there. They each had four additional magazines of fifteen rounds stuffed into their trouser pockets. Their weapons were freshly cleaned and oiled—this was not the time for a jammed weapon. A jam could spell the difference between a champagne reception back at the office with cheering colleagues thumping you on your back, or being zipped into a body bag and heading to the embalming room of the funeral parlor. Properly serviced, the actions of the weapons would cycle fast as lightning while the barrels flawlessly spat flame, smoke, and gleaming, spinning nine hundred feet-per-second, 9 mm projectiles.

Eyes darting around to detect danger, the two agents walked slowly, side-by-side, up the walk to the battered front door. Then standing to the right side, away from the window where they could be seen from inside, Nick reached over and gave five firm knocks on the door. They heard voices and motion inside—no one had ever knocked on this door unexpectedly. They waited ten long seconds, and then Nick gave another five raps. They saw the curtains stirring on the window on the other side of the door, but couldn't see the face behind them—nor could that face see them.

"Who it is?" inquired a heavily accented voice inside.

"FBI. Open up. You're under arrest for suspicion of complicity with terrorism. Open the door *now*," shouted Nick.

"Wait minute, wait minute," came the frightened male voice from inside. "We do nothing."

"Open the door, you're under arrest. Open the door NOW!"

The words hadn't escaped his lips for one second when a burst of ten high-powered rifle slugs ripped through the front door. Hiram could hear glass breaking as the rounds struck the car in front of the house.

"Christ, they've got a fuckin' AK in there," shouted Nick. "Hit the deck!"

As they both flattened themselves on the grass, another salvo from inside shattered the wood trim and shingled wall beside the door, precisely where they had been standing two seconds earlier. Both men withdrew their pistols from their holsters.

The sound of voices behind the house now carried to them. "Drop your weapons, FBI."

"They're tryin' the back door route, Nick," uttered Hi. "Watch out— the sonsabitches might be comin' out the front door."

And with that, the front door ripped open, and Anwar Azizhi appeared, AK-47 in his hands. As soon as he saw Hi and Nick, he opened up with a volley. One caught Nick square in the middle of the chest, and blew the breath out of him. He lay back, arms stretched out on the grass above his head, writhing. Another ripped into the top of his right shoulder, causing a sensation of heat, but not hitting any vital structures as it passed through into the grass. The third round penetrated Hi's left sleeve but missed his arm, and passed on into the grass between them.

By the time the volley was out, Hi had his 9mm up and fired two quick rounds. The first entered Azizhi under his left chin, ripping through and blowing out a three inch segment of the mandible on the right, with bone chunks and teeth cascading backward on to the front of the house. The second round, entered the terrorist's chest between the fourth and fifth rib, ripped through two chambers of the heart, and stopped inside the chest after fracturing the second rib on the right.

The SWAT members were in the action as well. Just as Hi's second slug ripped through Azizhi's torso, all four agents at the road, leaning on parked cars, opened up with their M-16's. Each fired three shots, and ten of the twelve rounds found their mark. Two passed through his face; one entered his left maxilla, and proceeded through to blow out the parietal section of his skull. Another entered his open mouth, chipping his left front incisor as it passed through the back of his pharynx, and exploded his brain stem out the occipital region of his skull. Bone and brain fragments mixed with bright red blood spattered up against the front of the house. Six rounds entered his chest, scattered like a good spread on a target at the range, and all carried on through, fracturing ribs both front and back, and spitting rib and lungs fragments on the house. Two rounds entered his abdomen, exploding his intestines from the hydraulic force, and ripping a two inch diameter hole on the left region of low back. Azizhi was dead within three seconds after firing his weapon. He collapsed forward, his momentum carrying him ten feet from the front door. Sprawled on the ground, his AK flying ten feet further than his corpse, he lay motionless, with pools of crimson gathering at his head and torso.

Now the air was crackling with M-16 fire from behind the house, preceded by the louder distinctive cracks of AK rounds. Nick & Hi could hear screams as some of the rounds found their marks. They would learn later that Mohammed Haneef had rushed out the back door, just as Azizhi had leaped out the front. He fired his AK at the agents he saw fifty feet in front of him. One round struck agent Hiatt in the left upper abdomen, just below his ballistic vest. The bullet penetrated the anterior abdominal wall, nicked the fundus of his stomach, traversed the transverse colon, shattered his kidney, and exited his left mid-back, splintering the left eleventh rib and spraying kidney and bone ten feet out behind him. Agent Hiatt went down in a heap, bleeding profusely out of the back wound. He hadn't yet fired his weapon – it's Agency policy to fire only in defense. But his three mates, as well as the two on the sides, were ready, and all five opened fire simultaneously.

Agents are taught to shoot for the thorax, because the target is large, and vital structures are compromised, immediately incapacitating the perpetrator. Accordingly, of the fifteen rounds fired, five missed entirely, six impacted his thorax, one shattered his left wrist, one entered his left lower abdomen, and one passed through his right thigh, ripping muscle but missing the bone, arteries, veins, and nerves. One of the missed rounds struck the magazine of his rifle where it joined the receiver, ripping the rifle from his hands and gouging a deep dent into the heavy steel of the receiver.

The thoracic shots were brutal. The first round entered his left upper chest just above the nipple, and ripped through the lung and its large blood vessels, exiting between the fifth and sixth ribs from the back. The next two struck his right mid-chest, one penetrating the nipple and the other one inch medially; the nipple round blew out the anterior rib, projecting twenty bone fragments through the lung, and the second passed through the lung, penetrating the right pulmonary artery and blowing out the right sixth rib near its origin at the spine.

The next two rounds struck his left lower chest, where they penetrated the base of the left lung, then the diaphragm, shattered the spleen, and continued through to cause the left kidney to virtually explode, ripping a large exit wound in his back where it shattered the ninth rib. The final shot was right straight down the middle: hitting him square in the sternum at the nipple line. The round shattered the sternum, then continued through the right atrium of the heart, and then demolished the eighth thoracic vertebra, producing a red shower of bone fragments and blood out the middle of his back.

Haneef remained conscious as he fell to the concrete walk, marveling at the firepower the Agency had mustered in his back yard. When his spine blew out, taking his spinal cord with it, he felt all sensation beneath the wound disappear. Then he saw and felt the thud of the concrete as his body crashed into it, looked up briefly to see the agents training their rifles on the door behind him, and then lapsed into a search for those virgins.

Feriz Hadba and Fatima witnessed the fate of their two partners, and decided to slug it out from inside the house. Hadba went to the rear window and began firing at the agents hiding behind the slender trees in the yard. He was instantly engaged by all seven of the uninjured SWAT members in the back and sides. Of the twenty-one rounds fired in the first fusillade, fourteen missed entirely, a number of them penetratng the thin shingled walls of the house and passing beside him. But five rounds passed through the wall and into his chest, with plenty of energy left to turn his heart and lungs into mincemeat. And the final two rounds found their mark in his head; one entered via his left eye, exploding the eyeball and passing through to burst out a four inch chunk of his posterior skull. The other struck his right upper forehead, blowing off the entire right scalp section of his skull. Instantly unconscious, he sank to the floor and lay on his knees, slumped half-sitting up, face into the wall, some slight quivering motion of his muscles, as a large pool of dark red blood formed under him.

Fatima was terrified by the sudden violent death of her comrades. Deciding that she'd go down fighting, she wanted only to take a few infidels with her. So calling out, she shouted, "No shoot, no shoot, I give oop, give oop." She sat on the floor at the junction of the living room and dining room, training her 9 mm automatic pistol at the front door.

"Drop your weapon, and come out with your hands up," Hiram commanded. "Come out NOW."

"No shoot, no shoot," Fatima repeated. "I cannot walk," she lied.

"Drop your weapon, and come out with your hands up," Hi repeated. "Crawl if you need to, but come out NOW!

"I cannot move," Fatima intoned. "I am hurt. I need doctor," she lied.

"This is your last chance. Throw out your weapon and come out, or we will kill you," Hi said, glancing down with fury over his injured buddy.

"I need help. Need doctor," she intoned again. "Help me."

At that, Hi was on his feet, advancing toward the open front door in a crouch. Peering in momentarily, he saw Fatima sitting on the floor fifteen feet in, but he couldn't see if she was armed. Collecting his strength, he dived into the front door, pistol arm first pointing in her direction.

BAM, BAM, Fatima's gun barked. BAM, BAM, BAM. Hi heard rounds whizzing past his head and splintering the wood behind him. Then his breath got knocked out of him, as a round impacted the porcelain plate of his vest, broke up, and the fragments continued into his right upper arm.

Now clearly seeing Fatima, he raised his 9 mm and fired out five shots in rapid succession. The first two went to Fatima's left, but the next three found their mark. The first entered her left hand, being used to support the pistol held in her right hand. Passing through the back of the hand, it shattered her wrist, jerking the arm back, and causing the unsupported pistol to point downward. The second round passed through the left portion of her neck, transecting her left carotid artery, instantly causing pulsating jets of bright red blood to spurt in front of her. The third round impacted her upper sternum, knocking her backwards. The round penetrated through the bone and on through her trachea and esophagus, finally lodging in her third thoracic vertebra, where it fractured the thick bone but lodged inside the body of the vertebra, shocking the spinal cord behind it such that she was instantly paralyzed below the chest.

As Hi began to stand up, he saw Fatima lying on her back, with blood spurting from her neck. Walking in a crouch toward her, he saw her right arm rise with the pistol pointing toward him. Leaping to the side as her pistol barked a final time, he shouted, "YOU BITCH," and fired off three more rounds, the first two of which crashed into the floor beside her head. The third round entered under her chin, continued upward through her mouth and tongue, crashed through her soft palate, through her nasopharynx and the base of her skull, penetrating the frontal lobe of her brain, where the bullet stopped after bouncing backward off the inside of the top of her skull. Her arm dropped instantly as she went limp with instant loss of consciousness and death.

Hi stood up and walked over to Fatima's limp body, still ejecting blood six inches into the air from her severed left carotid. Her eyes stared lifelessly at the ceiling, and her face was gray. He kicked the pistol away from her hand, and looked around, then shouted, "All clear inside, all clear inside. Two dead in here, two dead in here." He heard the SWAT team members approaching, so he turned and walked briskly outside to check on Nick.

Nick was now sitting up, taking off his ballistic vest.

"How ya doin, Buddy," Hi tenderly queried, as he squatted down beside Nick.

"Chest hurts like a sonofabitch, Hi," Nick responded, gently rubbing his sternum.

"Hey you're bleedin' from this left shoulder, Buddy," Hi observed, as the pulled Nick's shirt collar back to get a look at the wound. "You breathin' OK?"

"No, man, it hurts like hell to breathe here in the front where that prick nailed me with the AK." Lifting up his vest, he fingered the torn fabric where the AK round had penetrated the fabric, but was deflected by the porcelain plate. "Thank God for this thing, though, or I'd be feeling nothin' right now, man—I'd have transferred to the branch office in the sky."

Fingering the hole himself, Hi agreed, "Nick, my boy, it wasn't your time. You are one lucky son of a bitch. Thank God for the smart guys who designed this thing," he said as he gestured at the vest.

"So what's with my shoulder here, buddy," Nick asked, rolling the shoulder down and trying to see the wound.

Ripping the buttons open and exposing the wound, Hi said, "Looks like it's just superficial, buddy. An inch lower and he'd have air conditioned your lung for you."

"Christ, man, I got shot, but looks like it was my lucky day anyway."

"You can say that again. Let's get your sorry ass to the hospital and be sure there's nothin' else."

"What the hell happened in there?" Nick inquired, gesturing toward the open door.

"The bitch said she was hurt and needed help, but she tried to blow me away when I went in. Thank God I knew she was a lyin' sack o' shit, so I leaped in and she didn't get much of a shot. Hiram looked down at his own vest. "That twat, look what she did to my vest. Shit, she peppered my arm with bullet fragments," he uttered as he looked at his injured right upper arm, with a dozen tiny bleeding sites. "Doesn't look bad, but I guess I better get checked out along with you."

"Hey buddy, were these vests a smart decision, or what?" As I recall, you weren't so sweet on the idea, and I talked you into it. You owe me big league, Boy."

"Next root beer's on me, Bud."

"You're on. Let's get the hell outta here," Nick commented, as he struggled to stand up. After getting up and slowly standing upright, wincing with pain from his front chest, he said, "But first I wanna get a look at these turds who threaten kids."

Walking over to Azizhi's corpse, he looked at his lifeless face, and said, "So many things this jerk could have done with his life, but all he wanted to do was threaten babies. What a shithead."

The two of them then hobbled around the side of the house, where the SWAT team was loading Agent Hiatt into an ambulance. Hiatt had an IV running, but he was barely conscious and his face was gray. Each kidney receives 10% of total blood flow, so a ruptured kidney can cause hemorrhagic shock within minutes, proceeding to death within more a few more minutes if bleeding isn't stopped, and blood volume restored.

Addressing Agent Waseema Shaikh, Nick asked, "Is he gonna make it, Waseema?"

Her face distraught, with misty eyes, Agent Gude looked at Nick and said, "It's gonna be close, Nick. He needs to get into an operating room, fast. And he's gonna need a lot of blood.'

"We'll go and donate some right now, Waseema," commented Hi.

"It doesn't work that way anymore, boys. They use the blood they've already collected and processed. But you should donate regularly anyway.

That's where the blood he's gonna get, came from. Good citizens, eager to help, even with their own blood."

"Okay, Waseema. Anybody else hurt? Asked Nick.

"Just those scumbags," Waseema retorted, nodding toward the lifeless form of Haneef on the sidewalk, and the dead terrorists inside the house.

As they were speaking, the ambulance sped off, lights blinking and siren wailing.

"Okay, Waseema, Betty, Gloria, guys, we'll see ya. Thanks for the fab backup. We'll see you at the office. We're gonna go get checked out ourselves."

"Oh, Hi, I didn't know you were injured. What happened?" queried Betty.

"Fortunately nothing too bad. Nick caught an AK round on his chest plate, and a skin wound on his right shoulder. I stopped the bitch's 9 mm with my chest plate, and got a few bullet fragments in my arm here," he said as he demonstrated the arm wounds.

"Okay, guys, get outta here and get checked out," retorted Betty. "Congrats on a fantastic day. Nothin' I like more than bringing in dead baby-killers. Especially when we've already extracted all the intel from 'em that we need."

"Amen, sister," retorted Hi. We're outta here."

And with that, Hi and Nick walked gingerly back to their car, both of them wincing as they moved their bruised chest walls.

CHAPTER SEVENTY-THREE

THE INTERNATIONAL NOOSE TIGHTENS

Monday, 28 March

Alquieri was the starting point, leading to Saad, and on to the other twelve members of the leadership council, the Forum of the Avengers. Then on to the one hundred and four other members of the larger organization, Sacred Sword of The Avengers. That led to intensive monitoring of the activities of one hundred and sixteen sponsors of terror, and the results were vastly more productive than anyone could have dreamed. Between them, contacts with other executives of terror were identified in forty-one countries, including Canada, Mexico, Cuba, Venezuela, Colombia, Brazil, Ecuador, The Philippines, Australia, Indonesia, Thailand, China, Russia, Ukraine, Iran, Iraq, Bahrain, Yemen, Oman, Qatar, Dubai, Djibouti, Ethiopia, Somalia, Egypt, Algeria, Libya, Morocco, Turkey, Palestine, Germany, Denmark, Norway, Sweden, France, Belgium, Netherlands, the United Kingdom, Ireland, Spain, and Portugal.

Because of the risk of enemy agents going underground, coordinating the apprehension of these violent criminals was crucial. Keeping the magnitude of the dragnet under wraps was a brilliant achievement coordinated by CIA; each country was only told of its own cells, and plans for raids were coordinated one-on-one, so that only CIA knew of the world-wide D-Day for eradication of these termite nests. Mr. Arroyo, the coordinating officer for this massive project, knew well that Al Qaeda had infiltrated the security services of a number of these countries, and that the cells identified in their countries would be alerted and successfully melt away, but a few lost quarries only added to the credibility of the appearance that only small, local raids were planned. Only he and his colleagues knew of the spectacular blow about to be levied on the international organization of Al Qaeda.

Perhaps just as important, most of the funding sources of international terror were about to be brought to justice. And justice in many Arabic countries can be vastly more swift and decisive than the years of overpaid lawyers arguing before bored juries seen in the western world: a knock on the door, an arrest, a bullet in the back of the head in the rear seat of the van, and the body dumped into an excavation site, never to be found. Brutal, but effective. No junk science. No liar-for-hire spurious experts. No claims of insanity. No betrayal of state secrets. No appeal. No recidivism.

And the funds of families found to be sponsoring terror would be permanently appropriated by the state, from riches to poverty with a stroke of the pen. This measure assures that family will never again sponsor international murder, and sends a clarion message to as-yet undetected sponsors of terror: you're next. Your body will be consumed by worms underneath some new apartment building, and your family will be begging on the street. Your choice.

The Saudi king recognized that what goes around, comes around. The royal family had been fostering intolerance in madrassas around the world, teaching, under the guise of religion, hate and violence to millions of Muslim young. They had created a generation of intolerant young fanatics. And, predictably enough, now those angry, hateful young men were coming after the royal family itself. Saudi Arabia began propagating a peaceful, tolerant, mode of Islam, substituting economic fervor for violence. It would take a generation for the already inoculated young to grow out of their violent years, but the time was ripe for change, and the king was up to the challenge. Gradually the Muslim world would evolve out of the notion that their concept of the divine was the only legitimate one. The entire world was evolving toward the vastly more enlightened approach of the mantra, "The Light shines through many windows."

CHAPTER SEVENTY-FOUR

THAT WEEK: THE SAUDI CLEANSING

The evening was cool as the massive steel gates to the Saudi Army base slowly rolled open on their huge tractor tires. Because of the rise of terror within The Kingdom, security at all Saudi government facilities had been radically beefed up. And the military knew how to protect its resources.

One by one, the tanks rolled out, their 68-ton weight gliding amazingly smoothly on their precisely machined rubber-coated steel wheels on steel treads. Designed as stable weapons platforms, able to vaporize their target with their prodigiously powerful 5" cannon while screaming along at thirty-five miles per hour on rough terrain, these were no obsolete worn-out 1950s vintage Soviet junk like the fool Saddam sent his young men to war to die in. As major American allies, the Saudi Army fielded the premiere, best-of-all-time tank, ferocious American Abrams M1A1 main battle tank. And now they were being called to battle an insidious, unprincipled, murderous enemy within: Al Qaeda in Saudi Arabia.

On the outskirts of eight cities throughout the country, the scene was repeated: forty tanks rolling quietly into Riyadh and Jedda, squadrons of five each. Thirty tanks into each of Medina, Mecca, and Jubail. Twenty-five each into Khafji, Duba, Ta'if, and Dammam. The plan of battle had been meticulously laid out, and each squadron of five had its target.

The Saudi leadership knew that the stability of their country, and thereby every Arab nation, was in clear and present danger of being overrun by fools. Fools who thought the future of all Arabs, and the one billion Muslims in the world, lay in turning the clock back thirteen hundred years and living like animals. And after subjugating all the Muslims to their infantile ideology, they would export their message of vitriol to every other nation. Foolish but not cowards, they didn't fear death, and, in fact, longed for it.

The Saudi's reasoned that all the rules of all civilizations, from the time of the first human governance structure, were based on fear of punishment. But they were dealing with fanatics who harbored no such fear; they had no respect for their own survival, nor that of their families, and certainly not for anyone else's family. And so the usual rules of conflict were useless here. Geneva Convention conduct is absurd in the face of conscienceless butchers who attacked their restrained captives with chain saws, and filmed their savagery so they could savor the spectacle for years. Monsters who kidnapped unarmed, neutral journalists whose mission was to tell the unedited truth, and took pleasure in hacking their heads off with their bare hands, with glee.

Respecting the civil rights of such barbarians was an absurd notion. Promising not to listen to their international phone calls was not an approach intelligent people would choose in this situation. These were not people to be reasoned with, to be rehabilitated, to be given a second chance. These people were the Black Plague, smallpox and polio, all rolled into one deadly virus. They were not to be meddled with. Rather, they were to be extricated from the Family of Man, from the entire life cycle. It was them or everyone else's children—there was no in-between.

And to counter their propaganda of a rewarding life in their international recruiting efforts, a chilling example needed to be set, of how they would be dealt with. No mercy. No prisoners. No survival. The slate wiped clean of their existence.

The mission had been kept secret until the day of the operation, and all communication out of the bases was secured, except for the high command. Al Qaeda had infiltrated many a military, and it was likely that some of the Saudi soldiers were moles for the enemy. So all telephone service in the entire country was shut down—both land lines and cell phone service. Barracks were searched for walky-talkies or other mobile radios. There was to be no warning to the enemy. The strike was to be sudden, unexpected, ferociously violent, and scathingly lethal. Nationwide. Saudi Arabia was about to be purged of its version of Ebola. And the sterilization was to be so terrifying that potential recruits around the world would see the enemy's propaganda as suckers' traps, an invitation to a violent, instantaneous, and ignominious removal from the face of the earth.

The Saudi's had looked askance at brutal tactics in the past, but they were now experiencing a repeat of history within their own borders. A definitive response was necessary, and they rose to the occasion.

The homes of every member of the den of snakes, The Sacred Sword of the Avengers, was carefully identified and maps provided for the squadron leader of every tank group. Five tanks per house, each squadron supported by two truckloads of foot soldiers. Each house was to be silently surrounded. The commander of each detachment would approach the door of each house. Because all of the members of the terror group were wealthy, all of the homes were separate structures, with their entire compounds surrounded by walls. The commander would ask to speak to the master of the house. Not all would be home, but most would, since it was about nine at night. The terrorist would be advised that the home was to be destroyed, and he with it, but that the remainder of the family would be escorted to safety if they wished to leave, but they must walk out within sixty seconds.

Family would then be placed aboard the high bed of the troop truck, and would be required to watch as the tanks first bashed through the compound perimeter walls and then opened fire at the house with their main cannon. High-explosive rounds would be utilized—no armor-piercing required here. The buildings would be reduced to rubble with approximately five rounds per tank. The crumpled remains of the homes would be set ablaze with gasoline, such that all was reduced to ashes.

The terrorist would achieve his dream of dying for his cause. All of his assets would be confiscated by the state. The surviving families, formerly living a life of privilege, would be plunged into poverty. The destruction would be recorded by the military, for subsequent saturation broadcasts around the country, such that every Saudi, and eventually every person on earth with access to a television, would witness the Saudi approach to terror within. Sudden, meaningless death for the perpetrator; enduring disgrace and poverty for his family. An unattractive, less-than-glorious conclusion to a life of hate and violence. A legacy of shame and deprivation for the family. Anyone with half a brain would find this course of events to be an influential counter to Al Qaeda's deceitful overtures.

And so the tanks rumbled along, all over the country. The troops jostled silently as their trucks motored quietly behind the tanks. The troops were never briefed on their mission. Their orders to surround the compounds, allowing no one in or out, would be issued at each site.

Of the hundred and thirty-five members of the ill-fated Brotherhood, one hundred and twenty-three were at home. And so by 2100h that night, all hundred and twenty-three were buried alive inside the exploding and imploding walls of their homes. And by 2200h, their remains had been incinerated, their ashes entering the biologic cycle to perhaps be recycled into organisms better adapted to living within a communal world.

The Saudi government confiscated $55.7 billion from the families of the Islamists. Those funds were invested in expanding the Saudi economy instead of funding the destruction of other people's countries.

The twelve who were not home were rounded up one-by-one. Six were abroad, and Saudi agents were dispatched to retrieve them from the authorities of the countries wherein they were arrested. All twelve were taken to the public gallows in Riyadh precisely two weeks after the purge. And all twelve plunged through the platform, doing their dance of death at the end of a rope, like the common criminals they were. All were buried in unmarked paupers' graves, since they now all *were* paupers. They were to be denied the usual Muslim funeral rituals. They had violated the fundamental precepts of Islam, twisted it into monstrous distortions that desecrated its most sacred dicta. They were not to be afforded its dignifying dogma after their executions. And they weren't.

Allah had no use for this human garbage.

CHAPTER SEVENTY-FIVE

THE REST OF THE WORLD FOLLOWS SUIT

Canada was aghast at the extent of its infiltration with sleeper cells. Although there was no way of knowing how many cells persisted undetected, the apprehension of thirty-four such cells was obviously a massive blow to the enemy. Not to mention termination of the money flow that supported the remaining ones. The native Canadian lunatic fringe that had opposed inquiry into the presence of such cells in the past were humiliated and terminally disparaged; such asinine self-destructive conduct would not soon resurface in the proud land of the maple leaf.

Venezuela and Ecuador were particularly ashamed that their leadership was shown to be allied in terror with Al Qaeda. The regimes of Hugo Chavez and Rafael Correa were both deposed via impeachment, and free-market policies were restored to those ailing economies. Joy was rampant in the streets.

The continental Europeans got their act together, and acted with unprecedented rigid purpose in detaining and prosecuting the terrorists. The Brits had always taken firm action, with their domestic espionage unit M4 setting the standard for the world in monitoring the terrorists among themselves. Now the continent was catching up. The leaders of the western democracies there finally owned up that the world was a dangerous place, and that placating violent aggressors was no more successful in the twenty-first century than it had been in the twentieth.

Indonesia, the most populous Muslim nation on earth, finally grew some teeth in dealing with militant Islam. Following the lead of the U.S., Indonesia established military tribunals to deal with the unprincipled vicious practitioners of terror in the name of religion. Hundreds were tried, found guilty of treason and other high crimes, and were publicly hanged. The message went out, clarion clear, to the Indonesian street: live like a civilized human being, or die like an animal. No retreat. No mercy. The threat was too great for ambiguity. Abandon militancy, or disgrace your family by swinging from the rope of justice. The backbone of militant Islam in this pivotal nation was fractured for good.

In Ethiopia, the President discovered a number of Al Qaeda cells within his government. With the swiftness of an arrow, the traitors were arrested, tried, and executed for high treason. As in Indonesia, the message was clear: Ethiopia is a modernizing country that seeks commerce and enterprise, not infantile murderous religious dogma. Choose the other side, and you will promptly find yourself putrefying in a criminal's grave.

And so, originating from the purifying effect of maternal devotion, the forces of darkness around the world were dealt a paralyzing blow. Not only were most of the practitioners of terror permanently removed from the society of man, but most of its lifeblood of funding was abruptly terminated. Critical to its permanent vanquishing, the spiritual leaders who provided the impetus of its propagation were publicly labeled criminals and fools. The world would never again face the malignant threat of large-scale militant Islam.

But the diversity of mankind produces deviant individuals with sufficient charisma to win others to the course of evil. So long as free will exists, there will arise those who wish to control others, and who feel empowered to murder and destroy those who resist. It is for this reason that the civilized world must retain the capacity to detect, investigate, confront, and overwhelm evil in all its forms. It is narcissistic revelry to believe that freedom is free, that because people are good and honorable, that they need not preserve capacity to defend themselves. Such childish musing can ensure the triumph of evil over good. Only through the continuous copious expenditure of courage, treasure, blood, and some limited sacrifice of privacy, will humanity achieve its destiny of international harmony, prosperity, and spiritual fulfillment.

CHAPTER SEVENTY-SIX

AMERICAN HOMELAND PURGE

The scene was similar in all thirty-three American cities involved. Armies of special investigators, all with top secret clearances, had compiled phone records that identified one hundred and thirty-seven terror cells in cities across America. The larger cities were the ones infected, of course—where people with foreign accents would be common and therefore could allow terror cells to be established without suspicion.

The raids would be coordinated nationwide. It wasn't practical to shut down the phones of a nation of three hundred million, so the cell towers servicing the community of each cell were transiently disabled, and the land lines out of each terror group lair were cut.

It wasn't possible to assemble so many police officers at night without some type of explanation, so the word was out that clandestine raids on illicit drug manufacturing and distribution sites were to be conducted. Didn't matter if it leaked out, because such operations were fairly common, and therefore not suspicious. The true mission was revealed only after the officers were en route. They were already armored and heavily armed, because drug dealers are notoriously violent anyway.

Every residence was assaulted at roughly the same time across the nation. A few terrorist calls leaked out to alert others, but since all targets had already been surrounded by officers, it was to no avail. Three hundred and twenty-five of the four hundred and forty-two known terrorists were apprehended at their residences. Ninety-three of them went down in hails of gunfire, but the rest chose to surrender and hope for another chance to murder and maim, after the notoriously inept American criminal justice system would exonerate them, or release them after a desultory incarceration.

The remaining hundred and seventeen terrorists who had not been home, were then aggressively pursued. Ninety-two were readily tracked down. Ten were out of the country, and fifteen went underground.

The prosecutions proved vastly more decisive and effective than the authorities had hoped for. The evidence was incontrovertible. Of the 417 prosecutions, 403 resulted in prompt convictions. Sentences of 50 years were the norm, with a stipulation in every case of no possibility of parole. American juries had seen enough smoking holes in their country. The image of American business men and women leaping to their deaths from urban office towers was still fresh in their minds. These monsters before them would die in prison, or hobble out as feeble old scum.

Bills were introduced and entered debate in both houses of Congress, authorizing the death penalty for future individuals apprehended for promoting terror. America was recognizing the threat, and engaging in intelligent self-defense. Beyond preventing this slime from ever again harming innocents, the motivation for capital punishment was a society-wide revulsion against using tax money to keep feed, clothe, and provide medical care to criminals who plotted to murder their families.

CHAPTER SEVENTY-SEVEN

SAMIR HASHIMI SEEKS HIS REVENGE

It hadn't been a good day for Samir. In the morning, he had looked with the eyes of treachery at the Marines about him, all of whom he expected to be dead before sunset. He even hoped he would get to personally dispatch many of them. But when the TCNs had been rounded up and escorted into the dining hall before a shot was fired, he sensed a horrible foreboding. There should have been no break in routine on the base—the attack was to be a total surprise. Initially he hoped it was a coincidence —a drill perhaps. But just in case, he had evaded the Marine cordon that gathered up all the TCNs, and he had prudently decided to not report to work that morning anyway. So he had taken his cell phone and his weapons, walked behind the MWR building, and concealed himself in some bushes.

Things started to look worse when Samir opened his phone and realized that he couldn't receive a cell signal. The coincidences were adding up, and the sum didn't look good.

Then Samir recognized the ultimate truth: the Marines were aware of the impending attack, and seemed to have comprehensive strategies for dealing with it. Although he couldn't see the walls on the south side of the base, he could see the mannequins in the guard towers facing the river. Then he saw the Marines manning their machine gun emplacements on the ground facing the river, establishing lines of fire that no inbound boat could survive. He desperately wanted to get word to the insurgents that they were walking into a massive ambush, to call off the attack. But he was rendered mute and irrelevant by the foresight of the Marines. Worse yet, he now had to wonder if he had been discovered, and was in fact the key figure leading to the incipient slaughter of his cohorts.

It was a very long day for Samir. He was forced to watch, totally impotent, as the insurgent boats were blown out of the water, with the loss of all hands. He heard the fusillades of gunfire emanating from the south wall, followed by the huge *ka-booms* of tank and Stryker cannon. He was forced to listen to the terse communications of the leaders of the professional warriors around him, expertly executing combat arms with devastating effectiveness. Rubbing salt in his wounds, he could hear the upbeat tone of the Marine gun crews' communication as they massacred his colleagues.

Finally the battle had concluded. Samir was both hungry and thirsty, but he dared not leave his hiding place in daylight. Finally the night mercifully arrived, and Samir was able to surreptitiously sneak into the remains of the MWR building and steal some provisions. The base was alive with Marine work crews scurrying every which way. Armored vehicles were massing in Blue Diamond, with their noisy engines and treads. In this busy environment, with the benefit of darkness, Samir was finally able to stealthily creep away from his daytime concealment site. It was payback time.

During this longest day of his life, while he was listening to the devastation of his cohorts and his cause, Samir reflected on how things had gone so terribly askew. Slowly he pieced it together. The air officer had been around more than usual, and that woman Captain as well. She didn't belong in the COC, but had been there a number of times recently. And the General had started going to meetings on base without his usual comments to Samir about where he was going. The inspection of TCN quarters by KBR that had seemed so benign at the time. Gradually Samir put it together, and was confident he knew who had done him in: he had been ratted out by Major Baxter and Captain Curtis.

Although his cause was lost, and even if he himself survived this calamity, he now had no future. Samir had decided that getting even was more important than escape. He *must* kill those two. Their blood flowing onto his shoes would wash away at least some of the shame now consuming him. And he concocted a plan for his own sneak attack.

Having previously determined which Marine officer housing area Matt was quartered in, but not which individual "can," Samir found a new lair in bushes at the entrance to the officer housing area, where he could see anyone on the road approaching the area. He fondled his dagger, an exotic Arab model with curved blade a full six inches long, with sharp serrations on the blunt side of the blade and a gleaming razor on the cutting edge. He longed for the moment when he would plunge it into Matt's chest, and then slice Chris's neck ear to ear. He'd derive immense satisfaction pinning her down, seeing her terrified eyes staring into this, as her severed carotids and jugulars spurted her entire blood volume upward against his own neck. Then he'd hack her entire head off and hurl it against the wall. He hoped Matt would be too weak to move at that point, but able to watch the gruesome mauling. Then he'd return to Matt, and hack his head off while he was still alive. He'd set the heads together on the bunk, with the headless bodies strewn on the floor. Oh, how he longed for the moment. He would have his revenge. It would be brutal, and it would be delicious. He salivated, breathing heavy, and felt stirring in his groin from the perverted image of desecrating the body of the beautiful woman. He pondered if he would explore her private parts—she was so beautiful, he loved to look at her when she came by the COC. No, no, that would be contrary to Koranic teaching. After all, he was a man of profound spirituality and righteousness.

There was lots of commotion all around the base. Samir knew they'd be searching for him, and that they'd regard him as armed and exceedingly dangerous. He knew that his quarters would already have been searched, and would be under surveillance: no going back there. He knew they'd wonder if he had managed to slip over the wall and escape during the mop-up phase of the battle, when one dark figure might elude the guards, who were preoccupied with searching for more distant threats. The guards were watching the armored vehicles and foot soldiers counting the dead, retrieving the wounded, and clearing the remainder of the unexploded mines. There was the sound of voices and heavy military turbine and diesel engines all around, but no more explosions or gunshots. He hoped that the COC activities would wind up soon, and his quarry appear, but he knew that, after the largest battle in Iraq since the initial invasion in 2003, the COC would be humming with activity late into the night. He could wait. The battle was lost. He, the betrayer, had been betrayed. Like a dumb fish, he had been their sucker, their bitch, their whore.

He was so humiliated he could barely sit still. His hopes for a life of riches and leisure were now forever gone. He was an abominable failure, who had cost the insurgency nearly all its skilled fighters, their commanders, their equipment, their pride—everything. He didn't even want to speculate on whether he had led his Saudi handlers into discovery, and the vicious response that the Saudi government would have toward them. He was finished—he could never return to the life he once knew. Any of his handlers who survived would have him killed on sight. He had nothing to live for: even if he died in this final act of revenge, there was no real additional loss for him. He *must* kill the two devils that did this to him.

Samir drifted off to sleep, even though he was sitting uncomfortably, crouched in the bushes. His legs ached where the roots pushed mercilessly into his flesh. His back hurt from slumping forward. His neck pounded with pain from holding his head only semi-erect. He periodically awoke with a start, either to the sound of distant shouts of the Marines mopping up the battlefield, or nearby voices as Marine officers in singles or small groups returned to their quarters. Each time he awoke, he was transiently disoriented, then remembering his hopelessly miserable situation with a gasp, hands rising to his face, then drifting off again in troubled sleep. He tried to avoid any movement at all, increasing the aches all over his body.

Suddenly he jerked his head upward. Something had awakened him, but he was transiently confused as he shook the drowsiness from his mind. *There, there it is—the unmistakable sound of Chris's melodious voice.* She was only seventy-five feet from him, walking a path that would take her only fifteen feet from his position. *And yes, praise Allah, there was Matt trudging along beside her.* He could spring out on them and stab both of them from behind. But they could struggle, and might even survive. And even if they didn't, Samir wanted to revel in their murders and dismemberment. No, he would let them get settled into Matt's quarters, their guard fully relaxed. Then, he would have his revenge.

Samir seethed with resentment and hate as Chris and Matt strolled by, their conversation light, with occasional laughter. *How dare they be happy at a time like this? All my fighters slaughtered like sheep, their bodies being picked up this moment by the Marines, and piled in the beds of their huge seven-ton trucks. And I, the cause of it all, suckered like an amateur.* He trembled with rage. He was sweating now, despite the sixty degree cool of the evening. His body was preparing for battle.

Motionless, Samir peered after the two lovers as Matt unlocked the door to his quarters, and the two stepped inside, closing the door behind them. After the door closed, Samir heard the distinctive sound of the door lock being engaged. *Praise Allah for having the foresight to provide me instruction in picking flimsy locks like these. I will have that door open in seconds, and silently.* Samir's fingers now opened and closed repeatedly, eager to get on with his blood lust.

A few other Marines drifted by, entering their quarters and locking up. Samir waited, now palpitating with anticipation. At last the scene was quiet, lights in the windows of a third of the cans, some already having been extinguished as their occupants retired for the night. But the only lights he cared about were burning brightly. *They were in there. And he was coming for them. They were taking some of their last breaths, unaware of their imminent fate.* His body trembled from head to foot with excitement. The aches and pains were gone now, suppressed by the endorphins of fanatical hyper-arousal.

Now Samir was on the move. He silently parted the bushes in front of him, and crept to the three foot space between the first two cans, invisible in the darkness there. Matt's can was down the row, the fourth one. Now Samir was grateful for the remote noise of the battlefield sanitizing activities; the sounds of his movement, and of his attack, will be diluted out by the background noise.

One can at a time, Samir sinuously advanced to hide in the crevices between them. Finally he was at Matt's. His hands were shaking now, moist with sweat. His pupils were fully dilated by both the darkness and the excitement. He heard Chris' sweet, lighthearted voice inside. Again he felt fullness in his groin, as the erotic nature of Chris's murder overcame him with waves of pleasure. His lips were parted in a sardonic grin, his jaw gently opening and closing.

Samir crept to the dark area in back of Matt's can and crawled on top of the sandbags which protected the bottom five feet of the living space. Slowly bringing one eye to the corner of the window, he jerked to the sight of Chris's shoulder only a foot from his face! She was sitting on the bed, holding Matt's hand sitting to her right, both staring at the CD player as it canted Dionne Warwick's version of *I'll Never Fall In Love Again.*

Samir knew he couldn't overpower two able-bodied Marines with a knife, unless he could disable Matt before being detected. He would need to wait. Wait until his quarry was totally distracted. He was sure they would make love – it was their day of ultimate triumph. And they shared the victory. *They will make love. And they will die in the act. From ecstasy to catastrophe, in seconds. It will be sweet beyond all other experience.*

Samir peered through the other windows of the can. He observed that the front door opened into a small vestibule with the bathroom dead ahead and a room off to each side. The door to Matt's room was closed, and there was no lock. Matt's roomie wasn't in – Samir prayed he was deployed off base for the night. *No matter—after I overcome them, I can carve them slowly and silently, even with his roommate next door. And if he opens the door, I can take him with a sudden attack.*

After an interminable half hour of listening to music amid light chatter and kissing, Matt turned down the lights, only a dim corner table lamp providing muted illumination of the room. Samir now was trembling with eros, as he stole glances of Matt undressing Chris, finding the soft contours of her lithe body monumentally arousing as she was disrobed. Now her brassiere was off, and he could see the gentle curve of her right breast as she turned to embrace Matt. Passionately kissing her, Matt gently laid her back on the bed, and began kissing her torso. *It was time.*

Stealing a glance down the row to be sure all was still, Samir crept to Matt's door and silently tried to rotate the doorknob, confirming its secured status. Extracting from his pocket a wire tool he had fabricated weeks before, Samir silently probed the tool into the lock and initiated the repetitive motion of probing and rotating, while he repeatedly tried to rotate the knob. The music inside concealed the slight scratching sound of the tool. Suddenly the tool engaged a tumbler, and the knob rotated fully. He was in!

Pausing to look down the row, then listening to confirm continued music inside, Samir opened the door, slipped in, and silently reclosed and locked the door. He could feel his heart pounding like a battering ram, his palms slick with sweat. He could hear the frenzied breathing and moaning, with the rhythmic squeaking of the bed in the next room. He only had a few minutes; no man could last long, making love to such a spectacular woman.

His trembling suppressed, but not his heavy breathing, Samir rotated the doorknob and opened the door a crack. The lovers were five feet forward and to his right, the bed against the wall, beneath the window he had used for surveillance. They were totally absorbed with their lovemaking.

Extracting the knife from his belt, Samir grasped it firmly, and silently opened the door wide. Seeing the naked lovers writhing before him, his adrenaline rush put him in overdrive. Samir raised the dagger in his right arm as he hastily stepped into the room. But in the dim light, he didn't see Chris's boots just inside on the floor, and he tripped forward. The dagger was supposed to have plunged into the back of Matt's sweaty chest, but instead Samir's body lunged forward, and the knife only grazed Matts' back, and instead hit the wall behind them, sliding downward, imbedding in the mattress alongside Chris's waist. Samir was now lying on top of the lovers, a bizarre menage-a-trois. As Samir strived to raise his right arm, Matt rolled to his left, pinning Samir's arm against the wall as both Matt and Chris exclaimed warnings to one another. Now Samir and Matt's faces were touching, a deadly eye-to-eye encounter.

Without hesitating, Matt angled his head backward, then thrust it forward mercilessly, his forehead impacting Samir's nose in a bone-shattering impact. Samir's erotic and homicidal mania was now replaced with shooting pain, as crimson blood gushed from both his nostrils, and he was startled into inaction. Lifting his head, his arm still trapped, Matt's warrior instinct now took over. Samir's chin in front of his mouth, Matt opened his jaws and violently clamped down on it, sinking his teeth into the soft flesh overlying the mandible. As Samir pulled his head back further and Matt violently rotated his head like a great white shark feeding, Samir's chin was ripped to the bone, a new torrent of bright red blood cascading down on Matt and Chris's chests.

Samir shouted out and tried vainly to extract his right hand with the knife from under Matt's left shoulder, but Matt knew the danger and leaned firmly back. But now Matt's right arm was in action, although restricted by Samir's torso. Matt reached up and slipped two fingers into Samir's mouth, which opened as Samir howled. In one violent motion, Matt pulled lateral and downward, the huge muscles of his right shoulder pitted against Samir's delicate facial muscles. Without a sound, the tissues of Samir's mouth gave way, and Samir's lips split at their left commissure, the tissue ripping halfway to the ear.   Now Samir was struggling not to kill, but to escape. But it was not to be.

Striving to protect his face, Samir rotated his head laterally, away from the bed. But that was Matt's instant plan; Matt's index and middle fingers were extended ramrod straight and one inch apart as he violently jerked his right hand forward, the fingers entering Samir's eye sockets. The soft conjunctiva was no match for this force, and Matt's fingers ripped into the space between the bony orbit and Samir's eyeballs, which deviated wildly as the extraocular muscles were ripped from the globes. Samir instantly had double vision—but only transiently. Matt pulled the hand back, but now brought the two fingers together and shoved them into Samir's right eye to the back of the socket. Flexing the fingers, then ripping the hand back again, Matt avulsed the entire eyeball out of the socket, severing the optic nerve and artery. It was a nasty cure for diplopia.

Samir was stunned. He was blind in his right eye, which was dangling grotesquely out of its socket, suspended by the remaining three of its formerly six extraocular muscles. And Matt used that pause to continue the offense. Violently rolling left and grasping Samir's right arm with both hands, Matt sank his teeth to the bone of Samir's forearm. Yet a new hemorrhagic source erupted as Matt strived to break Samir's grip on the knife. But Samir's grip was tight, and Samir began pounding Matt's powerful back with this left hand, but he couldn't get any leverage, and the blows were desultory. Two of the blows slid off Matt's sweaty back and struck Chris in the ribs just below her left breast, causing her to shriek.

Matt slid his legs onto the floor and began to stand up. Samir's body slid upward, then fell on Chris's face. Samir managed to pull his right hand back six inches, and plunge it down again, slicing Chris's right lateral chest wall, adding her own bleeding to the gory scene. But now Matt had the advantage of having the power of his legs. With his back to Samir, holding Samir's knife hand down with his own left, Matt rotated his right elbow forward, then jerked it back violently into Samir's face. Samir grunted as his two front teeth fractured backward, bleeding violently, the last function of those teeth having been to lacerate Matt's elbow. Matt leaned forward, using all his weight to hold down Samir's right arm, as he pulled Chris off the bed with his right arm. Chris scrambled out onto the floor, blood streaking down her right side, and Samir's blood all over the front of her chest.

Samir's only seeing eye took faint pleasure in seeing blood all over the breasts of his beautiful quarry. But he used the distraction to shove the butt of his left hand upward under Matt's jaw, snapping Matt's head back and stunning him. In an instant Samir had freed his right hand, and plunged the blade toward Matt's chest. Reflexively, Matt deflected the blade with his forearm, but sustained a deep incision into the muscles, all the way to the bone. Punching forward with his right fist, Matt missed Samir clean, and Samir used the instant to withdraw and replant the knife into Matt's right chest, entering lateral to the nipple. Matt gasped at the sharp pain, and fell backward onto the bed.

Samir now leaped on top of Matt, and raised the knife again. This would be the mortal blow. Samir paused to revel in his victory, despite the one eye dangling, teeth out, ripped mouth. A crooked grin came over Samir's face as he raised his other arm, so as to use both arms to sink the knife to the hilt into Matt's heart. But it was a costly pause for pleasure.

BOOM! BOOM! The violent explosion instantly rendered all three combatants transiently deaf, with an overwhelmingly loud ringing in their ears. Samir looked to his left at the blood-covered naked woman half-lying, half-sitting on the floor over her trousers, where she had extracted her 9 mm Beretta. The first two shots went where they should, to the torso, because it's the biggest target, and usually lethal. Samir looked down at the two round holes in his shirt over his lateral chest. It was the last thing he ever saw. BOOM! BOOM! BOOM! The shell casings tinkled as they ricocheted off the floor, then all was silent.

The first of this volley paralleled the first two into Samir's left chest, ripping his left lung to shreds and embedding in his spinal column after penetrating his aorta. The next one angled upward, fracturing the second and third ribs. The bullet hurtled razor-sharp bony shrapnel backward into the lung, and then exited the skin, penetrating the sheet metal wall of the can, and into the night sky. The third round penetrated the mid thorax, a little anterior than the first two, and ripped holes through the left and right ventricles of the heart. In that instant, Samir knew he was in trouble, but he didn't get to think about it for long.

BOOM! BOOM! BOOM! The Beretta exploded again, and all three rounds penetrated Samir's skull, ripping through his deviant, hateful, deceitful, murderous brain, and exploding the skull out of his right side, leaving a bloody mess of bone and brain all over the wall. Samir slumped forward, the knife deflected aside into the wall by Samir's crumpling torso. The battle was over. The room was still. Samir's functional but now unseeing left eye stared down at the bizarrely erotic sight of the naked athletic woman, bloodied but still training the pistol at him.

Matt and Chris were both panting. Matt coughed, and spurted bright red blood. Chris was up in a second, pulling Samir's lifeless body off Matt, sobbing. Matt knew he was injured, and tried to sit up. Chris pushed him back down and pushed the pillow under his head.

"Oh Matt, Matt," Chris sobbed between words, "Matt, don't be hurt bad. Don't die on me, Matt!"

She embraced him, kissing him, but then realized she needed to act. She picked her blouse off the floor and found her cell phone in the breast pocket. When the dial tone appeared, she uttered a prayer of thanksgiving that the cell towers were back in operation. Dialing the base emergency number, she was greeted promptly by a junior Marine about three hundred yards away in Security.

"Blue Diamond Emergency, Lance Corporal Daniels."

"This is Captain Curtis. I'm in Blue Diamond Officers' Quarters 134. We've been attacked by an insurgent, and Major Baxter is severely injured. Send an ambulance immediately."

"Yes Ma'am, Major. Blue Diamond Quarters 134. Ambulance. Coming. Out."

The base emergency operator, LCpl Edie Daniels, promptly alerted the Blue Diamond Clinic. The doctor was exhausted after caring for so many USMC wounded and packaging them off to the surgical company across the river, but LT Will Alexander promptly arose from his bunk, and stumbled out to the ambulance while tightening his belt, his boots untied, his cover left behind. The ambulance pulled up to Matt's quarters.

Chris had hastily donned her uniform, no socks, and put a blanket over Matt, stepping over and on Samir's limp body as she ministered to Matt. Matt was ashen gray and cold and clammy to touch, with a rapid thready pulse, and taking rapid shallow breaths. Chris knew he was in shock, and near death. He coughed weakly, each time producing more red blood.

The corpsmen and doctor entered the room briskly. Seeing Samir on the floor and obviously dead, LT Alexander looked at Chris: "What happened?"

"He attacked us with a knife. He stabbed the Major in the left chest," Chris explained hastily, as she pulled the blanket down to demonstrate the wound.

LT Alexander felt Matt's pulse as he looked at his breathing pattern. "What do you feel, Major?" he queried, as much to determine Matt's level of consciousness as to truly inquire about symptoms.

"I—can't—breathe," Matt whispered between his rapid shallow breaths, now at fifty per minute.

LT Alexander listened to Matt's chest, and, even with the shallow breaths, he expertly observed breath sounds over Matt' right chest but not over his left. Using his fingers to percuss, LT Alexander found the sound produced to be normal over the right, but deeper in pitch on the left. "You've got air in your chest cavity, Major—a tension pneumothorax. I'm going to have to stick you." LT Alexander strived not to reveal to Matt and Chris that Matt had about two minutes to live, if he didn't act. In this state, CPR would be worthless; Matt needed the high-pressure air out of his chest, and he needed it out yesterday.

Turning to the Corpsmen, he ordered, "Gimme the biggest needle you got."

"I got a sixteen, Sir. Will that do?" responded HM3 Jennifer Mackey. "Perfect," responded the doctor, as he reached back for it. The needle was in fact designed for chest puncture, and was four inches long, with a plastic sheath over it. LT Alexander chose his spot, along the left lateral wall of Matt's cool and moist chest just above the knife wound. Looking at Matt's cyanotic and now-impassive face, it was clear that Matt was spiraling downward toward eternity. Seconds now counted.

Without delay, LT Alexander plunged the needle into Matt's chest a full two inches. There was an immediate hissing sound through the needle, confirming the high pressure air in Matt's chest cavity, which had been compressing the lung, and forcing the heart over into the right chest, impeding venous return to the heart.

Within ten seconds, Matt started to pink up. He began taking deeper breaths, and his left lung partially re-expanded. LT Alexander hastily advanced the blunt-tipped plastic catheter over the needle, and withdrew the needle, so as not to lacerate the lung as it re-approached the chest wall. He taped the catheter to Matt's skin, and inserted a connecting tube from the catheter into a Heimlich Valve, a one-way valve that lets air out but not back in.

The release of the tension pneumothorax doesn't stop hemorrhage from the lung, but it does resolve the acute emergency. Matt was still in danger from exsanguinating from his lung and chest wall wounds, but now there was time for transport to the nearby Navy Forward Resuscitative Surgical Suite, or FRSS. The Clinic on base had no O.R.—Matt needed to be transported across the Euphrates to Camp Ramadi, a much-larger base than Blue Diamond, where the nearest full O.R. and trauma surgeons were situated.

"Let's get him into the ambulance, Mackie," LT Alexander commanded. "He's gotta get to the friss [FRSS]."

"Aye, aye, Sir," HM3 Mackey responded, as she opened the field litter and lay it on the floor beside Matt's bed. The two skilled medics slid Matt off the bed onto the litter. They retrieved the blanket Chris had utilized and covered him. Mackie opened a warming clear-plastic pneumatic blanket and inflated it with the cartridge attached. They wrapped this device around Matt, keeping an eye on Matt's breathing, which was now slowing down to a normal pace.

"Check the pulse, Mackie", LT Alexander commanded, as he pulled the field telephone from his right thigh cargo pocket. Dialing base emergency, he heard, "Blue Diamond Emergency, LCpl Daniels."

"Emergency, this is LT Alexander. I have a critically injured Marine who needs to get to Ramadi FRISS immediately. I think a boat would be fastest. Can you get one?"

"Yes, Sir, we have a boat in service right now. I think I can have it ready for you by the time you get to the dock."

"Terrific, Lance Corporal Daniels, we're en route. Out."

The litter was slid into the back of the ambulance. Two corpsmen attended to Matt, while HM3 Mackey clambered into the driver's seat. LT Alexander slid into the passenger seat, and the ambulance turned around and headed for the main drag of Blue Diamond. The speed limit is five miles per hour, and vehicles usually travel with no illumination, making the situation extremely dangerous for pedestrians. Because the battle likely neutralized opposition, and there were plenty of juicier targets outside the walls cleaning up the battlefield, LT Alexander ordered the lights on, and to drive at twenty miles per hour. They arrived at the dock within three minutes.

"Unload the casualty, and bring him to the dock," commanded LT Alexander. "What are the vitals?"

"Sir, pulse one-sixteen, pressure ninety over eighty."

"He's in shock. Give him a bag of plasma, wide open. No time to get blood," barked LT Alexander.

"Plasma aye, Sir," came the response, as the corpsmen ripped the plastic packaging off the plasma bag, and hung it on the IV pole now attached to the litter. The corpsmen inserted an IV administration line into the bag, and plugged the other end into the IV they had inserted into Matt's arm during the three minute ride. The plasma began flowing rapidly into the drip chamber in the admin set.

Walking briskly to the dock, LT Alexander walked up to the boat and said, "I'm LT Alexander. Who's in charge here?"

"BM1 Lauren, Sir. What's the mission?" [BM1 = Boatswain's Mate First Class, possessing skills in small boat handling as well as large ship mooring, anchoring, etc.]

"Critical Marine, BM1. Need to get to the FRISS stat. Are you ready?"

"Yes Sir, ready to shove off. Bring your patient aboard, Sir."

The corpsmen already had Matt at the edge of the dock, and they advanced to the boat. Two corpsmen jumped aboard, and received the litter, being careful not to dump Matt out in the process. Patient transfers look simple, but they're fraught with hazard to both patient and crew, especially when there's a vertical drop as there was here. But Matt was strapped into the litter, and the corpsmen had practiced transfers endlessly, so Matt was loaded aboard without incident. LT Alexander jumped aboard."

"Cast off," ordered BM1 Johanna Lauren. The fore and aft crewmen deftly uncleated the lines from the dock, and pushed the twenty-six foot craft away from the dock. The two 125-horsepower Mercuries roared to life, and the boat cut smartly out into the current of the Euphrates. A rooster-tail wake arose from its stern as the craft accelerated.

Four minutes later, Navy boat RS3266 eased in beside the Camp Ar Ramadi dock. The receiving medics had convinced the Marine commander of the dock to switch on its lights, allowing a straight course to the destination. Two Marines were lying prone on the earth behind the dock, their SAWs on tripods and trained on the water just beyond the dock. A major battle had played out on the water before them just hours before, so this was still very much a war zone. Identification friend or foe was being accomplished by radio chatter and direct voice, but the Marines weren't taking any chances on an insurgent craft pulling up and ambushing them.

The litter was quickly handed up to the Ramadi medics, who immediately carried Matt up to their waiting ambulance, its diesel rumbling at idle. Matt was aboard in seconds, the door slammed shut, the corpsmen inside assessing Matt's vitals and taking down the now-depleted plasma bag. LT Alexander had joined Matt in the back.

Two minutes later, the ambulance pulled up to Casualty Receiving at Ramadi FRSS, and Matt was hastily carried past the waiting litter stands under tarpaulin covers outside, able to receive a dozen litters from a mass casualty event, to triage who gets into the ORs first.

One of the two ORs had just finished a case, so Matt was transported directly to the operating table of OR One. Matt was pink and conscious, but his heart rate was one hundred and twenty-five and he was breathing at twenty-four breaths/minute. His blood pressure had dropped a bit further, and was now at eighty-six over seventy-eight. Navy Commander and trauma surgeon Sean Doppelt was supervising the removal of Matt's blankets, and was examining every inch of him for wounds. When a trauma patient gets to an OR, severe and actively hemorrhaging wounds can be easily missed because of fixation on a readily visible wound, such that the patient is lost even though the visible wound is successfully addressed.

Matt was rolled from side to side, to convince CDR Doppelt that the chest wound and the lacerated arm were the only ones requiring his surgical skills. LCDR Ryan Howe, the anesthesiologist, had already summoned two bags of A-positive blood from the blood bank, based on the blood type cited on Matt's dog tags. Both bags of blood were hung, another IV started in Matt's right arm, and compression bags were placed over the blood bags, forcing the blood into Matt even faster than gravity would provide.

LCDR Howe gave Matt an IV injection of Versed, a sedative, followed immediately by succinyl choline, a paralytic. This allowed him to intubate Matt – place a breathing tube into Matt's trachea, allowing inflation of Matt's lungs with pressurized air and simultaneously protecting Matt's lungs from choking on vomit or other secretions. After the endotracheal tube was in place, LCDR Howe opened the valve of gas anesthetic into Matt's air supply. Matt was now in deep coma, and his muscles were totally flaccid.

CHAPTER SEVENTY-EIGHT

BACK AT BLUE DIAMOND

Chris was beside herself with anxiety. She didn't dare ask to ride along with Matt, knowing that she'd impede Matt's rapid transport. But now she wanted to get to him. Base security had taken custody of Samir's body, and was filling out reports. They asked Chris to come to the security office to give a statement, but she declined, saying she wished to get to Camp Ramadi to check on Matt and would do the reports in the morning. Such a response would never do in the civilian world, but in a war zone it was perfectly reasonable, so Gunnery Sergeant Mike Vemgrow, the senior Security officer attending, agreed to interview her in the morning.

Chris stepped into Matt's bathroom, since the bedroom was full of Marine security staff, and a very dead Samir. She put on her boots and straightened up her uniform. She brushed her hair quickly, put it in its workday bun, slipped on her cover, and headed out the door. She walked briskly toward the boat dock, hoping she could hitch a ride. Getting to Camp Ar Ramadi, only a half mile across the Euphrates, by helo or surface convoy, was always a challenging enterprise. But the Marines controlled the Euphrates between their two bases, so security wasn't nearly as much of an issue traveling by water.

Arriving at the dock, Chris found the dock security detachment in place with weapons trained on the water, but there was no boat. Inquiring of the commander of the detachment, she was advised that the boat that had transported the casualty to Ar Ramadi was en route back. She thanked him, and walked out on the dock. Her ear turned toward the far shore, Chris could now hear the distant growl of the twin Mercs. Standing very still, she could discern that the sound was growing closer. Three minutes later, Navy boat RS-3266 pulled alongside the dock. Chris identified the commander by her barking of orders to tie up. She advised BM1 Lauren that she needed to get to Ar Ramadi urgently, and asked if she could accommodate. Lauren asked the shore detail if there were any other requests, which there weren't, so she welcomed Chris aboard, and ordered the boat back "to sea."

Fifteen minutes later, Chris entered the FRSS and asked where the stabbing victim from Blue Diamond was. She was advised that he was in the O.R., and that she could wait. The desk staff knew he was critical, but nothing more. Chris sat down in the sand-bag surrounded facility, and began to pray.

Oh God, you've done so much good for the Marines today, for America, for Matt and me. You spared us both from Samir. But please don't abandon us now. I'll do anything for you. But please...please let Matt live. He's a good man. A good Marine. And I love him SO much. You brought him to me. Please, please don't take him away. Please.

She sank to her knees, turned toward the bench where she rested her elbows, her hands in praying pose, her head bowed, tears streaming down both cheeks. She started to sob outright. "In Jesus' name I pray, Amen." The sobs grew louder, her shoulders convulsing in grief.

A young female Navy corpsman came out and squatted beside her, embracing her. "CDR Doppelt is the best there is, Captain. He trained at the University of Maryland, the best trauma center in the world. He'll save him, Captain. He'll save him. Have faith."

Chris looked up slowly, her sobbing subsiding slowly. She wiped away her tears, and took HN Kranz's hands in hers. "Thank you, Doc," Chris whispered, "Thank you." (HN = Hospitalman, a junior Hospital Corpsman not yet a non-commissioned officer at rank E-3. The next rank up is HM3, rank E-4).

Chris stood up and sat on the bench. Staring into HN Kranz's eyes, she asked, "Is he really good, the surgeon?"

"He's saved a bunch of Marines that nobody thought would make it, Captain. He's truly a miracle worker. I saw your Major coming in. He was in trouble, but he was still responsive. That means his heart almost certainly wasn't hit, nor any of the big chest blood vessels. If they had been, he wouldn't have made it to us alive. I'm sure CDR Doppelt will save him, Captain. I'm certain of it."

Chris was now regaining her composure. She took the tissue HN Kranz offered her, dried up the last of the tears, and blew her nose. "Thank you, Doc. Any idea how long they'll be in surgery?"

"I'll check, Major," responded HN Kranz softly, and she disappeared back toward the OR. Then Kranz noticed the blood stain on the right side of Chris's blouse, and asked if she'd been injured. Chris had forgotten about the substantial laceration Samir's knife had wrought on her right chest wall, but now was acutely aware of it, and felt a little faint. HN Kranz immediately seated her, and called for a gurney. Within 3 minutes, Chris was in an exam room and all her clothes were promptly removed —following that first rule of trauma—to know what you're dealing with. She was rolled from side to side, and the chest wound was confirmed to be her only apparent injury. The 4-inch wound was probed and found to be superficial. Chris's vital signs were good. Her wound was cleansed and sterilized, and closed in two layers of sutures.

Inside the OR, Matt now had a foot-long incision between his fifth and sixth ribs, with a large retractor holding their ribs open, so that CDR Doppelt could access Matt's lacerated left lung. The knife wound was identified, and was probed. A vigorous bleeder was identified, and was promptly ligated with 2-0 synthetic suture. No other large intrapulmonary vessels had been severed. A few other small bleeders were cauterized, causing smoke with the smell of barbecued beef to waft out of Matt's chest. The lacerated lung was sutured closed. A chest tube was inserted into the open wound, to allow any blood or loose air to be drained out over the next several days. Then Matt's chest was closed with several layers of suture. Matt had now received four units of packed red cells and 5 liters of Ringers' Lactate [IV fluid], and his blood pressure was back to a not-yet-robust one hundred over seventy. His heart rate was still elevated, but much improved at 105. His lungs were working well, with the oxygen saturation of his blood, measured by a gauge on his finger, to be ninety-five percent. Matt was indeed going to make it. Chris's prayers were answered. The good man, the good Marine, Chris's true love, had been saved. Both Chris and Matt had survived Samir's attack. And Samir had not.

At that very moment, Samir's gray, lifeless, and disfigured body was being inserted into the refrigerated morgue at Blue Diamond, while Matt was being wheeled into a warm recovery room, or in modern parlance a Post Anesthesia Care Unit, or PACU. Chris was brought in, and was permitted to embrace Matt, even though he was still in deep coma from the anesthetic.

Matt didn't look too good. He had a tube through his nose to drain his stomach, and the endotracheal tube was in his mouth, connected to a wheezing ventilator. He had a tube in his urinary bladder, and the left chest tube. There were large-bore IV's in both arms, with fluids dripping. But he was pink, his vitals were stable, and his kidneys were making urine: the medics were pleased with his status.

Chris buried her face in Matt's chest. Despite the loud ringing in her ears from the multiple 9 mm rounds she fired into Samir, she could hear his heart beating, strong and regular. Once again she clasped her hands in prayer, and thanked God for sparing her lover. She was elated. And she suddenly realized that she was overwhelmingly fatigued. She had already had a very full day, before being attacked and wounded herself, then shot a man to death for the first time in her life. She had come very close to being decapitated in front of Matt—Samir's initial plan. If it weren't for her boots on the floor by the door... She didn't want to go there—far, far too close to a hideous, mutilated carnage of her and Matt. She and Matt had been incredibly lucky. But they were both elite warriors, so when the opportunity to save themselves arose, they seized it. And they had their lives to show for it.

CHAPTER SEVENTY-NINE

ONE WEEK LATER

Matt recovered fast, and was walking on his second post-op day. He was transferred by helo to the staging point for medevacs out of country at Balad, a large Air Force-run air base about forty miles north of Baghdad. He joined sixty-five other casualties aboard a gleaming new, massive USAF C-17 transport plane, destined to the large U.S. Army hospital at Landstuhl, Germany. [Medevacs also haul out of the war zone servicemen with non-battle-related injuries and illnesses—who usually vastly outnumber the combat injuries.]

Because of Chris's spectacular success in pulling off the sting operation, she requested and was given orders to Landstuhl to serve as the Assistant Marine Corps Liaison Officer to the Marine casualties being treated there. She stayed with Matt during his four days at LARMC (Landstuhl Army Regional Medical Center), then joined him, now on convalescent leave, in his C-5 medevac flight to Bethesda Naval Hospital, just outside Washington D.C. He was treated there another four days, then given convalescent leave and permission to go home. Chris accompanied him to his parents' home in St. Louis, where she met Matt's gracious and grateful mom and dad. After a week with them, Chris and Matt flew to upstate New York to visit the Curtis family.

Chris's mother had cruised through her excision biopsy, had been diagnosed with a mid-level aggressive breast cancer, and was undergoing radiation therapy. A little tired, overall she was doing very well. Chris's dad was ebullient that he had played a role in the stunningly successful detection of Samir's duplicity, and the subsequent international rout of the terrorist network. Several family dinners were convened in honor of Chris and Matt, with every family member managing to attend.

Renee was not prosecuted, because her confession and subsequent dangerous function as a double agent was considered sufficient payback for her crime. She lost her security clearance, and left the State Department. Her marriage survived after some tearful hours of confession to Don, and his acceptance of her moral lapse. She went on to finish her PhD, and became a popular professor at Duke University, and an international authority on Middle Eastern affairs. She and Don and their beloved Jackie and Sammy went on to rich and fulfilling lives.

Chris and Matt were now international celebrities. Although the U.S. military has celebrated individual heroes in prior wars, that form of honor and national pride had receded from the American press and presence. But these two handsome warriors, with their monumentally successful work, were now the darlings of all peace and civilization-loving people. Their photos were on the front pages of newspapers around the world. They were interviewed by every news organization in the world. Requests to speak were pouring in by the hundreds. America and the entire western world had been wounded repeatedly by the sinister forces of evil in the terror movement: this was their first massive world-wide victory, and the western world wanted to celebrate it with the two warriors most responsible for bringing it to fruition.

The military was supportive of these interviews and speaking engagements—good for recruiting, and good for military-civilian relations in general. And good for the country. So Matt and Chris were speaking at forums around the world. They strived to accept engagements together, or near one another, so that they could spend virtually every evening together. Life was good. Good for them. And good for mankind.

EPILOGUE

The terror movement wasn't abolished, but it was mortally wounded by the international raids that eliminated much of the infrastructure and financing of this movement of misfits and savages. Chris and Matt announced their engagement during his convalescence, and were subsequently married in the chapel of the U.S. Naval Academy in Annapolis, Maryland. Their wedding glittered with the best pomp and circumstance the Corps could muster. Pageantry is important to the military, and for the wedding they brought out their full Monty. Battle flags colorfully painted the breeze inside and out. A canopy of twenty gleaming swords, held high by white-gloved, muscular arms of fellow Marines in their finest dress blues, honored them as they emerged from the chapel as Major and Mrs. Matthew Baxter, United States Marine Corps.

The wedding was plastered on the cover of every major magazine in the world. The dignity, honor, and courage of the United States Marines came across brilliantly to the civilian public via all the coverage. Matt and Chris were thrilled that their union was beneficial to their beloved Corps, and to their entire nation.

Both Matt and Chris were subsequently awarded the Navy Cross, the maritime services' second highest award, second only to the Congressional Medal of Honor. In Matt's case, having already been awarded that extraordinary decoration for valor during the Gulf War, he was awarded a gold star in lieu of second award. The awards were pinned onto their uniforms by no less than the President of the United States, in the Rose Garden on the White House grounds. And on their shoulders were no longer pinned the gold leaf of major and the silver railroad-tracks of captain, because they were both field-promoted: she to major, and he to Lieutenant Colonel. So the silver leaf of the rank of 0-5 now gleamed on Matt's shoulders, and the gold leaf of Major on hers. And they were both a shoo-in for early promotion to 0-6, or full ("bird") Colonel, so named because the symbol of that rank is a silver eagle.

Matt and Chris were transferred to the Pentagon, as planners on the staff of the Commandant of the Marine Corps. They bought a lovely home in the nearby town of Great Falls, Virginia. Three months later, Chris was pregnant. Life was good. The world was good. It was all good.

Discipline, courage, intelligence, perseverance, and goodness had prevailed over raw evil. The ranks of the U.S. military swelled with highly talented recruits, inspired to serve their nation and the world by the sterling example set by Chris and Matt. America bathed in the pride of victory. The threat to western civilization had been severely reduced. The countries of the Middle East flourished with the rule of law and liberal policies. With free political expression, each society's art, academia, and commerce bloomed. Peace and prosperity reigned.

During Chris's six month of pregnancy, when her gait had somewhat evolved to the universal slightly-bowlegged walk of pregnant women, Matt and Chris drove home from the Pentagon on a lovely Wednesday evening. While Chris puttered around in the kitchen preparing dinner, Matt sorted through the mail they had picked up at the end of their driveway. The usual bills, the junk mail, the sundry military association periodicals, but one hand-written envelope stood out. It was postmarked Chicago, and the handwriting had a familiar lilt to it—something familiar about it to Matt's eye. Tearing open the envelope and extracting the enclosed letter, a 4 x 6 photograph dropped onto his lap. Examining it, he was horrified to see an image of pregnant Chris in civilian clothes emerging from the front door of their house. Then the letter: short and anything but sweet. "You kill our brothers. It not over."

And it wasn't...

www.signalmanpublishing.com

51619058R00174

Made in the USA
Charleston, SC
28 January 2016